CONTEMPORARY AMERICAN FICTION

# ORDINARY MONEY

Louis B. Jones is a graduate of the M.F.A. program at
the University of California at Irvine. He lives with his
wife, Brett, in Mill Valley, California.

# ORDINARY MONEY

LOUIS B. JONES

PENGUIN BOOKS

PENGUIN BOOKS
Published by the Penguin Group
Viking Penguin, a division of Penguin Books USA Inc.,
375 Hudson Street, New York, New York 10014, U.S.A.
Penguin Books Ltd, 27 Wrights Lane,
London W8 5TZ, England
Penguin Books Australia Ltd, Ringwood,
Victoria, Australia
Penguin Books Canada Ltd, 2801 John Street,
Markham, Ontario, Canada L3R 1B4
Penguin Books (N.Z.) Ltd, 182–190 Wairau Road,
Auckland 10, New Zealand

Penguin Books Ltd, Registered Offices:
Harmondsworth, Middlesex, England

First published in the United States of America by
Viking Penguin, a division of Penguin Books USA Inc., 1990
Published in Penguin Books 1991

1   3   5   7   9   10   8   6   4   2

LIBRARY OF CONGRESS CATALOGING IN PUBLICATION DATA
Jones, Louis B.
Ordinary money/Louis B. Jones.
p.    cm.
ISBN 0 14 01.4531 1
I. Title.
PS3560.O516O74    1990b
813'.54—dc20        90–41968

Printed in the United States of America

For Brett

# PART ONE

# 1

The first bill of Bim Auctor's currency to enter the economy
came into the hands of a temporarily unemployed housepainter
named Wayne Paschke, who lived with his wife and daughter
in Santa Venetia—which is before Terra Linda, one exit north
of San Rafael and out San Pedro Road past the La Brea apartments. There is a stop sign at the 7-Eleven, and you go left
onto Robin Song Lane, then right onto Sparrow Court, and
Wayne and Laura Paschke's house is the third on the left, the
same model as the neighbor's, but painted an out-of-date sher-
bet green, with a big chicken-wire thing on the side, left there
by the previous tenant—and the hard lawn and the oil-stained
driveway which always provide a landlord with a reason for
keeping the damage deposit.

Wayne noticed the envelope in the mailbox when, crippled

by the peculiarly glad stiffness of having slept well, he shuffled outside to get the Sunday paper. A large young man, with prematurely thinning hair still scraped into spikes by the rubbing of the pillow, he unbent himself slightly and held the envelope up to read his friend's familiar trickling scrawl:

Wayne—Check it out!
(LOOK CAREFULLY)

—Randy

Inside the envelope was nothing but a twenty-dollar bill. You always had to expect the unexpected from Randy Potts, who once picked up a girl at Rumplestiltskins during Happy Hour by throwing croutons and cheddar cheese dice across the room at her bare shoulders; who still wore the same size jeans as in high school; who had divorced Mary neatly and with good humor in a series of hectic anecdotal comedies, and in the same swift motion bought a convertible Camaro and started taking correspondence courses in real estate and French, which he never finished, but which lent him for a while a certain glamorous disloyalty. He and Randy had, in a single summer, dropped out of high school together and served as best man at each other's weddings in the Silverado Room at the Holiday Inn, their smirks keeping the marriages safely facetious.

The envelope was otherwise empty. He would have to wait to get an explanation from Randy on Monday. *If* Randy showed up on Monday. Lately he had seemed to depend less and less on carpentry.

Wayne padded back up the driveway toward the house, over the slight subliminal sin of the oilstains in the concrete, which probably even muriatic acid wouldn't completely bleach out, and he set the kettle on to boil and sat down in his swivel chair in the kitchen. Laura was still asleep, her breath and body warmth still flavoring the linen of their bed, an envelope of pleasure and responsibility which Wayne liked to desert before she did in the mornings, to recover briefly a risky, reminiscent shiver of bachelorhood. And Kim always slept late on weekends, rousing herself only for her favorite sugary vicious cartoon shows, which she willfully refused to outgrow as if thereby to preserve the glaze of childhood. He felt pleasantly custodial, shuffling about in the kitchen while his women slept.

The stale colors of the Sunday comics. The slew of slippery advertising inserts. The brief ache of the real estate section: this week's "Floor Plan of the Week" held his eye. He had often observed Laura poring over it on Sunday mornings lost in a kind of dollhouse reverie, contemplating the diagram as if she could imagine herself traversing its floors. He sunk his mind, still asleep, down into this Sunday's "Floor Plan"— which was headlined FREE FIREPLACE OFFERED AT COBBLE-STONE HEARTH VILLAGE TO FIRST FIFTY BUYERS—and he tried to imagine himself as a homeowner, a tiny stick figure in this origami condominium, with good posture and a nice sport jacket, standing by the fireplace, perhaps even a bit slimmer about the middle. Confetti-sized furniture surfaced in the diagram, and Laura cooked comma-sized pork chops on a transistor stove. A yet-unborn boy was asleep in the CHILDS BR, and there was a view to gesture out at as if he owned it, with the sturdy stance of a proprietor beside the mantelpiece. But at night in that bedroom, while Laura slept beside him, he would lie awake upon the breathing balloon of debt feeling as if he were in a motel room, in that odor of an empty drawer. He hated to conceive of the avalanche of six-digit mathematics that constitutes a "home loan." He had flunked algebra in high school simply because of a righteous unwillingness—morally justified in those blithe days when there was bloodshed in a distant jungle war—a righteous unwillingness to apply his mind to the impermeable pages of obvious text: "Or, plainly, if $x = x$, then: . . ."

And he had lived, ever since, a life of evasion of that eternally unsolved equation. The sight of the classified advertising pages stung his vision. He kept wafting the big pages past. Or if he looked, he let his eye run to those large contemptible ads promising to "dynamic" or "ambitious" candidates an unrealistically huge income in the first month, which to contemplate made him snugger in his torn bathrobe.

BIG INCOME IN COLLECTIBLES. Earn 6-figure income, first year with us, possible, promoting the #1 investment in America today. We train you to be a qualified Broker, there are 3 requirements. 1, dress well. 2, Speak English. 3, be willing to follow Proven Program . . .

It was the same ad he'd seen two Sundays ago. He had called the number in spite of the obvious fishiness, waiting until after Laura had left the house. And the young man he talked to had described an organization called Marketrend, which turned out to be one of those pyramid-sales organizations where you make money by bringing in other people. Except in this case it was rare coins; selling them over the telephone. When Wayne pointed this out, the young man said, "Well, Mr. Paschke, if you expected me to be a phony, why did you bother to call me? Obviously you're not used to getting what you want." It could still make him angry to think of it.

The kettle on the stove had been ticking, and now it started to make, like gravel stirred within, the sounds of waking. He picked up Randy's twenty-dollar bill to examine it. It was probably some kind of joke; Randy had probably defaced it in some funny way. There was the handsome, tousled President, "Jackson," looking out from his molding-rimmed oval window between stamped green sprockets. Above him on a wind-floated ribbon were the words *The United States of America*. Arcane little numbers and letters, some almost microscopic, appeared in spaces like official footnotes. The large numeral *20* was suspended in each corner among luminous silver spider webs, which hung above a dense and gloomy background, the dark atmosphere of an ancient vault, black air older even than "The United States of America," as ancient as the terrible and unfathomable secret of money. It repelled thought.

He turned the bill over to the lighter green side, where the corner numerals were set upon white doilies. There in the center of the bill was the White House, a two-story building beneath the pennant "In God We Trust" among the affluent old trees of Washington, D.C. Its miniature porch bulged outward, flanked by staircases. Its eaves were weighty ledgers, the kind that are hard to scrape and paint because flakes of tough old alligator-skin paint keep falling into your eyelashes. The lawn was as tranquil and flat as a pasture, bordered by shrubbery where Secret Service agents in dark business suits and sunglasses must crouch with their telescopic-sighted rifles and crackling walkie-talkies. Wayne looked to the four windows on the right-hand side of the upper story, where the President and the First Lady must live. They have sex there; or maybe sometimes they pass those difficult nights when he, out of some obscure anger, is unable to sleep, and she is aware of it. He could picture the First Lady rising from the President's bed with a sigh that condemned him. He could picture the two of them sitting up cross-legged in bed, facing each other, talking in bitter tones, with long silences, until three in the morning, sharing an ashtray. Or lying down side by side, alert in the dark, irreconcilable.

But of course in reality their marriage must be happy and quiet. In reality the President lies down each night stiff and doll-like, handsome in his expensive pajamas. It is essential for the President and the First Lady to sleep soundly, it keeps the land under its spell of happiness. Which is what the Secret Service agents are guarding. Wayne regarded the four upper-story windows closely, as if some etched detail of domestic life might almost be magically glimpsed, under close enough scrutiny, in the four small squares of darkness—a bedside lamp, or a favorite dressing gown on a chair back, limp with familiarity, or a palm-softened bedpost. But the discomfort of living for four years in the hotel-like White House must be that the edges of all the furniture stay so sharp and shiny, unbeveled by the rub of habit.

The kettle on the stove began, with a spit, to whistle, and Wayne lunged to silence it before Laura or Kim was awakened.

# 2

On that same Sunday morning, the second of Bim Auctor's twenty-dollar bills to appear in the local economy was stuck to the refrigerator at 2225 Las Gallinas in Terra Linda, where Randy's daughter Cindy would discover it when she awoke. Still rubbing crumbs of sleep from her eyes, she came barefoot into the kitchen to find it stuck under a ladybug magnet to the face of the refrigerator, with this note:

Dear Cindy—
This is for groceries and whatever. Buy anything you want, love. I'll be at Tom's again tonight. We need laundry detergent, could you pick some up? This is a responsibility I'm giving you. I trust you. I promise I'll pay the orthodontists bill, tell Dr. Bunton I PROMISE. Tell him

to start work on the upper bands in good faith. He hasn't
even done anything and he is already sending us bills.
Your dad was here last night and he says give you a big
kiss. Don't wear my clothes, you don't have my permission! And be wonderful!

· Love, Mom


Cindy read the note on tiptoe with her arms pulled inside
the huge NYMPHO VAMPIRE T-shirt that served as a nightgown,
pressing her fists together under her chin and knitting her
shoulders as if she were cold. It was obvious that the twenty
dollars had come from her dad, despite her mother's attempt
to make it look like her own gift. She stuck one hand out
through the neck hole of her T-shirt, plucked the bill from the
refrigerator, and drew it back inside her shirt; and she walked
out into the living room in her roomy straitjacket feeling a small
cramp of satisfaction in being worth, for the moment, twenty
dollars, indulging herself, as she walked, in her customary
game of not coming near anything as she veered among ma-
lignant furniture, not touching things. She used a single fingernail like a tapping claw to flip through her mother's record
collection of old rock and roll—music from that unimaginable
epoch of detergent-bright Kodak sunlight before she was born,
when her dad, in his innocence, could make the incredible
mistake of wearing tight bell-bottom jeans and high-heeled
boots and everybody listened to grotesque heavy-metal rock
and roll, which must have served as the anthems of her parents'
doomed romance, itself a kind of huge fashion mistake.

She set a Boz Skaggs album on the turntable and, using the
edge of a fingernail that would leave no clue, pressed the plastic
pill on the face of the amplifier. While the needle crackled in
the old groove, she bounced down onto the new mushroom-

colored couch, with its repellent department-store sheen that resisted body heat, and she pulled her legs up under her T-shirt and pulled her arms inside to hug her knees. To be home alone with the house all to herself—something about the sheer waste of space was sexy. Today could be the day she would disappear. She went back into her bedroom, where the air still smelled of her own sleep, and unzipped the secret compartment in Kermit the Frog to spill out her collection of suicide notes, on various kinds of stationery, folded or crumpled according to the circumstances of their composition. She began to unfold them and iron them on her thigh.

> Dear Mother and Father:
> You shouldn't blame yourselves . . .

Such a stupid letter it made her stomach squirm. She had written it in fifth-period study hall, on a difficult day when Jeff DeBono had been ignoring her totally and her face had looked so pasty in the bad light of the mirror in the second-floor girls' bathroom, and the flesh of her calves had looked so slapped, so raw, in her gym uniform. She remembered the moment perfectly, even to the hopeless smell of the lead-and-cedar pencil in her own moist palm.

> Dear Mother and Father—
> Please don't worry and don't panic. I am okay. My wrists
> are tied so tight that its cutting off my circulation and
> sometimes this one guy grabs my hair and pulls my head.
> But they give me food to eat . . .

She raised her eyes to regard her image in the opposite mirror to remind herself of her beauty. The clear gaze of her eyes, the soft flannel cushion of her lower lip, the new slope of flesh on her chest echoing the different slope at the narrow small of her back, the miraculous swelling of the hip. She was, more and more, conscious wherever she walked of leaving tiny eddies of discontentment spinning in her wake. Such beauty was not meant for this world: that would be the feeling of the mourners at her memorial service. Her flesh in the coffin would have the grace of relaxation that comes of complete surrender, the Mona Lisa smile of experience. Her lifeless corpse would be discovered somewhere, like at the bottom of a cliff, breasts thrust up, lips parted as if kissed, hips smashed by the consummation. Her mother, dressed and made-up for her interrupted date, would stand at the rim of the cliff above and look down to see where Cindy had gone before. Her bedroom would be kept intact as a shrine: the posters; the various embarrassing stuffed animals lining the shelf; the computer that hadn't worked since she spilled orangeade on it; the skis; the electric piano she never played, piled high with magazines and clothes. She had to decide what to take with her this morning. She could compose the right letter later. And she had to call Kim. And she had to shampoo her hair.

First of all, she lay face-down on the floor and pressed her front row of upper teeth against the palm of her hand as hard as she could, arching up to exert all her weight, an exercise she had started doing as often as possible recently to repair the slight imperfection of her two front teeth that vied like carelessly tossed throw pillows.

The phone on the nightstand rang. She knew it would be Kim Paschke.

"Hello?"

"Hi, it's me," said Kim. "Want to go to Northgate?"

"What are you doing?"

"Nothing. There's only cartoons."

"Can I sleep over?" said Cindy.

"At mine? Sure."

"But it has to be a secret. I don't want Wayne and Laura to know."

"How can my parents not know?"

"I'll sneak in after dark."

"How come?"

"I'm leaving home."

"Permanently? How long do you want to stay here?"

"Just a few days. Just until I get on my feet." That twenty dollars, crumpled now on her bedspread, would not be enough.

"You're really leaving home," Kim marveled. "This is cool."

"I'll meet you at Shakey's in an hour, okay?"

"I can't believe it. What are you going to do?"

"God, Kim, you're so retarded."

"What are you going to pack?"

"I'll meet you at Shakey's in an hour. Okay? Bye."

It took less than an hour. By the time she had descended the chain-link-fence-guarded steps of the freeway overpass— her jerkily orbiting suitcase banging her ankle and swinging her off balance, perspiration dampening strands of her hair— she had decided that literally running away from home at this moment was too problematic: the irksome and scary work of being out alone in the world, of suffering the necessary loss of soul that grown-ups undergo, the quenching of light in the eye, the loss of body and shine in the hair.

Shakey's Pizza, on the frontage road beside the freeway, had always been surrounded by a moat of torn-up asphalt, cut off from the world by striped hazard barriers whose flashing orange disks were extinguished by sunlight, erased by the dust that erases everything along the freeway. In spite of its huge sign, it was so nondescript as to be invisible, outshone by its sign, so that to cross over the sunny rubble and enter its shade was to vanish. When she got inside the building, darkness flooded her eyes and she had to stand there blinded for a minute, a new sheen of perspiration on her skin defined by the basementlike air. As usual, the place was empty of customers, silent except for the hum of refrigeration and the autistic whirr and blip of the video games along the back wall. Gradually the darkness paled. Kim was already sitting at the back in their usual booth.

"I can't believe it!" said Kim in greeting, and immediately Cindy was reminded why they had always been only on-and-off friends. Kim could be such an idiot sometimes, as only a good student could be, with this expression on her face of happy expectancy.

"Can't believe what?" said Cindy, shoving the suitcase under the table and sitting down.

"What are you going to do?"

"I got twenty dollars, I'm going to buy a quarter-gram of cocaine." She tapped Kim's drink. "Is that diet?"

"Yesss," said Kim. "Jeez."

"Good, because you're looking excellent. Jailbait, like."

Kim's eyes slid. "Oh God, shut up. What are you going to do? Are you really doing this?"

"Doing what?" said Cindy, standing up.

"Running away from home."

"I wish you wouldn't phrase it like that. You make it sound like I'm six years old." She turned and went to the counter, where the middle-aged manager was doing some kind of paperwork crouched behind the four soda spigots with their Coke, Sprite, Orange, and Diet Coke emblems. Cindy asked for a Double Slurp and fries. But he said, while he shook some already-cooked fries into a plastic basket lined with waxed paper, that the Double Slurp promotional was last month only. So she ordered a large Diet Coke, watching the manager as he moved with the sullen aplomb, the hooded eyes, that indicated either contempt or sexual admiration.

"You look cute," Kim told her when she returned to the booth with her food. Cindy regarded her ripped sweatshirt, the rummage-sale skirt designed for a much larger woman and taken in by a conspicuous safety pin, her frayed sneakers, her baggy socks. How could Kim—who wore mostly blouses and sweaters imbued with niceness—be sincere in such a compliment?

"Okay, tell me now," said Kim. "What are you going to do? Or first of all, tell me why you're running away."

"For one thing, I'm not 'running away,' I'm leaving." Ketchup from a squeeze bottle spat onto the waxed paper. "And I'm leaving because it's time. It's just time."

"Time for what?"

"Everything is always so normal."

"Yeah, but specifically."

Cindy sipped on her straw. "Well, I'm going to keep my plans to myself for a while."

"Can't you tell me?"

"Oh, you might misunderstand. You know, it's a very large, complicated world out there."

"Come on, you don't have any plans. You're just saying that."

Cindy shrugged. "I just want to explore my options."

"Does Jeff know?"

"Oh God, Jeff!" She rolled her eyes. "He's such a poodle."

"Aren't you going to tell him?"

"It's boys like Jeff I want to get away from. His tiny little peepee, you can't even find it. It's like a little rinky-dinky worm."

"Jeez, gross!" said Kim, smiling downward with shame.

"It keeps wriggling out of your mouth."

Kim slugged her in horror. "Shut up!"

"Well hey! If you're ever going to attract Jeff's brother? Without techniques? Do you think Eric DeBono is just going to want to hold hands?"

Kim showed the side of her face, watching the screen of a video game across the room. "Mmm," she said. They'd had this conversation before.

"You have to be more out there. If Eric knew the real you he'd be unable to resist. Like, you should get some weirder clothes. Want to go to Just Jeans? They have terrible security. And you have such nice features. Why don't you let me cut your hair?"

Kim wiped her bangs from her forehead, her eyes gliding away.

"I'm really not kidding. Trust me. Put yourself totally in my hands, and we'll do a complete make-over on you. You can get Eric in bed in a month, I promise you."

Kim sighed and said, "Yeah," faintly.

"Let's go get some earrings. You have to have your ears pierced. We can steal some earrings at the Emporium. And then let's go over to yours and I'll pierce your ears."

Kim touched her ear. "I can't. I'm getting a new one during vacation. I'm outgrowing this one."

"So? We can pierce this one now. And when you get a new

one we can pierce *it*. It's really easy, you just need an extra-large safety pin. Let's see," she said, and she reached over to draw aside the curtain of hair and softly pinch the lobe. "At least it will be more painless to pierce it. Won't it? God, it feels real."

"No, it's not like that."

Cindy ran her finger over the glossy outer curl. "You know, this does present a small problem, maybe. Because if Eric puts his tongue in here he might be able to tell it's a different temperature or something. The ear is one of the most important erogenous zones, and he's bound to stick his tongue in. They always do that. When you're in bed with him you should keep turning your head so the real ear sticks up. I mean this is incredible how real it seems, but Eric might be able to tell it's rubber."

"Latex," said Kim. "And besides, the latex part—"

"Latex, whatever, but Kim, the point is, I promise. Just put yourself in my hands. You have such wonderful features. Look at your nose. I'm so jealous of your nose. You can lose your virginity in a month if you just follow my program."

But Kim just sat there with her hands stuck under her thighs, so inert as to shed caresses. She leaned forward and sucked on her straw, making a snerfling sound among the ice cubes at the bottom of the cup.

"I'm going to get another Coke," she said, and slid out of the booth to stand up.

"Oh!" said Cindy. "I meant to tell you: Jeff said Eric was asking about you."

"About me? Why? What did he want to know?"

"You know how brothers talk. He just asked what year you are. And where you live." The lie was springing to her lips with the thoughtless ease of inspiration. "But Jeff said it was obvious Eric is interested in you. All he wanted to know was where you live and stuff."

"God, I hope he didn't tell him."

"Actually he didn't mention." She was going numb with inspiration. "But he did notice that Eric really is interested in you. He said, 'You know that Kim Paschke, with the cute eyes? Is she a sophomore or what?' And Jeff could tell he was really intrigued by you. He said he just asked, like, out of the blue."

Kim stood there in thought for a minute. Then, saying "Hm," she went up to the counter and ordered her Coke.

Cindy slid happily down in her seat, onto her spine. This lie had opened up a world of possibilities, like when, in geometry, the addition of a new axiom will make all the diagrams bulge up into a third dimension and permit an infinite number of new theorems and solutions and connections. She could tell a similar, complementary lie to Eric. She could arrange an accidental intersection between the two. She could forge notes. She would have to be careful. But beyond the risk lay the redeeming imaginary picture: Kim struggling beneath Eric.

When she came back to the table with her Coke, Cindy asked her, "So, could you at least see earrings?"

"I don't want to shoplift anything," said Kim, and Cindy knew she had won. The project of her own disappearance could wait.

Kim sat down, sipped on her Coke, and said, "What do you think? Hoops?"

"No, not for your face. You've got a sort of heart-shaped face. You need something long and hangy—but not too long— just tasteful. Maybe turquoise, for your eyes. But we don't have to shoplift them. We can get some cheap ones at that bead place. And look, I'll buy. My dad came by last night and he left me twenty dollars." She plucked the bill from her shirt pocket and uncrumpled it to show the magic rectangle.

"God, you have the nicest dad," said Kim. "My dad is such a blop."

# 3

Wayne the Blop was still sitting in the kitchen with the Sunday paper smoking his third cigarette, leafing through the Macy's magazine where a model in a Maidenform advertisement held open her fur coat to reveal her nakedness, as, with a grave plea in her eyes, she turned one thigh outward and pressed her hips in slight underpants against the fender of a solid car. He desired her so that his breath went secretly shallow; and for a moment he was an impostor in his own house, in this stupid ripped vinyl swivel chair, and this shabby bathrobe. This chair had never even felt like his, fully. It was a castoff from Laura's parents' cold and inhospitable rec room, left behind when they moved to retirement in a Santa Rosa trailer park and shrank to telescopic irrelevancy. With a peculiar intensity this morning, he hated its unstable rocking diagonally from leg to leg, which he had never bothered to fix but instead had resigned himself to tolerate all these years, living in the nauseous half-inch sway between the tap of the left leg and the tap of the right leg. The models in Macy's ads—it was obvious from the clarity in their gaze—had probably all gone to college. He stared at the gray sparse rectangle of a paragraph on the page before him, with unfocused eyes, seeing only the ravines of white-space that trickled vertically through the typeset lines.

He had almost had an extramarital affair last month—or, which was just as bad, he had wanted to. Simply because, at his age, it wasn't yet unthinkable or absurd; and obviously everybody else is doing it. He had gone to Rumplestiltskins alone on a Friday night while Laura was on the night shift. He had worn his denim shirt and combed his hair over his thinning spot, and he had stood at the end of the bar by the evil black amplifiers on the bandstand, ducking to pet the top of his head, probably looking like a total fool, a husband. But he could see from a few minutes of awkward conversation with this tiny-eyed, tiny-nostriled blonde who kept smoothing her sweater over her hips that it wouldn't work, that she lacked the omniscience he needed from Laura. Contritely, he came down with a prolonged snuffle and spent the rest of the weekend cleaning out the garage, sneezing gladly in the cloud of oregano-smelling dust he raised. Laura probably sensed his having wavered, for there was a peculiar new density to the air; across an arena of silence, she said oddly charged things, like asking him at breakfast what he wanted for dinner—which was something she hadn't asked in all their years of marriage. But she never said anything about his laboring in the garage. The garage was his province, his kitchen, and she pretended to dislike even entering it, always grasping her elbows when she did, and moving slightly tiptoed. And yet as he worked he felt he was moving within her. He preserved and restored to their exact position on the shelf even the crooked nails, even the Skippy peanut butter lid. He removed, dusted off, and replaced the unfixable bent and freckled frame of an incredibly heavy bicycle, the rotten shoes that didn't look familiar to anybody, the soggy-bottomed bushel basket with Kim's old Adidas sock on its rim, the column of old newspapers topped by a trowel, the baton dipped in housepaint, the torn envelope from a junk-mail circular, the erotic cadaver of a naked Barbie doll, the lost Tupperware lid, the handle from a forgotten rake, even the matchbook behind the water heater. After sweeping and washing, he returned each element to its original place, duplicating his memory, gratefully sneezing and sneezing. He had actually been frightened by his conversation with the girl in Rumplestiltskins, by her forced giggle, her monstrous rubbery sexiness, and now he kept shrugging as if to adjust the fit of his snug old role around the house, still chilly with reentry.

At thirty-four. The single steady point from which everything else drifts away. The money-market fund Laura had inherited—$5,001.60 according to the most recent statement—was their only property; and the one prosperity he could *see* was the increase of flesh, the visible manifestation of Laura's spell over him. "Love handles" she called the saddle of fat that this year had begun to show up undeniably around his hips. It was all that Stovetop Stuffing; and it was the complacency, the entitlement, with which he sat in this very chair after a day on the painting crew, his turpentine ghost sharpened by hunger in the cool air of evening.

He used to be so skinny in high school, so scrawny and awkward, his hair banging in his eyes, stunned or drugged all the time by the hormones of those blurred years. How had

Laura—then Laura Philips—chosen him? On their first date, he arrived late, with grass stains on his shoes, because his dad, who had grown merry from beer, had chained the steering wheel of the car to the garage doorpost, saying he couldn't go anywhere until he'd done his yardwork; as they descended her parents' front steps, he was too nervous to speak, trying to walk so that his cuffs would swing out over the green-stained toes. And she turned to him and said, "Here, could you take care of this? I don't have any pockets," and she handed him some folded cash. He was amazed. She hardly knew him. But he took the money like a diploma conferred in advance, supposing that maybe this was the usual etiquette on dates, that maybe it was intrinsic to girls winsomely to lack pockets; and he began imperceptibly at that moment to relax and expand. That very night, they wound up in her parents' rec room, kissing and stroking in the resinous smell of linoleum and new paneling; and from that summer onward, it now seemed to him, he had begun to put on weight, comfortably, to wax toward marriage. And then after they were married the flesh increased still further when Laura got hugely, scarily pregnant—so convex that it seemed to Wayne unnatural and dangerous, and he couldn't understand Laura's knowing patience as if she'd been through this before; and then Kim arrived with her few disturbing flaws—her ear, her nipple, her lip—and the medical bills started to pile up; and Wayne, who had always worked uninsured under-the-table, thinking himself shrewd on that account, couldn't find an insurer who would let him take out a policy covering such expensive cosmetic surgery.

And now she wanted another child. They had had two abortions since Kim's birth, now sacred in their unmentionability. "Dilation and curettage" had been the language on the bills that arrived, meaningless words, employed for their very meaninglessness, words from which the blood had been drained. During the healing weeks, Laura had seemed to mourn for the evaporative little souls that had vanished in the scent of iso-propyl alcohol. But he was in debt for years ahead; he couldn't afford another child. Though the topic was never brought up, he felt himself stuck in a protracted betrayal of Laura, whose efficient motions could now be heard in the bedroom as she got ready for work: the click of cosmetics, the rustle of her polyester uniform.

She came into the kitchen, radiant in her golden Denny's smock, singing out, "I'm gone!" and Wayne revolved his chair toward her—and then kept on revolving, a whorl spinning in her path, as she walked past him into the living room in quest of her purse—leaving in the air behind her that estranging scent of cosmetics which always made him faintly jealous. She said, "Did Kim go out?"

"Yeah, she went to the mall with Cindy."

"Can I have some money? I'm broke."

"I don't think I have very much . . ."

"Don't you have the thirty dollars I gave you from Friday night? Remember?"

"Oh, yeah. What did I do with that?"

"You put it in the jar on your dresser."

"Okay," he said, rising to get it.

"I just need ten dollars," she said.

While Wayne went into the bedroom he heard her call out, "Hey, what's this?" He knew she was referring to the twenty-dollar bill and in a frozen moment felt adulterous.

"What's what?" he said when he returned to the kitchen. "Oh, that. It's a twenty-dollar bill."

"Where did it come from?"

"Randy left it in our mailbox last night. Some kind of prank or something."

"He left it in our mailbox? Why?"

"I don't know. Some joke, I guess. I'll ask him about it when I see him."

"I love Randy Potts. Have you had any breakfast?"

"No, I don't want anything. I don't like my love handles."

"Still." She opened the refrigerator and took out some bacon and a carton of eggs, and she was already starting to pick at some strips of bacon with her fingernails. Wayne returned to his chair and slid down onto his back. Her forearms moved with exciting sureness in their ministrations.

"You look great," he said. Meaning she looked sexy.

"I'll just get this started." It was a rebuke. She set an egg on the counter.

"Do you have the long shift today?" he said.

"I'll be home about seven. This stupid faucet."

"I'll fix it. It's just a lot of mineral crap that gets stuck in the screen."

"I have to go." She had peeled up two strips of bacon and laid them in a pan. Her hands rubbed together under the faucet.

"Let's have some bizarre sex tonight."

"Well," she pulled her purse strap over her shoulder and walked around behind his chair to begin kneading his shoulder tendons, her fingers damp with tap water. "Let's be normal. It drives me wild when you're normal."

"Okay."

Her pinching fingers made his mind go blank.

She said, "Promise me you won't take yourself too seriously today."

"Okay." Maybe he would cut the grass or something. And

call McCrimmon to see if there would be work tomorrow. The problem was, all these rich childless couples were moving into Marin, nobody was building, painting crews kept getting laid off. And the rainy season was coming, which would mean more layoffs.

She bent over and set a kiss on his balding head and was suddenly gone, leaving a sung-out "See you!" hanging in the air. Wayne felt oddly anointed, peculiarly dissatisfied. The kiss, laid so gently upon the naked crown of his head where she located his fatal cuteness, had caused a kind of gentle, stunning stroke, and he sat there dazed, unable to analyze this predicament, unaware even of the bacon that was starting to spit in the pan. When, a minute later, Cindy and Kim came breathlessly in the door asking for an extra-large safety pin as if it were the most important thing in the world, Wayne was so lost in his daze that he looked up from the twenty-dollar bill at his own daughter in sudden astonishment as if she were a total stranger.

# 4

In Kim Paschke's bathroom, Cindy had laid out on a clean towel the pleasantly sinister tools of ear-piercing—a safety pin, Grand Marnier, some ice cubes, Kleenex, a hard new potato, a matchbook. "Plus, you should get drunk a lot," she said, speaking with plausible authority, "because it takes away your inhibitions, and pretty soon you get in the habit of not having inhibitions."

Kim was hopping on one foot to take off her tangled jeans. "I just hope I don't get cottage-cheese thighs."

"Celluloid," said Cindy.

"Cellulite."

"Whatever," Cindy said, and she popped out of her mouth the ice cube she'd been sucking on, now a translucent gray scarab. She slipped it back into her mouth and crunched it between her molars.

"That's a sign of sexual frustration," said Kim. "Eating ice."

"Who, me? Sexually frustrated? I'm *sure*," her throat pinched the word. "Don't bother with your underpants. Underpants don't weigh anything."

Kim slid the bathroom scale out from under the sink and stood on it, and Cindy crouched to read the trembling dial. "A hundred and five," she said. "You only need to take off five pounds. But it's like I say, attitude is everything."

"Really," Kim mooed.

"Hey, here's one thing. Try this. I always do this." She yanked her shirttails out and showed her torso. "Suck in your gut as far as you can, and hold your breath, and tense up your stomach muscles really hard." She demonstrated, throwing her shoulders forward and drawing her stomach in until it was grotesquely concave, stretched over the skeletal points of her hips. Her voice clenched, she grunted, "Hold it for twenty seconds. A few times a day. It's magic."

Kim tried it, gasping.

"You've already got a great body, basically. It's all attitude. Is that your plastic nipple?"

Kim nodded, still holding her breath.

"Cool. It looks like it's erect."

Kim let the air out and took a breath. "It always does. That's how they made it."

"It doesn't feel anything, does it?"

"Of course not."

"But the other one isn't erect."

"Yeah, but when it's erect they both match each other."

Cindy said, "Can I touch it? I'm really curious."

"Sure."

"I mean, I'm not a lesbian or anything, I just think it's cool."
She set her finger on the small pink tablet, a seed oddly
incapable of root. Beneath her finger, she rolled it back into
a fold of puckered flesh. The fact that it served no biological
purpose and was merely a plastic nub implanted by a surgeon
somehow made it sexier. The other nipple was now erect.

"They really do match. How did they get the right color?"

"They inject pigment. It's like a tattoo. Or part of it."

"Is this middle part the latex part?"

"Yeah, mainly, sort of. But it's inside."

"I wonder how they hold it in. I mean, is it sewed on, or
what?"

"I don't know, it's just sort of *in* there."

"Amazing!" she said. "Eric will never know the difference.
I bet even if he sucks on them, he'll never know. The rubber
one even feels like the same temperature. He's bound to suck
on them, you know."

"Yeah," said Kim, sighing.

"Hey, it's great when they suck on them. Don't keep thinking
of this like it's an English test or something. Is all the rest of
the breasts normal? How amazing!"

"I just wish I could do it my first time with somebody besides
Eric. I wish I could pay a male prostitute or something and
get it over with. I hate sex."

"You'll do fine. You just have to lose five pounds." She
waved at the vulnerable mound of Kim's stomach: "Suck in."
Kim's belly contracted. "You have to stay like that. Just keep
your gut sucked in and it will become a habit. And we'll fix
up your hair."

"I'm so grateful. I don't know what I'd do without you."

"Move your butt forward." She knelt before her and pressed
the small of Kim's back. "Like that. You have to lead with

your hips. You have to walk pelvis-first, so your hips are the first thing to pass through a doorway. You know what I always do?" She gripped the bowl of Kim's pelvis and scooped it forward. "I always do, like belly-dancing exercises." Her sculpting hands slid.

Kim said, "I just wish I could lose my virginity with a complete stranger."

"Hey!" Cindy sat back suddenly.

"What?" said Kim.

She stood up. She frowned and caught a bit of her lower lip between her teeth. "No," she said. "It's too crazy. Forget it."

"What?" said Kim.

"It's really crazy."

"What?"

"I mean, if you really want to have sex with Eric."

"What. Just tell me."

"No, Kim, forget it. You couldn't do it. You're just not the type."

"Come on."

"Maybe I'll tell you later." She picked up the bottle of liqueur and twisted the cap to break the paper seal with its pink governmental engraving. "Here's something, though. I'll tell you a secret. You have to masturbate a lot too. It's one of the most important secret exercises." She imagined the saliva of masturbation flowing in Kim's system to numb and shrink the overdeveloped brain tissues. "It makes you more feminine. It gives you the right body chemistry. Pretty soon you find you just naturally walk pelvis-first."

Kim looked thoughtful for a minute, inert with a fat-girl's inertia, and then she drew breath and whined, "God, I just hate this."

"What? I'm trying to do you a favor here."

"I mean, I hate sex. I wish you could have sex without—without—"

Cindy turned away and picked up the safety pin. "Well, I'm just saying," she said mysteriously. "But whatever. Whatever you're comfortable with."

"Cindy! What? Just tell me."

"No, maybe later." She had had a vision of Kim and Eric in total darkness—in the station wagon in her garage—maybe wearing masks or blindfolds—maybe a meeting arranged by anonymous letter. The blind anonymity of it would make the obscenity complete. But no, it would never work. "And besides," she said, "you have no idea how horrible it is the first time. The first time? It's incredibly painful, and there's blood all over the place. It's so embarrassing for both of you, you wouldn't believe it. It's not romantic. It's not romantic at all, it's just horrible. It's just gross."

She stopped herself. Her voice had risen unexpectedly, and her throat had swelled. Kim shone with new fear. Cindy thought about it and decided she hadn't gone too far: she was speaking from general knowledge, not from personal experience. Her own few grapplings with Jeff were so sticky and quiet, always interrupted by her fear, her stiffening with alarm . . .

"You'll see," she said, lighting a match to sterilize the pin.

"Come on, Cindy. Just tell me what you were thinking."

"Okay, but later. If you're nice."

"I'm nice."

Voices became audible in the kitchen: it was Cindy's father's voice. She set her finger on her lips, and the two girls stared magnetically into each other's eyes, setting up between them a sensitive charged field of listening. Then Wayne could be heard, along with the sound of the refrigerator door: "Want a beer, Randy?"

"It's my dad! Get dressed. Let's go out and see him." The unhealable ache of desertion—which must be love—panicked Cindy, and she dropped the pin and ran out through the corridor, shoved forward by joy, almost to the point of skipping. Her father was in the kitchen, just sitting down across the table from Wayne, and she landed drenchingly on him and threw her arms around his neck and smelled the fatherly scent of fabric, of work.

"How are you doing, Cindy?" he said, patting her behind.

"Fine," she said, hearing her own voice disconcertingly high and cute, suddenly the voice of an eight-year-old.

"I came by the house to see you last night, but you were asleep," he said.

"You should have woken me up."

Randy leaned away from her with a frown of appraisal. He was as handsome as the men in cigarette ads. "You look like a refugee. Doesn't your mother give you any money for clothes?"

Cindy raked over her hair to tousle it. "No, she's a bitch."

"Hey, why do you think I divorced her?"

"She steals all my records, she borrows all my clothes. I want you to come and rescue me."

"Oh, I meant to tell you," Randy said. "You know those little scooters?"

"Mopeds, you mean?"

"Whatever. The kind everybody has these days."

"Vespa, that's the good kind."

"I saw one for sale in San Rafael the other day, and it was only a hundred dollars. And I *almost* bought it, but then I realized your mother would have a cow."

"You should have bought it." She wriggled with disappointment.

"Well, honey, you know how your mom is. But I swear, I could just picture you zipping around on that thing, and I almost bought it. I came *so close*. I'm not lying."

Aware now that he was lying, she scrubbed her scalp to muss her hair and stood up, dangling one hip. "Well, maybe next time," she said. It was a sentence they might recall at her funeral, irrational with grief, realizing that "next time" had never come. She stretched her arms, pressing her breasts forward, holding before the two stupid men the great sorrow of her beauty.

"Cin?" said Randy, patting the back of her leg. "Could you run off and play, as they say in the movies? Wayne and I have some boring grown-up things to talk about."

"Probably sex, right?"

"Just go away, sweetheart."

"I hate you." She kissed him. And she left decisively, with a flounce, in order to create an impression of complete departure. For, in fact, she stopped and crept back behind the partition of the hallway, stopping Kim there—who was now dressed—and silencing her by setting a finger on her lips.

"Let's eavesdrop," she whispered.

"Why?" Kim mouthed.

"Shut up." She hung her head and stared, with eyes dulled by listening, at the pattern of parallel scuff-streaks printed on the linoleum tile squares. She heard Kim's father speak:

"So, Randy. How's everything? Are you a hotshot entrepreneur yet? You know, right now there isn't much work, but McCrimmon always says you could come back on the crew any time."

"No, I'm finished with that. It's too nice being my own master."

"What kinds of things are you looking at?"

"So, listen, Wayne. Did you get my twenty-dollar bill?"

"Yeah, what is that?" There was a rustling of newspapers. "It's under here somewhere."

Cindy was inexplicably excited. There was something in her dad's tone. Something Wayne wasn't aware of.

"What did you think? Did you notice anything about it?"

"Jesus, where is it?" said Wayne. "It was here a minute ago. Oh, here it is."

"Here, compare it with this one," said Randy. "Notice any difference? Just look at the front side. Don't you have anything but Budweiser?"

After a long pause, Wayne said, "I don't see anything. Looks normal to me."

"You know they brew this beer through horses?"

Wayne said, "You mean these numbers?"

"Exactly. They're missing. The four little twelves."

"So what?"

"But you can see a little ghost of a twelve where the twelves should be. Hold it up to the light. Except on that one, maybe it's eights or nines or something."

Wayne said, "Do you think this is counterfeit?"

"That's why I brought it here to show you. I want you to send it to the Secret Service and ask them to test it."

"Why?"

"Because if it's counterfeit it's cool! I'll frame it and hang it on the wall. Or I'll use it to pay my taxes."

"Why do you want *me* to send it in?"

"Well? Don't you want to?" Cindy heard her dad shift in his chair.

"Yeah, I guess so."

"So hey! And also, you're such an innocent kind of guy,

they'll never investigate you. Me, they'll investigate me. My car isn't insured. I always get unemployment payments in the winter when I work for Coast Improvement. And I stole that Jeep in high school? That'll still be on their computers. I'm just generally an asshole. Don't even mention me."

"Sure, I'll send it. I think it's interesting. I'll just tell them I found it in my change somewhere."

"They have a lab in Washington. They'll put it through all these tests."

"It looks like a real bill to me," said Wayne. "Because look. Do you see these little threads? There's little red and blue threads in the paper. They put them in at the mint . . ."

Kim had gone to her room, but now she had tiptoed back, and Cindy lifted her eyes to hold her gaze. She could tell, from the slight dent in Kim's brow, that Kim wasn't making out much of the conversation.

"Where did you get this?" said Wayne.

"I forget. I just noticed it, you know? It was in my wallet."

Cindy walked abruptly down the hallway towards the bathroom. For the first time in her life a peculiar swallowing motion in her vision rendered her unseeing, as if her smile were novocaine and had somehow spread to blind her.

"What?" said Kim when the door was closed.

"Nothing," said Cindy. "Where's that pin?" She picked up the Grand Marnier bottle and strummed the pink governmental seal she had broken. "I heard it hit the floor."

"C'mon, what?" said Kim.

"Nothing, nothing, nothing. Don't ask. Let's get back to your virginity." Something within felt emptied out, making room for this new rush of generosity. "I have an idea about how you could *be* a complete stranger. Does this interest you?"

# 5

The third bill of Bim Auctor's money to enter the local economy—and the last to enter singly—would be spent by Randy Potts on a Quarter Pounder with cheese and fries and a medium Coke at the McDonald's past Radio Shack at the far end of the Miracle Mile. Hunger completed his usual impatience as he sped south along the freeway after leaving the Paschkes' house, toward his appointment with Bim in the McDonald's parking lot.

Steering with a draped wrist, hanging one elbow out the window, thus catching himself feeling almost brainless with self-confidence, he straightened up and regripped the steering wheel, tapped the tape recorder hidden in his inner pocket, and pulled up on the accelerator a quarter inch, symbolic of a new policy of caution in his life—having passed the last mile sightless and unconscious. The circuitry of the Terra Linda neighborhood streets had always been so deeply implanted in his soul that he never watched where he was going, depending blindly on the radar of familiarity, swiping the steering wheel under his palm with invincible casualness. The town had always vanished beneath Randy's unfocused vision. The Sears Automotive Center was invisible, its strung-out Day-Glo plastic pennants rubbed from sight. The Civic Center statue was invisible, elevated above his notice. The huge script *E* of the Emporium, which presided over the Northgate Mall, the American flag above the Buick dealership, the sun-dulled aluminum cross atop the Congregational Church, the immense green exit signs that wafted overhead on the freeway—everything had been erased over the years by glimpsing, so that the whole of his neighborhood provided merely an even, washing, confirming pressure against the cornea.

But now the money had begun to make a tourist of him: the eternal Chevrolet billboard was still unchanged; the dirty-fluorescent Holiday Inn marquee was missing a letter; a willow grew by the San Rafael exit; a NOW HIRING banner was taped up on the window of the Taco Bell, which was separated from the Texaco by a sagging old chain-link fence beaten down by climbing kids. That "money is a necessarily imaginary stuff" is something Bim had said mysteriously a few weeks ago at one of their meetings. As he entered the traffic of the Miracle Mile, he felt the secret had lifted him to a comical new perspective above the ordinary drivers around him—simply because he had caught a flukish updraft, answering Bim Auctor's help-wanted ad in the *Independent-Journal* for a "general secretary/handy man, w/ some financial savvy" and then subjecting himself to a series of interviews, answering many questions which at the time struck him as oddly diagonal. By some miracle of luck, *he* was elected from among the applicants, and Bim at first put him to work doing miscellaneous jobs on a piece of unoccupied rental property in the Canal District; and then three weeks ago, after many apparently casual conversations in which Randy had felt himself nudged by some superimposed concept, Bim invited him to lunch and, with sighs and grimaces, gradually approached the topic: "Tell me, Randy," he said as the waitress was clearing their plates. "Do you think human nature is basically pretty good? Obviously it's a poor question."

Whatever Randy answered at the time, it must have been the right thing, because Bim leaned forward on his elbows and went on. "Do you trust me? Do you think I've got integrity?"

Randy regarded him—so small that he had brought a pillow into the restaurant to sit on, but perfectly handsome, in the bright-eyed way small people often are. Though he was probably in his forties, he looked like a teenager. His miniature hands held up the idea of "integrity" in air: a small globe.

"Well, sure, I guess." Until now, Randy had figured him to be harmless, merely too rich and too smart. He had a way of quoting Plato or Aristotle irrelevantly which unfitted him for normal life, and a kind of asexual sheen, as if he were lonely, isolated by being so much better than everybody.

"I wonder if your faith in me could withstand some rather severe tests."

He felt always with Bim as if some kind of stencil were being placed over him. He shifted in his chair. "Nobody's perfect, I guess."

"True. True. Exactly. I think there will come a time when you decide you don't trust me. In fact, it's essential to things that eventually you repudiate me. Yes, that is a notion you may resist now, which is gallant of you, Randy. But mark my words. The day will come when you decide you don't credit me anymore. Because you see, I've chosen you for a somewhat more difficult job than this carpentry on Medway Street."

"I'm not sure what you're getting at."

"All right, listen closely. I'm about to ask you to make the most important decision in your life. In a sense, the decision has already been made—and for that I apologize. I'm involved with a very important project, of which no one but myself is now aware. And at this juncture, I am placing my trust in you. It involves a great deal of currency. It might be considered illegal in a purely technical governmental sense. But if you follow my orders perfectly you yourself won't be inculpated, even in the virtually nonexistent chance that something goes wrong. There are a series of fail-safe mechanisms, which you'll get to know. Your job will be just to go on being yourself, in every way. First of all, you will know nothing of the project. This is to preserve your innocence. You will be told only about certain specific tasks. There will be an impermeable membrane between us blocking information flow, in either direction. You must be willing to follow my orders without any specific knowledge of the money's origin; and I must have no specific knowledge of your activities. This preserves us not only legally but ethically, you see . . ."

Bim had given him a week to consider his proposal. But his mind had been made up right away. Bim had made it sound foolproof, promising that he had already written and planted documents proving Randy's innocence; that there would always be scot-free bail-out procedures in case Randy should lose heart and want to quit his employment; that there was even a fail-safe mechanism in case of Bim's unexpected death. Bim was of course obviously peculiar; but he also really did have this thing integrity. Even his physical person seemed to radiate good will. At times since, in moments of worry, Randy had tried to lay upon him the image of a "criminal"; but such pictures immediately exploded as absurd. He'd said, "Just trust your own judgment, Randy. Trust your basic feelings about me. Because your basic instinctual feelings are all you ever have to fall back on. And I promise you, it will be hard. It will be hard to operate in ignorance. You will never know the uses of this money. Nor its origins. You must be able to carry out my instructions in the belief that my motives, and yours, are honorable. Naturally, you should reward yourself. You're free to spend any excess cash as you see fit. I mean that. Part of the protocol is that I may never ask you for an accounting. Because I too must be ignorant of your half of the project. The protocol is designed to keep us both innocent. Literally."

It was still a strange, slow surprise some mornings when he woke up amidst the divorcé's squalor of his apartment, to feel gradually unweighted against the mattress with the remembrance of this new force in his life. By danger he felt rescued. There were no longer those vague awakenings alone in the night, the feeling of permanent lovelessness in his bones, the tidal pull of his marrow toward the sick moon. Even now, driving along the Miracle Mile obeying all the traffic rules, he sensed himself a disguised god. Every cute little blonde in tight blue jeans was sexier, more vulnerable. He would be as irresponsible as he liked. For indeed, that was Bim's plan; Bim had designed the whole thing to protect him from responsibility. Even now, if he were interrogated by police, he could honestly say that his employer had simply given him some cash and told him to send it to the Secret Service; and that was all he knew.

Still, he had decided to take a few self-protective measures of his own. Bim sometimes seemed so peculiar, in a worrisome sort of way—his seeping little smile, his saintly gaze, his occasional flights of irrelevant moralizing—Randy had decided to create some evidence that might be useful later. The little tape recorder in his inner pocket was cued to begin recording at a single tap of the pause button. The conversation with Bim would be trapped permanently on magnetic tape, so that he would have a document, just in case, to prove that he was merely a passive employee taking orders in ignorance. He wasn't trying to fabricate anything. All he needed was a little something to prove the truth.

He found Bim parked in the back corner of the McDonald's lot in a long white car. So slight, he looked like a little boy sitting in the driver's seat, reading a book, stroking each page vertically as he read with those small artistic hands that seemed in gesture always to wash or bless. When Randy approached the car—like any ordinary American sedan, but unlike any he had ever seen—the side window retracted humming into the door and the film of reflected Miracle Mile traffic slid down to reveal a clearer view of Bim, marking his place in his book and setting it aside. "Good morning, Randy," he said. "How punctual you are!"

"Hey . . . !" Randy tossed up his arms to accept the applause.

"Hop in." The electronic door lock on the passenger side sent out a click. He jogged around the car's funny grille and got in, sliding into a leather seat as big as an airplane seat— and swinging shut the door with a vaultlike sound of steel embracing steel.

"This is a different car, is it American?" he said, fingering a pressure-sensitive lozenge of walnut in the door panel which made his window glide down with surprising slowness.

"Randy? I'm sorry, could you put the window up? All the lead in the air."

"Oh, of course." He pressed the other square of wood. "What's it called?"

"It's called a LaGonda, actually. It's English. They don't make many of them."

"On the outside it just looks like a plain old Ford or something."

"No, it isn't very flashy, is it. But tell me, how did it go with your friend?" He tossed himself into a sideways position in his seat, drawing up his tiny legs.

"Fine. Perfect. He said he'd send the bill. And he doesn't suspect a thing. He looked at it for a long time, and he said it looked genuine to him. But hey, what does Wayne know?"

"Randy, I have to remind you not to mention your friend's name to me. Remember the protocol."

"Oh, yes, I'm sorry. Anyway, the point is, he didn't suspect a thing."

"Randy? Didn't we have an agreement?"

"I'm sorry. Really. I just wasn't thinking for a second."

"But that was an important second. Do you understand? There are *reasons* for the protocol, Randy. If you continue to permit yourself these errors . . ."

"I'm sorry, I promise I'll remember the protocol from now on."

"Well, all right," said Bim. "I think we're justified in proceeding with the next stage. What do you think? Do you think we'd be premature in going ahead, on the assumption that we'll pass the test?"

"Sure. Full speed ahead. Don't ask *me*." His right hand slipped up inside his coat and pressed the pause button on his tape recorder. He could feel against his breast the closure of the electronic circuit, and immediately he hated himself for his duplicity.

Bim slid the book he had been reading into a console between the seats, and he drew himself up to sit on one ankle. "Now listen closely. I want you to be in Curaçao on the fifth of next month. There is a resort called Las Palmas, and I want you to be there at noon on the fifth. Outside the lobby is a pay phone, which will ring at noon. And when you pick it up, I'll be on the line to give you further directions." He paused. "Randy, you don't know where Curaçao is, do you."

"No." The idea of foreign travel hadn't occurred to him. It worried him.

"Curaçao is an island in the Antilles, in the Caribbean. The Las Palmas Resort and Casino is outside Willemstad. That is the big town on the island."

"Why Curaçao?"

"You ought not to ask, but I'll tell you since you'll soon find out: I want you to do some banking there. I want you to set up accounts denominated in various foreign currencies."

"Wait, do you have a pencil?" he said, trying to seem earnest in spite of this new-kindled misgiving. The whole idea of traveling bothered him. The scale of activity was growing too large. It occurred to him that maybe now he was recording an incriminating conversation and would have to erase this tape.

"No, these are verbal instructions. You mustn't write anything down. You'll find a single page in the Canal District house next week with some specific information, but today I want you to depend on your memory. Leave all the writing to me. Can you remember that? Be outside the Las Palmas lobby in Curaçao on the fifth, and the phone will ring at noon. Get there any way you like."

"Okay, sure."

"Good. Now then. Until that time, I have another job for you. You must find all the safety-deposit-vault companies in the area and open accounts. The storage of all the physical product is our biggest problem, and it will occupy most of your time in the next few months. You'll now find a large number of twenty-dollar bills in the Canal District house."

"Twenty-dollar bills! Is it just sitting there?"

"In cardboard boxes. You'll have to build some proper crates. That's the first thing."

"It's just sitting there by itself?"

"Yes, it's safe. What I want you to do is to set up a number of accounts in safe deposits."

"Should these accounts be in fake names?"

"I don't need to know. Do it any way you like. But as always, I recommend prudence. This is a million bills."

He had said a million bills. That would be twenty million dollars.

"How much space does it take up?" Randy said, his voice springing lightly in this throat while his heart quickened against the tape recorder. A million bills would stack up as high as a refrigerator. Or several refrigerators.

"You'll see. You'll find it all in the kitchen."

He looked out the window, unseeing, his imagination dilating under the concussion of this realization: storing the "physical product" will "occupy most of your time in the next few months."

"You'll have a great number of storage sites."

"Why?"

"Well, Randy, the sheer physical volume of product."

"No . . . I mean . . ." This feeling worsened—of getting pushed by a force which if he stood still would snap him off.

"I'm sorry," said Bim. "It's essential to both of us that you not ask."

"Well, yeah, but . . ." He cast his eyes upward and winced sneakily to indicate moral qualms.

"Randy, governments themselves have always been more shameless circulators of money."

"No, it's just." He was pitching his voice to the tape recorder. "It's just it goes against my instincts. This whole thing where I don't know what you're doing."

"Randy, listen to me now. There's a wonderful old book, from the Middle Ages, by a fellow who was very famous at the time. His point is that separation from God consists in selfishness. It's a book about motives, really. And the point is that 'sin' consists precisely in establishing a 'self' separate from God's will. These are outmoded concepts these days, aren't they? But the fact of psychology is still valid. We must guard against our motives' ever becoming self-serving."

Bim always got heavy-lidded and mild-smiled when he slipped into this tone. Randy looked down at his sneakers on the thick carpeting, his hearing stopped by the roar of his thoughts; that he wasn't basically sneaky enough to be a criminal; that a circle of imaginary detectives listening to this tape in a possible future wouldn't know what to make of Bim's sermon; that Bim Auctor might turn out to be crazy, too crazy to trust.

"Or does all this sound insane?" Bim said. "Don't think I'm insane. I'm as aware as you of the risks here, and I'm taking every measure to protect you. You have no idea how carefully I've designed our procedures. Just trust me. All right? Randy? If you have any doubts, we should talk about them."

"Well, here's one thing," he said finally, deflecting the topic.

"This old Camaro of mine. If I'm going to be hauling around crates of cash . . ."

"Randy, please, the protocol! Do you know what *literally* means? Don't consult me on trivial matters like car purchases. The legal fact is that the money is now yours to dispose as you please. I've told you you should use it to meet any expenses. I trust you. Do you keep that constantly in your mind? That I trust you? I think this interview is at an end. Tell me if you're clear on your duties."

"Yes," said Randy. "Build crates for the twenties and rent some vaults to store them." His breath had gone shallow, and his head light with betrayal. Within his soul was the vacuum left by throwing everything away in order to gain everything. If Bim knew about the small wheels of the tape recorder revolving next to his heart, the whole plan would be suddenly finished.

Bim said, "And be in Curaçao at noon on the fifth."

"Hm."

"Randy. Wait. I'm sorry. It's clear to me right now that you're losing heart. Didn't I warn you that it would be hard to go on believing in me?"

"Well, Bim!"

"Yes?"

"Isn't it normal? To be a little apprehensive?"

"It's true, I'm sorry, the apparently shady aspects of this are troubling, aren't they? I apologize for that. There's an old Confucian saying, Randy—just hold this in your mind: *If a man handle chrysanthemums, he will smell good; if a man handle pitch, his hands will get black.*"

"Yes, okay," he said, getting out of the car, unable to file this flimsy strip of a maxim anywhere. "I'll remember that."

"It's advice to the spirit," Bim said. "Since you're so obviously confused, just now, why don't you take the day and relax. I advise you to meditate actively. Think about what I've said. Sleep on it, and see how you feel tomorrow. It would be awful for you to go on collaborating with me if you've lost heart."

"I'm okay. Really. It's just weird."

Bim turned the ignition key and the car started, not with the whinny and roar of American cars but with a click and a hum. "I have confidence in you. Relax. And leave a signal for me at the Canal District house when your friend gets a response from the Secret Service. You won't hear from me for a while."

"Yes. Okay." He was crouching now in the open door.

"I want you to feel free to discuss any misgivings with me."

"No, Bim, it's okay. It's just that it goes against your instincts to operate in the dark; because when you do something, you need to have some idea exactly—"

"I understand, Randy. Just keep me informed. Don't stop communicating how you feel. That's the important thing. I wouldn't ask you to do anything against the law. But right now I have to go. Good-bye. And good luck."

"So long, Bim."

With an inner crunch of satisfaction since he now had on tape exactly what he needed, he pressed the door shut, sealing in the atmosphere. As the car backed up, the reflected images of the sunny neighborhood began to bulge and pinch, sliding down the windshield. He walked back across the parking lot relaxing his shoulders in an effort to feel again the warm surrounding liquid of his confidence in Bim. I wouldn't ask you to do anything against the law, he had said unmistakably.

Why had his fear come on so suddenly? At the mention of the money. Twenty million dollars. The reality of it. As he sat there in that leather seat, he had felt in his lungs a falling sensation. Helplessly, he had seen the glisten of irrecoverability on ordinary objects in the sunshine outside.

He took out the tape recorder and pressed the rewind button.

But when he pressed play all he got was woolly rustling sounds—his own shirt—and occasionally the distorted rumble of his own voice through his ribs; the words were unintelligible. Bim wasn't there at all.

The only thing to do was relax. Bim was perfectly right in saying that he hadn't yet done anything "illegal"; the technical miracle of this distinction still guarded him. He should just try to relax and wait to see if the Secret Service would call the specimen genuine or counterfeit. If they wrote back to say it was counterfeit, he might almost feel slightly relieved to abandon the project.

But these were supernaturally perfect bills. Bim had such confidence in them that he had told Randy that, if the lab declared the specimen genuine the first time, he should send it back a second time, insisting they had made a mistake and it really was counterfeit, asking them to give it a more thorough test. If it passed a second time, then surely it was foolproof.

First of all—as an experiment with himself as much as with the money—he could try spending this bill, ceremonially, to make it real. He veered away toward the McDonald's, to spend the last of the extra twenties in return for a Quarter Pounder, french fries, a Coke, and a handful of ordinary money in change.

# 6

A scissoring whir rose up in sighs from Wayne's back yard into the neighborhood sky. The old lawn mower was hard to shove and jab through the tall, for some reason wet grass, and a vinegar dew was distilled in Wayne's hairline. He always hated the prospect of cutting the grass until he finally got going—until, driven out of the house by the ache of Sunday afternoon, he went out into the back yard to unpadlock the prefab aluminum English Tudor shed on cinder blocks, and released from within it that dissolving childhood fragrance of the power-driven lawn mower: the smell of spilled, rinsing gasoline and that intensely green fibrous paste that clung to the metal skirt and almost gagged him with the scent of fermenting vitamins. But the gas tank was empty. And the bonking goose-neck gas can in the cold shadows gave up only a thin urinary dribble. So he had pulled out the old manual lawn mower—Laura's father's—whose handle was missing one bolt and therefore wobbled trickily like a compound fracture. After five or ten minutes of lunging forward against the forest of wet green spears, he had reached that pleasant deaf aerobic intensity of meditation that solitary work provides, his mind like a racing flywheel on the machinery of his work, growing angry: his little brother, who was attending a series of graduate schools in the rectangular, pastel middle states, had phoned long-distance six months ago to ask for his kidney.

"Well, Tim, I'm using it at the moment," Wayne had said.

"I'm talking about way off, Wayne. My kidneys are fine now. Besides, you've got two, I only need one." His brother's voice, thinned by long-distance, had grown even smarter over the years.

"Don't they have donors for kidneys? People who die in car crashes?"

"You're my brother. The genes are better. Or the blood types are more closely matched or something."

Wayne had always been the lucky one, the one to get a pickup truck, the one to go to Disneyland. Their father, especially after dinner when he had had enough to drink that he became cruelly merry, would ignore everything Tim said, while always bending an ear attentively to Wayne. He would never forget the fear in his brother's blue eyes, across the dinner table. *My God*, his dad turned to shout, *learn to take a fucking joke*.

But the fearful prosper. Now Tim kept winning grant money, getting too smart to communicate with Wayne anymore. He had actually bought his own house, a big Midwestern three-story farmhouse. When their parents died, leaving no estate at all, it was as if an ocean had receded from the earth and left them stranded too far apart to be any help to each other. When Tim bought his house he sent a snapshot of it in an otherwise empty envelope.

"Well, yeah, you asshole," Wayne said. "I guess I'll give you my goddamned kidney. Jesus, you're an asshole."

"Look, I'll pay you," said Tim. "How much do you want? It's about two dollars a pound at the supermarket."

"How much does a kidney weigh?"

"I don't know. I don't even know what they look like. Four or five pounds?"

"That's ten dollars."

"Wayne, I appreciate it."

Tim's diabetes came on a foggy Halloween Night in the late fifties: he had tagged along behind Wayne dressed as Mighty Mouse in a dime-store costume held on by apron strings, dragging his paper shopping bag full of candy on the rain-soaked pavement. And when he got home to discover that all his candy had fallen through a soggy hole in the corner, and that he had left a trail on all the neighborhood sidewalks, his despair was oddly satisfactory to Wayne. Though Tim wept, Wayne refused to share any of his candy; and after his mother had rushed out to the store to buy Tim some candy of his own and establish justice, Tim gorged himself vengefully. He drank eight glasses of milk while they watched the sherbet-colored cartoons of "The Huckleberry Hound Show" on TV, both sickened by their wealth in the narcotic light of the screen. And then Tim began to feel weak, twitchy, and he fell into a deep lustrous coma, from which he emerged two days later a very different person, a pale boy in a hospital gown, less fidgety, more serious. And somehow more valuable than before—refined. His pancreas, which Wayne imagined as a tiny oyster-shaped thing among the intestines, had stopped secreting its necessary juice. There

was talk above his head of complications in later adulthood—
circulation problems, blindness, gangrene in the extremities,
kidney failure—but "adulthood" was still a dinosaurian fable,
unthinkable. Since then the seas had receded, the sun had
shrunk to a sequin, Wayne and Tim had actually grown into
these ambiguous and fumbling doomed dinosaurs. And the
doctors' predictions were coming true with comedic, Aesopian
inevitability.

Wayne had sighed into the telephone. "So look," he said.
"When do you need this kidney?"

"Years and years from now. Maybe never. I'm just asking
ahead."

"Five pounds."

"Four, five, yeah."

"Five pounds is what I'm trying to lose," Wayne said. "I'm
fat and bald now."

"Hey, Wayne, I'm sure it's a lovely kidney. I'm sure it's a
*fun* kidney."

But now he felt angry, jabbing the lawn mower harder. It
was a dangerous operation. The survival rate for donors wasn't
a hundred percent. And he would have to take time off work
he couldn't afford. Which was a concept totally foreign to his
brother, who had no family responsibilities and lived in a
bachelor's luxurious impoverishment on the ebb and flow of
university grants, while hypocritically buying his own house,
sleeping with all the young girls in graduate school. Wayne
kept ramming the lawn mower into the tall grass at the back
corner of the yard, where it stuffed the rolling cylinder of blades
to make them stop. He was reaching an age in his life when
he would have to recognize that he had always lacked some
mysterious element in his personality. That he would just get

poorer and poorer. A scent was growing in the pink air of dusk, a clove scent of somebody resurfacing a tar roof somewhere in the neighborhood.

He stopped work to stand still in the steam of his own body heat and breathe deeply of the faint, probably carcinogenic licorice, the smell of many summers past. He had remained faithful to Terra Linda, he hadn't gone on to college. It was a kind of vigil. It was a kind of virtue—his pact with Randy Potts to drop out of high school together and thus elevate themselves morally into permanent sarcasm. He breathed deep, flushing his lungs of the greasy nicotine film of Marlboro Lights.

"Looks great, honey," said Laura's voice. He turned.

She was sliding aside the screen door and stepping out onto the patio in her uniform, with that uncertain step she used when she was entering upon his projects. "What's wrong with the power mower?"

"No gas. How was work?"

"Is 'Tater Tots and Salisbury steak okay?" She held up the usual tinfoil pods from work.

"Sure. Where's Kim?"

"I don't know. Want a beer? Work was weird," she said, going into the refrigerator and raising her voice. "You know Brenda? I told you about her? She's the new hostess?"

He sat down on the edge of the patio, and Laura came back with two cans of beer, handing them both to Wayne to open. The misty silver cylinders were cold and healing against Wayne's palms, which had grown grimy with work. The aluminum tab yielded to his fingers with a kissing sound that punctured the afternoon heat, and smoke curled in the hole. He held the can out to Laura, but pulled it teasingly away from her, and, when she came closer, set his salty lips on her forearm. She knelt beside him and put her arms around his neck, but Wayne shrugged. "I'm dirty."

"I know. I like it." She lifted her crisp Denny's skirt almost to the central white pad between her thighs and swung a leg over to straddle his lap facing him. Wayne dropped back to prop his elbows on the concrete of the patio. "You smell good," she said, sitting on his thighs.

"Hm." He swigged from his beer.

"So anyway. She's got this roommate? And the roommate started to get fat? And feel sick? And she thought she was pregnant?"

Laura drank from her beer, and Wayne now lay out fully on his back beneath her on the concrete, pillowing his head on one forearm, closing his eyes against the blue sky. Pregnancy kept getting mentioned more and more often. With a feeling like the desolation of nightmares, he pictured a second CHILDS BR trying to wedge its way crushingly down into the floor plan of this rented house. After each abortion, he had felt estranged from her by intervening silences. The hovering angel kept being driven away.

"But Brenda says then they thought it was an ectopic pregnancy."

"Which is like a false pregnancy?"

"The baby gets stuck in the fallopian tubes or something. I don't know. Or else the sperm travels way up and fertilizes an egg in the ovary. It's supposed to be really horrible."

He wanted to wriggle out from beneath her straddle. "Well, anyway"—he shouldered himself up on his elbows—"I should finish before dinner."

"But then?" she went on. "Then they decided it was cancer

of the ovaries. It's a long story, they went around and around, and finally they decided to operate. And you know what?"

"What."

"This is horrible. They operated on her ovaries and took out the tumor, and you know what? It was as big as a grapefruit, she said."

"Yuck."

"But this is the horrible part. It had hair and teeth."

"What did?"

"The tumor. Can you imagine? I mean, it didn't have a jaw or anything. But it had, like, the seeds of teeth embedded. And it had hair."

His image of the thing surged up in his mind. He struggled out from beneath Laura's hips. "Jesus," he said.

"Isn't that disgusting?" she said.

"Who was it?"

"What do you mean, 'Who was it'?"

"I mean . . ." He didn't know what he meant. "I mean, was it alive?"

"Well, sure it was alive. A tumor is living tissue."

"But I mean, was it supposed to be a person."

"Yes, Brenda says maybe it was a partly fertilized egg or something. Like there were chromosomes in it."

"Can that happen?"

"They said maybe if you get cancer of an ovary. But isn't that just the most horrible thing? It was living inside her like a parasite."

The thought made him shiver. He picked up his icy beer but set it down again. "I have to finish up," he said, his eyes scanning the yard. He wasn't hungry anymore; he wanted to *earn* an appetite, working so hard his eyes would lose their focus amidst the smell of cut stems. A strong appetite was starting to be an elusive thing; everything was simpler in the days when he was always hungry. That Randy Potts, he was always hungry. He could eat two hamburgers rapidly, and then walk away with a cheerful predatory spring in his step.

"Oh, yeah," he said. "Randy came over. You know that twenty-dollar bill? He thinks it's counterfeit. We mailed it to the Secret Service."

"Really? Where'd he get it?"

"I don't know," said Wayne, pushing himself up, back toward work. "Somewhere."

And two hours later, over gravy-smeared plates, Laura said, "I bet Randy counterfeited it himself. I wouldn't put it past him." Wayne smiled sadly—it was the old after-dinner sadness of overeating.

"That Randy," Laura said, lifting the plates with the automatic swiftness of her waitress's training. His smile expanded again in agreement, and then died. All those carbohydrates were spreading in his blood, drugging him.

She began to rinse the dishes. "I think Cindy is planning on sleeping here tonight, but I think we're not supposed to know."

He heard the sound of the television in Kim's room, where the two girls were secreted. He said, "What makes you think so?"

She shrugged.

Cindy Potts was so much better-looking than his own daughter, so prematurely wise and sexy. She was getting almost to the state of perfection where Playboy recruits them for centerfolds. It was always astonishing to read, on the biographical page of the Playmate of the Month, how young those girls are. Some of them were born while he was in high school. Maybe

Kim was a late bloomer, but when she did finally bloom she would have no physical imperfections to hold her back in life. On the morning she was born, he had leaned over her sterile Plexiglas cube in the hospital nursery: the unfair slash in her lip, the downy blank space where her ear should have been, the salamandrine webbing of her fingers. Now the years of surgery were almost at an end, and all that was left was this cosmically huge debt to the doctors. It had almost reached a point where just the interest on the debt was outstripping his salary as a housepainter. He could never have foreseen this, that the early years of his life would be mortgaged to the purchase of an ear, a nipple, some cartilage. He kept resolving to find a part-time job for a second income. Ever since McCrimmon had reduced him to half time, Laura had been telling him he ought to place an ad himself, advertising his services as an independent painter. As if it were that easy. As if you could just go out and place an ad. Defeated now by these Salisbury steaks, he felt the necessary energy to be unobtainable, and he lit up a Marlboro Light—in spite of the knowledge that the smoke would intensify the faint headache which had been growing all evening, an accumulated amber spot in the center of his brain. A sort of nightmare feeling of a curse had been clinging to him, climbing on him since nightfall. And later when he finally lay himself down in bed he felt he was installing himself in the imprint of an insomniac, a wrestler lying down to resume a struggle. And indeed, he couldn't get to sleep. He tried to calm himself by picturing the well-trimmed back yard, the interior of the aluminum tool shed, where he had restored the lawn mowers and the clippers and everything to exactly the positions of disarray he had found them in. But he lay awake, a tightening strand in an immense knot. He kept getting angry. He didn't want to give his kidney

to his lucky brother, and simultaneously he hated himself for
feeling this way. It worried him that he had never mentioned
the problem to Laura, whom he told everything . . .

But it relaxed him to keep imagining the interior of the
aluminum shed, where all the work-worn implements of gardening lay unobserved, arranged in the total inertia of neglect,
the utter peace of dishevelment. Finally, as he sank centimeter
by centimeter into a gritty, clammy plane at the surface of
sleep, he began to feel gangrene like Tim's soften his arms
and legs, and suddenly the thing that had been gathering and
clenching within him punched up from beneath: a tumor with
hair and teeth. Who was that?

He jerked awake. Laura was sitting up beside him, her hand
on his shoulder. He had yelped.

"Wayne?" she said. "What's wrong?"

# 7

In the secret hours after midnight, Kim lay stranded in her bathtub almost naked, but wearing her father's ancient stiff Boy Scout poncho, her hair spiked out in twists of aluminum foil, her earlobe still aching. She listened for sounds from her parents' room, poised to seize her glass of Grand Marnier and dump it out in case they should come looking for her. They had gone to sleep hours ago, but now she had heard their voices. Holding herself motionless to prevent the loud crunching of the poncho, she listened until she was sure they had fallen silent to roll back together into the giant sleep of adults, then she lifted the glass of Grand Marnier and poured a little bit down the bathtub's drain, so that when Cindy came back she would think she had been drinking it.

She should have come back by now. The 7-Eleven was only

two blocks away. And Kim had begun to worry about the tint on her hair inside the twists of foil—whether it might bleach the strands if it were left on too long. Fifteen minutes, Cindy had said. She had promised it would bring out only the highlights, so that even her parents wouldn't notice anything. But the chemicals' smell, which flared like a match behind her eyes when she first put her nose into the dish to sniff the black jam of the tint, seemed poisonous; and she had begun to have frightening visions of her hair all streaked and chemical-singed. If she had to go to school with stripes of sulphur in her hair, her only consolation would be the moral satisfaction of knowing it was Cindy's fault; and the familiar inner warmth of being misunderstood.

The bathroom door opened.

It was Cindy. Kim set a finger on her lips and whispered, "My parents."

"What, were they up and about?" Cindy said. She had a bottle of Stop 'N' Go vermouth.

"I think they've gone back to sleep."

"I should have taken that with me and ditched it," Cindy said, gesturing toward the empty Grand Marnier bottle hidden behind the shower curtain. "I know: I'll fill it with water and put it in the toilet tank. Then we can ditch it later."

"Good idea," said Kim, though of course it wasn't.

"So are we wrecked?"

"Really," Kim lied, voluptuously arching an eyebrow. She lifted her glass and sipped. "How'd you get the booze?"

"I cruised it. These guys came up. They said this was all they could get with three dollars: Stop 'N' Go . . . I bet it's terrible."

"Cindy, hasn't this stuff been on my hair long enough?"

"How about this?" said Cindy, uncapping the vermouth and frowning at the label. "You could wear a mask. They have nice-looking masks, like feminine, with pointy eyes."

"Eric would know it was me. Let's wash this stuff out. It's been fifteen minutes."

Cindy drank from the bottle and made a grin of distaste. "And I suppose you couldn't kiss him with a mask on."

"Cindy, can't we take off the foil?"

"Oh, God, you're such a retard. Put your head over the sink."

With a rustle of the poncho, she got up out of the tub and saw her foil-fringed face rise into the mirror.

"Kim. Pelvis?"

"Oh, yeah, I forgot, I'm so retarded," she said in her elite sadness.

"Or!" said Cindy, plucking out twists of foil. She was obviously getting drunk. "Or, you could be so famous that you have to keep your identity a secret. You're a famous princess, who's also a model, and everywhere you go guys in tuxedos are throwing themselves at you. But you're lusting after this dorky high-school boy, so you have to meet him in complete darkness. Drink up."

Kim drained the last of the Grand Marnier, sustaining Cindy's intoxication, and she put her head down into the sink.

"I'll just wash this out and you'll be amazed. You'll be sorry you didn't trust me."

"I trust you," said Kim, her voice muffled pitifully by mask-close porcelain. Cindy splashed handfuls of hot water over her head, and then began to spread over her scalp a cold dose of her refrigerated apricot-smelling shampoo.

"I promise," said Cindy, scrubbing hard. "Within a month,

Eric DeBono will be deflowering you. I've got some books, with techniques and everything. Like, there's a lot of stuff you're supposed to say during."

She felt sick whenever she pictured it, sick with a fear greater than she had felt before any of her operations, which in fact she had always undergone with a kind of mellow trustfulness that, since, struck her as amazing. And Cindy always talked about it so gaily and casually as if Kim had a normal body. In her worst imaginings, Eric would draw back in horror. Or, to touch her latex parts would turn out to be a prank, a dare he had accepted among scornful friends.

Cindy stopped scrubbing to take a swallow of the vermouth. "Stop 'N' Go," she gasped with disgust, and then took another swallow. "Okay, rinse out."

Kim let the water run over her scalp, tossing sheets of it back over her neck, and then she straightened up—starting to feel the liquor now like a queasy sunburn—and accepted the towel Cindy handed her. Wet, her hair didn't look any different in the mirror. Her face was plain, incapable of beauty.

"Or we could say the police are after you or something. You're a runaway. Or you're a nymphomaniac. That way, you could be really lustful. Pelvis."

Kim pressed her forgetful hips against the sink. As she toweled her hair dry, it was a relief to see that the color seemed to be emerging unchanged.

"Let's go in your room to blow-dry it," said Cindy. "We can be quieter in there. This is cool, I'm drunk. Hey, Kim?"

"Hm."

"You know what would be fun? This occurred to me."

A weaving tone had entered Cindy's voice.

"What."

"You know that bill your dad is sending to the police? We should intercept the letter."

"Why? And Cindy, he already sent it."

"No, we should intercept the police letter when it comes back—just check the mail slot every afternoon. We could steam it open."

"Why?"

"Just 'cause it would be fun."

Kim didn't answer, but let the subject drop, saying merely, "Hm," as if to indicate indifference. She pulled her head out of the noisy poncho—which was so old it had shed flakes of its stale green skin all over the room, to be swept up tomorrow—and she put on her nightgown and followed Cindy into the bedroom, bringing with her, unmentioned, the empty Grand Marnier bottle, to get rid of it in a less ingenious way than through the toilet tank. She was aware of an indigestible stone in her stomach. What Cindy had said—about the things one must say during—had fixed like a germ inside her: Cindy's fictions would inevitably bring about a specific reality. A boy's penis and testes, which she had seen only in cross-section illustrations in anatomy textbooks where they looked like halved gourds, must be the strangest, most pitiful appendage. But she had to go through with this, to break the spell that had been laid upon her flesh like an imagined whiff of rubber in the nose. And Cindy was necessary.

"Better texture." She rubbed some strands of Kim's hair in her fingers. "And see? Just highlights."

Kim turned on the blow-dryer. While Cindy sat cross-legged on the bed and began to write on a sheet of notebook paper, Kim prodded her hair with the blow-dryer before her reflection in the mirror, until it smelled of hot plastic, snarled with crackling electricity; and astonishingly, a new head of hair emerged—the same but better, with lights in its depths. And there was a springy new resiliency to it.

She turned off the blower and said, "This is incredible. It's exactly like the girl in the Opium commercial."

Cindy glanced up, and then returned to her page, saying, "Well, we'll check it in the light of day tomorrow. You're looking good. Masturbate tonight."

She set aside her writing, with a slap, and came to stand behind Kim, grasping through the nightgown a pinch of flesh on her thigh, and on her inner arm. "This and this," she said.

"What are you writing?" said Kim.

"Just a first draft of a note to Eric."

"Let's see," said Kim, and she bounced cross-legged on the bed to read it. Cindy sat down opposite her, took a drink from the bottle, and passed it to Kim. "Have a slug." Kim wriggled closer on her buns and took a drink as reckless as Cindy's. They were close enough to bump foreheads, their secrecy intensified by being squashed between them like the balloon of power that holds apart two positive-poled magnets.

Dear Eric—

Do not read this note in the presence of any other people. You must never reveal this note and it's contents to anybody. If you are now reading it with people around, fold it up and go somewhere to be alone . . . . . . . .

Are you alone? Good.

I am your secret admirer. I want to have a secret rhondevous with you but you must never reveal this to anybody, or else there will be terrible consequences. You have never met me I dont go to your school or anything. My identity must remain forever anonymous

Kim was ashamed beforehand. This would never work, it was destined to fail.

"That's as far as I got. We have to decide who you are."

"You decide," said Kim, with a feeling of willful blindness coming into her eyes.

"Come on, you have to decide," said Cindy. "You can be anything. A model, a prostitute . . ."

"No, just . . . just you decide, and tell me what to do. I can't . . ."

"You can't what?"

"It's just so hopeless.

"It isn't hopeless. You wait and see. Eric will be there."

"Yeah, but I don't know anything."

"Wait till you see these books. There's illustrations and everything. It's really step-by-step. They tell you what to do with your tongue and what to say during and what to say after. It's guaranteed."

"It's just so weird." Kim felt herself receding, drawing Cindy onward.

"What's weird?" Cindy pursued.

Suspended together in the ghost-crowded ether of this generalization, the two girls fell silent and stared off into space. They each took a swallow from the bottle of vermouth.

"Know what I like?" said Cindy, setting her ear on her shoulder. She was so drunk now that she had to prop herself on her arms. She had finished most of that first bottle herself.

"What."

"Boys' hips. They're so funny and bony. The leg attaches to the body in a neat way."

"Like pliers," said Kim.

"I guess." Cindy took another sip from the bottle and handed it over. "You should think about your hymen," she said.

"Why?"

"You might want to take care of it beforehand. Like with a sharp object. Lots of girls do."

"Oh, God!" said Kim. "I don't even know what my hymen *looks* like." Her soul had made a sick spasm. Cindy was too drunk.

"It's like the tamper-proof seal on vitamins, but with some people it's really painful. And it's like I said: it'll be embarrassing if it happens with Eric. He'll just be grossed out. The smart thing to do is, do it at home by yourself beforehand."

Slipping upward into forgiveness, Kim pulled away from the topic: "Well, I'm too much of a coward. Let's just work on my hair for the time being."

"Oh. Speaking of hair . . ." Cindy put on a somber leer.

"Oh, jeez, Cindy!"

"Well, look, do you want to be perfect or not? What do you think making love is *about?* The hymen, the pubic hair, you have to think about these things. You just have no idea."

"Okay, okay, I'm sorry," said Kim. "But listen, though. I'm serious. Just don't tell me about the arrangements. Okay? You write a letter to Eric, and you tell him where to be and whatever. And then surprise me with it. Just surprise me. I can't be part of it."

"Surprise you?" Cindy accepted the bottle from Kim. She was lit by an artificial fever, her eyelids closing blissfully. "What do you mean surprise you?"

"Like, you plan the whole thing. You send the notes and everything without telling me. And then just bring me over to your house one night without telling me Eric will be there. I won't have the courage if I know. You have to trick me into it. Is that okay? I'm serious."

"It's because you're so *nice*."

"No I'm not."

Cindy's eyes were closed. "I hate you."

"Come on, Cin."

"Will you at least help me make up a few notes?" She dropped backward on the mattress to stretch toward the floor where the paper had fallen. Her fingertips barely grazed the paper, trembling with the effort of reaching, but then she gave up and relaxed and lay there in a slain position.

"I'm too comfortable to move," Cindy said, her voice slurred, her breath stirring strands of hair that had fallen over her mouth. "Just help me do one letter."

Kim regarded her. She decided to go along with the scheme of checking the mail slot every day and steaming open the letter from the police; letting the subject drop had signaled her acquiescence. "No," she said, "you do the whole thing. I'm too much of a coward. You tell Eric whatever."

Cindy didn't respond.

"Cindy? Are you asleep?"

Kim unwound her legs and stood up to get the sleeping bag. "I'll sleep on the floor." Cindy's corpse bounced listlessly when the mattress was sprung by Kim's standing up.

# PART TWO

# 8

It took almost three weeks for the Secret Service to return the specimen of Bim's twenty-dollar bill. Randy in his edgy new life had kept himself distracted, filling out forms to establish paper corporations, running errands in the immaculate brochurelike interior of the new panel truck whose fragrance made him feel like an impostor, jingling unfamiliar keys in his pocket, walking through unaccustomed doorways squaring his shoulders, with a constant sensation of soundless hyperreality as if his ears hadn't yet popped—and he had so far been able to feel detached, like merely an "employee." But when one rainy morning at breakfast his phone rang and it was Wayne saying the letter had arrived from the Secret Service, he experienced an ecstatic momentary cramp of justice in his very flesh, a sensation almost like abject prayer: I never meant any harm, I take it all back, it wasn't my idea—

"What did they say?"

"Nothing." Wayne sounded crestfallen. "It says the note in question enclosed herewith is genuine."

"Be right over," said Randy, and he hung up, with a deep lung-searching breath of, unexpectedly, regret: there was no going back now. The wedge of refrigerator-cold pizza in his hand was from a former life; he set it down. He wished there was some way he could get in touch with Bim. But it was Bim's policy to remain totally inaccessible; and, strangely, he had failed to show at an appointed meeting yesterday in the McDonald's parking lot. It was unlike him. There hadn't been any of the usual signals in the Canal District apartment. The last thing Randy had found in the kitchen cupboard was a one-page "Itinerary," which contained only a couple of names and addresses in Curaçao, and some sketchy instructions involving the specific questions he was supposed to ask of this offshore banker. But since then, there had been no communication.

But he knew that he was supposed to send the specimen back to the Secret Service for a second inspection; he could do that much without consulting Bim. He found the aluminum keys to the truck, unlike his old Camaro keys, too light in his pocket to feel potent or genuine, and he ran out the door leaving his pizza half eaten on its cardboard circle, rising and falling on the still-undulating waterbed.

The truck always started immediately, as in an implausible ad for a truck. He jammed amidst complacent wifely Volvos along Third Street toward the freeway beneath the regular snick of the windshield wipers that kept snipping off his forward push. Bim's silence worried him. In the past three weeks he had built ten wooden crates for twenty million dollars—two million dollars per crate—and he had committed the independent felony, or maybe misdemeanor, of renting safe-deposit vaults under assumed identities; he couldn't go on simply being grateful for the close pane of ignorance that protected him from complete vision. Maybe he would go ahead and buy a plane ticket for Curaçao; and he would go ahead and send the specimen back to the Secret Service. He would stick to the plan. But as soon as he could reach Bim, he wanted to discuss changing the arrangement somehow. He didn't have the guts for the life of a criminal, and each new success scared him further. He found, when he got to Wayne's, that the bill had been unceremoniously enclosed in an envelope with a brief letter typed on a Xerox of Secret Service letterhead, as if the office were economizing. It was almost a form letter:

Dear Mr. Paschke:
    Examination has determined that the note in question enclosed herewith is genuine showing evidence of minor defacement. Thank you.

                            Bob Ludex,
                            Senior Investigator

"So there you are, huh?" said Wayne. "Want some coffee?"

"Sure, yeah. But look, Wayne. This time, *ask* them about the missing numbers."

"If you insist," said Wayne. "But I'm sure that's what the defacement is. Somebody just rubbed them off."

"Oh, and could you do me a minor favor?"

"Hey, if you want me to send it back again you shouldn't curl it up like that."

Randy had been unconsciously rolling the bill into a cylinder against his thigh. "Oops," he said, unscrolling it on the formica table to flatten it under his palm. "But look, could you do me a minor favor? I've got this crate in the truck I need to store."

"This is your new truck?"

"Yeah, but I have to store this crate. It was in that Self-Store place on Francisco Boulevard. Can I put it in your garage for a short time?"

"Sure," said Wayne.

"It's small," said Randy. "Just a bunch of stuff left over from the divorce, like probably pots and pans. But it's heavy. Will you help me put it in the garage? It's just in the truck. Why aren't you at work?"

"McCrimmon's an asshole," said Wayne, stabbing his cigarette into an ashtray to go out into the rain. "With this weather they aren't doing exteriors, and I don't have any seniority. Marin County isn't what it used to be."

Randy had always been guilty of luckiness. When they got outside, Wayne said hopelessly, "Nice truck."

"The payments are killing me. But I've been getting some good jobs lately." He unlocked the rear doors and opened them to reveal—along with the crate—the further embarrassment of a new scooter he had bought for Cindy, one of those ugly little amphibious-looking European mopeds which the salesman in Marin Cyclery had said was the only model to satisfy a fifteen-year-old girl.

"Wow," said Wayne. "Is that for Cindy?"

"Yeah, I'm a jerk."

"What are all these jobs you're getting?"

"Same old shit," Randy said. "The usual bullshit carpentry. I just charge more. People will pay anything."

"Whoa," said Wayne, patting the crate. "This looks like you *built* it."

It was true. Why would he build such a solid crate—of sharp-scented new two-by-fours and plywood, with counter-sunk bolts—just to store household odds and ends? Wayne coughed with the effort of lifting his end.

"What the hell kind of pots and pans are in here?"

"Solid granite pots and pans," said Randy.

"Like on the Flintstones," said Wayne, as the two men shuffled into the garage, each holding up an end, to stow the crate in a corner beneath Wayne's workbench. And here was Randy taking advantage of him. Just because it was easier than starting another phony bank account. It felt wrong.

They shoved it back against the wall under the workbench, where it sat with such inertia it seemed permanent. They both straightened up and stretched their backs, two old buddies, partnered by their shared fatigue, by a sense of common mis-chief extending way back into high school days when they were too happy for ambition, content to be swimming and sunbath-ing in the secret lake, biking on the fire roads, pissing in the 7-Eleven phone booth, lying around in their half-completed hut in the depths of Big Cat Canyon. Wayne was so doting, such a constant buddy. Randy always had to keep insulting him to keep him at a distance.

They stood there looking at the crate while the rain sizzled on the roof.

Wayne said, "Laura is pregnant."

"You're joking! That's great!" said Randy, feeling an un-comfortable mental flinch.

"Yeah," said Wayne. He averted his eyes and patted his breast pocket for his cigarettes—which weren't there—which he had left on the kitchen table. They went through the door that joined the garage with the kitchen.

"Well, here's to Laura," Randy said, lifting his coffee cup in toast. He clinked it against Wayne's cup, which sat on the table.

"Definitely," said Wayne, lowering himself into his chair. "That's why I'm looking around for a job. Rent is already a problem. And you know," he nodded toward the bedroom, "with everything."

The remark somehow blamed Randy. Married, Wayne sat so inert, his eyes downcast. It made Randy want to get away, to get back on the road. Besides, Wayne was fortunate; he'd married one of the few halfway decent women left in the world; Laura never bought too many clothes or too many magazines, she had never developed that harsh shine in her personality; and she still had a great body. Their marriage even after all these years still had that mysterious formulaic magic which was defined by Randy's exclusion from it on account of his happy lack of integrity, his charm.

Still he felt a small ache of guilt, of luckiness; maybe some time down the line, when things were more settled, he could pass on a little bit of this cash to Wayne. Without Wayne's knowing. He was supposed to spill a little bit here and there if he felt like it. He was *supposed* to do whatever he pleased. He said, "Where's Laura? At work?"

"She can work there until she starts to show. But they don't have a maternity leave thing."

"Well, you'll just have to hit up McCrimmon."

"I wanted to ask you if you knew of any other jobs around. Who are all these other people you've been working for?"

"Yeah," he said flimsily, "I've been pretty fortunate lately with lucrative jobs. But right now I don't know of anything. You ought to place a classified ad."

"Well, let me know. Not even painting necessarily. Just anything."

"Hey, I wouldn't worry. You know what they say: 'There's always room for one more.' And it's such a miraculous experience. The creation of a totally new human being. It's such a totally amazing thing . . ." The annoying kazoo of his own voice stopped.

After a pause, Wayne said, "Yeah."

"But look," Randy said, standing up. "This is me leaving. I've got a million things to do."

And Wayne, who had zero things to do, nevertheless slapped his thighs and stood up as if filled with cheerful resolve. "Okay, I'll send the twenty-dollar bill back to Washington, right?"

"Right," said Randy. Now *he* was Wayne's employer, was the feeling. "And tell them you think they must have missed something because it really looks like counterfeit. Point out those little numbers where they're missing and ask specifically. Some time why don't we go out and hit Uncle Charlie's or the Beef 'n' Brew, like old times?"

"Yeah, well . . . ," said Wayne in a tone that was like a loosening embrace.

"And hey! Give my congratulations to Laura," said Randy, edging toward the door. "Really."

"Sure."

"You guys must be really happy." And with that remark, Randy walked out into the rain and freed himself from the creeping vines of responsibility, glad to be uncomfortable and rained-on outside. Leaving was his specialty. He loved it, especially in bad weather, the plunge of icy oxygen into the lungs, liberty, moving against the current.

He was somebody else now, the new-car smell kept reminding him; he ought to get used to it: have faith, take a risk, relax. Everything was going according to plan: the Secret Service laboratories had actually passed the twenty as genuine; millions and millions of dollars' worth of twenties were safely stashed all over the Bay Area, in locations known only to Randy, not even to Bim. He ought to go ahead with the trip next week, even if Bim had not contacted him by then. It was of course possible that the Secret Service had in fact determined the bill to be a fake, and had sent it back just to see what would happen next. But this second inspection would solve that.

On the way out of the neighborhood, he stopped at the Civic Center post office to mail a bundle of envelopes—articles of incorporation for two new fictitious businesses, which he had to file with the secretary of state, along with proof of workers' compensation insurance for each of the companies. He had stayed up late last night doing all this paperwork, and now he slid the envelopes into the OUT OF TOWN slot with a satisfaction as if he were banking them. Also, later today, he would drive into San Francisco to rent two more post-office boxes in some forlorn neighborhood, because he had received two new forged birth certificates and he had to begin the process of acquiring Social Security numbers for these two imaginary people who would be directors of two more paper corporations.

He drove out San Pedro Road and headed north on the freeway two exits, to drop off the scooter at Mary's house. Cindy would probably be at school, and Mary would be at her office, so the house should be empty. Whenever he drove this familiar route, swinging off at the Terra Linda exit and arcing over the Freitas Parkway overpass, the car taking each turn and lane change as if habit had put kinks in space, hitting every green light, and finally turning right onto Las Gallinas, he always felt himself reentering that world in which he was a creep. In the past few years he had found a new life in south Marin, where he had recovered himself as the nice guy he always meant to be. San Anselmo, Larkspur, Sausalito. But whenever he swung over this familiar route he felt his momentum guided by enclosing circumstances back into the groove of meanness. It was spooky. Mary like a witch conjured about her circumstances which conspired to make a creep of her ex-husband. It was all those magazines and books she started bringing into the house. They had had a perfectly fine marriage, everything was great, until Mary started to get so smart and not cook dinner because she was too wrapped up in her latest book. Or not stay home to watch their favorite TV shows because she had a stupid class at the College of Marin to go to. She was always looking up from her reading to regard him thoughtfully, so that he kept getting this feeling of being judged in his own house, like invisible cobwebs were breaking across his face. He never thought to do the laundry, he hated those boring PBS "educational" shows, he kept doing some mysteriously wrong things in bed so that Mary would go as limp as a martyr. And he wasn't good at *processing*, as Mary called their arguments. One time, having taken a stab at reading one of her articles, "Why Men Fear Intimacy," he tried to destroy the whole idea once and for all, by sitting down willingly to "process."

But he kept saying the wrong things, and all their discussions kept ending in anger, and Randy started to think, "Well, sure, what the fuck, if this is intimacy, I guess men do fear intimacy. Fuck it. Fuck the whole thing." He hated the magazines arrayed on the coffee table in a fan so that all the articles' titles showed—half of them mentioning "orgasm," it seemed, as if the writers could have some peeking spectatorship of his own

precious, ashamed gifts to Mary in the dark sloshing waterbed—and he used to come home and purposely mess up
the arrangement on the coffee table. He started to get so mad
all the time—about little things, about his inability to pronounce *croissant* correctly; you're supposed to somehow hold
the *r* in the back of your throat and gargle it, and at the mall
the new La Petite Boulangerie, which was taking business away
from Hunt's Donuts, was full of ordinary housewives jutting
out their chins to pronounce *croissant* correctly, so that once
even Mary smirked when he tried—he was getting permanent
shoulder aches, waking up in the morning with a headache
and going through the day angry, ready to hit somebody. He
actually could have struck Mary. There were times when he
wanted to grab her and shake her, as if it would clear her eyes.
And one night as he washed dishes in the kitchen, while they
were processing, Mary said something in that serene, complacent tone which implied her superior knowledge of his deficient
male psychology, and a cast-iron frying pan leaped from his
hand and he turned toward her with violence frozen in his
muscles. He didn't hit her, but the intention had been clear,
a spasm had been printed in a flash on both their memories.
Randy felt transformed into a textbook illustration of her feminism. She slowly smiled, while the clanging of the pan in the
sink died away. In that smile was predestined her successful
career as a real-estate agent, her B.A. in psychology from
Sunset College, her ability to run five miles every morning
working up a sexy sweat alone, her purchase of a Porsche, her
ski trips to Tahoe.

It was amazing, she actually *owned* that wall-to-wall carpeted
house, or at least she was making the payments. And she kept
adding improvements on it, installing a hot tub or a disposal—
so that Randy's apartment's only redeeming comparison was

that at least you could relax there, at least it wasn't cluttered with phony shit like wine racks or framed art posters or knick-knacks, and there was room for a man's elbows. Women apparently preferred to keep everything in their environment pertly in suspense, with small breakable objects near a man's elbows to keep him on edge; whereas Randy needed to scatter a newspaper or smudge a squeaky surface or something, before those bands of muscle between his shoulderblades, after a day's work, gave up their healthy wrath. And now whenever he was at Mary's, he always put his feet up on the coffee table slowly and gently in a delicate act of territorial conquest, his heels nudging those magazines a bit.

But when he pulled up in front of the house, he found Mary's famous purple Porsche in the driveway. She was home.

So he parked—about two doors down the street—and quietly unloaded the new scooter. He left it around the corner of the garage with a note, "For Cindy, from her DAD, RANDY POTTS," because he just didn't want to face Mary. He dreaded the abrupt happiness, the quicker pace she moved in.

After he had propped the scooter on its stand beside the garage and sneaked back unobserved to his truck, as he started the engine and pulled out, he almost regretted a little that he hadn't stopped in for a conversation with her. He would have liked telling her about his trip to the Antilles next week, which of course he would have said was purely for recreation. Last week, just for the hell of it, he had taken an Alfa Romeo on a test drive; and he had found himself explaining to her ghost, in the passenger seat, the workings of the dashboard controls. Some night soon, after things had settled down a bit, he would get dressed and go out to Uncle Charlie's or someplace, and take advantage of the famous aphrodisiac effects of money. Every girl's ass in blue jeans was sexier now, with his money.

Wayne and Laura, whose unborn child might have defects like Kim's, would have to get some of this money. Bim would never have to know about it—indeed, *didn't want* to know. He had told Randy to spend small amounts any way he liked, and never report it. Just as he had insulated Randy from guilt, so Randy could further insulate the Paschkes, and only the cash, leached pure, would filter through to them.

# 9

When Cindy first found the scooter it scared her. She was home alone at dinnertime in that infinite minute of twilight when everything turns the purple of vanishing. The only light in the house was the television, to which she had turned her bright back, and she was wading aimlessly off the back patio, ascending into the darkness, protected by the halo of self-contemplation: thinking of the sinking, grappling doom of sex, of Jeff's eyelashes, the licks of hair behind his ears, his hard ropy hips, the flicker of his smile. Though she felt all hollowed out at the mere thought of his eyelashes, still something always made her sit up scalded and tug her disintegrating clothes together. Over the lawn she drifted further from the planetary light of the television, disappearing into darkness where the neighbors' square ports of exclusive yellow lamplight established the various distances of her neighborhood and the unfair smell of barbecues lingered over the back yards.

And when she wandered around the side of the garage in the shadows and came across the scooter, it frightened her. It actually made her ill. She came upon it deep in thought, eyes dimmed; and it gleamed so slick and repulsive, it made her draw back in fright. Even after she bent over it to read the note her father had left under the seat strap, still she didn't want to touch it. It was the perfect scooter, more perfect than any specific scooter she could have hoped for, yet it made her ill to look at it, there was a permanent, ready kink in her intestines. She didn't know how to start it or ride it, and she wished never to have to learn. The nausea of the whole thing suddenly grabbed her and she turned and walked quickly back around to the patio on a rink of panicky fear, simply putting it out of her mind as if it were a sea-lion carcass she had stumbled over behind the garage which would just go away if unmentioned.

She went back inside, into the kitchen, and dialed the telephone.

"Hello?" Her mother's boyfriend answered.

"Hello. May I please speak to Mary Potts?"

He gave the phone over, and her mother said hello levelly, perhaps already suspecting it was Cindy.

"Mom?"

"Hi, Cindy."

"Mom, there's something in the house." She was whispering.

"What do you mean?"

"There's something." Her heart began to beat harder. The darkness in far doorways began to shimmer with possibility.

"How do you know?"

"Well for one thing, these boys drove past. They've been

driving past all night. Remember I told you about those boys who are always freebasing in the bathroom?"

"Punkin, did you find the quiche?"

"The DeBono boys? They bring cocaine to school? They've been driving back and forth all night really slow, and you know what? Jeff DeBono, he's the worst one, he said at school yesterday he'd come and get me and bring me to a party."

"Punkin, listen. I want you to do me a favor—"

"But Mom . . ."

"What."

A crucial silence. "Mom."

"Cindy, it's obvious what you're doing. It's so obvious. Just look at what you're doing. How many times do we have to have this discussion?"

"There really is something."

"If you truly think there's something, then call the police. Besides, Dick and I will be dropping by any minute—"

"You will?"

"You're a big girl, Cindy. All this dramatizing only makes you small again."

"Mom, there really is something."

"Okay, Cindy? Could you do me a favor? Could you move my stuff from the washer to the dryer? And set it on delicate. It's mostly lingerie, so set it on delicate or you'll melt my teddy. Dick and I will be stopping by soon."

"Okay."

"And Cindy, why not go out with the DeBono boy? My opinion is, he's a fox. Wouldn't it be fun? Call him up. Girls can call boys these days."

"Mm."

"Cindy? Remember the quality of your experience? We've had this discussion. You're a big girl now, and you can't keep making me responsible for the quality of your experience."

"When are you coming over? I could thaw something."

"No, we've already eaten, punkin, thanks. Dick made delicious Rock Cornish game hen, he's such a perfect man, isn't he?"

"Okay."

"But honey? I love you. You ought to feel assurance about that. You don't need to keep calling me with these crisis situations. 'Authenticity,' remember?"

"I love you too, Mom."

"Okay, and move my stuff, will you? Do it right now. If you don't do it right when you hang up, you'll forget."

"I won't forget."

"Bye, punkin."

She set the receiver back in the cradle. It was unfair having a genuine child psychologist for a mother, who always knew the truth. Cindy had once secretly paged through the huge eighteen-page thesis her mother had written to graduate, on the topic of psychokinesis, whose sheer dazzling unintelligibility made her realize as a child that her mother was smart. She seemed omniscient sometimes, there was so much light, Cindy felt herself a spot of indigestible darkness struggling to be swallowed in transparency. It was the Embracing Abundance workshop after the divorce that seemed to give her mother the magic power. She lost all that weight. She started her own business. Now whenever Cindy heard the familiar fading song of the Porsche climbing through its gears disappearing toward the freeway, it seemed the sound of abundance no longer resisted.

She had opened the box of an Insta-Pizza—the packet of powdered tomato paste and the pouch of the few tissue-thin pepperoni slices—and she found that she could dip the pepperoni slices in the powdered tomato sauce for a not-too-bad flavor. She went into the bathroom and lay in the tub. The TV screen, which was the only light in the house, flickered through the doorways like fireplace light, casting bursts of radiation on the orange coins of meat and the pink powder. Her spine couldn't quite get comfortable on the porcelain curve of the tub, and she kept slipping down. She finished the last of the pepperoni disks and put her head back against the hard porcelain and closed her eyes, slipping further down, her body pooling in the tub.

Suddenly she sat up and went back into the kitchen and dialed the phone again.

"Hello?" said her mother's boyfriend.

"May I please speak to Mary Potts?"

"Who is calling?"

"This is Cynthia. Hi, Dick."

"Hey! Cindy! Good to hear from you. How's everything?"

"Fine," she said. Dick hated her.

"Haven't heard from you in a while. How's school? Boring?"

"It's okay."

"Oh! Congratulations! Your mom says she found a present from your dad today—one of those motorcycle things. That must be pretty neat, huh?"

"Yeah, really." She wished she hadn't called.

"Have you been riding it yet?"

"No. I don't know how to start it."

"Why don't I come over some time and show you how. I'd be glad to."

"No, that's okay. It's probably easy to figure out."

"Want to talk to your mom? She's sitting right here."

"Yeah, okay, thanks."

Her mother first smothered the mouthpiece against her scratchy sweater. Then she came on. "Hi, punkin. How are you. About that scooter from your father, I just want to say one thing to you. You are aware that things aren't always the way they seem on the surface. Aren't you?"

Cindy didn't know what she meant, but feared getting into it. "Yes, Mom," she sang, in the two notes of exasperation.

"A word to the wise. Now, what did you call about?"

"Just one more thing. We need groceries, so could I have some money? We're out of everything."

"Of course, yes, love. I'll be dropping by soon, and I'll write a check. Is that all?"

"Actually, I've got a problem." Her breath had gone short again, and her heart was pounding in her throat. "I'm making ravioli, you know? The boil-in-bag stuff in the freezer? But the thing is, I can't fit the bag in, because, you know, that little pot? I was trying to squish it down so it would be all underwater, but it keeps popping up, so only half of it will be boiled . . ."

"Cindy, you're a lot smarter than this."

Cindy said, "Yeah? I guess."

"Cindy, you know what this is really about? This is about me being a bad mother. Isn't it."

"Mom . . ."

"Just put yourself in my position. That's one of the skills of maturity, putting yourself in other people's shoes. So imagine yourself in my shoes. I'm a single mom. I have to work to support us, so I can't be there all the time. And I need my fun time too. Grown-ups need their fun time just as kids do. And sex. Sex is a part of life too, Cindy. It's natural for you to resent the fact that I have sex with Dick."

"Yes, Mom."

"Children don't want to think of their parents as people with vaginas and penises. But sex organs are perfectly natural. These are new times, Cindy. I'm a single parent. You have to own that. This is an important distinction I want you to see. On the one hand, you have to know I love you; but on the other hand, I can't be responsible for the quality of your experience. So when you keep *testing* my love, well . . . ? I've got my life to lead. And your dad, well, he's on his own trip, and you have to own that too."

"Okay, okay, I won't call again."

"Oh, God, Cindy, please don't use that accusatory tone. I'm not a bad mother. Really I'm not. I'd love to be the sort of little birdbrain housewife that stays home and bakes cookies and knits potholders, but that's just not reality."

"Mom, I said okay."

"You have a responsibility to give me the strokes I deserve."

"I know, Mom. You're the most wonderful mother."

"Okay? Whenever you stop being totally authentic with me, it just destroys me. I don't have any defenses against that."

"I'm sorry, Mom, really. I'm sorry."

"Fine. Now Dick and I will be dropping by there soon. We're actually on our way out the door. Did you move my stuff?"

"Yes. And I set it on delicate."

"Are you sure?"

"Mom, I'm sure."

"All right, well, just in case you forgot, why don't you do it now."

"Okay."

"See you soon, punkin."

Cindy set the receiver back in the cradle, numb. Was it gratitude she felt? It was just a matter of becoming an adult. Of becoming as wise as her mother. She went into the attached garage, where the washer and dryer were, and she transferred a strange escaping armful of lingerie into the dryer and set it on delicate. This was what it felt like to grow up. It was simply to breathe a colder, clearer air. After the dryer had begun its roar and rhythmic button-click, tumbling her mother's sexy nylon ghosts, she sighed—and stretched as if to add an inch to her spine—and she went back into the kitchen.

The TV was still on. She had finished all the pepperoni, but the pouch of powdered tomato sauce was left, which she took into the living room sampling it with her finger. She decided that this feeling—of a tiny wheel spinning uselessly to a blur in her chest—was boredom. Maybe she should write love letters for Kim Paschke, since writing her own suicide notes was no longer interesting. She kept dipping her finger in the tomato powder and sucking it, picturing herself lying face-down on the rocks at the roadside below the Pacific Coast Highway, at that bend in the treacherous part where the road swings you centrifugally out over the bulge of the ocean. Her body was flung out relaxed in the form of flight that her impact had thrown her into, in that moment when the flesh meets rock and the wraith flies on unstopped. Her pelvis was held up without shame. Her thighs relaxed in total submission. She was lit by the twitching beams of police flashlights. In the months of grief to come, her mother would prove to be stronger than the sorrow. She would join a Grief Group in Berkeley composed of parents recovering from similar tragedies. And gradually she would learn to stop blaming herself. That would be the first stage. There would be stages. She would read books about it and discuss it in her group. The second stage would be anger, anger at Cindy. Which was perfectly natural. But then this would subside and eventually she would learn to forgive Cindy, to forgive herself, everybody is forgiven, nothing is remembered, life goes on by self-forgiveness. The snapshot in memory—the gorgeous horror of Cindy's angel's imprint at the roadside, prodded by flashlight beams—would fade.

She dipped her finger and it came up coated with pink powder. Just then, she heard the familiar sound of her mother's car taking the corner and halting in the driveway—and then the crunch of the parking brake, which in its swiftness was a characteristic signal of her mother's whole personality, her whole world, which came flooding into the house buoying and lifting Cindy from the floor. She ran around turning on lamps in the living room, the kitchen, so that the house was all lit up when Dick and Mary came in the front door and Dick called out, "Hi, Cindy, are you home?"

Just in time, she got a bag of ravioli out of the freezer and stuck it in a pan of water.

"Hi, you guys," she said.

"Hi, punkin," said her mother. "I see you've got everything under control around here." And she went into the garage to check her laundry, saying, "Thanks for moving my stuff."

"Yeah, sure. But it's probably not dry yet. It's only been in there a few minutes."

"No problem. Rayon doesn't take long." She came into the kitchen and gave Cindy a big ceremonial hug. "I don't tell you often enough how wonderful you are. I appreciate you moving them for me, and I think you're the most wonderful daughter in the whole world. I know what I'll do, I'll separate out the unimportant stuff." She went back into the garage. "This will only take a few minutes, honey; and besides they always start late because the band doesn't come on time."

Cindy and Dick were left facing each other in the kitchen. Dick folded his arms and said, "So. How's school? Boring?"

"No, it's fine."

"Oh, say! Let's see your new moped. Where is it?"

"It's out there."

"Where? Come on, let's see. I can show you how to work it."

"No, it's no big deal. It can wait till daylight."

"Hey, come on, aren't you excited? If your dad left the key, we can get it started."

"Go ahead, punkin," said her mother, raking at her laundry in the garage. "We can't leave for a few minutes anyway."

So she followed Dick out the front door, turning on the porch lamp as they passed it; and they walked around to the side of the garage where the scooter crouched gleaming in the shadows.

"Oh, wow, it's a Vespa," said Dick. "Excellent."

Cindy hung back in the light while Dick gripped it by its handlebars and jerked it like a stubborn animal out of the shadows.

"Didn't your dad leave an operator's manual or anything? Here's the key. I wonder if it's already in gear. Isn't this the greatest, Cindy?"

"Yeah."

Why had her father bought this? Something strange and permanent was happening. With a sneezing tremor, the scooter started. Dick said over the engine noise, "Hop on."

"No, that's okay. I think I'll wait till daylight." Her heart ached hearing the birth of the healthy little engine. She resolved never to ride it—ever—nor even to touch it.

"Well, I'll just give it a little test run," said Dick, swinging a leg over the saddle. She stood back while he revved the motor and bounced testingly on the suspension. With a lurch, it started moving, and he pulled out into the street calling back over his shoulder, "Tell your mom good-bye for me. Tell her it's been nice knowing her."

# 10

---

With the thought that he was beginning either the smartest or the stupidest enterprise of his life—unsure which—Wayne picked up the telephone in his small acoustic-tiled carrel and dialed the top number on his computer-printout list of leads, while his trainer Buddy hovered over his shoulder to listen in on the monitor. This was his first call. Buddy whispered, "Now call on your power, Wayne." Brokers' Training Week was full of such minor humiliations as this being supervised, this being spoken to like a child in slogans, with a bunch of other trainees all looking miscellaneously deficient or hopeless. But he was trying to have an open mind, having decided for once in his life to throw himself into something without ruining it before-hand by the usual cynicism—which he had now come to think was just laziness, just arrogant laziness.

"Hello?" said a creaky, polite woman's voice. And Buddy, a skinny, radiantly self-confident kid at least ten years younger than Wayne—who had just been lucky, who had smartened up earlier in life—winked and patted Wayne's shoulder.

He began to read from his prompt sheet. "Good morning. Is this Mrs. Irving?"

"Yes?" Already suspicious.

"Mrs. Irving, I'm Wayne Paschke, an agent for Marketrend Numismatic Investments. I hope you have a moment to discuss Marketrend's exciting investment program with me. Are you presently happy with the rate of return on your savings, or would you prefer to have your money working harder for you?"

"Well, naturally, I'd prefer . . ." She was elegant; she was sitting on a nice new couch; she went to art shows; she was just leaving the house wearing white gloves; or his call had interrupted an important conversation she was having with her husband, who was making eye contact with her at this moment. To make things worse, he'd gotten a bad phone connection: a blizzard of static rose up.

She had left the sentence aristocratically unfinished. Buddy tapped the next paragraph on the prompt sheet, and Wayne read on through the static:

"In these times of scarcity and uncertainty, the market for collectible coins has become an important haven for the smart investor. While some may profit in the stock market or money-market funds, a great many people lose. Some lose their entire life savings on such paper investments. But the great advantage of investing in rare and collectible coins is that they are not paper. They are physical, tangible possessions. Many of them are made of precious or semiprecious metals. Such as gold or silver. For this reason, they will always have market value. No matter what happens to the stock market or the prime rate or inflation. Some of Marketrend's recommended coins have actually tripled in value over an eighteen-month period. That's equivalent to a two-hundred-percent rate of return. Have you ever heard of a secure investment that yields a two-hundred-percent profit in a year?"

He paused for her answer, as the prompt sheet directed.

Mrs. Irving said, "I'm sorry," and hung up, and Wayne was immediately certain he would fail at this. The pressure of future obstetrician's bills swelled larger. Buddy patted him on the back. "Excellent! I've never seen anybody do anything like that on their first call." He stretched himself taller to address the other brokers at their carrels. "Hey, everybody, this is incredible. Wayne just made a Stage Two contact on his first call."

"No kidding, Wayne," he said, sitting down in the chair beside him. "That might have felt like a failure to you, right? I mean, she hung up, right? Somebody hangs up, it's insulting. Probably right at this moment you're pissed off, right? And embarrassed, because you feel like you failed. Right?

"Well, I'm telling you from my experience, you did excellent. Because it takes a hell of a lot of hung-ups to get the one big-commission call. Because, see, the prompt is designed to be a filter. The hung-ups are designed in. You have to get used to them. That first paragraph is designed to scare off the dorks. You sit here all day and dial a thousand numbers, nine hundred will be nobody-homes; and fifty will be hung-ups like Mrs. Irving; but you'll get a few talkers; and any one of those talkers will be the big-commission call. That's the thing. And here's the other thing: some of those talkers will be interested in earning some extra income, you just chat, you know, la-di-da, and pretty soon you're on the road to being a Head Broker, which is where the total gravy comes in. You just shouldn't have waited so long for the old lady to respond. You develop a sixth sense after a while."

"I know what you mean," said Wayne, recalling the sensation of his voice foredoomed in the static. She had seemed, he felt furtively, too nice a woman to buy Marketrend coins. "Even while I was talking, I could sort of *hear* her losing interest."

"Yes, it's a mystical thing. I've seen Brokers like you develop it in a week. Just don't let the hung-ups get you down. Actually, the nobody-homes get to be more of a pisser. But just cruise. Just keep cruising on the prompt. The prompt is magic."

He set his hand on Wayne's shoulder and gave it a couple of kneading pinches. "I'm going to go help Farouk. You just cruise along the list for a while. You're clear on how to follow the dialogue tree, aren't you? Okay, then. Keep up the good work. Call on your power. I know it sounds silly, but it works. That's the miraculous thing about Marketrend. You don't even have to consciously believe it yet. And be sure to raise your hand if you get another talker."

Wayne turned back to face his carrel with a spine-straightening resolution not to be pessimistic in spite of the obvious dubiousness, and he jabbed the phone's push buttons impatiently. Out there on the infinitely branching network of telephone lines there were rich old Mrs. Irvings, a few in every thousand calls. One single successful contact could net him five hundred dollars, even if he just sold the smallest Starter Portfolio. If he were really shrewd, he might get two phone lines installed, so that he could be constantly dialing two numbers at once and thereby eliminate all the nobody-homes twice as fast. After the training period was over and he was turned loose to set up his own Marketrend Brokerage at home, he would do just that: install two separate phones on his ply-wood workbench in the garage, and listen to two unanswered ringings simultaneously, cutting off the one whenever he got a "hello" on the other. For that matter, maybe a machine could be devised to automatically dial several numbers at once, elim-inating the nobody-homes.

Such an idea could revolutionize telemarketing. But he would keep it to himself until his training period was over. It was the first of many such creative ideas that could launch a man on the road to success, the kind of idea he could never have put to use as a housepainter. For the first time in his life, he was "unlearning the habit of failure," as it said in *Unlock the Dynamic Power Within*. Even a week ago, he'd been a different man. As he sat there at his carrel listening to a distant phone ring unanswered, he remembered his slouch in the white vinyl swivel chair in the kitchen; and the very remembrance made him sit up straighter and grow impatient with the ringing, as if by force of will he could make the bell telepathically more urgent and compelling. He had been sitting in his kitchen sunk in exactly the apathy that the speaker at the Marketrend Op-portunity Meeting described with clairvoyant accuracy: "the *effect* of events rather than the *cause*." The Marin Medical Center had given notice that they were turning the Paschkes' account over to a collection agency, which meant their cars might be confiscated or Laura's wages might be attached. And it meant they would have to find an obstetrician who was willing to take them on in spite of their credit history. Then Mc-Crimmon had sent the legal layoff notice to protect his own ass. Wayne started looking over the infinite flat waste of em-ployment ads, with a pen poised to draw one of his usual stupid awkward high-school rectangles around any ad for a job that seemed lowly enough for him—housepainting or handywork or something, just anything—with his shoelaces untied and that paralyzing cigarette burning in an ashtray beside him. He called every painting contractor in the county, only to find that everybody had about ten in-laws or buddies who were already lined up for job openings. As he scanned down the columns of fine-print ads, each little box—"Accountant," "RN," "LVN,"—seemed a trap, yet an inaccessible trap. The newsprint page of flush rectangles made a sheer surface which his mind kept sizzling off of. But there was this one, the same one he had seen before:

BIG INCOME IN COLLECTIBLES. Earn 6-figure income, first year with us, possible, promoting the #1 investment in America today. We train you to be a qualified Broker, there are 3 requirements. 1, dress well. 2, Speak English. 3, be willing to follow Proven Program . . .

He knew it sounded phony. And Laura said so too, reminding him that when he called them before he had decided they were actually dishonest. But he pointed out that they couldn't say six figures if it weren't literally true, at least in some cases, because the Better Business Bureau or somebody would prosecute them. Plus, they paid you for your training period, so you couldn't lose. And besides, he wasn't doing anything in particular the following night, when there was to be an Opportunity Meeting at the Holiday Inn. Despite Laura's suspiciousness, he went—relaxed by skepticism, and protected by the attitude of permanent hopelessness which, he realized now, he had always employed to elevate himself righteously and humorously above his failures. He was going to sit at the back of the Holiday Inn banquet room with his arms crossed, unpersuadable.

But it was amazing. As soon as he signed in at the door and got his name tag, this young guy Buddy introduced himself and offered to answer any questions. Wayne had always hated those "Hi-My-Name-Is" stickers, and he tried to fold it away in his pocket, but Buddy told him, "Yes, I know they're dumb-looking. I feel the same way. But think of it this way, Mr. Paschke. Within five years, eight percent of the people in this room will be wealthy. That's a statistical fact we know from experience. Those who are going to seriously stick with us will want to declare themselves early. Get started now. Me, I gave in and wore my name sticker at my first Opportunity Meeting, and the speaker at that meeting remembered who I was because of that sticker. Two months ago, that same man signed the papers for my promotion to Head Broker."

Wayne said, "Magic sticker, huh? If I wear it, I'll be a millionaire."

Buddy didn't laugh. He leaned back slightly, almost appraisingly, and said, "You know, Mr. Paschke, very few people catch on so early. That's literally true, in a way. If you don't wear it, you've already signed a kind of contract that says, 'I'm not taking this seriously,' and you might as well go home now."

Wayne hadn't expected such directness, but supposed that this was how people in business dealt with each other: bracing and insulting.

"Wearing this sticker," said Buddy, "is the first of many decisions you'll have to make tonight."

"Well, hell, I'll wear the damn sticker."

Buddy smiled. "You've signed a very different kind of contract, in that case, and I'm glad. Want some coffee? Mr. Paschke, forgive me for being so candid so early. But you know, you really have made an important decision. I'm glad your mind is open to Marketrend."

"Well, you know, I was intrigued. I'm always in the market for new investment angles."

"Yes, and obviously you've got the acumen to decide for yourself whether or not Marketrend is right for you. I'm going to mingle a bit, which of course is my job. Just make yourself at home. The presentation will start soon. But please don't leave without speaking to me. Hey, look, I'll be honest. We Head Brokers get commissions on the recruits, so you're a sort of 'fish' I've caught. But you're an exceptionally good fish, if you'll forgive my putting it that way. My organization needs mature men like you who already have some business experience. And I've never yet dealt with a recruit who caught on so quickly to the real truth of Marketrend—that you make a sort of contract with each little decision."

"Well, I'm not going to be convinced too easily," said Wayne.

"Good. Excellent. One of the purposes of these meetings is to weed out the people who don't mean business. Talk to me before you leave. I want to get your opinions."

Buddy left, and Wayne turned to survey the room feeling patted into a better posture, and he found a seat in the very back row that would give him a feeling of a noncommittal vantage point on the presentation that followed. The speaker turned out to be a bona fide millionaire, who had made his fortune solely through Marketrend. But the surprising thing he said was, he realized at the end he hadn't done it for the money. His personal story was exactly like Wayne's. He had been a loser basically, surpassed by his friends, until at the age of thirty-eight he had joined Marketrend at the bottom, as a trainee Broker. In his prior life he had done all kinds of jobs as the victim of his employers, the passive tool. He had always been exploited by other men, because his motto had always been "Work harder," rather than "Work smarter." In his speech, he made a comparison between the eagle and the oyster, the one sunk in comfortable muck, the other soaring free through the risky heights. He said that it was the Marketrend philosophy that had transformed him from an oyster to an eagle. Tonight, he said, all of the people in the room were being offered an invitation to fly. But he said that if they should accept this invitation, it would mean they must change their very selves, they must transcend the muck of habitual failure, they must actually become new people. When he started, he'd thought money was important; but not anymore. Wealth, he said, was only a negligible side effect of Marketrend; money was a much-overrated commodity in the world, a mere by-product; the greatest benefit was the transformation of the self into a new and free being, a master of destiny.

Wayne sneaked out of the Opportunity Meeting that night, actually skulking behind the easel of coin displays to avoid Buddy. And he reported to Laura that it had been boring and unimpressive—that the whole operation had an air of hucksterism about it. It was just one of those pyramid sales schemes where you get rich by getting other people to join the organization. "Well, too bad," she said sleepily, rolling away from him in bed and curling up to continue this drowsy mysterious incubation he was excluded from. But for hours he lay awake beside her, unable to fall asleep. One phrase of the speaker's speech kept returning to him: "living below the line." Transforming the personality consisted in elevating your thought until you were "living above the line." When you lived above the line, you were the cause of events in your life, rather than the effect. And Wayne knew with filthy intimacy exactly what it felt like to be the mere effect of everything. Even his daughter, even Kim lived above the line, and was able to push him around, was able to be instantaneously right about everything, while Wayne at his age was increasingly slow and paunchy and deliberate and confused, nudged this way and that by the conflicting ambiguities of life around him like an aging fighter in slow motion.

It was just that he had developed the wrong habits of thought. What he had always supposed was his being a nice guy was really just a kind of laziness. The Marketrend people had discovered a program to raise people above that line, and the program was entirely contained in the Broker's Starter Kit, which cost $179.95, complete with a Broker's License and a sheet of sample coins and a list of phone leads—which according to statistics would yield at least ten for-sure sales and thus would recoup the initial investment easily. If he ever wanted to drop the admittedly dubious job of selling coins over the phone, he could quit after recovering his investment, and he would retain the kit, including *Unlock the Dynamic Power Within,* by Fortinbras Armstrong, which the speaker had called "the second most powerful book ever written." All these people were a little bit on the corny side; but if it worked for them it should certainly work for somebody smarter. Wayne was still young enough. Plenty of great men, as the speaker had said at the meeting, had accomplished a turnaround in their lives at an even later age. He didn't want to spend the second half of his life below the line. He didn't want his children to have an out-of-work housepainter for a father, the whole family sitting around watching television commercials and sitcoms where the fathers had that clear, college-educated gaze and that affluent spring in their step. He lay in bed paralyzed as if a tree's great roots were planted in his chest and were groping slowly to squeeze him, ticking and creaking. This was death.

He sprung awake into a sitting position, his soul distorted from its bulge in the vacuum of panic.

The next morning at breakfast, feeling sprained, he slumped forward to sip the surface of his coffee as if medicinally—almost guilty for some reason about his nightmare. He said, "I think I'm going to drop by the Holiday Inn tonight. There's a follow-up meeting, and some of that stuff was kind of intriguing."

"Are you actually thinking of doing that?" said Laura.

"No, it's all pretty hokey. I'm just going to check it out a little more."

And that night he came home from the follow-up meeting with his Starter Kit—a vinyl briefcase containing his sheet of sample coins, the Personal Transformation literature, his certificate of membership in the Brokers Guild, his prompt sheets and brochures and *Broker's Guide*, and all kinds of other pamphlets and manuals describing the bonus system and the commission rates and the procedures for recruiting other Brokers. Laura was angry. She couldn't believe he'd spent nearly two hundred dollars on this, and she wouldn't listen to reason. The pregnancy had been making her unaccountably clumsy, and she knocked over a carton of milk, then swept the pool of milk off the table with her palm and cried, "Two hundred dollars, Wayne!" and went into the bedroom crying.

Wayne had started to sponge up the spilled milk when she came back into the kitchen saying, "Weren't you telling me just last night that they were a bunch of hucksters? You were saying it's a rip-off. How could you turn right around and buy this thing?"

"Honey, please, just calm down and listen. First of all, it's easy to get back the two hundred dollars and quit. You're self-employed with Marketrend, so I can quit any time I like. And second of all, I can see that these people are jerks. I mean, I'm not interested in them, I'm interested in the business. I have to do something. I'm unemployed, honey. And this is something. It won't cost us to try this out, and it might turn out to be a good thing."

"How can it be a good thing if the people are jerks?"

"Oh, I don't mean 'jerks.' I don't know, I just have a good feeling about this. If we're ever going to get anywhere, we have to take some risks. Marketrend is something besides the same old eight-dollar-an-hour housepainting. Don't you see? If we go on like we've been doing, we'll be poor all our lives. This is a start on something else, something new. You have to get on the right side of the money river," he went on, borrowing the metaphor from the Marketrend speaker. "We've always lived on the wrong side of the money river. But successful people have to do one thing to get on the right side of the river. They invent some invention, or rob a bank, or make a crazy investment that everyone tells them is crazy. Or they get an education. Or you know. They have to cross that river."

He knew she had acquiesced when she sat down in her chair and brought her palms to her eyes in a splashing gesture that continued over her head to smooth back her hair. She snuffled and rubbed her nose with her wrist. She was beautiful. He was filled with love, with duty. He dragged his chair around next to hers and sat down, taking both her hands in his. "And, Laura," he said, "if it looks like I've made the wrong decision, it's easy to quit. I'm just as suspicious as you. Believe me. I can see the weird stuff in this. They've got all these stupid bonus prizes and Cadillacs and stupid mottoes. I'm just as suspicious as you are. But I think there might be something good in it too. Just let me tell you about it. The people who designed the program are pretty smart, and they're really onto something."

"You'll still do housepainting part time?"

"Yes, yes, the Broker's Training is only in the mornings; and it's only for a week. After that, I'm on my own. This can be totally part time. Just let me explain how the commission system works. I can buy these valuable coins for thirty percent off their market value." He reached for his fragrant new briefcase and rummaged through it for the chart explaining the discounts. "See, I buy the coins for thirty percent off. And then I turn around and sell them for the full price."

Laura reached into the case to pull out the sheet of sample coins in rows of clear plastic pockets. "Pakistan, 1948," she said. "Liberty Head, 1907. England, 1967. Hong Kong, 1975. Just so long as you promise to get out of it as soon as it starts to look crummy."

In those first days the briefcase gave off a sacramental glamour like a kit for performing magic, and each morning a whiff of that sharp new scent of factory vinyl was a caffeine stimulant. By the time the training period commenced the next week, he had secretly begun to feel sure of defeat whenever he smelled that smart black plastic and those insufficiently studied brochures sliding around together within. But that was perfectly natural, as he came to understand: the one object in the kit that unfailingly felt good in his hands was the paperback *Unlock the Dynamic Power Within*. The author Fortinbras Armstrong had devoted his life to studying the secrets that great men had discovered to overcome adversity and rise to unprecedented achievements. He had actually traveled around for many years and interviewed hundreds of millionaires and artistic geniuses and leaders of men, like Andrew Carnegie and Henry Ford and Thomas Edison. Wayne cleared his workbench in the garage and created an area for an imaginary blotter, telephone, filing cabinets, "in" and "out" baskets. Randy's crate of pots and pans was too big and heavy to be put anywhere else, so he just left it under the workbench and worked around it. He hung a hundred-watt light bulb from the ceiling with an aluminum pie-tin reflector, whose mote-suspending warmth created a sense of shelter. And he began to retreat there to study Fortinbras Armstrong with the door closed, in the solace of the cluttered garage's complex silence beside the warm digestive noises of the water heater. In an almost hallucinatory trance of expectation, he crouched, as if perched for a leap, over the pages of Armstrong's book, which began, "The book you are now holding in your hands will transmit to you the simple secret of attaining riches, or attaining any goal—provided you are ready to receive it. In reality, you already possess the secret, but you have failed to recognize it and put it to work."

He actually began trying to forget that he needed money desperately—that Laura's paycheck only covered the rent, that her pregnancy would soon become expensive—because for the first time in his life he could see that these were the motives of a loser. Motives based on a fear of failure rather than on a confidence in success. The motive of need rather than desire. He didn't know when—in childhood?—he had lost the essential self-esteem; yet he knew that too much such introspection would only reinforce the old habits. Now he wanted to begin to think like a success, to have faith in himself. And thus it was with a pang of fear that he opened his briefcase and released the guilty scent of vinyl in his telephone carrel at the end of his first morning of Broker's Training with Buddy; and he looked forward to hiding again in his garage and reading another chapter of Fortinbras Armstrong in the warmth of his hundred-watt bulb and the reassuring atmosphere of old concrete flooring. He had made 112 calls, 71 of which had been nobody-homes. The rest had been hung-ups, except for just two talkers—one of whom was a babysitter too broke to buy anything, and the other of whom was a very talkative old lady who kept going on and on about a bad investment her husband had made before he died, while Wayne sat there in an agony of impatience, tossing himself into new positions in his seat and drawing breath quickly every few minutes to try to interrupt her. But he wasn't discouraged; he had already absorbed enough of Armstrong's philosophy to realize that it wasn't the sale of a few coins that was at stake here; and it wasn't even the immediate need for income. It wouldn't have mattered if he was "selling ice to Eskimos," as F. W. Woolworth had been quoted in the book; in fact, it was altogether fitting that Wayne should face such early discouragement. He actually *agreed* with Laura. He *knew* this Marketrend operation was rinky-dink; this Buddy was such an arrogant, glib kid; and he certainly didn't plan on spending his life as a Marketrend Broker. But he had made a decision to seize himself at this midpoint of his life. He almost welcomed the early ill omens. It was true what the speaker had said at the first Opportunity Meeting: A true eagle doesn't put in any time as an oyster. He starts flying right away. Wayne's job was to hold that image in his mind.

He had reached the chapters where Armstrong was recommending daily mental exercises for the alteration of subconscious patterns of thought. They seemed silly on the surface, but they made sense. You had to play tricks on your subconscious mind; you had to imagine yourself in situations of success and fulfillment, and thus you would instill new habits of expectation. So he repressed skepticism and spread a canvas tarp on the floor to protect his flesh from the chill of the

concrete, and began the relaxation exercises that were supposed to lower the metabolism and sink the consciousness to
a level of suggestibility. He lay as still as a corpse, relaxing
his muscles one by one, concentrating first on his toes, then
on his feet and ankles and calves, then on his thighs, then on
his buttocks, picturing the red fibers of muscle as soft and
nerveless as the large cellophane-skinned roasts at Safeway.
Finally, having pressed the flushing wave of relaxation up to
his forehead and out to the tips of his fingers, he was defense-
less, vulnerable to suggestion; and he began to imagine himself
in scenarios of happiness, success, fulfillment. He was writing
a large check in an automobile showroom while the salesman
looked on deferentially. Then he was driving a new BMW
through the sunny forested countryside of Lucas Valley Road,
with shadows of overhanging boughs splashing on the windshield, taking turns like the cars in commercials. Even though
maybe he wasn't the BMW type, it would serve for the purpose
of the exercise.

Then his family was with him, riding in the BMW over the
winding road. The baby had been born. He was riding in a
car seat. It was a boy, born wholly without defect or malfor-
mation. In fact, there was a look of such intelligence in his
infant eyes that he seemed already philosophical, destined to
be a professor. Everybody had his seat belt on. They were
driving out to a ranch in west Marin where Kim would go
horseback riding. She had her own horse, which was stabled
out there somewhere. And of course they would own a house.
And he would read a lot. He would sit in a lawn chair in the
back yard wearing a sport coat—the one affectation he would
permit himself. Laura would quit her job and go back to school
to get a college degree, while he would educate himself by a
program of self-directed study. His afternoons would be free,

because his Brokerage business would occupy only his mornings. He would be a Head Broker by then, with an organization of ambitious people working for him. Buddy had told him to get started right away building an organization, by getting in touch with all his friends and enrolling them. There was a booklet in the Starter Kit which gave sample dialogues: "Hi, Ted, this is Jim from work. I'm calling because I've discovered an exciting new way of life, and I want to help you get in on it too . . ." He would be the laughingstock of the painting crew.

He was messing up the exercise, and he sat up. The implausible sport coat had been the first ruining detail. Armstrong had warned that the first few times would probably fizzle out, because the subconscious mind holds stubbornly to its old habits. So he stood up and went into the kitchen to make a cup of coffee; then he returned to the garage and opened the book to go on with his reading. At this rate, he would finish the book in a day or two—and then begin to reread it. For Armstrong recommended that the book be reread several times, the more the better, to magnetize the subconscious with optimism. He had to keep repressing the persistent thought of how stupid all this seemed. As Armstrong promised, these exercises begin to have an effect before faith. And it was precisely his faithlessness—his snug contempt—that had prevented him from trying anything in life. He could see that now. Or his conscious mind could.

Ten minutes later, when he heard Laura come home from work, he was deep into another auto-suggestion exercise, leaning back in his chair with his feet up comfortably on Randy's crate of pots and pans, talking on an imaginary phone to an imaginary client. He heard the front door close with Laura's characteristic cheerfulness, and with a start he jackknifed up into a standing position. Laura called out, "So how was it?" and she opened the garage door just as Wayne got the book out of sight, stowing it under the workbench on top of the crate.

"Fine," he said. "Just about like I expected. I didn't make any sales, but nobody does on their first day."

When Laura turned away with her grocery bag, he began to kick the tarp together into a pile under the shelf—into the same crumpled bundle as always.

He emerged into the kitchen. She was on tiptoe swimming through cupboards, a can in each hand.

"Tell me all about it," she said. "Did other people make sales while you were there?"

"Well, no, just a couple. But see, it's not like you make a sale on every call. It's a statistical thing. You sit there all day making a thousand calls, and nine hundred of them are nobody-homes; but a few of them are guaranteed to be sales. You just have to keep trying. But it feels like an incredible waste of time. I spent the whole morning listening to phones ringing."

She said, "Maybe phoning isn't the best way to reach the right people."

"No, there's no other way. I mean, it's telemarketing, right?"

"Yes, but maybe you could find other ways to find the people who might be interested. It *is* a waste of time to sit around calling people who aren't home. And when you get somebody, it's probably just somebody sitting around watching a soap opera. Maybe you should place ads in business newspapers or something—find the right customers. Or, don't they have conventions for investors? Where you could, like, set up a booth or something?"

"No, Laura, you don't know anything about it." Her new expertise angered him.

"Well, I'm just saying." She started to take groceries out of the bag.

"But I appreciate the suggestion," said Wayne, grazing her hip with his palm as she passed.

Just then, Cindy Potts came out of the hallway leading to Kim's bedroom.

"Hey," said Wayne. "How long have you guys been here?"

"Forever," said Cindy. "Were you home?"

"I was in the garage. How long have you been here?"

"I've been making Kim up."

"You didn't make any noise." He was thinking of his conversation on the imaginary phone in the garage, wondering if any of it had been audible.

Laura said, "Tonight is the night you girls are sleeping at your house, isn't it?"

Then Kim emerged into the kitchen, shockingly transformed into a seductive young woman. Her hair was teased out into that horrible new messed-up style girls were wearing that made them look like they'd just been molested. She was wearing a sleeveless T-shirt and her breasts were disturbingly prominent.

"My God, Kim!" he said.

"I'm a genius," said Cindy. "I'm a bad influence."

"What are you girls going to do tonight?"

"Nothing," they both said.

Laura said, speaking into the refrigerator, "Do you like your hair that way?"

"Oh, God, Mom."

Cindy said, "It's just a phase we're going through."

Kim thrust out one breast with whorish aplomb, her hip pivoting slightly, and said, "We're going to Cindy's now. I'm bringing all my homework stuff."

Laura said, "Do you have your regular clothes for school tomorrow?"

"Yes, Mom," said Kim, holding up her sleeping bag.

Wayne was paralyzed. He would chastise her, but suddenly she was too grown-up, he too hypnotized. Before he knew it, they were gone, Kim carrying her sleeping bag and her SuperCat pillow, exiting through the front door with a provocative sway of the hips. His gaze was riveted to the flicking crease in her jeans.

"Jesus Christ," he hissed after they had gone. "Are you going to let her get out of the house like that?"

The faint darts of a smile appeared in the corners of Laura's mouth as she installed plastic-bagged vegetables in the refrigerator and moved things about on the shelves with the confident grasp of a gardener weeding and planting. She said, "There's been talk of an Eric DeBono."

"All the more reason!" He sensed himself buzzing around her. "That Mary Potts is never home, you know. God knows what will happen with the two girls alone in that house."

Laura sighed. "Kim has been looking forward to this for a long time. We both gave her permission weeks ago. I have a feeling she's going out with Eric tonight."

"But, Jesus Christ!" He recalled the sight of her breasts nosing against the fabric of the T-shirt, the dented softness of her lips under scarlet wax, the slight, skilled revolving of her hip whose impact on his gaze had caused a reeling planetary concussion. He was senile. The backs of his legs bumped into his chair.

"Oh, Wayne," she said. "Maybe you're losing Kim, but you've still got me."

He sat ponderously down in his chair in this atmosphere of feminine conspiracy. He felt baffled, newly stuck, as solidly planted as a streambed rock. The next child would be a boy, about whom everything would be more obvious. Laura set a bunch of grapes before him, just washed, covered with shining beads of tap water. She returned to her groceries, saying, "Kim is a smart girl. She'll be fine. You just have to trust people to go through things and come out okay. The people you love, of *course* you're worried. But you can't *tell* them."

# 11

"Do you have the condom?"

"Oh God."

"Don't be like that. This is a full dress rehearsal."

"I'm sorry, it's just this is weird."

"Well, it gets weirder, so please just get used to it. Try laying down."

Kim pinched her shirt pocket to check for—along with the crisp sound of Cindy's twenty-dollar bill—the rubber ring of the condom, whose particular diameter in her palm had been so strange and sobering. The station wagon in Cindy's garage was shrouded in blankets, safety-pinned together; the garage window was covered in Hefty bags and duct tape; even the dashboard lights were taped so Kim could listen to the radio without its red ember shedding a glow on her face. Cindy held aside the shroud: "Just try laying down to see how you fit."

Kim wriggled into the backseat in her bandage-like skirt with a slight bleat pretending annoyance. But the greater pretense, which made her as numb as a mannequin, was that this was just a "dress rehearsal"; she was supposed to believe that this was merely a test for light-leaks. But they both knew that tonight was the night. The whole project was so doomed that she could never have gone through with it except by mistake, in rigid passivity. She and Cindy had shared the knowledge only telepathically, that tonight, probably within a half hour, Eric himself would actually come groping into the dark garage. There was a blur on Cindy's smile when she said, "See? Plenty of room!" regarding Kim's mummy on the back seat of the Chevrolet—which smelled inside degradingly like an old car, that popcorn-and-cigarette smell.

"Okay, I'm going to close the door and turn out the light. I'll be right in the house, so don't come out till I say. Your eyes take a long time to adjust."

"Okay," said Kim.

"Okay?"

"Okay."

Cindy closed the door. The blanket fell over again. But she had lingered too long, awkwardly, and now in the ear-squashing silence of the compartment, Kim knew for sure that tonight was the night.

When the overhead garage light was turned off, the interior of the car went totally black.

She sat up and slid over against the armrest, trying to be detached: her physical body could go through these motions without her mind's constant criticism. Even if it turned out to be the worst thing she had ever done, it could still be partly Cindy Potts's fault. She sat with her shoulders hunched curling

forward over her knees. She tried to imagine herself in Eric's
arms, arching her back in the bliss that was promised in Cindy's
manuals, whispering the recommended obscenities. Somewhere out there, though the darkness would save her from
actually seeing it, would be the attached candle of his erect
penis, which she was supposed to grasp. But she had this
flickering nightmare pre-vision: that Eric would open the crypt-
like door of the station wagon, sit down beside her obscure
form in the embalmment of all this makeup, take her tentatively
in his arms, and then gradually realize he was touching plastic
parts—and scramble back against the door in bright-eyed horror. She had always been the girl, famous on the playground,
whose surgical aura prevented touching; excused from classes
for medical reasons, walking down the school corridors alone,
prematurely adult, while all the other children were audible
in classrooms. As a kindergarten child listening to stories
cross-legged on the schoolroom floor, among the other children
who squirmed so unself-consciously in their bodies, she used
to hear of magical spells in fairy tales, and she had believed
in them as the other children could not, because there was an
actual spell on her, whose necessary breaking kiss was incon-
ceivable.

Armless with her hands stuffed under her thighs in the
station wagon's complete darkness, she had let her forehead
drop almost to her knees. Weirdly, she could have almost, in
her anxiety, taken the hem of her skirt between her teeth.
Which would print lipstick on the fabric. She sat up straight.
The darkness was so total that her spirit had bled out through
her dilated pupils; and her body, invisible and bereft of soul,
kept wanting to drift slowly into seaweed figures. She set an
anchoring elbow on the armrest to orient herself.

She was anonymous. In this experimental vacuum, she kept telling herself, Eric need never know who she was. She would never identify herself by using her voice—she would only whisper—and their two bodies would remain imaginary. Eric would touch her lips, perfectly sculpted by scalpel. His mouth would enclose her nipple, with its latex core, on the breast which—out of flesh borrowed from her buttocks, and mysterious yeasty tissue borrowed from her normal breast—had been reconstructed so skillfully that as she grew older the two hillocks remained miraculously symmetrical, equal in contour. All the sutures had been invisible, stitched with absorbable collagen thread. She had spent many intense solitary hours, over the years, examining herself in the mirror, marveling at the perfection, in the grip of beauty's melancholy like any ordinary girl. According to her doctors, it was through some luck of the hormones and the genes that her body was achieving symmetry. It had occurred to her—almost humorously, in a clenched sort of way—that since the areola had been grafted from labial tissue, Eric's advances would be, technically, swifter than he imagined.

She heard the sound of the garage door closing outside, softly. That would be Eric. Cindy must have telephoned him. He must have been waiting somewhere nearby for her signal. She wished she were doing this with someone besides Eric, someone she didn't care about.

Then there were shuffling, tentative footsteps. Cindy would never tread so carefully in her own garage, even in the dark. It must be Eric. She could feel her heartbeat in her skull. If she got sick, Eric would be embarrassed and leave. And then he would know it was her, Kim Paschke. He would tell people at school.

Wasn't he bound to identify her anyway? And wouldn't he naturally tell people? Hadn't he already guessed her identity? And hadn't he probably already told people?

This was all wrong, it was stupid from the start, she had to get away. There was still time to sneak out the door on her side of the car—and creep out of the garage undetected while Eric was still groping around.

She found the door handle. The door released a tremendous ringing bang when she opened it, its rusty springs stiff from disuse. She pushed it out against the blanket which enshrouded the car, and she felt for its hem. The darkness was like clusters of bees on her eyes—

But Eric was right there. She touched his actual knee. For some reason, he had felt his way around to the far side of the car.

She got back in and slid along the seat, deeper into the car. Eric crawled in, closed the door, and sat there on his side, at a distance she could hear. She knew it was him. He smelled like the hallways at school. She perched on the edge of the seat.

"Hi," he said.

In reply, she made a slight rustling motion. If she had to speak, she would whisper. To use her voice would be to connect her soul with her body, whereas a whisper was just a nameless product of the black air.

Eric moved and Kim froze in fear, her eyes useless. At his motion, she lowered her arms and turned slightly toward him, offering herself stiffly to his embrace.

But nothing happened. He just sat there. He had merely shifted position.

Finally he drew breath to speak: "I'm interested in normalcy," he said.

The pulse of her brain increased. For a perilous moment, sparks crept in her vision. If she could hold herself perfectly motionless, she would not get sick and faint.

Eric spoke again. "Allow me to define that term *normalcy*."

The faintness was passing its peak. She realized as she subsided into nausea's trough that he was nervous. His throat was gripping the words.

"I'm talking about the usual things. All the boring things. A house, children, a job with the right mix of creativity and security. A dog if the yard is enclosed. I mean, I'm not proposing marriage or anything. But I think it's because I'm the middle child in my family: I'm logical and clear, and I'm always striving for harmony and normalness. I'm not like my older brother. He's interested in everything weird and bizarre. I don't play guitar or anything."

He waited.

Kim sat back invisibly in the darkness and folded her arms. What had Cindy told him in her note?

"Don't get the wrong idea. I'm not incapable of deep romantic feelings. There is definitely a proverbial jungle animal trapped inside me. Just because I'm in the Debating Society and I edit *Highlights*, people think I'm an intellectual, but that doesn't mean I don't have stormy passions. I'm just saying that I have plans for my future which are pretty much on the boring side. Doctor, lawyer, et cetera. I put in for early application at some of the best schools, and I'm a National Merit Scholar. And I won first place in the American Cancer Society's Youth Essay Contest . . ."

She whispered, "What did Cynthia Potts tell you about our meeting?"

"Well, she's so imaginative, she said you were a nymphomaniac orphan. But I knew."

"You knew what?"

"I knew it was you. You probably don't remember, but we had the same section in the S.A.T. . . ."

"You knew it was me? How did you know?"

"I deduced that it was you. You probably don't remember but we happened to be in the same section for the S.A.T.s . . ."

She did remember. She had sat at the desk right beside his. He was the reason she hadn't tested as high as she could have, because just his presence in the next row had made her stupid, as if her stupidity could help *him* be smarter by some irrational voodoo of seduction.

". . . But even before then, at Dixie School. I moved here in the eighth grade, so I didn't know anybody, which is how I got to be a nerd. I'm not like Jeff, I can't just go up and talk to people. But I've always been attracted to you, not just because of your physical attractiveness, but because I admire your courage. When I first saw you by the book rack at Dixie, you probably don't remember—"

"You admire my 'courage'?"

He had said the wrong thing. He paused. But then apparently deciding to plunge deeper into error, he said, "Well, yes. Your surgery and everything. I think you've got values."

"My surgery!" Humiliation swarmed all over her.

"Wait, Kim, I just meant to say that your artificial parts don't bother me. I think they're kind of interesting, actually, in a way. Other than that, I'm indifferent to them. Or, that is, not indifferent. 'Indifferent' has the wrong connotations . . ."

She let out a cough of frustration.

"Wait. Let's be frank. I'm just trying to explain everything. There obviously is an interesting quality about prosthetic implants. I mean just technically. Not morbidly, or sexwise or anything. I didn't mean to bring this up and make a big deal out of it, because it's not a big deal, but at least we have to get it out of the way, and we just have to admit that it's kind of interesting . . ."

"This is your idea of *normal*?" She began to grope for the door handle on her side of the car.

"Oh, Kim, wait. I'm just trying to say."

She gave up searching for the door handle, slapped the wall, and sat back against the seat, arms folded.

After a silence, he said, "Can I just start over? Kim?"

She was newly pleased to realize that she hated him. He was a jerk. Now that she had spoken to him she could define her disgust specifically. His voice. His haircut. His overlarge eyes in the S.A.T. testing office, overlarge with impolite curiosity. It was not innocence that showed in his unkempt haircut, but a kind of arrogance. Some of the things he'd said were incredible. Not even to be remembered or considered until she could be alone by herself. She only wanted to get him out of here.

"Is Cindy's father really a counterfeiter?" he said. "Brilliantly changing the subject."

"What gave you that stupid idea?"

"Everybody at school says so. Cindy says so herself. That's what she told Jeff."

"That's the stupidest idea I've ever heard," she said, though she felt unexpectedly lifted into doubt. "Is that what you came here to talk about?"

"Well, he's been buying a lot of expensive stuff like that moped. And he's been giving Cindy all these twenty-dollar bills. Certainly not sufficient evidence to convict. But it's interesting."

One of the selfsame twenty-dollar bills was at that moment buttoned into her shirt pocket. Cindy had given it to her when they thought the condoms would be expensive, and had told her to hang on to it just in case Eric brought cocaine and wanted her to help pay.

Kim said, "It's really malicious, a rumor like that."

"Cindy told Jeff she heard her dad talking to your dad."

"Oh! All that was, was he found a twenty-dollar bill he thought might be counterfeit. So he and my dad sent it in to the government. But it turned out it wasn't counterfeit. I can't believe how malicious!"

"*They* said it was real? Well then, it can't be counterfeit. The paper is the tough part. You can't duplicate the paper. It's got microscopic red and blue threads in it." He stirred against the upholstery. "Can we just get out of this automobile? We could get out into the fresh air. Cindy is crazy."

"We can't leave. Cindy thinks we're . . ." She spoke with disgust. "Little does she know!" Her new hatred for Eric was starting to feel like a whole world she could begin to explore now slowly, with specificity and relish. For example, there was his vast assumption that—after this!—she would want to go outside with him. No doubt his eyes at this moment were unblinkingly wide in the darkness, with bland self-confidence.

"We could sneak out by a window," he said. "There has to be a window here according to California building code. I thought maybe we could go to Baskin-Robbins."

Just to think of his use of the word *interesting* gave her wings of anger. "Well, Eric," she said gently, "I'm afraid this was all a big mistake. Now, I have one of the twenty-dollar bills—"

"You have one? Really? Can I trade you for it? Because even if it isn't counterfeit—"

"Pay attention, Eric. I'll show it to you if you never mention this whole stupid incident to anybody. Do you promise? We have to keep this meeting a secret. Because I'd be incredibly embarrassed if anybody knew I'd . . . met you."

"Kim."

"Let's just get you outside, and I'll show you the bill, and then you can go away. The window is on this side."

He didn't respond.

"And Baskin-Robbins is out of the question, Eric, because it would be too humiliating if somebody from school saw us."

"I'm just trying to say . . ."

She opened the car door. "Here, give me your hand."

As they moved toward the window, his hand found hers in the blackness; it was large and strong, a male's errant hand. She could smell his sweater—and realized that was what she had loved: his sweater, the expanse of it, the dizzying smell of it. For a minute, his sexy slight overbite came to mind. But then she twisted her hand out of his grasp to take firm hold of his wrist, wringing out of her own shoulder this satisfying new anger. Of course he was "just trying to say." He just wanted to say he "understands"—"understands how she feels"—but how could he? How could anyone understand how it feels, to be the girl of whom there are no baby pictures?

# 12

Cindy was going through one of her ugly days, when her thighs in corduroy looked squashed fat on study-hall seats and her posture glimpsed in shop windows had an evil slouch. She sat across from Kim in Shakey's after school, supposedly doing her homework by the light of the video screen, but really just doodling—her usual stupid doodle, the fat daisy so swollen with cuteness that she hated it. She hated the very smell of her moist palm like the sweat smell of her steel locker in the hallway at school—whose chill metal against her forehead this morning, while she turned the combination-lock tumbler, had felt like the temperature of absolute boredom against her skull.

Kim looked up from her algebra and said, "What." It was annoying, her prying, as if everything were so simple. Kim had set her pencil down on the rows of unfolding quadratic equations which always came so easy to her somehow as logical corollaries to her having both parents at home.

"This is so dumb."

"Read me what you've got so far."

Cindy sighed against the flu. " 'The comparison/contrast of the Greeks and Romans is a very important comparison/contrast. Since the beginning of time, people have pondered this question. In the hustle-bustle world of today, the comparison/contrast of the Greeks and Romans is very important and relevant. For example, the Romans were after the Greeks and therefore they had a more technology-oriented advancement. For example, they had plumbing and flush toilets and they had lead in the pipes which made everybody gradually insane. For example, Caligula, which caused the Decline and Fall of the Roman Empire.' "

"Too many for-examples," said Kim.

"She likes for-examples. 'Another comparison/contrast of the Greeks and Romans is, the Greeks were very sane. For example, Plato and other world-famous philosophers pondered the greatest questions of all time. Plato believed that everything was ideal. This is still true today.' "

She stopped reading and reached for her Coke. "It's completely bullshit, but Orbach never notices. It's a hundred and forty-two words if I count 'comparison/contrast' as two words."

Kim said, "You should ask Eric. He's already had Civ, and he probably got an A. He said he'd come by here today."

"Here? Now? You told him to come by Shakey's?"

"Yeah." Kim averted her eyes, her pencil poised again above the rows of quadratic equations. "He had a yearbook committee meeting, but he's coming right after."

"I thought you hated him."

"I do." Kim's pencil began to move through the equations again. "He's the most arrogant! Conceited!"

This was a kind of betrayal. Shakey's had been their exclusive meeting place, where their faster, surer girls' wit could flicker unembarrassed among their webs of shared assumptions and ancient jokes. But the presence of a boy at their table would transform it into the usual complicated, shallow arena of performance and flirtation.

What was wrong with her? Insulated by this strange new feeling of brushing the surface of things without really touching them, Cindy pretended to return to her essay, but just began to run her pencil over the outline of her stupid daisy, increasing the pressure until the pencil point left trembling black crumbs in its path, not quite ripping the paper. Jeff DeBono hadn't called her in weeks, and the certainty of solitude was a new comfort. She could feel the knot, high in her chest, relieved every time she returned home alone and closed the front door in the empty house. She was happy. The more solitary she became, the more she was repelled even by physical things, weakened just by the sight of this varnish-tacky table, so near and inescapable.

"Is something the matter? You seem weird."

"I'm not weird."

"You know, I want to confess something," said Kim, and Cindy got angry.

"What," she said dryly.

"You know last week? When Eric and I were in the station wagon?"

"Yeah?"

"You know how I said we fooled around?"

"Yeah?"

"Well, we didn't. We didn't do anything. It was too bizarre.

But I told you we did because . . . I don't know . . . we thought you'd be mad. I mean, I still hate him. He's so incredibly arrogant. And you know the way he talks."

"It was 'too bizarre'?" said Cindy. "Since when is sex bizarre?"

"We were nervous, I guess. And he's a jerk."

"You're such a baby. You're both such babies. How perfectly matched you are!" She expelled breath through a faint smile, and she turned to her Coke, blowing bubbles through the straw to take out the carbonation. "You should both get married— get married and never have sex, because it's too bizarre."

"Come on, don't be like that. It was just too weird. He was so nervous. We went to get ice cream instead, at Baskin-Robbins."

"You snuck out?"

"Don't be mad, Cin."

"You snuck out? While I was spending the whole night standing guard in the kitchen?"

"Come on, Cin. Don't be mad. Keep your voice down."

"I can't believe how immature you both are. You probably haven't even held hands."

Kim stuck her hands in her armpits and leaned back.

"Okay then," said Cindy, temporarily epileptic with the impulse to say this reckless thing. "I've got a secret for you. Your dad is a counterfeiter. He's involved with this thing just like my dad is."

"What 'thing'? All this talk about counterfeiting is stupid."

"Hey, you heard them just like I did. Remember? When I was piercing your ears?" Cindy was surprised at this strange spasm of anger, which suddenly brought out as certain truths what had been merely shadows. "They were talking about it right there in the kitchen."

"That doesn't mean anything. They got that letter. What about that letter?"

"You know the wooden crate you said they put in your garage? I bet you anything it's full of money."

"How do you know?"

"Intuition," said Cindy. "But my intuition is never wrong."

"It's pots and pans and kitchen utensils. Your dad said so himself."

"Yeah, sure," said Cindy, turning to scan the room as she expelled breath again through that faint smile, a new mannerism. It felt good; it felt somehow like a new kind of solution she'd discovered. "I can really picture my dad making a big deal out of a bunch of kitchen utensils. I can really picture him building this incredibly strong crate to store a frying pan and a mixing bowl and a *spatula*."

"God, you're so mean sometimes. You don't have any proof of any kind."

"I don't need any proof. I know."

"Okay," said Kim. "There's only one thing to do."

"When, now?"

"My dad is always on the phone. We'll have to wait for a time when he's not there."

"Okay."

"Okay," said Kim. "Some time when there's nobody home."

Agreed, they looked around the room.

"*Wayne*," Cindy said, putting a nasal diphthong in the name to hold up its ridiculousness; and again she expelled that sarcastic sneeze through her smile, looking impatiently away from the table.

The compact sealed, Kim pretended to return to her algebra. And Cindy picked up her pencil and began to gouge a new daisy into the paper—the central ring, then the vicious dental petals moving clockwise—that same unwiltable daisy that existed in a Platonic and ideal world of crayon-bright sunshine, a changeless world where a daisy, a house, a lollipoplike tree, and a family trinity all loomed the same size, all sprouting together from a horizon. A cramped, sick world, locked into a state of glee, it had the dreamy horror of a forgery: she imagined herself as a stick-figure, the child in the center, trapped in a two-dimensional world where her only facial expression could be that scrawled smile, unable to slide her eyes to the left or the right to behold the stick-figure parents who gripped her either hand. She felt queasy in the video light.

Kim—who, Cindy was aware, had not been working, her pencil hovering in the breathless air above an incomplete equation—dropped suddenly back in her chair and said, "Let's go there now."

"Where?"

"My house. Maybe my dad isn't there now. I mean, when Eric gets here."

"Okay."

"I can't believe it," said Kim under her breath.

Cindy threw down the bouncing pencil. "You're such an infant. You can't even get laid. By the biggest fag in school. You don't know anything, you've been so sheltered."

"I know one thing, I know my dad isn't a criminal."

"No, he's too smart to be criminal, isn't he. He's the smartest guy in the world. That's why he drives a ten-year-old truck; that's why he rents a house in Santa Venetia; he's too smart to *own* a house. That's why he got a part-time job trying to gyp people over the telephone."

"You shut up. He's not gypping people. Some of those coins are worth thousands of dollars."

"I know you're not that dumb, Kim Paschke. You always make me look like the asshole."

"Let's go there now." Kim slapped her book shut. "Even if he is home. Let's go there and open the crate. I promise you it's full of pots and pans. I promise you. Even if my dad is there, we'll just go ahead and tell him why we need to open it."

At that moment, Eric came in the door, with that goofy bounce in his step that always reminded Cindy of phys ed, and his sketchy haircut, and the nylon backpack always heavy with textbooks slung over one shoulder. When he approached the table, she and Kim fell abruptly silent. He stood flatfooted beside the table looking from one to the other, and then he said, "Maybe I should come back later."

Neither girl said anything.

"Or," he said, shrugging off his backpack and letting it drop to arm's length, "now that I'm here we could just pretend everything's normal."

Still neither girl said anything, but Kim started sliding her papers together.

Eric said, "If you just pretend everything's okay, sometimes it gets actually okay. It seems illogical, but if you think about it it's really very logical."

Kim came to his rescue. "Come on, Eric, we're all going to my house."

"Why?"

Cindy shoved her essay into her purse and got up to leave, trying to beat them out into the parking lot. She knew what would happen now: Kim and Eric would form a conspiracy of innocence against her. As she opened the door to the roar of the freeway, she could hear Kim say, "We're going to open the crate."

"Ah! Terrific!" she heard Eric reply. Obviously he knew

exactly which crate Kim was referring to. Cindy waited outside in the blindingly bright parking lot where, after the darkness of Shakey's, the mind vanishes like a flame in sunshine—stuffing her books and papers angrily deeper into her purse.

As they came out, Kim was telling Eric, "It just seems mean, to sneak around and suspect him and everything."

"No," said Eric. "It's better not to ask him straight out. Why get him angry unnecessarily?"

The three of them started up the frontage road toward the freeway overpass, Kim and Eric in the lead, Cindy following. Kim turned to say babyishly, "If it's pots and pans, I get to slug you ten times in the shoulder."

As they walked over the overpass, Cindy ran her fingertips flutteringly along the mesh of the chain-link fence that guarded against suicides, until she discovered that she was picking up the fine gray flour of deposited carbon monoxide which like the Romans' lead was driving everyone crazy; so she reached into her purse and tore a page from her *Story of Civilization* textbook to wipe her fingers on. Kim and Eric were talking together exclusively several paces ahead. She could tell, by the agreed-upon distance between them as they walked, or by the way Eric's shoulder prodded Kim's aura tentatively, that there probably had been some kind of physical intimacy between them, or there soon would be.

They walked up Freitas Parkway, past the Northgate II mall, a cheap imitation of the Northgate Mall beyond it—with a Safeway and a laundromat, and a Piccadilly discount fashion outlet which was always trying to catch up with the styles and stapled that low-class REG PRICE, OUR PRICE ticket to every sleeve, and a Dunkin' Donuts where a cute greasy boy worked as morning fry cook. Next to the drive-in bank, the Jack-in-the-Box clown was saying, through the sizzle and spit of static,

"Okay, that's one Jumbo Jack, one large fries, and a Diet Coke. How about some onion rings today?" But the driver who had placed the order had already pulled away. Kim and Eric turned onto Northgate Drive and Cindy followed, past the repellent Exxon station with its armored-glass booth occupied by a grouchy old Vietnamese man, who always pretended that his English was so bad that he could never give kids change for the Coke machine or let them use the bathroom. Gradually the freeway rumble fell away, baffled acoustically by the trees that had begun to mature in the relatively new tract housing developments. The lawns had filled out and the houses had begun to acquire distinguishing differences. Rec rooms had been added, and better cars had appeared in the driveways; skylights had been cut in the roofs. Her mother had put in new carpeting in Cindy's bedroom, which glowed with newness in the moonlight as if Cindy were trying to fall asleep on the surface of a swimming pool. And now her father had become so recklessly rich. She had to take a deep breath to loosen her lungs as she thought: Now we are going to see if it's true.

Ahead, Kim and Eric cut behind the huge billboard— INFORMATION 389-9229—to go diagonally across the new Leisure Village Estates development, where new young couples bought little bobbing stucco houses on churned-up ground, so new that tractor-treads were hardened in the baked-white mud outside their patios, and wires protruded from the undulating earth. Crashing through the scratchy bushes at the back of the development, Kim—then Eric, then Cindy—slid down a flinty cliff behind the Union 76 station, and they picked their way through the familiar heap of bald tires, emerging onto the street without yet having spoken a word.

They passed under the freeway, past the huge ugly Civic Center building, and turned finally onto Robin Song Lane, into the shabbier neighborhood of Santa Venetia, where the streets lacked curbs and most of the houses were rented, the lawns unkempt, a neighborhood where the sun always seemed suddenly hotter. Then, as they rounded the curve, the Paschkes' house came into view: there were no cars in the driveway.

"Looks like nobody's home," said Eric over his shoulder to Cindy.

They waited for Cindy to catch up, and the three of them stood at the roadside regarding the house.

Kim said, "Let's look in the mail slot to be sure."

They continued to stand there.

"I can't believe this," said Kim. Then she took the initiative and crossed the street.

The mail slot on the Paschkes' house communicated with the garage. By lifting the lid they could peer in and get a good periscopelike view of the interior. They moved quietly over the driveway, and Kim lifted the lid to find that it was dark and silent inside. Wayne was not there. So she said, "Okay, let's do this quickly," and they went in the front door.

"Mom? Dad?" Kim walked through the house, calling. Cindy and Eric went into the garage.

The crate was there, under the workbench. Without being instructed, as smoothly as a well-rehearsed commando, Eric got down on his knees and, with effort, slid it out, making a tremendous scraping noise of crunching granules on the cement. "It's money," he said expertly. "It's exactly as heavy as if it were full of paper. And there's no clanking sound."

"We'll need a screwdriver," Kim said. "There's one in the drawer by the fridge." Cindy, trying not to seem useless, followed Kim out into the kitchen to look for a screwdriver, while Eric remained in the garage pressing the panels and corners of the crate as if for a secret latch.

In the kitchen, Kim opened the drawer, but couldn't find the screwdriver, swatting aside flimsy supermarket produce bags and clipped discount coupons. "Not here." She went into the bedrooms. Cindy remained at the drawer to give it a more thorough, or redundant, search. There were rubber bands, a warranty certificate, a hammer, stingily saved sheets of folded aluminum foil, a button, a pinch-pot ashtray from ceramics at school, a Tinker Toy piece, thumbtacks—and a nostalgic smell like the smell of Play-Doh.

"Okay," said Kim, returning with a screwdriver. "We've got to be fast. If we get caught I'll die." Cindy followed her back to the garage.

Eight shiny screws held down the lid of the crate.

Cindy looked on, shouldered aside by Kim and Eric, while Eric turned the screwdriver. To break the tension, she moved away and scanned about the garage, picking up the plastic cap of a Bic pen which lay in the bowl of a hubcap, examining it as if it were interesting. She supposed it must have been Kim's once, because it was dented with the marks of molars. Or else her dad chews on his pen like a kid. She wandered off toward a corner, where a smashed radio sat on a shelf.

Eric said, "Okay, last screw." She set the pen cap down and returned to peer over Kim's shoulder at the lifting of the lid.

It was full of money. There were twenty-dollar bills bundled together with rubber bands, filling the crate to the rim. Eric reached to pick up a bundle, but Kim said, "No, don't touch it," and he removed his hand.

"Put the lid back on," Kim said dreamily, staring at the money.

Nobody did anything. They just gazed at the green rectangles.

"We should get out of here," said Eric, but nobody moved,

or even turned away from the sight of the cash. The three of them were trapped in a prism.

Eric eclipsed the money with the lid. He said, "Let's be calm."

Cindy turned away and blinked the strangeness from her eyes. She went out to the kitchen and looked through the front window to be sure that no one was coming; the neighborhood looked deceptively ordinary. When she came back, Eric was tightening the screws on the crate while Kim leaned listlessly against the workbench under the influence of the rectangles of green.

"What should we do?" she said.

Cindy thrilled at the word *we*. She would have expected to feel fearful, but for some reason she was excited, guilty, thrilled to be an inoculating influence in this household. She hadn't expected such gladness, or such an immediate warm sense of being locked into a crystal of companionship.

"Well, we have to be logical," said Eric. "I think we should make a list."

Kim said, "First, just put it back under the workbench. Exactly like it was. Exactly."

Eric got down to put his shoulder to the crate, saying, "The first thing you learn in Toastmaster's Club is the value of lists. Because you can organize all your options. And then make sublists of the advantages and disadvantages of each option."

"What are we going to do?" said Cindy.

"Nothing," said Kim. "Let's just wait and see what happens."

Eric nudged the crate a bit further and said, "First of all, we should come back in a week or two to see if any has been spent. We're not sure what's going on yet. Or we could just come out and ask what it's doing here. I really think we should make a list to evaluate the pros and cons systematically." He nudged the crate. "Is that exactly how it was?"

"More into the corner," Cindy said, from her vantage point by the door.

Eric wiggled the crate further back and stood up. "Here. I suppose you want to put this back exactly where it was." He handed Cindy the screwdriver. She accepted the wand but couldn't discharge the responsibility, not knowing where Kim had found it.

Eric said, "First of all, we should do nothing for the time being. That's the main thing. We should just go on like normal."

Kim was still leaning against the workbench. Cindy said, "Come on, Kim. What are we going to do?"

Kim began to amble toward the doorway. "Could you just leave us alone, Cindy? I want to be alone."

"Leave you alone!" said Cindy. Anger flew all over her and irrational arguments crowded her mind: You can't leave me out, I was the one to first tell you about this, you wouldn't even have this crate of money if it weren't for my dad . . .

Eric followed Kim out into the kitchen and put an arm around her shoulder as she walked. She said, "I just want to be alone." She shrugged away Eric's arm and turned on Cindy: *"Would you please just leave us alone!"*

Cindy's flesh tingled. She flung the screwdriver at Kim's feet and grabbed her purse and walked out the front door, darkness welling in her vision. She breathed deep to stretch the closing ring of muscle in her throat. She began to run, trying not to cry, tears jingling in her eyes. She increased her pace until she was sprinting at top speed through the sunny neighborhood, around the corner, down San Pedro Road. The faster she ran, the less she felt like crying.

# PART THREE

# 13

The months went by, and the rains of winter came, and the foil sleighs rose and fell on the lampposts in Bon Aire Shopping Center; an immense Pay 'n' Save arose from the tossing earth where the Twin Bowl used to be, and the Burger King on Francisco Boulevard added the classy touch of a salad bar with croutons and bacon-flavored confetti and jittery elusive sprouts; Century 21 pickets kept appearing and disappearing on lawns; the Beef 'n' Brew on Lincoln Avenue was replaced by something in pink script with an exclamation point; and they began widening San Anselmo Avenue, Day-Glo cones appearing along its custom-hardened banks; and then, as flocks of high school girls became more visible, the rains departed, withdrawing in misty veils over the supine hip of Mount Tamalpais—and still Randy had heard nothing from Bim. Holed up in his apartment in San Anselmo, at first he had been too fearful even to go out much, or to put his Social Security number on a job application. The smartest thing he'd done was to cancel the trip to Curaçao, to let fear hold him in place waiting for further instructions that would never come, and thus stay blameless. In his worst periods of fear, which seemed to come and go in cycles like relapses into a persistent virus, he lay awake at night watching parallelograms of headlamp light scan the ceiling, picturing himself under constant surveillance by the F.B.I. or somebody, tossing on his waterbed mattress, whose undulations cut him off queasily from reality. He finally quit sleeping on it and moved with uprooted blankets to the solid couch, where he could worry better.

It began to occur to him that Bim might even have died or something. The Secret Service had approved the twenty-dollar bill for a second time—sending it back to the Paschkes with an irritable note asking them not to send it again, explaining that it was a genuine twenty "from which the Reserve Branch Numerals have been partially effaced with a common rubber pencil eraser. This according to Treasury standards is not mutilation sufficient to warrant recall, nor does this constitute a violation of Federal utterance laws." But Randy couldn't find Bim. Mostly he just hid in his apartment, doing occasional carpentry work as if he needed the money. And staying away from everybody. He began driving aimlessly around Marin's affluent neighborhoods looking for Bim, looking for that peculiar long white car which Bim had called a LaGonda—but soon he gave this up, and resigned himself to living indefinitely in a state of apostolic expectation, looking for signs, visiting the Canal District apartment often, looking for him when he turned streetcorners, listening for him when he picked up the telephone. One night, in the illogical but pious hope that Bim had somehow planted a microphone in his apartment, he tilted back his head and addressed the ceiling: "I just need to know what to do. Did I do something wrong? Tell me what I've done wrong. Give me a sign."

Finally, as the winter rains withdrew over the mountains, he began to feel permanently deserted; he had to face the likelihood that Bim might have vanished for good, and he started trying to think of himself as independent. The first specific pictures emerged only dimly, of what his life would be like if Bim never came back at all. He had lived so long on a thin hibernatory trickle of anxiety, he began now to feel released, skinny, clearer-eyed, as if a glacier had receded from the world leaving a strangely scooped moraine strewn with some few immovable new facts: he was altogether alone in this now; he had not been detected by the police, having not himself committed any act that was, strictly speaking, "illegal"; and he was the sole possessor of about a million perfect twenty-dollar bills. Which had been tested twice in the Secret Service's forensic laboratories and both times been determined to be "genuine." Didn't that make it truly "genuine"? Even if the Secret Service was bluffing, he would still be able to claim that he had *tried* to submit it. It was genuine. He bought a Ferrari.

Because over the months Randy had developed a philosophy of economics, the basic idea of which was that cash is a force for good in the world; when you spend it, you spread it around. Everybody benefits. The Ferrari dealer prospers and decides to put in a pool at home, so the pool contractor prospers and decides to hire more people. And so on. Bim's plan had probably been something like this, something philanthropic, because he had always insisted that personal gain was not his goal. And so Randy's first acquisitions were a house and a car—which would be useful not so much for themselves, but for the sort of people they would let him associate with: he needed to fade into social circles where people knew how to dispose of money.

Deciding that he would always be morally in the clear if he retained forever a willingness happily to give it all back, he removed two of the crates from a safe-deposit vault in San Jose, and he deposited the cash in a number of small checking accounts in various banks, using the false identities he'd acquired when he was working for Bim. Then he brought the checking accounts together in larger sums by buying Certificates of Deposit, to make it seem that the money was abiding in stabler forms. And when he bought the Ferrari, he used the CDs to arrange for long-term financing rather than buying it outright for cash, in order not to seem suspicious. Gradually and cautiously, he would spend the cash on real estate and other tangible possessions, diluting it in the general economy and washing himself of the idea of a "crime." He drove around Tiburon and Belvedere and Ross looking for a suitable big house to purchase, feeling satisfactorily feeble and lightweight as if he were recovering from a long illness, while a few spring rains continued to sprinkle occasionally in sunshine. He finally found the right house in Ross, a town so austerely upper-class that there was no postal delivery at all—you had to have a P.O. box to live there. This was one thing Randy had started to pick up: that the upper class prefer a kind of inconvenience, a kind of impoverishment. He had already realized he might start to regret having bought a conspicuous candy-red Ferrari, which, as he walked alone over the grounds of his new house after closing the deal with the realtor, was parked in the leaf-strewn driveway, transcendent like a cinematic special effect. But he loved the way it made him nervous, like dating a model.

He told himself, with self-forgiveness, This is a stage I have to go through.

He had even pictured cute young women going dull-eyed and unbuttoning their blouses under the spell of money. The house was really a sort of mansion—an old three-story shingled mass of unexpected rooms and porches, set back among huge trees on Shady Lane, with a haunted-looking turret; age-dimpled glass panes; high ceilings enclosing volumes of plaster-smelling space that would have to be filled with furniture, and thus, by implication, with new friends; a defunct Victorian turntable in the rear driveway for reversing the direction of the car; a large lawn heavily invested with immense old trees that seemed vaguely ancestral, watchful. Beneath a cloudy sky that lent an appropriate Englishness to his tour of his property, Randy passed an oak and brushed his palm against its rough bark, thinking, This is "my" tree. He set his foot on the stair of the porch and mounted the steps, thinking, This is the tread of "the owner."

He opened the door. The daunting air of the empty rooms could only be warmed by throwing parties, making new friends. He had restricted all his old friends to a separate, shrinking world, in order to keep intact the membrane between the "ethical" and the "unethical." He had completely avoided Cindy and her mom, which no doubt irked them both, in different ways. He had not answered any of the peculiarly self-burying messages Cindy left on his phone machine, mostly appeals for help in the usual pretended catastrophes. And of course Wayne and Laura Paschke were not to know about any of this. Not for a long time. Their not knowing saved them from complicity. That crate was still in their garage, and it must remain unopened until Randy had learned how to dispose his property legally. Which is where rich friends would be useful. That was the next, the most important step: finding rich people to associate with so that this new money could melt naturally into the world.

But he wasn't sure how people in this neighborhood made friends, they all seemed so aloof. They didn't go to bars: the center of town had only a post office, a public library, an antique store, and a concrete-floored grocery that closed at five o'clock. And one dumpy office building that seemed to be occupied only by lawyers and child psychiatrists. Randy Potts would be a refreshing new element in the neighborhood, the new owner of the run-down house on Shady Lane—which had previously been tenanted, on a month-to-month lease, by some hippie religious cult, and which had therefore already acquired a bad reputation. They had left the interior rooms with a sour, postcoital feeling. A hippie girl's paisley shawl was still tacked up over one of the front windows, sun-faded almost to translucency, and Randy walked across the living room floor and tore down the shawl to look out on the lawn. Through the mass of his own unkempt foliage, he could see the neighbor's house, more impressive than his own, bigger, built of red brick and bristling with chimneys. The neighbor's grounds were as well-kept as a fairway. Randy would have to hire gardeners too.

But he didn't want to spend too much money at one time; he didn't want to attract the notice of the Internal Revenue Service. From now on, he would be more cautious. He had heard that big-time criminals hide large flows of cash by owning laundromats or liquor stores. Maybe he should buy laundromats, on timid little down payments, and then hire a sleazy lawyer to help him do his taxes. He almost wished blasphemously that the money had never entered his life: he would almost rather be here at this big troublesome house as a hired carpenter than as the owner. But he had decided to cooperate with fate, to observe himself with detachment going through the motions of this new force. His idea was, as long as he remains a basically nice guy, everything will turn out all right. Wasn't that right? He hadn't manufactured it. He had simply been given a great deal of "money." It hadn't been his idea to begin with.

Somebody was moving in the bushes outside. The branches of the hedge trembled. Randy drew back and peered around the window frame. The branches shook again.

It was an old bum. His clothes were stained as if he'd slept on the ground. How had he found his way into this neighborhood? Randy went outside.

"Hey, friend," he said, descending the steps and crunching through the layer of fallen leaves, taking some pleasure in the peremptoriness of his tone. "Are you looking for something?" Driving off an intruder made him feel for the first time like a proprietor, primitively.

The old man revolved amidst snagging branches. "Ah! Hello!" he said, seeming to focus on Randy gradually through milky eyes. He had an oddly pouched face and rubbed-off white hair. "The bees," he said, gesturing about him.

"The bees?" said Randy.

"To see what they're harvesting, you know. I hope you'll forgive my trespass. I just wanted to have a look at your blossoms here."

"Well, there aren't any bees," said Randy. "Were you trying to get to someplace?"

"You're with the religious community. My name is Arthur." He slapped his palm back and forth on his pants and extended it in a handshake.

Randy realized that he was the neighbor's groundskeeper, and, deciding with rapid intuitive firmness that he liked the old man, he returned the handshake. "I live here. Just bought the house. My name is Randy."

"How in the world did you get the money to buy that place?"

His face felt stretched tight as he smiled. He said, "I made the money."

"Which doesn't pose an ethical problem for you?"

"What's wrong with making money?" He tried to casually toss a hand, but there was something involuntarily spastic in the motion. "That's what it's all about, isn't it?"

The old man's eyes narrowed. "Well, I'm disappointed. A great tall fellow. With a blond pony tail. Said his name was Ananda. I was in town last month, and I ran into him out here playing a sort of flute instrument. We had a rewarding conversation."

"No, no, I *live* here. The hippies left. I bought the house."

"Oh, of course! Well then! I feel I must shake your hand again. I feel I'm meeting a different man. Arthur Van Sichlyn. And you're Randy . . ."

"Potts."

"Potts. Potts. Yes. I must say, I'm sorry to see the pilgrims go . . ."

Now, as if delayed, the symptoms of panic were passing over—a prickle at the hairline, a dimming of the vision—while Arthur went on talking about the hippies and the nobility of their poverty. He was obviously not the groundskeeper but the owner himself, stumbling around his property in rags. Visionless, Randy shifted his weight on his knees to occupy the zone his ghost had been displaced to—realizing that he would have to recover his poise and act quickly. Somebody like Arthur would know what to do with large amounts of money. Or he would have friends who would. And he would be an example of behavior to Randy, who could be immediately so perfect an impostor as to achieve actual sincerity.

". . . They gave me some of their literature to read, and it was surprisingly impressive. One of those popular philosophies with some Oriental inspiration, but really just plain common sense. They were so poor, I offered to help them, but they actually refused my offer. They were quite indifferent to their poverty. I thought, well, at least I could give them an old truck, something practical. But you know, they had their feet planted on the ground. On the ground."

"They sound really nice."

"Of course, they weren't popular in Ross. People imagined Druidic rites, actually."

"Yeah, I wish I'd known them. They left a bicycle in the garage."

Strangely, Arthur backed further into the shrubbery and narrowed his eyes at Randy. A leprechaun.

It made Randy nervous. "Bees?" he said.

"Hm? Yes. A few apiaries."

"What were you saying about bees before?"

"Agh, I visit so seldom. Though my daughter-in-law has dogs, you know. Bees are my preference. I thought today I might smoke them out."

"Smoke won't kill them. Malathion is the only thing. If you use smoke they'll just get sleepy, it won't kill them."

"Oh, my goodness, I don't want to kill them. But tell me, Randy, may we get acquainted, you and I? Actually, I'm returning to England on Friday. But I do like to be a good neighbor. I was planning to go into Fairfax this afternoon, and I see the sun is coming out. Would you like to come with me? Do. Actually, I thought I'd ride my bicycle. Do you suppose that bicycle in the garage is in working condition? If not, I can lend you one. Ah, but I see you're not dressed for a ride. Much of it is uphill and strenuous; I know an old fire road behind San Anselmo."

"Oh, these old clothes?" said Randy. "I don't mind sweating in them."

"Ah!" said Arthur happily. "Well, then!"

"What's in Fairfax?"

"My wayward son. He's putting in some sort of bullshit installation."

"Well . . . ," said Randy, "I guess I'll go check out this bicycle. Should I meet you out front?"

"Yes, excellent, wonderful," said Arthur, making breast-stroke motions as, with a senile scowl, he made his way back through the bushes.

So Randy ran around to the far side of the house and started the Ferrari, moving it into the garage; and he found the hippies' bicycle to be in good condition—an old Schwinn ten-speed with hard tires and a shinily oiled chain. These hippies, who had actually turned down the offer of free money, must have migrated to someplace where they wouldn't need a perfectly good bicycle. Why couldn't they have simply strapped it to the front of their bus as other hippies do?

He hadn't been on a bicycle since he'd gotten his driver's license, and it felt awkward—his Italian mushroom-leather shoes on the pedals, his new silk shirt straining across his shoulders—but he found that as soon as he was in motion he had recovered the momentum of youth. He rode on popping gravel down to the bottom of his driveway, where Arthur was already waiting on an old-fashioned Raleigh. Maybe he shouldn't have consented so easily to this ride. Maybe his courtship of Arthur would appear too eager. It would have been better to wait for another chance encounter.

"So, anyway," he said. "What sort of installation is this?"

"Kevin's? Agh." The old man winced. "Who knows. Last one, he drove sixteen tiny silver stakes into the lawn. It's a dirty great lawn, you know. It's the IBM corporate flagship building, so they have a dirty great lawn. These poor Fairfax people have no idea what they've bought."

They began to wobble side-by-side down Shady Lane, which was empty of automobile traffic. Here he was beginning a new life in a situation he could never have anticipated: his suddenly oversized knees, polyester-clad, prodding arcs in air beneath his chest, his spine curved, his handlebars floating steadily in remembrance, intermittent sunshine and shade flickering in his eyelashes. His every remark felt like a test.

He said, "He drove silver stakes into the lawn?"

"Agh, yes. That's exactly what I told him. The stakes were planted in some sort of arcane pattern, you see, which had to do with the yes-no, positive-negative language of computers. But then, you're not supposed to interpret it. You ruin it if you look for meaning. There's supposed to be some sort of mysterious Heideggerian trance you enter, wherein Being Itself is disclosed."

Arthur turned to Randy in appeal for his opinion. Randy said recklessly, "It must be hell for the poor guy who mows the lawn."

"Pardon me?" said Arthur. Then he started to laugh. "Yes! Those silver stakes! I suppose it takes him three times as long now to do his job." He started to chortle so that the shaking of his laughter chucked him this way and that, and his bicycle began to veer. It was genuine laughter. Randy felt he hadn't heard genuine laughter in years. "Ah, Randy, Kevin would be angry. He takes it all very seriously. He can be quite a prick about it. Tell me, are you free for dinner tonight? At my place? It'll be just me and Kevin and Kevin's wife. My own wife is dead, actually."

"Well, sure, I . . ."

"Are you from around here?"

"Yes," said Randy. "Marin County."

"Where did you go to school?"

There was no way to lie about it, so he leaped straight to the truth: "I didn't go to college."

"Agh," said Arthur, "Kevin did. All his friends were going to college, and it was important to him at the time. And at that age, boys are still adolescents. They don't know what they want."

Randy regarded Arthur with a sidelong glance.

"His mother's influence. My opinion, a bit of public school is fine. So long as it stops there. And so long as they keep the boys out in the fresh air on the playing field, rather than indoors feeling each other's willies. His mother's ambition from the start was to turn him into a homo. If not for a few homo professors, he wouldn't be taking himself so seriously today."

Randy's guess coalesced into a conclusion: that this was art. Kevin was an artist. Possibly a gay artist. And immediately he knew he should launder his cash by investing it in art, in Kevin's art. Or in some other art Kevin and Arthur recommended. It would seem the most natural thing. He had to keep grasping at each oncoming handhold.

He asked an intelligent question, perfectly phrased: "What does Kevin title the IBM piece?"

"He doesn't use titles anymore. Can you imagine? He refuses even to call them 'Untitled.' The only way to refer to them is to say, 'the silver stakes in the lawn of the IBM building,' or 'that bundle of mylar in Chicago.' Or, 'those bits of gravel under the freeway foundation in Los Angeles.' It makes conversation about them very awkward, you can imagine."

The rich seemed almost to have different-shaped souls, enfeebled by their leisure. Did "art lovers," like burnt-out perverts in search of some faint new shiver, actually travel to Los Angeles to look at the stretch of freeway with the bits of gravel underneath? But Randy told himself to reserve judgment. Adaptability would be the key to his survival. He and Arthur were approaching a dead-end in the street, where a stile marked the beginning of a gravel fire road.

"Stupid. Effete." Arthur was muttering. "Went away to one of his mother's schools and started straightaway behaving like a fucking poofter."

He fell silent as their tires entered on the gravel of the fire road and they began to climb into the hills behind Ross, embarking on an arduous trip that would have taken about two minutes if they'd driven his Ferrari. They didn't speak at all during the ride, too winded for speech, and isolated by the necessity to travel single-file through the unpredictable ruts. The clouds had burned off and the sun heated Randy's back, so that his new silk shirt was soaked by the sweat of all the accumulated poisons of the winter's nervousness—the distillation of his unkempt felonious-looking apartment, with its discarded clothes and old Styrofoam Tap Ramen cups and the bathtub-ring film of worry on everything. When they finally came up into the full blue sky at the top of the hill at the point where the earth pivoted beneath them, the cool breeze from the Pacific began to whip at him, tearing away the sweat in chilly sheets as he and Arthur coasted bumpily, brakes squeaking, down the squirming road, swerving to avoid big rocks,

vibrating their bones, making tiny suede-gray lizards scamper
for roadside weeds. This area felt slightly familiar. It looked
a bit like where he used to drink beer with the crowd from
Terra Linda High School. But no, that was somewhere else—
unreal—a slope had whipped past like a slope he and Mary
had once had an argument on. An argument that had ended
in love. But the rinsing scenery kept flying, and the road ahead
kept slipping out from beneath his expectation. His limbs were
rattled to limpness by the stones under his tires. Finally, they
rejoined an asphalt road and, still single-file at the roadside,
coasted down to Bolinas Road, which Randy recognized and
felt reoriented to see, and which emptied out finally in the
middle of downtown Fairfax.

Kevin—rising from his seat at the bus stop at the sight of
the old man—was about Randy's age, an ordinary-looking man
in jeans and a sweatshirt, drinking coffee out of a paper cup.
He had apparently been sitting there on the bus stop bench
all day. There were no tools, nor any evidence of art. In fact,
he looked like he was waiting for a bus. The rich don't look
any different.

The old man, getting off his bicycle less winded than Randy,
said, "Kevin, this is our new neighbor. I told him to come to
dinner tonight. Randy Potts. Bought the house those spiritual
kids had been renting."

Kevin extended a handshake. "The town council will be
glad to hear that," he said grimly, prolonging the handshake.
"Horrible shoes."

"So you see, Randy," said Arthur, looking around the parking lot, which was situated exactly in the middle of everything,
surrounded by a theater, a pharmacy, a delicatessen, restaurants, a bakery. "I'm sure he has no idea what he's going to
do here."

Kevin pushed his hands into his pockets, which thrust his shoulders up around his ears, and he began slowly to revolve, saying, "Strict territories. An arena, really. There's a group of boys with cars who hang around the east end down there, but they're usually gone by some time after dusk. When they greet each other, they say, 'Any parties?' And there's a group of mountain bikers who hang around this part here. And then, you see the gas station. On Saturday nights, that's where the skateboard punk rockers hang out. It's an ecosystem. There's all this competition for territory . . ."

"But you see," Arthur murmured into Randy's ear, "he hasn't yet decided what sort of 'installation' to . . . 'install.' "

"Has my father already been telling you how fraudulent my art is? I'm a horrible disappointment as a son?"

Randy just smiled filmily. He used to hang out here too. Down on the east end looking for parties, that was his crowd.

Arthur took Randy's elbow and lowered his voice: "No doubt he'll finally do something absurd like drawing a chalk line on the pavement, calling it, *Chalk Line on the Pavement*, and charging the city of Fairfax thousands of dollars . . ."

"Actually, I sort of like that."

". . . and it will be described glowingly in journals . . ."

"How far did he get, Randy? Did he get as far as 'The boy should have been murdered in the womb'? Has he already got onto the subject of homosexuality?"

"It's humiliating . . . ," said Arthur. "Randy, this is a father's worst nightmare."

"What you're seeing here is an oedipal conflict in its later stages. The woman in contention is dead, but—"

"Jesus bloody Christ, it's humiliating. Here's my son, talking like this, sitting here bilking a nice little American village out of several thousand dollars . . ."

Arthur's sentence trailed off, and, in a lull, they both looked at Randy as if expecting some sort of response. He just shrugged, searching his mind for a plausible remark. "Where will the kids go when it's changed?"

"Oh!" cried Arthur, pulling a folded slip of paper from his pocket. "That person Bowsher from Los Angeles rang up again. I promised him I'd get some information."

"My father tries to make himself useful while he's in town," said Kevin. He began to spin slowly away again, stretching his arms sleepily wide, and then clasping his hands behind his neck with his stomach stuck out.

"First of all," Arthur said, consulting his slip of paper, "he wants to know how much room *Requiescat 1972* will require."

"Just tell him that'll take up half a room," Kevin said, but speaking to Randy. "He knows my work well enough."

Arthur said, jotting with a pencil, "Then there's *Room*."

"*Room* is a room. And tell him to use a light meter to set the light level. It's important. Tell him it's between five and eight foot-candles."

Arthur kept writing. "Then there's *Pleiades*."

"That's a room. A light-sealed room."

"*Vertical Twelve*."

"A room."

Arthur was writing awkwardly on his thigh, his pencil puncturing the paper. In a moment of silence, Randy, off whom this whole dialogue had been rebounding, felt cued to say something. "I thought you didn't title your pieces. Your father told me you didn't like titles."

"I don't."

"*Vertical Fifteen*," said Arthur.

"That's just a wall. That's lasers and polyethylene. It could go anywhere."

Randy said, "I think I'll go across and get a cup of coffee to go," wishing for the defensive distraction of a cup to hold before him. "Anybody want some?"

Neither of them responded.

"Anybody want a cup of coffee?"

Arthur said, "They want to know about recent work."

"The turf in Providence has been photographed," Kevin said, turning to Randy. "And the IBM lawn has been photographed. Tell him I'll send it all with the blueprints. And tell him there's a video of the sandheap at Carnegie-Mellon, with interviews of all these disgruntled administrators who were unwilling to pay my commission. It's wonderful." He kept addressing Randy rather than his father.

Arthur stopped writing and looked up to Randy. "Isn't this bullshit?"

"Also!" Kevin actually kicked Randy's toe. "It would be good to have a video crew for the glass at the LACMA museum."

"Jesus fucking Christ!" said Arthur, folding away his paper and standing up.

Kevin explained, "I'm going to lay out twelve large panes of glass on the lawn of the Los Angeles County Museum. Just twelve unframed panes, in a three-by-four grid."

"Won't that kill the grass?" said Randy.

"Yeah, it'll leave a pattern of twelve square dead spots, with green borders separating them like mullions."

"Like a window," said Randy. "I like that."

"No you don't," said Kevin. "When Duchamp did the urinal, there was still an 'artist.' I want the *urinal*. It's necessary to leave the urinal in the bathroom. I don't even need to come *near* the urinal."

Arthur plucked at Randy's shirtsleeve. "Let's go. He's going to begin explaining all this. It's simply fraud."

"Well, yes, Randy, of course it is. Because the point is, I'm not here anymore. I'm no longer present. I recommend the coffee at Perry's. It's powdered instant, but it's better. And it's only twenty cents."

"No, let's go," said Arthur. "Don't let him trap you. He's about to get theoretical."

Kevin said, "Glad to meet you, Randy. See you tonight then." With a wave of dismissal he turned and trotted across the street and into Perry's Delicatessen.

"Isn't he awful?" said Arthur, his eyes shining.

# 14

Eric said, his breath stirring the hairs on her forearm, his finger drawing lazy tingling figure-eights on her knee, "I am the *abstract concept* of a boyfriend."

"C-plus," Kim said, and she shifted her chin in the turf. "Maybe B-minus." She loved to hear him talk, loved the laboring of his Adam's apple, the clarinet tone of cartilage in his voice, the seriousness, the grammar.

"Okay, you're not even seeing that shopping cart over there. You're limited to seeing your *concept* of a shopping cart. That shopping cart is wasted on you."

Kim lifted her chin, tickled by the ends of lawn-mower-torn grass.

"Which explains the divorce rate, my theory is."

"You're so smart. Let's sit someplace else."

"Where?"

"Anyplace. Someplace nice. We're out here in the middle of everything." They were lying on a triangular island of grass in the Northgate Mall parking lot, beside a trash dumpster that had begun to send out a sweet clove smell of rot as the Saturday morning sun warmed it. Reclining in a public place had always been the sort of thing that Kim, retarded by niceness, had never been able to get away with—unlike Cindy Potts, who was constantly doing things like sitting on dirty curbs, or wearing ragged disintegrating jackets or little-old-lady skirts, sarcastically, so that her beauty shone through. But Kim with the vindicating new presence of Eric beside her had begun to develop a confidence almost like revenge. In a way, he was right, he had started out as the concept of a boyfriend, a rectangular presence at her elbow. As if she were now only gradually coming into her five senses, his image kept resolving into more particular focus. What a surprise his actual pores had been! The lone twig of hair between his eyebrows. The iridescent rips in his colorless irises. The tuck of his lip. The earnest vulnerability.

She rolled her shoulder softly into him. It had been Cindy Potts's presumed attitudes, always ambient, which had provided for so long an excuse for her not trusting him. The beginning of sex had unpinned so many ancient gathering tensions in her body, that now a kind of minute, continuous choreography was growing between her and Eric which would have been impossible before. He brought his chin into contact with her skull and looked out over the parking lot, saying, "This is perfectly normal at our age."

"Still," she said, irritated. His comment was connected obliquely to his running joke about their eventual marriage—an easy jocosity which always struck her as, in a male, unfair.

"We could check the money," he said.

"We just checked it. Besides, my dad is probably home."

Eric's finger renewed its teasing on her knee as if to say she was being cutely irrational. She bent her leg to harden her kneecap against it. He made a humming sound of satisfaction. His very voice had been changed. Changed by the many late hours they'd spent in his family's rec room, slipping through each other's shifting embraces, sliding toward that precipice of pleasure where her self-consciousness of her body fell away and a dark muscular angel arose within her, an angel that could carry them both. His voice was losing its monotone, acquiring various pitches. Infinite subtle shades of humor were appearing in the breath-scented intimate space between them, a space minutely fraught with dense codes: she relaxed her knees slightly.

"I'm just saying," said Eric, his cheek slipping downward against hers, "I'm more obnoxious than you think."

"Are you obnoxious?"

"Of course I'm obnoxious." He was whispering now. "Everybody's obnoxious."

"No you're not."

"I'm obnoxious." His lips brushed her ear.

"You're a gentleman."

"I'm a concept of a gentleman."

She sighed. And from within the deep breath, as if stored at the base of her lungs, rose the chronic irrelevant worry about her father. Since they first discovered it, she and Eric had been sneaking in to check the crate every few days; and still none of the money had disappeared. It was amazing how ordinary her house continued to appear among the other houses on Sparrow Court. Continuing to hope her father thought it was pots and pans, she concentrated the diffuse guilt in the house as a diamond concentrates light, so that a new expectancy kept her tense, bright-eyed, regarding her ordinary dad from the corner of her vision, listening for the sounds of his motions in other rooms. As a precaution, Eric had persuaded her to go to PayLess and buy a package of pink gummed seals—actually price stickers—and they had stuck one on the border of the lid. Then he had photographed it and mailed himself the photograph, in order to have a postmarked, dated record of the crate's sealing. And he said they should photograph the seal again at intervals, as proof that it was still inviolate. All this was to provide evidence of her father's innocence in case there was trouble—a scheme she had at first objected to, but finally, after considering all the other alternatives, consented to. All they could do prudently was wait, be watchful. But every time they sneaked into the garage to check it, they couldn't resist lifting the lid to check the money—which broke the seal. And then they had to apply a new one identically. Fortunately, she had bought a package of five hundred at PayLess, which she'd hidden in her room, and a new seal was easy to apply to the exact same spot. Eric had a strongbox in his closet where he kept the photo in the unopened envelope—which she pictured being torn open one day in a courtroom by a defending attorney. Eric had said, *This is serious, Kim. Probably only organized crime could make such a good counterfeit. Randy Potts is in real trouble, and we're the only ones who can protect your dad.*

His body tensed. "You want to see the concept of obnoxiousness?"

"No tickling, Eric."

His hand darted to her ribs and she rolled away. "Don't."

"Just an illustration."

"Let's go check the crate," she said. "Maybe my dad isn't home."

He propped his head. "Look, Kim, don't worry. Why would he be involved with the coin business if he knew it was there? I'm absolutely certain, Cindy's father lied to him about it."

She stood up slapping her hips. "Come on." She turned away toward home. "It's something to do."

"How will it affect your strategy if you do find some of the money missing?"

But she had already started walking across the asphalt toward the freeway. It felt good to get fresh air in the face, to tear away from the humidity-fogged breath of love. He said, catching up to her, "And we have to talk to Cindy about this."

"Mm," she said coolly as she walked on, preventing the idea of Cindy Potts from condensing. Ever since they had discovered the money, Cindy had made herself invisible. She seemed to have no friends at all anymore. She could be glimpsed only occasionally at school, in the far distances of the corridors, and seemed to be taking the back way to and from school. The one time Kim had cornered her in the cafeteria to try to talk to her about the money, she glazed over angrily and walked away. And last week, when assigned to write an in-class essay on American history, Cindy wrote instead on the topic of her future career as a glamorous European model and heiress to a fortune in counterfeit money; when the teacher called her into his office, Cindy retracted it all, saying it was all an invention of her imagination. Kim now feared to befriend her, feared to jiggle the apparently schizophrenic balance. There was no way of knowing whether she had yet told anybody about the crate in the Paschkes' garage, or whom she might have told. Would anybody believe her if she did?

"We're the only ones who can take responsibility," Eric said, humping along lovably, loyally, beside her. "It's obvious your dad is innocent, but he's in danger of being caught. We're the only ones in a position."

Kim said, "I don't know, Eric," and hastened a little to speed their pace; but he managed to keep his arm around her shoulder as they walked under the freeway and toward the now-visible palm tree of the distant 7-Eleven that marked the entrance to her neighborhood. He was wrong about one thing: she loved him specifically, particularly. Somehow, it was his particular flaws that gave her that sweet, sick, chiming in the chest: his hopeless haircut, his way of filling the air with words as if in the expectation of being disliked, the slurping tuck of his mouth. She had first felt her love leap irrecoverably on the day, in algebra, when she noticed that there was an almost middle-aged finickiness in his way of holding a pen. His hair was so badly cut as to look lopsided. How thin his neck was! It had once annoyed her that he persisted in coming up to her in the hallways at school and saying things like, "Here I am, making conversation," or, "Let's have some casual small talk and begin a lasting relationship," as if he were trying to embarrass her by referring, in his facetious monotone, to their encounter in Cindy's blanket-enshrouded car. But on that day in algebra, after she'd heard he had lost in a track meet, she noticed him in class picking up his pen with the same confident fussiness as always; and that was the moment of loss. His plucky failure on the track team had lent him a doom that was hers alone. The whole idea of Eric DeBono came together in her mind—his continual generous self-parody. His gallant intellect. And he was so interested in everything. After class, she maneuvered to precede him out the door in the crowd of exiting students, and turned around to say, with remarkable poise, "Casual small talk about what?"

As they passed the 7-Eleven, approaching her neighborhood, she shrugged off his draped arm. "Would we . . . ," she said, reverting to a former topic. "Would we report it anonymously?"

"They don't take anonymous tips seriously."

"I just need proof," she said. Coming into her neighborhood now, they had begun to whisper.

"He doesn't know. It's obvious."

"What would they do?"

"Nothing," said Eric. "They would hand the information over to the Secret Service. The Secret Service does counterfeiting crimes."

"And then they would follow Randy Potts around . . . ?"

"Kim, we wouldn't even have to mention the crate in your garage. We could just tell them a certain Randy Potts is a counterfeiter. If it is counterfeit. Or we could just say a certain Randy Potts is carrying around bizarre amounts of cash. They would never think of including your father in the investigation. Or even if they did, he's totally unaware of the money in the crate. He's obviously innocent. See, that's why we have to hurry. If he finds out there's money in the crate, he'll start behaving guiltily. Or Cindy will start blabbing. Then he'll be implicated. And besides, Kim, we have the photographs of the seal."

She quieted him with a glare, for they had come around the corner of Robin Song and Sparrow, and they were about to go through the preliminary routine of stealing up the driveway and lifting the lid of the mailbox.

He dropped back while they tiptoed toward the front of the house—both cars were in the driveway—and she listened at the closed lid with her good ear. The other ear had received its final latex implant a few weeks ago, and was still slightly tender on the underside. Within the garage, she thought she heard her father's voice. Then, just as she got her fingernail under the lid of the mailbox, she heard somebody behind her humming loudly, tunelessly.

It was the mailman, his heavy black shoes slapping the pavement, his three-wheeled cart squeaking. Kim and Eric backed away from the mailbox and sidled artlessly from the house.

Wayne heard the day's mail fall through the slot onto the shelf while he was on the phone with a Mrs. Olin from Mountain View. "But the great advantage of investing in rare and collectible coins," he read from the prompt, "is that they are not paper. They are physical, tangible possessions. Many of them are made of precious or semiprecious metals. Such as gold or silver. For this reason, they will always have a market value—"

Mrs. Olin, obviously too smart to buy, interrupted him: "But certainly if your organization expects these coins to appreciate, they wouldn't put them on the market. They'd keep them."

"Good point, Mrs. Olin!" he said, flipping to Stage C in the prompt and reading, "I'm glad you asked that. Because Marketrend is not looking for casual or incautious investors . . ."

Just then, Laura opened the door and entered the garage. He glanced at her and started to read on, but Mrs. Olin interrupted again:

"I'm sorry, but we already have set up the investments we want."

"Good point!" he said, flipping to Stage D. Laura came up behind him and began to knead the ropy tendons that always lifted his shoulders while he talked on the phone. "Marketrend's trained staff of expert researchers is able to recommend purchases. And while of course risk is an essential ingredient in any investment, it is important to bear in mind that—"

Mrs. Olin said, "I'm sorry, but we're really not interested."

"Of course, Mrs. Olin. I understand. But if you give me your address I'll put you on our mailing list, so that if at any time in the future . . ."

She hung up.

"Thanks, Mrs. Olin, have a nice day," he said for Laura's benefit, and he hung up.

"How is it going?" she said.

"Great. Two call-backs and one mailing-list. Saturdays are good. How are you feeling?" he asked, referring to her pregnancy. The impossible swell was getting to be plainly visible. His own blood seemed, lately, to be moving with slow, placental melancholy. In fact, his sales weren't going well at all, but he felt he had to provide an atmosphere of optimism around the house.

"Had a nap," she said. "Egg salad?"

"Whatever." He leaned his head back against the new lens shape of her belly, and he closed his eyes to discover light-headedness, feeling hyperventilated from the persistence, all morning, of his own pleading voice on the telephone.

But he knew that such feelings were just the habitual negativity Fortinbras Armstrong warned of. It shouldn't matter what specific activity brings the wealth, nor even how discouraging it may be. What matters is his faith in himself. He turned his chair around to face Laura, deciding to confront her abruptly with a proposal that had been on his mind all week, acting according to Armstrong's dictum that one must never hesitate or mull things over, but assert oneself with perfect confidence and immediacy.

"Laura, I want to cash in the money-market fund and invest it in the business," he said, and regretted saying it right away, seeing her grow thoughtful. Pregnancy had made her girlish again, with bright skin and fluffy hair. She sucked her lower lip back between her teeth. It was really her money: five thousand dollars saved from tips, begun on an inheritance from her parents. It had been set aside for Kim's education, or maybe for purchasing a house some day.

She said solemnly, "Okay."

She could have said no, but she didn't; and Wayne felt the floor of his stomach rise. That money was their last security. After he'd spent it, they could never recover it. And he knew that she secretly thought it was a bad investment.

"Because, see," he said, "I have to get a Retail Bonus Volume of ten thousand dollars in one month, and then I'll be locked in as a Head Broker. First I can buy the inventory—"

"You have to sell ten thousand dollars' worth of coins in a month?"

"No, it's RBV. Retail Bonus Volume. I just have to *generate a flow* of ten thousand dollars. But see, the deal is, if I can do just one ten-thousand-dollar month, I'll be locked in for life as a Head Broker. Which means I'll be able to build an organization and hire other brokers underneath me. That's the whole secret. That's the pyramid. You get other people. But I have to get just one single ten-thousand-dollar month—which I can do by just buying the coins myself. Lots of people do it to get their start. That's how Buddy did it. It's called 'buying in.' "

"Well," she said, rubbing her upper arms, "how about an egg salad sandwich? You can take it back up on your pyramid to eat it if you like." She grinned, reaching out to pluck at his shirt.

"Honey, it isn't like we're getting nothing in exchange. We'll get a shitload of valuable coins. And I'm not being totally committed if I hang back with something in reserve."

"No, it's fine, Wayne. I think it would be wonderful for you to make Head Broker in your first year."

"Yes, but do you see the principle?" he went on. "I have to be totally committed. If we try to keep that safety net under us, it means we don't have faith. It means we expect to fail. The safety net means I'm *planning* to fall . . .

"And look, I did some calculations. I can buy the ten thousand dollars' worth for sixty-five hundred, as a Lieutenant Broker. But I've already bought some this month, so it's really just fifty-seven hundred. And the money-market fund is five thousand. So, see? I'll only need to sell seven hundred dollars' worth of coins before the month is out. I can do that. Any imbecile can do that."

"Wayne," she sang, "I said it's all right."

"It's just ten days, but Jesus! If I work like crazy. And then I'll be over the top."

She dabbed at his temple to press down some stray hair. "How much RV have you made so far this month?"

"R*B*V. About eight hundred dollars."

"Great. Of which you get to keep . . ."

"Thirty percent. But it doesn't work like that. See, I haven't actually sold eight hundred dollars' worth. That's my RBV."

"How much have you sold?"

"Three hundred and some. That's a ninety-dollar profit. Which, for three weeks' work, isn't so great. I know. But don't be pessimistic, honey." Evading her response to this revelation, he got up and wandered over toward the shelves, saying, "The next ten days includes two weekends. I'm sure I can sell seven hundred dollars' worth." He found himself looking down at the smashed Zenith which had been his brother's as a teen-ager. On top of it, he discovered the chewed Bic pen cap that usually lay in the bowl of the hubcap on the far table. How long had it been here?

"Has somebody been fooling around in here?" he said, picking it up.

Laura said mildly, "You know, it's reaching a point where we'll have to decide which bills not to pay. Marin Medical gave us to a collection agency." She went to the basket beneath the mail chute to pick up the day's mail. "And the amniocentesis will probably be expensive."

Yes, the amniocentesis: he had pictured them sliding a long needle into her womb, taking a nick of the new flesh, and analyzing it to see if its genes were deformed. People like Mrs. Olin led untroubled lives. They just hung up the phone and went back outside to their gardening or whatever. When he had stood over Kim's Plexiglas crib in the maternity ward fifteen years ago, he had felt a curse settle on the name of Paschke.

"Whatever," he said. "I think I'll take a break"—even though this was a stupid time to take a break: midday Saturday, when all the potential buyers were at home—and even though he had to sell seven hundred dollars' worth of coins in the next ten days or lose the entire investment of Laura's money, seeing his slate wiped clean at the end of the month.

But he had to recover his optimism. If a safety net invites failure, then having no safety net will guarantee success; it was a galvanizing thought he had to hold in his mind. He said, "At least there's always San Francisco County General." Supposedly they had a sliding scale for people who could prove they were poor. Laura would be there waiting in the corridor with all the destitute welfare mothers.

"No, I heard from them," she said, sorting through the mail.

"We're too bad a credit risk. They have some limit for debt delinquency, and we're over it."

"You mean we're not eligible? We're not eligible?"

"Wayne . . ."

"How could we not be eligible?"

"Something will turn up . . ."

"God damn it, Laura, I swear to you. Any fool can sell—"

They both looked over to the mail slot, which had—maybe because of a breeze—given out a faint clank.

He turned back. "Laura, listen. Any fool can sell seven hundred dollars' worth of coins over the goddamn telephone. The whole program was designed to be foolproof."

"Wayne, don't get mad at me. If you don't sell the coins, we'll pay the midwife with them." She walked out the door opening envelopes. "Egg salad."

How could it be so easy to say good-bye to five thousand dollars? She seemed to be sleepwalking through it. Especially with a baby coming.

But he had to spend it. There was no other way. For once in his life, he had to do something with good faith. It shouldn't matter that Marketrend seemed at times so corny and hopeless. The old Wayne Paschke would have found Marketrend ridiculous. But exactly when things seemed most absurd, that was the moment when the successful man plunges forward without admitting the possibility of defeat, almost irrationally. Then people look back later and call such a man not stupid but courageous. Fortinbras Armstrong would say it was a coward's natural contempt of the brave which had kept him at home for ten years comfortably smoking cigarettes and getting fatter and explaining away his failures by adopting the popular excuses like "the class system" or "lack of education" or "luck."

His voice had risen unreasonably. He relaxed his shoulders

and began to close up his files, taking a deep breath to flush out skeptical thoughts. Everything would look brighter after he had taken a break for lunch. Reversing the habit of failure was painful; it was just as Armstrong had warned: now that achieving Head Broker was actually within his grasp, the prospect had given him a self-defeating sensation of precariousness.

# 15

When the Secret Service first called on Randy, he was home alone at his place in Ross, happily busy. He had bought two pictures at the Brent-Heimetz Gallery in the city—a huge green abstract oil painting as big as a garage door by an artist named Diebenkorn, and a dingy, cramped etching called *The Distrest Poet* by an old Englishman with an illegible name like Hobart— and he was hanging them on the living room walls, wielding again the familiar live weight of a hammer, which the tendons of his forearms were grateful for the remembered heft of. Hauling this sixty-pound painting around, flashing reflected chlorophyll light on the newly painted walls, Randy was enjoying the labor as if he could get the illusion of earning these implausible objects. He leaned the expensive quadrangle of green against the wall and sat down out of breath on the new carpet to bathe in the view. It was just a green square, like an aerial view of an acre, but already it irradiated the room with the aphrodisiac glamour of art, relaxing to the gullible girls he would soon find a way to bring home. Even the most aloof would pull off their little underpants and, beneath a bona fide work of art, fuck without shame. The artist had been recommended by the experts at the gallery. And Kevin Van Sichlyn would like it, it was his kind of art. Kevin—who was in Fairfax today wrangling with the Fairfax Improvement Committee over his installation for the parking lot—had perceived in Randy a natural instinct for art. He had even given Randy one of his installations, a pile of grass clippings entitled "a pile of grass clippings," which Randy had placed on the front lawn beside the driveway, and which, last week, he had gone through the hassle of having appraised by a gallery and insured and registered with the Library of Congress.

Because over the last few weeks Randy had, astonishingly, discovered himself an appreciator of art, though of a new and more radical kind of art. He had always been bored by pictures of fat women on couches, and so was Kevin. Randy had only wanted to learn enough about it to acquire camouflage for his money—but it took all his patience. When there was a new construction site in Marin Kevin would call him up and bring him along for a tour of the torn-up earth, the little boulders of dirt, the fluorescent-tagged wooden stakes. And Randy would have to pretend to share Kevin's enthusiasm, while his heart hardened: the further he ventured into Kevin's imaginary terrain, the more he felt like an angry spy. Kevin would drop down on his knees to contemplate a scrap of dust-powdered wood half-embedded in clay, or a chain-link fence that had been dragged down into mud; or he would walk around and around hillocks of bulldozed earth to consider their undulations. One Sunday morning he insisted that Randy come along to the site of the new shopping center in Corte Madera, where bulldozers had been gouging new contours into the earth, and he led Randy over the curves and cuts among the debris in total silence, in a kind of reverent daze. The next week Kevin persuaded him to fly on a day trip to Los Angeles, where, at a museum called The Temporary Contemporary, a conceptual artist named Chris Burden had actually excavated the floor of the gallery itself, and titled the installation with the obvious joke *Exposing the Museum's Foundation*. Randy agreed with achingly feigned delight; he had intended to spend the day stripping woodwork in his dining room.

But when he got into the museum—separated for a minute from Kevin, who was parking the car—he stood alone at the rubble-strewn rim of the installation and felt a cold new draft rise before him. There were rude wooden stairs descending into the excavation, so that viewers were supposed to climb down and stand for a minute in the pit, and maybe get their hands dirty or soil the hem of their skirts. So remorseless was the truth that, in obedience to it, the artist had jackhammered up the floor and dug fifteen feet down into the subsoil beneath the museum, exposing a quiet, archaeological dimension beneath the parquet. It was beautiful. It was sacred. It was a grave. The crumbling laminated horizons of red California clay and the polished museum floor had become, in a moment of blinding fission, *concepts* juxtaposed. And Randy, who had sat beside Kevin on the plane still protected by his secret anger, stood there at the brink of the hole actually feeling the idea of "art" evaporate from the world. Here was pure misunderstanding, in all its serenity. . . .

Suddenly, with a crackle of fallen leaves under tires, a car drove up the driveway under the living room window. Randy staggered to his feet, supposing it would be somebody deliv-

ering something: furniture or appliances, or another delivery
from the Brent-Heimetz Gallery. He had also bought a small
lithograph for the front hallway, but it had needed matting and
framing, and he supposed the gallery had now sent the delivery
truck—

But it was a police car.

It pulled up to the rear and stopped in the wide space before
the garage. Nobody got out. The car just sat there. At that
same moment, the front doorbell rang. He looked out through
the dining room window to see a second police car moving into
position out front at the curb. He jogged to the hall, stopped,
and turned back, retracing his steps to the living room, past
the incriminating painting, and went into the kitchen, where
for some reason he opened an empty cupboard, gazed into it,
and then shut it. His blood was thudding; he felt like sitting
down on the kitchen floor. Instead he leaned over the old
porcelain sink and stared down at the drain. There was something soothing in the sight of the rough old porcelain, some
nostalgic anesthesia.

But the sink wasn't "his" any longer. He was already looking
at it from a great historical distance. He should have known
this would never work; you have to be brilliant to get away
with a crime like this, or at least basically criminal by nature.
Bim Auctor had plainly been insane, Randy should have seen.
With a sudden sensation of new freedom, like ears popping,
he felt the house itself cease to be "his." It was just an empty
house. All the integers in his life had switched in a minute
from positive to negative, and he was released into the vacuum
of surrender. He would just turn himself over and—how
strange!—feel freer after being caught. The doorbell rang
again, and he stood up as straight as a sleepwalker, going to
the front hall to answer it.

There were two men on the doorstep, in those cheap suits one expects of plainclothes police. One was Mr. Hodges from the Treasury Department and the other was Mr. Ludex from the Secret Service; they flashed badges in leather wallets, just as on television, and they asked if he was Randy Potts and they apologized for bothering him and they wondered if they could ask him a few questions. They moved past him through the door, shifting bars of gray blocking the light, and walked ahead of him down the corridor toward the kitchen, where the only furniture in the house was, and they sat down at the folding card table looking about them as affably as if they were neighbors paying a friendly visit, making bland observations about the house. Mr. Ludex asked if there was any coffee.

"Yeah, I've got a Mister Coffee thing," said Randy, his voice sounding dubbed, and he turned away to a cupboard watching his fingers as, without trembling, they separated a filter from its nested stack and measured spoonfuls of the expensive French-roast grounds he had been trying to develop a taste for.

Ludex cleared his throat and said he apologized for the show of police cars, it was merely routine procedure.

Randy poured water into the top of the Mister Coffee machine, and as it started to trickle, he squirmed up to sit on the counter and said, "So, what can I do for you gentlemen?" He realized it would have seemed more natural if he'd said this earlier—as soon as they'd arrived. But his voice had been suave. He could feel a faint smile on his face.

Ludex looked at Hodges, who was cued to reach inside his inner coat pocket and pull out some papers, which he spread on the table. They were Xeroxes of bank statements.

"Do you know anything about these?" asked Ludex. "We traced them to your post office boxes."

"Okay," said Randy. "It's counterfeit."

Now he had uttered it, and he couldn't take it back: the word remained printed on the silence of this resonant house. He would just hand himself over, so limp as to be unbruisable. Bim Auctor had forsaken him. It would be a relief not to have to be so cunning anymore. And maybe finally to find out what had happened to Bim, who Bim was.

But Ludex and Hodges were just looking at each other.

"What's counterfeit?" said Hodges.

"The money."

Nobody said anything. The Mister Coffee machine was belching and spitting.

Hodges cleared his throat again and said, "All this money?," tapping the bank statements with his finger. "Counterfeit?"

They hadn't suspected yet. They had come calling for some other reason.

But they would have found out anyway. They were on his trail, and he would have had to explain the money somehow. It was all over: he had never gotten around to the parties, the women, the gifts to Wayne and Laura. The coffee would soon finish brewing: Would it be wrong for him to offer them coffee, hostlike? He wanted even the coffee, now, to feel like impounded government property.

"I see," said Hodges.

"No, it really is," said Randy.

"How was this counterfeit manufactured?"

"I don't know," said Randy—the truth. But it would make his story all the more incredible.

"Well, how did you obtain it?"

"Wait. I shouldn't be saying anything, should I? I should talk to a lawyer first. But you have to put me under arrest. So everything I've said so far doesn't count, right? Does it count if I say something before I'm arrested?"

"No, Mr. Potts, we're not going to arrest you. You're not yet charged with any crime."

"I have the 'right to remain silent,' the 'right to an attorney' . . ."

Ludex finally spoke. "Mr. Potts, do you have a sample of this counterfeit currency? Something we could take with us?"

"Well, yeah, but I don't think I should give it to you. Don't you need a search warrant to get it? I mean, I don't mean to be hard-ass, but I'm entitled to confer with my lawyer, aren't I?"

Ludex didn't answer.

Hodges said, "Mr. Potts, we could arrest you right now if we wanted to. On suspicion."

Randy said, "Well, I'll need my checkbook, so I can pay my bail."

Ludex's eye met Randy's and they almost shared the humor of the idea. He got the sudden irrelevant feeling that Ludex was a nice guy.

"We're not going to arrest you at the present time," he said.

"Why not?"

Ludex turned to Hodges. "Frank, radio downtown and have Wanda courier one of these banks." Hodges slid the Xeroxes together and got up and headed toward the door, apparently to go outside to one of the police cars.

He stopped and said, "Bob, did your people examine it?"

"Just the usual."

The two men looked at each other for a minute, and Hodges shrugged.

Ludex said, "Wait, let's both go," and he stood up.

They seemed to be leaving.

"What am I supposed to do?" said Randy.

"Nothing," said Ludex, handing him a business card. "We're grateful for your help in this. We'd like to ask that you remain available for further questioning."

Ludex turned toward the corridor, and Randy followed him to the front door.

"Don't you even advise me not to leave town?"

"Okay, don't leave town. And my number is on that card if you want to contact me."

When Randy had closed the door, he was alone in the listening house. What had just happened? It had all taken place so quickly. He felt oddly swindled. The smell of fresh-brewed French-roast filled the air; he was disappointed that they had forgotten all about their coffee.

# 16

The television commercials for the Satin Kitten chain showed a handsome couple being seated by a waitress in the presence of a chef who smiled and wrung his hands; then the woman gazed lovingly into the man's eyes while her index finger pointed to something on the menu; then they toasted each other with glasses of wine, with such poise and politeness that you could tell they both did something smart for a living like programming computers or running their own business. Wayne had only been inside the Terra Linda Satin Kitten once in his life, and that was because he had to use the pay phone because his car was broken down on the freeway exit ramp, and he got engine grease on the push buttons and the air-conditioning-chilled phone book; and since then he had held the place, high on a hill above the freeway by the new Fireman's Fund building, in contempt. He remembered when it was built, in the late sixties, on a slope that had been perfect for box-sliding. His father, who was still alive at the time, had remarked with wonder on the cheapness of building materials these days, the hastiness of the construction, the greenness of the wood, the flimsiness of the drywall; and Wayne recalled his father's insight every time he drove past the place, taking some native satisfaction in the thought that all those rich people who weren't born in Terra Linda, the new invaders whose swiftness rendered Wayne and Laura stationary, were in there being hoodwinked. But today Randy Potts had called to tell Wayne and Laura to meet him there, to go ahead and reserve a table for three, because he had something urgent to discuss with them. When Wayne hung up and looked down at his half-eaten egg salad sandwich on the kitchen table, he said, "Jesus Christ, Randy's going to pay for lunch at the Satin Kitten and I've almost killed my appetite."

"What did he say?" said Laura.

"Nothing. He sounded worried."

Laura left the room. "Where has he been all this time?" Her voice was muffled by the hall closet.

"Mm," said Wayne, thinking of the two hours he would lose in going to lunch, when he could be on the phone reading the prompt. There were only ten days left in the month to raise his RBV above the crucial line. If he were truly committed to Marketrend, he would mention it to Randy at lunch; he would try to involve Randy in it, try to bring him to an Opportunity Meeting. But he had already mentioned it to him in the most self-defeating way—snorting, in an unfamiliar voice, about the stupid incentive system that involved Cadillacs and trips to Hawaii. Why did he say things like that when he was around Randy?

"Does he ever visit that daughter of his?" Laura's voice continued to drift from the smothering depths of the closet.

Wayne called out to her, "He said we shouldn't tell anybody we're meeting him there. He said he had an amazing secret. What do you think about that?"

As thumps and rustles continued to issue from the closet, Laura's ever-fainter voice listed the possibilities. "Crazy new business scheme . . . statutory rape charges . . . wants to borrow bail money . . ." Her sad clowning was a way of forgiving him for his having annexed so easily her money-market fund. Every few weeks she had been reminding him that he should place his own ad in the paper for his housepainting services. As if it were that easy! As if you could simply place an ad! Carrying a pair of Kim's shoes, she returned in time to snatch the sandwich from him just as he was about to bite into it absentmindedly. "I'll call," she said.

So Laura called the restaurant to make the reservation, and they put on some nice clothes and drove over in Wayne's truck, parking it in the sun at the far edge of the parking lot. Inside, the light was so expensively murky that they had to stand still for a minute to overcome their blindness and Wayne nearly bumped into a big antique gadget, like a copper coffee grinder on wheels. The darkness seething in carpet patterns in his eyes gradually faded to reveal soft zones of light on scarlet wallpaper with embossed fuzz raised on a satin background. Wayne, although it was surely uncouth, furtively ran his fingers over its rich braille. Everything was opulent like that. The girl who approached them to ask if they had a reservation wore a low-cut dress whose skirt was so large with petticoats that she had a hard time squeezing among the tables, and the menus she handed them were as big as tombstones, printed on rigid wood-grain plastic.

Randy was already there, sitting behind his menu, looking rather surprisingly relaxed in this expensive place. It was a new haircut, Wayne decided. And a costly-looking leather jacket. After they were seated Randy said, "I'm glad you came right away."

"Would you like anything to drink?" said the hostess.

"Go for it," said Randy gloomily. He already had a drink.

With a glance, Wayne checked with Laura and said, "Sure, I'll have a Michelob."

"Ma'am?" said the hostess.

"No, nothing for me. Do you have Tab?"

"We have Diet Coke."

"That will be fine." Laura had this nice way of settling herself in a chair and smoothing the fabric over her thighs, with the same gentle authority in her hands as when they folded linen. Wayne felt an irrelevant inhalation of pride, of guardianship. He looked around the room, still tingling with outdoor sunshine, still adjusting to the atmosphere like a fallen-asleep limb shimmering with sensation.

After the hostess had gone, Randy leaned around the obstacle of his menu and said, "Okay, this is weird. This is incredibly weird. I hope you guys are ready for some weird, weird stuff."

"What," said Wayne.

"I'm such an asshole."

"Is that your amazing secret?" said Laura.

"No, wait. I'm really an asshole. You remember that twenty-dollar bill we kept sending back to the Secret Service laboratories? That really was counterfeit."

"No," said Wayne simply. He knew it was the wrong thing to feel, but he was joyful as if this were a prank.

"Yes," said Randy.

"Well, Jesus Christ, Randy."

Laura said, "We could have been . . ." She left the sentence blank as possibilities flooded in.

"You asshole," said Wayne thoughtfully, trying to be gradually saturated by the idea that Randy Potts was a criminal, but finding the notion just beaded up and rolled off.

"Yeah, but look. It's not as bad as you think. You know that crate in your garage?"

Laura said, "Oh, no. Randy!"

"You're joking," said Wayne.

Randy said, "Yeah. All this time."

"All this time? It's been sitting there?"

"How much?" said Laura.

"In that crate, just under two million." Randy raised his menu, looking shifty.

Laura stated the query, "There are other crates."

Peering around his menu, Randy said, "But hey . . ." He hoisted the menu out of his lap and set it on the floor, leaning it against the arm of his chair. "But hey, that's the bad news. The rest is good news."

Laura said, "How in the world did you get into this?"

"Okay. I'm not going to tell you anything about it. In fact, I'm not even telling you this. I'm not even here now. Because I'm already going to jail for sure, but you guys are about to be rich. That's the one crate nobody knows about. I just put it in your garage because it was the last one, and I was sick and tired of driving to safe-deposit vaults all over the place. Nobody knows about that money. And it's perfect. It's perfect. The paper is perfect, the ink is perfect, the printing is perfect. It's money. Remember, Wayne? Remember we sent it in to the police? Twice? And they tested it chemically and everything. And both times they said it was genuine."

Their drinks arrived: all three leaned away from the table. Then when the hostess had gone, they drew close again. But not Laura, Wayne noticed. His heart felt like a stone suddenly as he began to realize what danger Randy had carelessly put them in.

Randy said, "You guys are still innocent. And we're not having this conversation, so you're going to stay innocent. You don't know what's in that crate."

"How much money is there altogether?" said Wayne.

"I'm not saying. You guys don't know *anything.*"

"But Randy," said Laura, "how was it printed? It's hard to believe."

"No, I'm not telling you anything. I'm just saying you have to take that crate—whatever is inside, you don't know—and bury it someplace for a few years. You guys have to stay innocent."

A waitress appeared in a costume like an Old West prostitute with red satin cat's ears on her head. "Hello, ladies and gentlemen," she said with a smile. "Welcome to the Terra Linda Satin Kitten. My name is Mindy. I'll be your server today. I am at your beck and call, to ensure that your meal at the Terra Linda Satin Kitten is a memorable one. Today we are featuring the following chef's specials—tenderloin of beef en brochette, which consists of nuggets of succulent USDA Choice beef marinated in a tangy sauce . . ." She went on, but Wayne wasn't listening. Through the new clang of silence in his ears, he heard himself ordering a chicken dish, which swam up to his eyes easily from the illegibly calligraphic menu—and making irritating decisions between mashed and home fries, between soup and salad, between French and Thousand Island; and he sat back and folded his arms amidst this air-conditioned candlelit scene, with his skin crawling like a plaid TV character superimposed edgily on a background. A sick germ had begun to grow in his stomach. That crate in his garage was a black hole, through which all the value in the universe flooded away. Everything in his life had suddenly become merely imaginary, merely clouds of atoms. When she had gone, Randy leaned forward over the table again.

"Because my ass is grass," he said. "There were two guys from the Treasury Department at my house today. I bought a house."

"You bought a house?" said Laura.

"Yeah. In Ross."

"You bought a house in Ross?"

"I bought a Ferrari too."

"Wow, Randy," said Wayne. "That was dumb."

Laura said, "We didn't see it in the lot outside."

"Yeah, I left it at where the Beef 'n' Brew used to be, and I took a cab to the Holiday Inn, and then I walked across the freeway. I'm not here now, see."

"You had police at your house this morning?" said Wayne.

"Yeah, but see, the way they got on to me, I think, was through bank records. I'm such a jerk, I just started depositing all this cash in banks. But listen, there's absolutely no record of that one crate. They wouldn't have caught me just by looking at the bills. The bills are perfect. They didn't believe they were counterfeit."

"Yeah, but Randy!" said Wayne. "Somebody helped you print this. I mean, what is this? I mean, somebody will come looking for that crate."

"No, take my word for it. That's the one crate nobody knows about, not even the people who may or may not have been involved with me. And the people who may or may not have been involved with me are now totally out of the picture. Take my word for it. I wouldn't propose all this to you if I thought you weren't completely safe."

Wayne began to try to picture it: driving up into the Sierras with a lot of camping gear, and the money sealed in waterproof canisters, say. And burying the canisters in obscure canyons in national forests. And making out genuine treasure maps, with dotted lines and $X$s. And maybe marking the burial spots in some tricky way. And hiding the treasure maps at home in his socks-and-underwear drawer. Which, however, was the same drawer his envelope of World Series Candlestick Park dirt had been hidden in when Laura found it and threw it out— for which, still, he'd never quite forgiven her. That's the first place the police would look.

Randy was saying he himself would almost certainly go to jail—and that maybe after a twenty-year prison sentence there might still be a little money in the crate, but that he didn't require Wayne and Laura to save it for him. It was a gift, no strings attached.

"Have you hired a lawyer?" said Wayne.

The waitress interrupted them with salads, carrying a huge, batonlike pepper grinder under her arm, and they all had to wait while she went through the irksome ritual of grinding pepper over each of the three salads. When she had gone, Wayne said, "I'm not hungry." It was true, he felt suddenly nauseated by the swoop of life.

Laura said, "Have you hired a lawyer?"

Randy stuffed a big forkful of lettuce into his mouth and said unhappily through the crunch of roughage, "Lawyers cost money." He patted his mouth with his napkin, like a rich man. Like a man with a Ferrari and a house in Ross. A man who can afford to give his daughter dangerous little motor scooters. The money explained his new handsomeness. "Because, see,

I think they'll impound all my cash. They know where it all is, because they've been investigating me. The only cash they don't know about is the one crate in your garage. And, obviously . . ." He shrugged.

"Obviously what?" said Wayne.

"Obviously everything I have will be confiscated. Except for that one crate."

"Randy," said Laura, "what about the serial numbers? Don't they . . ."

"All different," said Randy. "No two serial numbers alike. I'm telling you, this is perfect."

"It's unbelievable," said Laura. "Are you sure . . ."

Her voice trailed off, and Randy said, "Wayne, you saw it. You saw how good it is."

Laura said, "Maybe these people have given you real money and told you it's counterfeit. If it's so perfect."

Randy looked back and forth between the two of them. "You guys! God damn it!"

She changed posture, sighed, and said, "Randy, we have to think about this."

Protest rose from Wayne's heart. "Honey!" It was almost a whine.

Randy said, "Laura, wait till you get a look at the money. Just go home and look at it. It's perfect. These scientists at the Secret Service put it through all kinds of tests. Like they scrape off some ink and analyze the chemicals; and they test the paper and everything, to see if it has exactly the same fucking molecules as the real paper. And we sent a bill in twice, and both times they said it was genuine."

"I'm just saying we have to consider this very carefully," said Laura. She wasn't eating her salad either. "And there's no special hurry, because, as you say, nobody but us knows about that crate. Like for one, I'd like to go home and at least look at the money."

But Wayne could tell that her skepticism was deeper than that. If they considered this with much care they would obviously never do it. "Honey," he said, "this is the chance of a lifetime. It's like they say in Marketrend, about how you have to do something in your life that will jump you over to the right side of the money river . . ."

"Wayne, I'm only saying we should think about this. Do you realize the risks?"

His voice sharpened as anger began to clarify things. "Look, Laura, do you think I like sitting there all day talking on the phone? Trying to get little old ladies to invest their life savings in these stupid coins?" Or painting houses for less than union wage, without benefits? Or worrying about this second baby, the likelihood of its deformity? Or fearing a phone call from his little brother saying that it was time for a kidney transplant operation, which would lay him up weeks in the hospital and finally leave him even worse equipped for the competition of life? While the money river went on flowing in the wrong direction, wearing him down? While it built other people up?

Laura's mouth hardened. "Wayne, you're such a baby, I'm tired of being the responsible one," she hissed, heedless of Randy's embarrassment. "I'm tired of all this self-esteem nonsense. As if you always had to be propped up by me."

"But Laura!" he said, scared by the unexpected high yelp in his voice. "Two million dollars—"

"All these self-esteem exercises are just self-pity exercises. We don't need the money."

"We don't? We don't need it?"

"Oh, Wayne." She looked down at her plate, and her lip began to tremble. She got up and left.

Randy had leaned back from the table, keeping his eyes on his salad.

She crossed the room—heading toward the bathroom, Wayne supposed. Suddenly moist-eyed for some reason—or, perhaps obviously, for Laura's having married the wrong man—he waved dispellingly at Randy and stood up. Outside in the parking lot, his tears stung his eyes, and he swept them aside with his white cloth napkin, which he was still carrying. Laura was there, across the parking lot getting into the cab of the truck, the wind whipping her skirt around and stuffing it between her legs to paste the fabric to her pregnancy. Strands of her fine brown hair blew across her mouth. Her getting into the truck meant she would forgive him. He left his napkin on the hedge, a misplaced bandage, and crossed the pavement to get in beside her and drive home in silence.

# 17

On a rainy Wednesday morning Randy was at his house in Ross waiting for the Secret Service investigator and the Treasury Department lawyer to arrive for an appointed meeting, at which he would learn where he stood; or at which he supposed he might even be handcuffed and taken permanently away— he had no idea; yet for some reason he was full of abiding joy. He had spent the past few days in cheery numb psychosis as if nothing were amiss, accomplishing his ordinary householder's errands, furnishing this mansion like a burglar. In furniture stores, landscape contractors' offices, fixture shops, art galleries, he stood on the floor smiling, signing orders to have merchandise delivered, spending cash as fast as possible with a feeling of outflowing blood keeping a wound clean. He just kept moving, keeping a breeze in his face, keeping the psychedelic sunshine of ordinary California neighborhoods in his eyes, parking his Ferrari heedlessly in No Parking zones, bossing sales clerks around on showroom floors with happy anger, saved minute-to-minute by impatience. He was getting to know passages of the yellow pages he had never given a thought to.

And when he was at home encamped like a trespasser in this imaginary idea of a home, he kept the Mister Coffee machine and the stereo going all the time, as he moved without respite from one distracting task to another, a stage hand moving props—knocking out the pantry wall, shelving expensive books in the library, stripping and staining woodwork on the bannister, refinishing the hardwood floors of the third-story guest rooms with a rented rotary sander, hanging paintings until he was dizzy. Today, with the panicky joy mounting in him against the hour of Ludex's arrival, he was staggering through the job of shelving books in the various bedroom bookshelves. A shipment had arrived the day before, deposited in the garage, and he was hauling the boxes into the house in a light, atomized rain, slamming volumes into the shelves by the handful. Every time he stopped to catch his breath, he was yanked back into action by the rapid coagulation of the thought that he had so little time left. The day before yesterday he had signed an order for a custom-built hot tub, whose rim he'd imagined himself bracing girls' hips against. More and more, Mary's astonished, remorseful ghost followed him through the rooms as he worked, sharpening to presence as new arguments occurred to him of the stupidity of feminism, the selfishness of woman's desire to look like the girl on magazine covers: sexy as a porn star, but with an executive briefcase; no longer needing a man, actually now independent of any man, aglow aerobically with success. He was driven today, kept from rest, by a feeling that the house wasn't sexy enough yet, at this last minute before the police came to end his short career.

His lawyer, Dan, newly hired, was supposed to get here before Ludex and Hodges. Randy had found an agency called The People's Attorney in Berkeley that permitted a half hour of free telephone consultation, and which offered sliding-scale rates for low-income clients; it seemed a prudent choice of attorney, on the assumption that all his assets would soon be taken away. And he had spoken with a smart-sounding young lawyer named Dan McBride, whom he had liked for his candor. Dan had said, "This isn't exactly my specialty, and we may have to bring in consulting lawyers. But I'd almost work pro bono on a case like this." *Pro bono* meant "for free."

But Dan McBride, when Randy went to meet him in Berkeley, turned out to be totally blind—a twenty-seven-year-old kid who had somehow actually gone through Harvard Law School without any vision, in these times when disabled people were supposed to get an even break. His two eyes, wide and pure with the clarity of never having seen anything, seemed to be focused on that abstract point in the distance where parallel lines theoretically meet. Randy's first, uncharitable impulse was to go back out front and ask for another lawyer— especially when Dan knocked his telephone off his desk in their first interview—but he finally decided that on the whole having a blind lawyer would be okay, that maybe it might even draw sympathy from the jury. Besides, you can't get through Harvard Law School without learning something. And Dan turned out to be smart. And funny. He said, "Don't worry, Randy, I'm not a groper. I don't need to feel your face or anything."

And it was surprising: he didn't sit still in the paranoid solemnity one expects; he moved freely and restlessly around the office without bumping into anything, using broad gestures; and he spoke so loudly, from within his enveloping darkness, making thrashing gestures with his hands and forays into open floor space, as if to try to dominate these rooms that sighted people had such an unfair advantage in. The skin of his forehead and chin was fraught with dents and pewter scars; Randy pictured him bumping into cupboard doors and low-hanging branches ever since he was a child. But, as Randy learned when they went out for coffee at their second meeting, the scars were from the track field: he had actually sprinted competitively in college, and still ran five miles a day on an enclosed circular track, where sometimes he smashed into a pillar or a fellow club member. It was interesting, seeing how he'd adapted, keeping clutter to a minimum, touching familiar points; when Randy first entered, he turned on a tape recorder; and occasionally he made notes to himself on a little twelve-key braillewriter on his desk. He listened to Randy's entire story with intensity, asking acute, angled questions that cut an unexpected slice across the story and made Randy feel surprisingly exposed in guiltlessness. And finally he said, "Well, the smartest thing you did was send in those bills for analysis, through your friend Wayne. It wouldn't be too optimistic to hope we can get you off light."

"Hey, I don't want to get Wayne Paschke in trouble." The one fact Randy had withheld from him was the existence of that tenth crate in the Paschkes' garage. He still intended for that crate to vanish into Wayne's possession, no matter what else happened.

"Don't worry, I don't intend to frame him. Just don't say anything about this to anybody unless I'm present. Not even to Wayne. Not anything." Randy liked him. After he had been with him for thirty minutes, watching in suspense as he moved around his office without bumping into things, he stopped worrying and began to feel peculiarly *more* relaxed than with a sighted person, to feel comfortably invisible, and he sensed his own sight starting to atrophy empathically.

He went outside into the light rain to get another box of books from the garage. The more he furnished his house, the more certain was his case: the weight of his furniture would make him immovable. As he walked back toward the garage, Kevin Van Sichlyn's truck pulled in at the driveway next door. When Kevin got out, Randy called a greeting through the interceding shrubbery, and was simultaneously struck by a premature nostalgia for the pleasures of neighborliness. He would miss Kevin—with his chinless face and his juvenile tennis shoes and his slept-on hair.

"Wankers," said Kevin, slamming the truck door. "They had a little private séance last night and came up with the ultimate excuse: They say they *don't have* the money now."

"I thought they already budgeted for it."

"They're lying of course. Their story is that that 'fund' has been 'diverted.' To creekbed management, of all things! A creek is a creek. It's *already* a creek. How do you 'manage' a creekbed?"

"Don't you have a contract?"

"No, Randy, don't be stupid. The *proposal* was what we were dickering about today. Hang on, I'll come round." He walked down toward the street to get around the bushes that separated the two driveways.

"Come on in out of the rain," Randy called, getting one more box. Then it came to him in a flash of obviousness, inevitably, that *he* would provide the cash for the City of Fairfax to purchase Kevin's installation; there would probably still be time. He could donate it anonymously. Because it was partly a suggestion of his own that Kevin had finally acted on: he had decided to call it "the Fairfax parking lot"; and at Randy's suggestion—preferring especially that the idea was not his own but a bystander's—he had proposed to drive sixty pine stakes into the ground around the perimeter of the parking lot and to string it off with rough twine, leaving the parking lot otherwise unchanged. The Fairfax Improvement Committee was angry and had refused to pay for the installation, saying that first of all it would make the parking lot useless for traffic; and secondly they didn't care about his international reputation, it just wasn't art.

He came up the driveway scowling. "Want me to take a load?"

Randy handed over his box and went back for another.

"Drink?" said Kevin.

"No, I'm expecting some people."

"Wankers. Can you imagine?"

"How much money are you talking about?"

"Eighteen. But they fronted two for development, and they say they want *that* back. They say it's just a roped-off parking lot. It got a big laugh when they said they'd be willing to pay my hardware-store bill for fifteen dollars. And then the Mother Superior said she could get the police to charge me with vagrancy and littering."

They got the boxes into the kitchen and set them on the counter. Kevin poured himself some coffee without asking, an intimate presumption that sealed their friendship on the spot. Prematurely nostalgic about everything, Randy was watching himself from a hovering point outside himself, as he handed Kevin a dish towel to dry off his rain-damp hair.

"Well, it *is* just a roped-off parking lot, isn't it?" he said avidly, brainlessly, waxing perilously jolly in these last minutes. "Didn't you say you'd let them start parking on it?"

"Yes, but not until the money changes hands. I know that sounds mercenary, but I'm talking about principles. That's the big lesson I learned when I was with the Velvet Underground."

"You were with the Velvet Underground? You never told me that. Did you know Lou Reed? And that Nico girl?"

"I was just a kid, I was a groupie on the periphery. I was probably thirteen at the time, and I was instructed to go to supermarkets and buy cases and cases of Campbell's tomato soup. And then I'd bring them back to the Factory and Andy would put his signature on the label and sell them. Six dollars apiece. And so I've always said to myself, *That* was the moment of transubstantiation, when it turned from soup to art, because then it has *value*."

"Well, fuck 'em." Randy banged his fist on the table. "That's what I say, fuck 'em." In another hour he might be in jail, a merry thought. He wished he could tell Kevin the whole story of the counterfeiting, as if it were a story from somebody else's life. The burnt-earth smell of coffee, so much more intimate on a rainy day, gave him an intense feeling of being indoors, made him harden his shoulders in a shiver of coziness; it was something he would remember in the series of drafty courtrooms that, strung together, would be the corridor of his future, lit by long fluorescent tubes in ice-tray grilles. If the meeting with Ludex turned out to be inconclusive, he would run over to Fairfax to find out how he could become an anonymous patron of the arts. And then he would churn himself into even more frantic thrashing in the effort to scatter as much money as possible before it was all taken away.

"Cheer up, Kevin," he said. "Tell you what you do. Just

call all the reporters in the world. Wouldn't this make a good magazine story?"

Kevin looked at Randy with his mouth slightly ajar, and Randy realized he'd had a good idea. He couldn't do anything wrong anymore. In his moment of perishing, he turned to gold anything he touched. "Didn't you have a friend who writes for—"

"The Wall Street Journal, yes."

"Well, there you are. Plus any other newspapers or magazines you can think of."

"My goodness, Randy. New York would love this. It's provincial! I don't know which of my elves is here today, but whoever it is she'll be immediately on the phone."

The front doorbell rang—that would be Dan McBride. Now the legal machinery would begin to grind.

Kevin said, "Maybe I really should get myself arrested for littering."

"Take the coffee with you. Take the cup."

"No, that's okay. Randy, listen. If I get myself arrested, will you bail me out?"

"No. Keep the cup, will you?" Randy picked up the coffee cup and thrust it into Kevin's hands.

"Ah, Randy, I'm a litterbug now."

"Go. Fuck off."

"How can I ever repay you?" Kevin went outside with his coffee, and Randy turned inward to answer the front door. He ran his fingers through his hair. He had chosen his clothes this morning with a view to the possibility of going to jail, where they take away your shoes.

Dan was standing there on the doorstep in a three-piece suit, supernaturally undampened by the rain, folding up a white metal cane that collapsed ingeniously into a pocket-sized cylinder. He slipped it into his inner coat pocket, saying, "Randy!" with his hand extended.

"Yeah, it's me." He took Dan's elbow to guide him into the house.

Dan pulled his elbow free and grasped Randy's arm. "Relax," he said. "There's nothing to worry about. Have a drink. This will be an uneventful meeting."

"What do you think will happen?" It occurred to him only now that maybe he should have unplugged all the appliances in the house.

"I'm serious, Randy. Have a drink. I'll have one too. Scotch."

"Sure." He decided he could fill Dan's glass only halfway to make it harder to spill. He watched him apprehensively as he moved across the floor toward a chair and grasped its back as if he had expected it to be exactly there.

"Nice place," he said. "On the rocks, with a splash of water. And I insist you have a little drink too, Randy. It's early in the day, but I'm not going to have you sitting here nervous."

"Hold on." Randy almost ran into the kitchen.

"Change the music, will you?" Dan called. "Something quieter."

When Randy came back with the drinks, Dan was sitting there in the chair with his briefcase open—full of nothing but cassettes marked with braille tape—and he was rummaging through them pinching each cassette to find the correct one, his head cocked quizzically as if he were *listening* to the silent code of braille through his fingertips.

"All new furniture?" said Dan.

"Yeah, I know, it looks suspicious."

"No, we can have all that ruled irrelevant. The house and everything."

"How did you get here from Berkeley?"

"Judy. But she can wait in the car. She's fine, she has a book. And I don't think this will take long." He accepted the clinking glass of Scotch, dipping a testing finger inside the rim, and he felt for a table at his side to set it on. Randy smelled his own Scotch—sour, disgusting—and set it aside to forget about it.

"Now, Randy," said Dan, "you're going to have to say very little during this interview. I need to assess the kind of case the Treasury Department is going to build against you. I'm told this person Bob Ludex is very good. So we both have to do a lot of listening. Especially you. Don't say anything unless I say it's all right. Is that clear?" He pressed a button on his wristwatch to make the crystal flip up, and he set his finger on the dial.

"What if they arrest me now? What should I do?"

"Nothing. Just be arrested. We'll post bail. I hope that doesn't happen, because I have a million things to do today."

They fell silent. Randy started to rub his palms together nervously, but stopped, realizing the friction was audible to Dan.

"Just relax, Randy. You don't have to do anything but listen. Drink that Scotch. It's your job to relax in this."

"Oh, the music." He got to his feet and turned down the rock-and-roll station, and found instead KJAZ, where they were playing the usual apathetic jazz as if this were any ordinary day—which, for most people in their gray rainy broadcasting radius, it probably was. He sat down again and rubbed his upper arms. "So! Tell me! Why don't you have one of those seeing-eye dogs?"

Dan didn't answer. He was loading a cassette into his tape recorder.

"Oh, I do," he finally said. "His name is Specks. But you know, that's a big myth. Just a minute."

He turned on the tape recorder, to hear a voice, like a young college student's tonsilly voice, chanting legal statutes with maximum ennui. He turned off the machine and sat back. "But that's really a myth. Specks is a wonderful dog, but he'll literally drag me into the middle of traffic if I let him. I'm not the kind of cruel disciplinarian you have to be with those dogs. I kept him finally just because I got to love him. And he's a great way to meet girls. People really think they're magic dogs. I take him to a bar, and he bounces around wagging his tail and charming all the girls in the place."

Randy's spine was cold, and he kept hunching his shoulders. "I thought they were totally trained and everything."

"No, when you first get them they're fine. But you have to *keep* them in training, which I never did. Specks is very emotional. Now he actually chases pigeons."

The sound of Ludex's horrible heavy black cop-shoes was audible on the boards of the front porch, and Randy sprang out of his chair.

The doorbell rang.

"Relax, Randy," said Dan. "Your only job is to say nothing."

He was more frightened than he had expected to be: something infantile within him desired that this scene should stop now, that all these summoned people should just go away, so that he could return to the reality of carrying boxes of wisdom-heavy books. Dan's presiding blindness struck him as newly sinister. I never meant any harm, was what he wanted to tell them all—as if Dan and the cops were all conspiring together against him.

"Answer the door," said Dan. "If I answer it, they'll get the heebie-jeebies."

Was that a joke? Randy couldn't believe it: here he was with a blind lawyer. He could have just gone back to the front desk at the People's Attorney and requested a real lawyer. But he was moving across the hall to open the door under the spell of the inevitable. Ludex was there, and so was Hodges. But this time there were no uniformed policemen, no creeping police cars. Which he took as a good sign.

"Good morning, Mr. Potts," said Ludex, who looked exactly like a detective on one of those old television cop shows. Round-faced, slot-mouthed, with black felt eyebrows. Hodges was fairer, less consequential.

Dan had followed Randy to the door; his radar was perfect. He extended a hand. "Mr. Ludex? I'm Dan McBride, Mr. Potts's attorney."

"This is Mr. Hodges, from the Treasury Department."

"Glad to meet you, Mr. McBride."

"Yes, Treasury Department," said Dan. "Interesting work."

They were all going into the living room to sit down while Randy drifted among them mute as a child among grown-ups, feeling already guilty.

"And you?" said Hodges.

"The People's Attorney, in Berkeley. It's fun."

"Hastings?" said Hodges.

"No, Harvard."

"Ah."

"And a bit of time as Assistant U.S. Attorney in Chicago."

"Ah," said Hodges again.

The three men sat down, and then Randy last of all. He was trying to be passive, Exhibit A. He crossed his legs confidently and guiltlessly.

"You see, I'm blind," Dan said, tapping his temple, simultaneously reaching with perfect accuracy for his glass of

Scotch. "I hope that doesn't make anybody ill at ease. Please don't make silly faces, or pull down your pants. I'll hear the snickering."

Hodges and Ludex didn't laugh, though Randy looked around feeling a filmy smile slip across his face. He supposed he should follow Dan's example, and lifted his glass to take a small sip of sour liquor. Nobody was offering the two cops anything to drink.

Dan pressed a tab on his cassette recorder and leaned back. "So, what are we looking at here?"

Hodges placed a plastic envelope in Ludex's outstretched hand. Since Ludex didn't say anything, Hodges ventured: "A counterfeit."

"Yes?" said Dan.

Hodges said, "Mr. Potts deposited a total of about eighteen million dollars' worth of this currency in twenty-eight different bank accounts and security-deposit vaults, under assumed identities."

"Allegedly," said Dan.

Ludex finally spoke. "Mr. Potts," he said, putting Randy onstage, "we were hoping you'd have another specimen here. To compare."

Dan halted the transaction with an upraised finger: "Sorry."

"May we ask Mr. Potts a question?"

Dan shrugged.

"You stated you did not print this money. Do you have any idea how it was printed?"

Randy glanced at Dan, who said, "Just answer honestly, yes or no." His X-ray eyes were fixed on far planets.

"No," said Randy.

Ludex said, "May we assume someone gave it to you?"

Dan answered for him, "You may assume what you like."

Ludex's mouth had hardened. "Okay, then. Supposing someone *gave* you this currency—"

"Excuse me," said Dan. "Is Mr. Potts under investigation?"

Hodges answered for Ludex, "Yes, Mr. Potts is under investigation."

Dan said, "Is Mr. Potts accused of a crime?"

"Not at this point," said Hodges. Something had happened. Like a shift in the wind.

"May I see the specimens?" said Dan, holding out his hand. "What evidence do you have?" He accepted a twenty-dollar bill.

"Well, for one thing," said Hodges, "we have all these bank accounts under assumed names. And for another, the Federal Reserve auditors have no explanation for the sudden appearance of eighteen million dollars. It's a bubble."

"The Fed keeps records?" said Dan.

"They measure the velocity of currency in the economy. And these bills have come from nowhere."

"What about the serial numbers?"

"We're working on that. There are two high-speed currency verification machines in the Market Street Fed."

"What about laboratory tests?"

"Not finished yet. The bills are in Washington now." Hodges glanced at Ludex, who, silent, had leaned back behind the steeple of his joined fingertips.

"What sort of tests will be used?" Dan said. He was massaging one bill beneath his thumb.

"Enlarged acetate overlay. Spectral pattern recognition. They're very thorough. Things like the pH of the paper."

Dan handed the bill back to Hodges, but addressed Ludex. "This meeting is over," he said. "You shouldn't have come to us until you had test results."

Ludex made an impatient motion in his chair, tossing himself against one arm, but did not seem ready to leave.

Dan stood up and started to stroll aimlessly out into the open space of the room. He said, "I'm asking you now, on Mr. Potts's behalf, to leave his house. Everything you've said today has been recorded and may be produced in a court of law."

"Wait a minute," said Ludex. He leaned forward over his knees. "Mr. Potts—Randy—I'm asking you now to surrender to us any currency which was unlawfully gotten by you."

"No, Randy," said Dan. He had arrived at a window which he seemed to be looking out of. "You don't have to do anything. Now, I'm sorry, but I have to ask you gentlemen to leave. We'll be happy to have another interview any time. Here's my card."

As Dan crossed the room confidently to open the door, the two men began to pluck themselves together, sighing, and Hodges scooped the money off the coffee table. Randy just sat there in his chair confused, tied down by the cobweblike network of contradictory surmises—and now stung, paralyzed, by the realization that nothing, nothing at all, would happen. He almost felt disappointed.

Ludex stopped at the door and turned back. "Randy, you and your confederates are the subject of a federal investigation. Everybody you've ever known will be under investigation. Do you understand?"

Ignoring him, Dan said cordially, "Nice to meet you, Mr. Hodges. May I know your first name?"

"Frank," said Hodges.

"I'm Dan, Frank." Dan offered his hand. "I hope to see more of you. In fact, I'm sure we'll be seeing each other. This is a fascinating case."

Hodges smiled uncertainly and turned to follow Ludex outside. Dan closed the front door after them.

He walked back into the living room, and Randy levered himself out of his moist print in his chair, trying to feel tentatively that this new reprieve fit perfectly with his abiding fundamental sensation of guiltlessness.

"So Dan," he said. "What am I guilty of?"

"First of all, look. When your friend Wayne sent in the one bill, who did he get the letter *back* from? Whose office checked out the bill? Do you think it might have been Bob Ludex? I mean, do you remember?"

"No, why? Or actually, it might have been. At least it was a San Francisco office. Why?"

Dan picked up his Scotch. "Do you really have no idea how that money was manufactured? This 'Bim Auctor' just *gave* it to you?"

"Yes, Dan, I *told* you."

"I think we have to find this Bim Auctor person."

# 18

"Good morning, is this Mrs. Tielis?" said Wayne in lively pitches, with the fakey kink in his throat that made of his voice a suave saxophone. "This is Wayne Paschke—"

"I'm not interested," said Mrs. Tielis, and she hung up.

He set the receiver back in the cradle watching his well-dressed reflection in the mirror he had set up on the workbench in these last crucial days, as an additional charm for sales—on the premise that a man's voice will sound more persuasive when he's wearing a tie and sitting up straight and can actually see himself making an impression. Like everything about Marketrend, it was a stupid idea but it worked. He looked good in the superimposed coat and tie, though with something strangled about his complexion, or something like a fever that pulled his eyes away. After every call, he looked again under the workbench at the crate of impossible money which cast new shadows and lights everywhere and reversed the meanings of everything. Beside it, four new cardboard cartons were stacked, the purchase of Laura's inheritance—each carton stamped with the Marketrend logo (a doubloon that shone with unattainability, as indicated by radiating wavy lines)—which contained the thousands of dollars' worth of coins Buddy had dropped off on Wednesday along with a celebratory six-pack. Beside the cartons were five Starter Kits in vinyl briefcases, and a box of the new color-illustrated booklets *Numismatic Investment for You*, and a lot of forms and brochures and coin displays and balance sheets and income reports and miscellaneous stuff whose specific use was obscure but which he hoped vaguely he would never have to learn about. The suppressed thought of how stupid Marketrend was had become a permanent high chest-ache.

And yet he had no choice but to go on. It was Friday already. There were only two days left in the month and he still needed that last seven hundred dollars in RBV to achieve Head Broker. He had been a star at the Regional Opportunity Jamboree at the Oakland Marriott, where he was announced from the podium as the newest member of the Medallion Club, and he'd had to acknowledge everybody's applause by standing up from his folding chair among the hundreds and bobbing his head, so nervous he knocked a weightless stamped-foil ashtray off the table when he rose; and at the local Opportunity Meeting last night Buddy had mentioned that, after Wayne had made the ten-thousand-dollar mark, he would give him some leads for Lieutenant Brokers to hire in beneath him. He had quoted Fortinbras Armstrong: "That old reassuring confidence that you will remain miserable has begun to desert you, and the worrisome prospect of happiness is looming." If he didn't make the grade in two days, the month's RBV tally would be erased and he'd be back at zero; all of Laura's money would have been spent for naught. But dipping into Randy's crate for the necessary seven hundred was unthinkable. It repulsed touch.

When, on that first night, he and Laura opened it and saw the money, they felt irradiated by it and—after Laura reached out to stroke the paper once—they closed the lid and pushed it back under the workbench with blanched vision. Since then they had pulled it out again only one time to replace the pink circular stick-on seal on the lid which they had broken, but which fortunately could be exactly duplicated by price stickers available in the Northgate PayLess stationery aisle. After they had applied an identical new seal and wiped their fingerprints off it, the crate had just gone on sitting there under his workbench. He hadn't even brought his knee closer to it than twelve or fourteen inches since they first unscrewed the lid to reveal the vision of rows of identical green rectangles. It was like one of those surrealist paintings where a boulder or a tuba appears blandly in the bedroom, preposterously. He started setting the table without being asked. Laura fell into reveries which made him somehow jealous. Every passing car seemed louder. Whenever Kim came unsuspecting home from school, Wayne felt she was in some way physically imperiled by its presence in the house, whose walls were now diagrammatically transparent. The crate would end his new habit of visiting Rumplestiltskins. After Opportunity Meetings, rather than going straight home, he had been stopping in to encounter, sitting at the bar, that young blonde, Tina, to whom he never quite mentioned his being married, describing himself as an investment broker, letting his eyes drop frankly over the parts of her body, which shifted in response with equal frankness. She talked and talked idiotically, never letting him say a word, which he was grateful for, mortified by the secret clutch of his groin. His darkness-congested vision magnified the parts of her body it traveled over.

But now the crate would scare him back onto his usual paths. On that Saturday evening when he and Laura examined the cash, they replaced the lid and went in to sit in silence and darkness at the kitchen table, their very marriage still sprained. It was his role to say something decisive; but, sickened by the sudden swerve of possibility, he could only sit there in the dark hoping for the telepathy of her guidance. Finally he said, "I'm still Randy's friend."

"It is awfully realistic," she said softly.

A passing car made the front window blaze. They had waited until nightfall to open the crate; Kim had been home all day.

"At first, we shouldn't do anything," Wayne said. "Just go on as usual."

"It was submitted twice?" she said. As she stood up and walked around the table to the refrigerator, she dragged her fingertips across his shoulders.

"We have two possibilities," he said. "Give it to Randy or give it to the police. Or destroy it, that's three."

The declaration, he felt, hadn't bounced but had melted in. She stood in the milky light of the refrigerator door, her head bowed.

"Or, for the time being, pretend we don't know what's in it. As Randy says. We can't do anything unusual now."

"Kim," said Laura.

"Yeah," said Wayne.

"It's amazing how good it is. You know, you're innocent because you sent in a sample. You're fine."

"Hm."

But then she left the kitchen. He sat in the dark deserted,

for a moment closer than she to the crate on the floor plan of the house. He watched the door through which she had exited; it was filled with the angelic yellow illumination of the bedroom lamp.

She returned and stood in the light with an envelope, from which she drew the checkbook, never once used, for her money-market fund. She set it before Wayne on the table with his can of beer.

"Oh yeah," he said. "I'll see Buddy at the meeting tomorrow night."

She turned on the overhead lights, to reveal that all the ordinary objects in their kitchen still looked like themselves, hard in the light.

"Just think. We could have bought Ferraris."

"And mink coats and yachts."

But Wayne was weak. He sat there now at his workbench, so tired of repeating this reedy-sounding sales pitch on the phone that he had begun to think of how much he was missing by standing so still in this shifting world. The perfect crime is solitary, he had once heard. It was true: he could keep Randy's money easily if there were no Laura or Kim. They provided the triangularity to necessarily fix his position. Of a solitary crime, the only observer is God, who had only mattered when there was space enough in the world, and boredom enough, to accommodate Him. Yesterday, having spread his tarp to do his visualization exercises, Wayne had laid himself down and imagined himself standing in Rumplestiltskins laying a hand on Tina's hip with a confidence that he had lacked at the age when he was still free to do such things. He had stood up and put away the tarp and got out of the garage to do some work, to wash his truck so thoroughly that he even hooked up the vacuum cleaner and cleaned under the seats. Then he cut the grass, and, still breathless from the exertion, telephoned Laura at work to ask if there was anything he should pick up at the supermarket. She said, baffled, "No—no—nothing I can think of. But I'll call you if I think of anything." Anything! This large coefficient of two million dollars had thrown all equations out of balance. And the fact that it was so perfect, that it was an impossibly good counterfeit, made it a kind of imponderable zero containing infinity. He kept veering between belief and complete disbelief. The crate was making them all look away from each other, raise their eyes to the horizons. Laura had ceased her customary wishful pencil cipherings in the margins of the "Floor Plan of the Week" column—which she used to love doing, sleepily tallying what the monthly payments would be if they were rich, simply as a kind of arithmetical dreaming on Sunday mornings with the complacency of a crossword-puzzler comfortably assured of futility. But last Sunday Wayne had seen her actually slide aside the "Floor Plan of the Week" page as if she hadn't noticed it.

Or as if Wayne's wishing for a girl in a bar had somehow broadened her own horizons. For she could read his mind. The crate had atomized the walls. Tina in Rumplestiltskins had offered herself shamelessly, almost urgently. There was a kind of wisdom in her eyes. There was an imperious generosity in her hips. Her hands had kept alighting on him while she talked. According to Oprah Winfrey—whose show he had watched furtively when he was first unemployed—most husbands commit adultery during the wife's second pregnancy, a statistic which seemed to provide camouflage. Or almost to mock him for his faithfulness.

In his squeaky chair, he pushed himself up from his position of reclining on his spine, and he met his well-dressed reflection in the mirror, prepared to dial another number from his phone list: a Charles Schneider in Daly City. He dialed the number with the untiring words already in his mind like discovering a headache: "Good morning, Mr. Schneider, this is Wayne Paschke"; but the phone just went on ringing and ringing— at some house in Daly City where Charles Schneider was too busy to stay home and answer the phone. He lifted his pencil and poised it above Mr. Schneider's name on the list, to chalk up another victory for the losers of the world, another victory for God.

With a surge, the repressed thought flew up: he was a fool, he would lose all their money, he had to get out of Marketrend now. It wasn't too late to get Laura's money back. He dialed Buddy's home number, knowing he would regret it.

"Hello?"

"Hi, Buddy? Wayne Paschke here."

"Wayne! How's it going? I was just going to call you. What can I do for you?"

"Fine, Buddy, fine, it's just, I was wondering, have the papers gone through on all these coins by now?" Already his resolve was weakening, having struck the soft expanse of Buddy's reasonableness.

"Yes, of course, you saw them. You loaded the boxes on the truck with me, Wayne. Wayne, I'm getting a strange vibe from your voice. Are you getting discouraged?"

"No, no, it's just that there's only two days left in the month . . ."

"Uh-oh. Okay, now listen up. I can tell you're getting discouraged. I'm going to give you a talking-to right now. And when I'm done, you're going to feel better; and you're going to owe me a drink for being such a good friend. What you're going through now, everybody goes through. All new brokers have to get over this hurdle. I know it seems impossible. To you, it seems like you're different from all those successful lucky brokers, it seems like you've got special circumstances in your life. But Wayne, everybody's got special circumstances. Everybody's different."

"Buddy, my wife is pregnant!"

"All the more reason! All the more reason!"

"Buddy, I'm not kidding. That was five thousand dollars."

"Okay, calm down. Listen, I can guess what you've called about. You want to give back the coins and get your money back. And Wayne, even though that's against every Marketrend rule, I'm willing to get you a refund. I'm willing to personally risk my reputation and try to get your money back. But first I want to talk to you. I want you to calm down and get some perspective. Because you have to think first. I really believe you'd be making a big mistake by pulling out now. You're on the brink of being a Head Broker. And this last inch looks like a mile. Doesn't it? Doesn't this last inch look like a mile?"

"I'll say."

"First of all, Wayne?"

"Yeah."

"Are you with me, Wayne?"

"Yes."

"First of all, just tell me what's on your mind. Tell me how you feel, and we'll figure out what to do about it. Even if it does mean quitting. But just tell me what's going on for you."

"Well, how about this?" Wayne said, knowing however that it was strictly forbidden by the Marketrend code: "You could buy the last seven hundred dollars' worth of coins. That's all I need to be over the top, and I'd pay you back . . ."

"No. Categorically. I'd rather give you the whole amount back and be honest about your failure, than loan you seven hundred so we could pretend you're a success. One: It's against the rules and it would mean my ass—though that's actually the minor consideration. Because two: it lacks integrity. You have to succeed with integrity. It's like Fortinbras Armstrong says. Marketrend is about personal integrity. If you get rich without that, you're very poor indeed. So Wayne, if you're not going to do this, I'd really rather give you back the whole entire amount. But listen, you haven't told me what your thinking is on this. What was it that got you down?"

"I've just been sitting here all morning getting hung-ups and nobody homes. And I guess my thinking is, I just blew away five thousand dollars that my wife needs for doctor bills. And you know about my situation . . ."

"It feels wobbly—"

"Wobbly! My daughter had all this medical work done. And my wife is due any month. And I haven't had any income. All I do with Marketrend is put money *in*."

"And nobody's been buying?"

"Entirely hung-ups. Entirely."

"Yeah. You know, maybe I should have Bill Wilson phone you about this."

"Jesus! No!" Big Bill Wilson, the founder, with his Arkansas grin implying any idiot could do what he'd done. Whose color photograph appeared in all the Marketrend literature alongside his gleaming ten-room house. Or alongside his yacht or his photogenic family or his immense desk. Wayne had only seen him in an inspirational film screened at Opportunity Meetings. "I'm sure that isn't necessary, Buddy."

"Necessary! Wayne, do you know who you are? You're one of the most important, most watched people in Marketrend."

"Do you know him? Can you just call up Bill Wilson, for a little thing like this?"

"Wayne, this is not little. This is not little. You're an im-

portant Broker in danger of losing motivation. Don't you remember the Jamboree? If you start thinking of yourself as
insignificant and negligible—"

"I don't. I don't."

"Just tell me what you want, Wayne. Let's start there. Just
tell me what you want. You're valuable to Marketrend, and
it's my job to keep you happy, so let's start by you just telling
me what you want."

"Buddy, I'm sure Marketrend works for some people. I'm
sure all these millionaires at the Jamboree weren't lying or
anything . . ."

"But it won't work for you?"

"Well, yeah, I guess."

"You guess what?"

"I guess it won't work for me."

"Why not? What's the difference between you and all those
millionaires who got what they wanted?"

"I don't know, Buddy."

"Now, don't misunderstand me. I'm not trying to talk you
into anything. If you want to try returning those coins for a
refund, we'll try to swing it somehow. Because if we're taking
a trip you don't want to take, then you won't be a very useful
passenger and you should get off the boat right away. There's
nothing worse than having one member of the team who isn't
really playing. But before you do, I just want you to think first
and get some perspective. I believe that if you quit, it'd be a
heck of a loss to all of us. And remember that Fortinbras
Armstrong story? About the miner who gave up when he was
six inches from the mother lode?"

"Yes, yes—"

"Don't you see how you're truly six inches from the mother
lode right now? Do you know what it'll be like being a Head

Broker? You bring in new recruits. And then just stay on the phone all day motivating. Like I'm doing right now. You know, I'm making a heck of a good percentage off your efforts. I just pocketed an easy two thousand dollars on that load of coins. And all I do is get on the phone all day motivating with my brokers."

"Yeah," Wayne said noncommittally.

"And see? I profit by your profits. And we'll *both* profit when you bring in your own organization. And a few of them will go Head, and then you'll be soaking *that* up. But it has to begin with attitude. That's the secret: desire. You have to desire it. Which brings me back to my main question: What is on your mind? How do you feel? What's the difference between you and all those Marketrend successes? Because I'm not your enemy here. I want to help you get what you want. If pulling out of Marketrend is the right thing, then so be it. But if you're going to stay, then I say: Let's do it right."

"Okay, Buddy, one difference with me is, my wife is pregnant and we need emergency money."

"I know! I know! All the more reason! That's why I personally feel it's a privilege for me, to be helping you get over this hurdle. Because, Wayne, the secret of Marketrend isn't money. The money is shit. The money is strictly a by-product of success. The real secret is a whole way of life. The habit of success.

"Or think about this, Wayne: Maybe you don't really want money badly enough. Have you ever considered that? Not everybody needs to be rich, you know. Success can be, you know, writing a symphony or picking up girls or winning at tennis, or anything. That's what Fortinbras Armstrong is all about. Nobody says you have to be rich."

"Okay, look, Buddy." Wayne just wished he hadn't called

him. "I just need time to think. Can I just have some time to think?"

"That's exactly what I was going to recommend. Because that's what Fortinbras Armstrong is all about. You get what you desire, but you have to *desire* it. Right now you're *already* getting what you desire; it just doesn't happen to be money. So what I'm saying is, look at what you're already getting. We only go around once in life, so don't sit around getting things you don't want. I don't intend to resist you. If you want to be rich, then let's work together. If you don't, then do quit. There's plenty of other things to do besides get rich. Like I say, there's picking up girls, and football, and a million things. And Marketrend does not need halfway-committed people . . ."

"No, Buddy, I really do desire this. It just seems pretty useless when I sit here all day getting hung-ups. You're right, I need to think."

"Call me back, Wayne. Read your Fortinbras Armstrong. He truly is magnetizing, just like it says. I mean, it's bullshit, but it's magnetizing. It's proven. And if you want to pull out, fine. I'm not kidding. It's fine. I'm your friend in this thing, and I want you to get what you want. Although, personally my feeling is, you'd be throwing away money precisely when you need it—and precisely when you're about to get it. And the worst thing is, you'd be compromising. You'd be saying, Okay, I'm willing to live at this level."

"No, don't worry about me, Buddy. I don't want to quit. I'm just starting to feel, you know—"

"Hey, Wayne, this is the dark hour every new Broker goes through. It's hell. But on the other side of it is a changed man. In fact, this is exactly the critical moment. If it weren't impossibly hard it wouldn't be the critical moment. Right? This

is the point where an ordinary reasonable man would give up.
You have to keep on going after it's no longer reasonable.
That's what all those great men did, in *Unlock the Dynamic
Power Within*. Then you can burst through the barrier of or-
dinariness, and you achieve unordinariness . . . Well, you get
my meaning. When I broke through this barrier—did I ever
tell you this?—when I broke through this barrier I did the
same thing: I wanted my money back. But I was really a hard-
ass; I actually threatened to sue and everything. And my Head
Broker, Kurt, who worked under Bill Wilson, he did the same
thing with me. He offered to refund my money. But after I
faced myself, I decided I really didn't want to be a failure. I'd
still be assembling computer chassis for four dollars an hour
if Kurt hadn't called my bluff. He motivated with me for about
six hours one night. It's the Dark Night of the Soul, Wayne.
All you need is somebody like me to motivate with. Because
that's when you unlock the dynamic power within: Marketrend
isn't about money, it's about you. You have the key to everything."

"I appreciate it, Buddy."

"Hey, it'll be your job when you get to be Head Broker.
And look, I intend to collect on that drink. Say, next summer,
when you're a famous Head Broker, you have to buy me a
Scotch and soda. Chivas Regal with Perrier. At the Top o' the
Mark."

"You know, I should get back to work."

"Is it a date? Let's just say, June twenty-first. At the Top
o' the Mark. A Chivas and Perrier. Okay?"

"Okay, but look, let me get back to work."

"But call me. Will you? Call me later. Call me tonight and
tell me what your thoughts are."

"Sure, Buddy."

He hung up.

Wayne leaned back in his chair. How had he, in the legendary time of infancy and childhood, suffered the original loss of confidence? It had seemed so logical, his imaginary picture of financial crash. But enslavement to mere logic is exactly what true success transcends. Every failure is perfectly logical. Things always looked bad when he started letting himself think of Marketrend as stupid. The very word *stupid*, freighted with slow pain, came down to him from high school, the years when the word was most often in his mouth, the years when he and Randy Potts went around town barefoot, hated by waitresses and shopkeepers—when, amidst assassinations and undeclared wars, things stopped meaning anything, or when things first started to mean their opposite; when he and Randy learned their incessant sarcastic "talking in quotes," in the specious baritone of ad announcers. It provided a refuge, a personal charmed protection against the school system that was designed to weed him out, against "wars" and "presidents." Even at the dramatic moment of walking out of Miss Roup's economics class, when Randy leaned over and whispered, "Hey, 'Let's Drop Out,' " even then the words had been enclosed in quotes. When they walked out the school's front door, Randy said, "Now We Enter the Ranks of America's Disaffected and Disillusioned."

"Here's to Success!" Wayne had jeered later, lifting a beer above the horizon: he and Randy lay side-by-side on the golden hillside above town on that May afternoon of the Nixon administration. It was Randy, always ahead, who had taught him how to surround everything with treacherous irony. Even at his wedding, Randy was elbowing him and murmuring of "Becoming a Solid Citizen" and "Being a Loving Husband and Responsible Father," alluding to the irrecoverable days before

girls when they were a pair of untrappable outlaws. For once
in his life, if only to save himself, Wayne had to do something
whole-hearted.

"Wayne?" Laura's voice came through the kitchen door.
"Wayne, Randy Potts just drove past the house in his goddamned Ferrari."

He went out into the kitchen. Laura was looking out the
front window with a section of the newspaper trailing behind
her.

"Twice," she said. "The first time, he slowed up and almost
stopped. But the second time he was going the other way."

"Which way did he go?"

"Toward San Pedro. Why would he be spying on us?"

"Who says he's spying? Do we have to assume Randy's an
asshole?"

"Why else would he come to this neighborhood? Maybe he
means well sometimes, but Wayne! He *is* an asshole. He put
that crate in our garage."

"All I'm saying is, we don't know that he's spying."

"Well, all right," she said, in that finalizing tone that, by
yielding him the point, made him contemptibly fascist, and
she walked away in the wounded gait of pregnancy.

Something dark rose in him. "Okay!" he shouted. Suddenly
he was angry. "Maybe he is spying! Who the fuck cares? Who
the fuck cares?" He swept up the weekend newspaper and
whipped it at the floor.

"All right then!" Laura shouted, her voice rising to the same
pitch of fury as his, actually almost imitating his tone, as
different musical instruments raise the same motif; and he
realized that in a moment of effortless self-sacrifice she was
touching him to ground the charge. "Let's go ahead and spend
the goddamned shitty money. What do you want? A house? A

car? Let's all become assholes like Randy Potts. With his big mansion in Ross. What do you want, Wayne? You want a fancy car? You want a, a fucking butler?"

She fell silent, and the air rang. Wayne said softly, "Let's just drop it." He was still looking away from her, out the window.

He heard her shuffle off toward the kitchen, where she sat down with her section of the newspaper, rattling it to restore the peaceful noises of ennui. Then she said, "I want a peacock."

"A peacock?" he said, with the quick sting of a tear in his eye. He knew all the things she really wanted.

She sighed. "I've always thought you're really rich when you have a peacock on your property. People in Belvedere and Tiburon all have peacocks wandering around on their property. And a llama."

His throat large with the plum of emotion, he responded only with a small querying noise. "Hm?"

"They have a weird cry," her voice went on. "And they just hang around and look beautiful. And I think I'd want a butler. With an English accent and a gray vest and everything. But a nice butler. A butler you could be friends with. A butler you could hang around and talk with. Or I can sit around and drink coffee all morning with the maid. I think that's the real reason people have servants: so they'll have people around the house." The newspaper rattled. "Wouldn't that be nice? Wayne? Just have all these maids and butlers around the house to chat with and hang around with?"

He took a deep breath. "Yeah," he said, his voice even.

"What about you?" she said. "What do you want to buy?"

"Nothing."

"Nothing? With two million dollars?"

"A trampoline," he said off the top of his head.

"A trampoline!" she said.

"It's like peacocks."

"You've got two million dollars, Wayne. Nice rich people *we* are."

"It's because, remember Johnnie Guinn's trampoline? I always thought he was the luckiest kid in the world because his parents got him a trampoline. Randy and I used to go over there all the time. But one time he went up on the Guinns' roof and threw a bowling ball down on the trampoline, and Mrs. Guinn saw him doing it. So we were never allowed to come back."

The newspaper in the kitchen rattled again. "I wonder what happened to Johnnie Guinn."

Wayne's voice was coming to him from far away. "That bowling ball bounced way over the garage. If it had hit anything we would have been in deep shit."

At that moment, Randy Potts himself—twenty years older, but with the same walk, the same eager lift off the heel in midstride—came around the corner. He must have parked his car in the 7-Eleven lot.

"Here he comes now," said Wayne.

"Uh-oh." Laura came out of the kitchen and opened the front door.

"Where's Kim?" said Wayne, following her.

"Don't worry, she's somewhere," said Laura, tugging her sash tighter as she went outside.

Randy stopped. "Wait, you guys," he said, showing his palms in surrender as he stood on a corner of the lawn. "I just want to talk."

"Did you park at 7-Eleven?"

"Yeah. Nobody is following me or tapping my phone or anything. I'm just trying to take extra precautions."

"Okay, Randy, let's all get inside," said Laura, looking up and down the street clasping a bunch of fabric at the throat of her nightgown.

Randy skipped in the door ahead of Wayne and Laura, saying, "I've had two or three meetings now with the Secret Service, and I've got a lawyer. There's been some really bizarre developments. What is this?" He halted, blocking the passage, having come across a pile of Cindy's belongings by the door. "This is my daughter's computer. And her skis and her guitar and her bird cage. I *gave* her this computer. And look at it now."

"Randy, get in, I want to close the door."

"Why is all this here?"

Wayne said, "Cindy seems to be giving it to Kim. We found it the other morning with a note that said something about 'Keep this or pass on to Goodwill or some charity.' Kim says she doesn't know what it's all about."

Randy picked up the note, which lay on the Coke-sticky ruined computer, and, scanning it, said, "My weird daughter."

Wayne went into the kitchen. "Come on."

"Look at all this shit," Randy marveled.

"Randy," he said, "you're putting *us* in danger by coming here."

"Okay"—he tore himself away—"well, I couldn't phone, just in case they are tapping me. Believe me, I'm doing everything I can to protect you guys."

"You realize, we might be considered accomplices," said Laura.

"Exactly. But just tell me. Does Kim have any idea why Cindy is giving away all her shit?"

Laura said, "Randy, you're sure—aren't you—that the girls have no idea about any of this."

"Positive. There's no way."

"What does your lawyer say," asked Wayne. "You said you had a lawyer."

"Okay." Randy pulled his chair in to the table. "There's been some new developments. You guys have to act fast. The Secret Service took some of those twenties and tested them *again*. And this time they really tested them. And whatever tests they did, they couldn't prove it was counterfeit. There's no way science can tell the difference. So, see, the money you have in that crate? It's, A, completely perfect, and B, nobody knows you've got it."

"What about the paper?" said Wayne. "With the tiny threads."

"No, see, even the paper is the same. They thought this guy—the person or persons who gave me the money—they thought he must have purchased the paper from the Crane Paper Corporation. Because it turns out Crane is the supplier of paper for the mint, right?"

"You mean, like *Crane?*" said Laura. "The stationery company?"

"Yeah, Crane has an exclusive government contract to make the paper. But if you purchase it from them you have to register yourself and everything, but Crane said nobody weird had purchased weird amounts of it. So then they thought the person or persons might have figured out how to manufacture his own paper exactly like Crane—like the exact same recipe for pulp. But they're completely unable to explain it. Don't you see? That crate of money is the same as real. That's what I'm trying to say."

Laura said, "Have you considered that it might *not* be counterfeit? Maybe the person or persons is passing out real money and calling it counterfeit."

"What about the serial numbers?" said Wayne.

"Yeah. Okay. That's the thing. They went through all the cash. Which they've impounded and gave me a receipt for. Can you imagine? They gave me a receipt for eighteen million dollars."

"That's how much it is? Jesus!" The windows seemed to loom larger as suddenly Wayne lost his sense of shelter in his own house.

"So they went through it all. They have these amazing machines which they call CVCS machines. They feed the money in one end, and it *reads* the bills at an incredible rate, like five hundred per minute or something. And it even weighs each bill, because supposedly a genuine bill weighs a certain exact amount."

"This is in Washington?" said Laura.

"No, this is here. They've got two of these machines in the Federal Reserve Bank on Market Street. But so the machine read all the serial numbers on my bills and recorded them, and it turned out that no two bills have the same serial number. All the bills are a little worn, and they're all from different issues. Or different series. I forget. Like issued at different times."

"Randy," said Laura, "it's real money. The person or persons is passing out real money. It's a *counterfeit* counterfeit."

"No, but wait. Now they're running *actual real* twenties through the machines to read the serial numbers, because eventually they want to find a real bill from general circulation that has the same serial number as one of my bills. My lawyer says they'll probably succeed. They have these CVCS machines running all day and all night, and they're using computers to compare the numbers. Eventually they'll find two bills with the same serial number, and they'll know that mine is counterfeit. They'll have proof."

Laura sighed, what Wayne thought of as her pregnancy sigh. "What makes them so sure it's counterfeit?"

"Well, there's other things," said Randy. "Like the Federal Reserve has economists, and they can't explain where a million twenty-dollar bills could suddenly come from. A million bills is a lot. It fucks up their graphs. It seems to have come out of nowhere."

On the word 'nowhere' a silence accumulated, locking the three of them together. Wayne glanced at Laura, whose eyes were downcast; and he broke the triangle by revolving in his swivel chair slightly away from the table. He got up and went to the refrigerator, saying, "Beer?" while he reached in and got one for himself and one for Randy.

He set the cold can of Budweiser unopened before Randy, who ignored it, saying in a lower tone of voice, "And nobody—nobody—knows about that one crate. Except us three. Not even my lawyer."

Laura drew breath and pleaded, "Randy!"

"There's still time."

"Randy, even if it's real! I mean, it's extremely hard to believe there can be a counterfeit so real. Even if it's genuine money, we still don't know . . . We don't know where it came from . . ."

"Can you just take my word for it? As long as I don't tell you anything about it, you're not guilty of anything; you're not an accomplice to anything. I still haven't told you a single fact about it. The only thing I said was, I told Wayne it was a box of Mary's old kitchen stuff. Now I'm saying, 'Go bury that box of old kitchen stuff.' This way you're not guilty of anything. Can't you just take my word for it?"

"Randy, Kim is still in school. And I'm pregnant. And we like this town. And my gosh, Randy! Money doesn't just come out of nowhere."

"Wait, you don't understand. My goose is cooked. And the jail sentence is twenty-five years. And even when I get out of jail, at the age of like sixty, they'll be watching me to see if I start spending lots of money. And besides, they've got me on other charges, like setting up bank accounts under false identities. But you guys. You guys are in the clear . . ."

"Randy," said Laura, her eyes still downcast to evade Randy's steady imploring gaze. "Please just."

There was final decision in her voice.

"Wayne?" Randy said. Wayne just shrugged. He might always regret this.

Randy stood up like a shot. His chair slid back. He walked rapidly out the door with such disgust that Wayne knew he wouldn't come back for the crate. Laura continued to stare at the formica before her while Randy slammed the door. His Budweiser still stood on the table unopened, the ornate red etching on the can developing a silky mist.

# 19

Sitting alone against the wall in Ludex's outer waiting room at the Secret Service office, Randy was reminded of the criminals on TV who sit in court with their obvious guilt prefigured in the very slope in their shoulders, and he realized it was these tubular-steel government chairs that make you crouch looking convicted, these armrests; so he stood up and, like the handsomer actor who plays the innocent accused, walked in his buoyant new suit to stand by the window as if he were looking out at the view, though there wasn't much to be seen through the Venetian blinds except for a tiled corridor, this being an interior window. He adjusted his lapels. Remaining unconvicted was just a matter of attitude—of shrugging off the silhouetting diagram of guiltiness in spite of the apparently, now, irrefutable proof that the money was counterfeit.

It hadn't taken them long: their computerized machines had found two bills of the same serial number. It was like a distant abstraction of theoretical physics which proved something unthinkable: in those two bills, now probably clipped together in an official drawer somewhere, Ludex had located a point of tangency between the real world and a world that had come to seem increasingly imaginary. For, lately more and more, Randy had come to think of Bim's money as genuine, and even, in a way, to think of Bim Auctor himself as unbelievable. Dan McBride had hired a private investigator to search for Bim— or for anyone who might have been posing as "Bim Auctor"— and he had turned up no trace. The restaurants that, according to Randy's memory, he and Bim had eaten in, had no records. The Canal District apartment, which had recently changed hands, had been owned and ignored by a harmless group of ecological antinuke fund-raiser physicians, none of whose members could have been Bim, even in disguise, and none of whom were connected with anyone remotely like Bim. The rooms themselves were now rented by a rock-and-roll band who had covered all clues with black paint. The parking space behind the McDonald's had been occupied over the seasons by thousands of cars erasing the incriminating conversations he recalled having there with Bim. Randy's heart told him Bim had died and, according to his protocol, left behind no evidence of his existence. The whole idea of Bim Auctor, refracted by the new legal context, had come to seem miragelike; it felt right when Dan told him, last week, that Bim had "started to seem so nonexistent that we can treat him as irrelevant." Randy glanced back at Ludex's receptionist, who was busy doing something at her desk, and he pulled out his wallet to look at one of the twenty-dollar bills—which he was continuing to carry and spend, his boldness keeping him innocent. Within the defensive arc of his shoulder, he parted the lips of his wallet to reveal a green corner: "20." It was real; this had been one solid "fact" amidst the shimmer of Bim's evaporation. But now it was contradicted by this other fact: that there existed two bills of the same serial number.

Also visible in his wallet was the slip of paper bearing Arthur Van Sichlyn's venerable English address—simply "Slade Park, Hart-'pon-Bent"—which at this dire moment felt like an unspent certificate of value equal to any of the cash folded together with it. Arthur had given it to Randy before departing on his most recent trip, saying he should drop by any time; and now Randy had been wishing he could actually go—but *with* somebody, so that the experience wouldn't be wasted. On that plot of ground, Slade Park, was the tree Arthur had told him about, in which the ancient jawbone of a boar, the totem of his family's defeated enemies, was embedded. Randy wanted to actually run his fingers over the molars that, as he imagined, broke through the bark of the oak undigested. He imagined Arthur and himself sipping old sherry in a slate-floored hall as if they themselves had just conquered this plot of turf from which the shrieks of ancient, unappeased ghosts rose up crying for justice. The fact that Arthur's real estate had been won by carnage, in the days when families were mere tribes warring in the constant mud, lent his position in Marin County an impressive cruelty, an authenticity.

*Cindy* could come with him to England; a trip to England was something her mother could never afford. And his gift of an expensive scooter had been so casually devalued—Cindy never once rode it, finally claimed she had "lost" it, never even thanked him for it—the whole scooter idea had been a strategy that, when it backfired, had turned somehow to her mother's advantage. Ever since, Cindy had seemed to sulk, to remove herself from the world, staying in her room whenever he called. Her mother had shouted through the bedroom door, "Cindy, your Dad's on the phone," and after a long moment she'd responded, "I'm busy right now." When finally she came to the phone, he'd wanted to know why she was giving away all her prized possessions to Kim Paschke, and she'd answered forlornly that Kim or some other less fortunate girl could use them, while she herself would get the satisfaction of knowing she had made this world a little brighter for someone . . .

The outer door opened. Led by the paunchy old security guard from the lobby, Dan arrived, slipping his collapsible cane into his coat pocket, catching his hip awkwardly on the doorknob, smiling warily. Randy felt his heart sink with loyalty. "Morning, Dan," he said.

"Randy," said Dan. "A little late. Sorry." As usual, he was perfectly dressed; he must have had his secretary look him over whenever he went out. Randy guided him to a chair.

"Now, Randy. I have no idea what will transpire. Anything could happen at this point, and we're simply unprepared. Your job is to say as little as possible. Okay? Just like the other meetings." Randy watched in sympathetic suspense while Dan groped for a blank cassette in his briefcase and slipped it into his tape recorder.

The receptionist, who had lifted her phone when Dan entered, now replaced it and rose, saying, "Would you gentlemen like to follow me?" She preceded them down a corridor, Dan lightly holding Randy's elbow. Randy watched—what Dan couldn't see—her body moving beneath her dress as she walked ahead of him through the bureaucratic scents of the corridor, and he thought: I've wasted this money. The toss of her hair, the weightless ticktock of her hips, filled him with the old doomed longing for eternity.

They arrived at a room guarded by two armed officers in white billed caps and white gloves. Inside the room, at a long conference table, were Hodges and a young man in a gray suit—younger than Randy, almost college-age, and somehow Washingtonian: the glasses, the haircut, the shoeshine; something pre-senatorial about him. He didn't rise when Randy and Dan entered, though Hodges did.

"Morning, Mr. McBride. Mr. Potts. Investigator Ludex will be here in a minute. This is Ralph Conlin."

Ralph Conlin said good morning.

"So," said Dan. "It's just the five of us? After Mr. Ludex arrives? You see, I'm blind, Mr. Conlin. I usually mention a Helen Keller joke or two, to put people at ease."

Mr. Conlin made a fake chuckle audible.

"Tell me," Dan said to him. "Which side are you on in this mess?"

"Oh, I'm just going to sit in," said Mr. Conlin.

"As . . . ? As an interested party?"

"Well, you must admit, it's an interesting case."

"Ah, but you represent . . . ?"

Hodges interrupted, "Mr. Conlin won't be contributing to our discussion today. He's just going to listen in."

"I understand that," said Dan. "What I want to know is, whom does he represent? Why is he here? Is he Treasury?"

Conlin said, "I'm with the State Department."

Dan simply said, "Oh. I see." And that was all. Randy got the feeling they'd met some insurmountable setback.

Ludex came in and sat down at the head of the table with a manila folder and a zippered nylon pouch, from which he drew two clear plastic envelopes. "No preamble," he said. "Good morning, Mr. Potts. Mr. McBride. Here are the bills. This one"—he held up an envelope marked SPECIMEN— "comes from the cash Mr. Potts is known to have deposited in Eureka Federal Savings of Walnut Creek on November seventeen of last year."

He held up the other, unmarked, envelope. "This one was found by our currency verification system in the Kansas City branch of the Federal Reserve. It is a genuine note taken from circulation in the general economy. Here also is a copy of a statement from Robert Loove at the Bureau of Engraving and Printing, indicating that this bill was issued in 1981 through the Chicago Federal Reserve Branch. You'll see they are identical in every way, including serial numbers."

He passed the two clear plastic envelopes to Hodges on his right, and he turned to Randy. "Mr. Potts, the purpose of this meeting is to ascertain three things: Do we have all of the money? Who manufactured this money? And how did these people manufacture it? We need your help in answering these three questions. Do you understand?"

Dan said, "Why is Mr. Conlin here?"

Ludex said, "Mr. Conlin is irrelevant."

"This is a criminal case . . ."

"Our information may be furnished to any government branch," said Ludex. "Mr. McBride, is that thing running?"

"What," said Dan, "my tape recorder?"

"I'm sorry, but you'll have to turn it off, and surrender that cassette to us."

Which Dan actually did, without any protest. Was it even legal for the police to make such a request? With passive compliance, Dan turned off the machine, pressed the eject button, and slid the cassette into the center of the table.

Dan said, "Why isn't the U.S. Attorney here? This would be U.S. Attorney jurisdiction."

Ludex said, "The case has been passed upward. The U.S. Attorney will—"

Dan leaned forward over the table. "You can't tell the difference, can you?"

A glance passed between Ludex and Conlin.

Ludex said, "That is correct."

"I'll want a lab report furnished to me."

Ludex took some pages from his manila folder and slid them toward Dan. "This is the lab report. You may keep this copy. But all evidence is confidential. You understand that, Mr. McBride."

Hodges said, "You may want to bring in another lawyer on this."

Dan didn't reply. His eyes were fixed on something worrisome out there where parallel lines abstractly meet.

"So," said Ludex. "Let me repeat. This meeting has three goals. We have to determine who was making this currency, how they were making it, and where all the existing currency is."

"What tests were run?" said Dan. "Can I see the bills? How thorough were they in their testing?"

Hodges said, "It's the best forensic laboratory in the world, Mr. McBride. Actually, it went to the F.B.I. labs. They have the best facilities."

The two bills, which had worked their way around the table to Conlin, were passed to Dan, who rubbed the paper between the pinch of his thumb and forefinger.

Randy looked at the lab report which lay open before him on the table, printed out by computer in ghostly dot matrix. "Sizing hydrophbc," was jotted in pen at the bottom of the first page. The second page, which was headed "Paper Composition," seemed to contain a long list of numbers rating the surprisingly bread-like ingredients of the paper: "alpha-cellulose, beta-cellulose, gamma-cellulose, lignin, carbohydrates, carboxyl and carbonyl groups, copper number, monomeric sugars . . ."

Ludex said, "You see, Mr. McBride, the question of whether or not you'll cooperate is already settled. This meeting isn't taking place. We have to answer these questions immediately: especially who was manufacturing this currency and how."

"Why they are manufacturing it is a further question," said Mr. Conlin, from behind the rock of his joined hands. The assertion, his first, was made in a level drawl that halted dialogue for a moment. The other men shifted slightly in their chairs.

Dan sighed and set the two bills on the table and folded his arms. "Gentlemen, I have an obligation to my client," he said. Everybody seemed to be somehow disappointed by the remark, or angered. Dan was smiling unconsciously to himself, his head listing in that blind way of his, as if obeying the gyroscope of his inner ear. Randy picked up the two bills. In parsley-green ink, the serial number "G 35749008B" was printed on the face of the one bill; and on the other was the same number: "G 35749008B."

"Mr. McBride," said Ludex, "you may not be aware . . ."

"I'm aware of an obligation to my client," said Dan. "Everything loses meaning if a lawyer can simply break his contract. And the fact is"— he leaned out over the table addressing himself to thin air opposite, where Ludex wasn't—"the fact is, you have no evidence. Those two bills aren't evidence of counterfeiting. He can't be found in court for utterance. This is genuine." Three times he tapped the empty spot on the table where the bills had been before Randy picked them up. "These two bills are equal."

Randy, the last to examine the bills, set them down in front of Ludex.

Dan added, "Define *genuine* for me."

Ludex snatched the bills up. "Who removed these from the envelopes?"

"Not me," said Randy.

Hodges said, "I took them out of the envelopes, Bob."

"Well, do you remember?" said Ludex. "If these get mixed up . . ."

"Aren't they marked?"

"No, of course not. They're specimens. They were in marked envelopes."

"Well, won't they be able to tell the difference at the lab?"

Ludex stuffed both bills into one of the envelopes, and he turned to Dan. "Look, Mr. McBride. We all know that a crime of utterance has been committed."

"But it can't be proved," said Dan. "The bills can't be produced in court, because they're perfect. They're money. They aren't evidence of counterfeiting."

"But two bills of the same serial number—" said Hodges.

"Well, then you're asking a metaphysical question," said Dan. "This whole case hangs on a metaphysical question. If you produce these bills before a jury, I'll have them excluded as evidence. There's no evidence of a crime here. If money consists of a certain configuration of ink on paper, then my client is in possession of money. I'm going to stick to this."

Ludex said, "Do you understand why Mr. Conlin is here today?"

"Yes. Yes I do," said Dan. Randy realized that the two

guards in white gloves had come with Conlin; there had been something Washingtonian about them too.

"Yes," said Dan again. "But I think we'd like some time to think about our position. Maybe you're right, Frank." He addressed Hodges, surprisingly, by his first name. "Maybe I should take on a consulting lawyer. And of course we may modify our position. But I think Mr. Conlin—whom I know by reputation, and who is a lawyer himself by training—I think Mr. Conlin will understand that for the moment we'll have to take a hard line and protect the client." Dan turned toward Conlin and said conversationally, "Eddie Mensinger at Brookings, in 1979."

"Eddie Mensinger!" said Conlin.

"Same house at Harvard," said Dan.

"Where is Eddie Mensinger?"

"SRI. Just south of here."

"Palo Alto?" said Conlin.

"Yes," said Dan.

"Hm!" said Conlin, frowning. And then again, "Hm!"

Ludex seemed to resent this inscrutable exchange. "Mr. McBride, Randy knows who did this and how they did it."

"No really I don't," Randy blurted out, sincerely. He had spoken without Dan's permission, but Dan didn't seem to object.

Dan said, "We actually retained a private investigator, and he found absolutely nothing. The only legal reality is that Mr. Potts came into possession of eighteen million dollars. He'd pay a tax penalty on that. And maybe he'd be found on the bank fraud."

"Giving false information to an agency of the U.S. government," Hodges put in.

Randy said, "What's the jail sentence for that?"

"Negligible," said Hodges.

Dan said, "A fine maybe. Probation maybe." He turned toward Conlin. "He found it in the woods. He stumbled across the crates while he was hiking on Mount Tamalpais. They washed up on the beach. Which would perhaps solve your problem too."

Conlin said, "No. Wouldn't solve my problem at all." Again a lull succeeded his remark.

"Randy," Ludex said, more quietly now, with fake friendliness. "You could lead us straight to the printing presses."

"No, I'm not kidding," said Randy, conscious of the name Bim Auctor like a pill under his tongue, "I really don't know how it was printed. The guy just gave it to me. All I ever saw was the ten crates of bills. That's the complete total of what I knew."

"He's telling the truth, it's *factor nesciens,*" said Dan. "We've had a private investigator looking for this person; he's vanished without a trace. They had a few meetings behind a McDonald's restaurant in San Rafael, and all their contacts were *designed* to frustrate evidence. He told Randy nothing."

"That's right, I only had about six or eight meetings with the guy," Randy went on. "And because, the whole idea was to keep me in the dark. All I know is, this guy in a big white car met me in the parking lot behind a McDonald's and gave me specific verbal instructions to take care of his money. That's the complete story. I was his employee. He made a point of never telling me anything. He designed the whole thing that way."

Dan said, "It's a foolproof mope defense."

Ludex leaned forward. "Randy, where's the tenth crate?"

They were too quick for him. "What tenth crate?"

"This isn't the first time you've mentioned a tenth crate. And as you know, we've only accounted for nine."

"You've accounted for it all," Dan said with confidence.

But Ludex went on addressing Randy. "Are you aware that all your activities and contacts over the last year will be thoroughly investigated?"

"Frank," Dan said to Hodges. "You guys should be very careful about procedure. I can have that thrown out."

Ludex said, "We just don't believe you, Randy. We don't believe an individual can manufacture money this good in his basement."

Hodges turned and said, "It sounds believable to me, Bob. The technology is getting good enough these days. Isn't that right, Mr. Conlin? I heard the Treasury was making plans to change the currency to make it harder to counterfeit. Because the technology is getting good enough that they were starting to be afraid of this kind of thing. Isn't that right?"

"I can't say," said Conlin.

"I heard they were going to put a magnetic strip in the paper or something? Or print it finer?"

Conlin tossed his hand. Randy began to catch on that Hodges was the sympathetic guy of the pair.

Hodges went on. "Somebody who has the personal financial means. This mysterious guy in his big white Cadillac—"

Ludex caught Hodges's eye, glaring at him to silence him. Hodges was too nice a guy to be a cop.

"Mr. Potts," said Ludex. "There are serious consequences to your not helping us. This missing person is the key. And we just don't believe you. It isn't believable that this person would have enough personal wealth to buy the equipment for such a sophisticated counterfeit, even if he could afford a Cadillac. A white Cadillac is not evidence of great wealth. In a thousand little details, like that, your story just doesn't hold together."

"No, this guy was wealthy. You have no idea. This was no Cadillac, it was this custom-built El Gondo or something. This person was wealthier than you can imagine. Whatever kind of technology was necessary, he could have afforded it."

Hodges—addressing Randy though catching Ludex's eye— lifted a pen and asked, "How do you spell that?"

# 20

Inside a corral of striped hazard barriers, Randy was laboring like a convict in the hot morning sun in the Fairfax parking lot, with a hoe and a tire iron and a Polaroid and a clipboard. He and Kevin Van Sichlyn had spent the previous day breaking the old asphalt into manageable pieces with a rented air hammer; and today while Kevin was out talking to shipping contractors Randy had been assigned the job of chalking each piece with a legible identification number, recording the number on the reassembly chart, photographing it "in situ," as Kevin said, and then using his tire iron or his hoe to pry it away from its embedded position——to ensure that each piece would be lifted easily and without breakage into a shipping crate. He was grateful for the island of work, keeping his gaze lowered to the ground, visored. The Secret Service was still out there searching for Bim Auctor with a professional fierce patience that, as Dan McBride seemed to feel, made their eventually finding him inevitable; and Randy had come to dread the cool, silent rooms of his house, which still didn't feel like his own, as if it were in escrow while Bim was sought, and whose every piece of furniture stung him with the static electricity of expensiveness, of fraud. Slapping and wrestling these chunks of asphalt with dusty palms, feeling the salt slime in his armpits, Randy was able to distract himself from the constant pulsing thought of how unexpectedly large his crime had grown, how global. After their meeting with Ludex in San Francisco, he and Dan had gone outside, and Dan had stopped him at the street corner to shout through the roar of ocean wind, "Randy, the State Department is involved in this. They believe you're a threat to national security." Simply because of a counterfeit? Randy's words were torn off in the wind as he shouted, blind in sympathy with Dan. Dan called back, clinging, "No, Randy, it's perfect. The dollar is the most important currency in the world. This hasn't happened before. This is perfect." As they turned the corner onto Golden Gate Avenue, bumping together buffeted by the wind, Dan's trench coat whipping up around his head, he had shouted, "Randy! Is there a tenth crate?"

Randy just kept working harder, wanting the labor in the sun to feel futile, not redemptive or expiatory but simply sweaty, unconnected to everything. The more he worked, the crazier he felt; and the more his pace quickened; so that now, when he had chalked a number on a new chunk of asphalt, he almost *lunged* to the bed of Kevin's truck to get the camera, take the shot, lever the floe up atilt, and drop the clanging tire iron to move on to the next floe. He was a madman in Fairfax, tearing up the parking lot among striped wooden hazard barriers, feeling himself digging himself deeper and deeper in this bizarre and mostly imaginary predicament—while all around him the indifferent citizens went about their errands and the suburban trees breathed the breeze he had known so well since his childhood. He remembered how this parking lot used to be, years ago, in those infinitely mischievous moments of summer dusk when the last light of the sunset exactly equals the first light of the neon Schlitz and Texaco signs around; and the air, radiating heat from the paving, exactly equals skin temperature—so that everything floats in perfect equilibrium, and the injustice of homework is far away in another country. Before he got his driver's license, Randy used to hitchhike here from Terra Linda—down Third Street, out Sir Francis Drake Boulevard—to gather with his friends around the bright delicatessen while the sky in the west went as red as barbecue sauce, stopping customers as they entered to ask them to buy a six-pack.

Sometimes Wayne Paschke came along too. Long after dark, the paving released the sun's stored heat under their bare feet. They would sit on a cement tire-stop under the usual oak and have unembarrassed philosophical discussions in the dark, or debate the comparative virtues of their preferred cars—Randy's was the Maserati, Wayne's the Corvette Sting Ray. Wayne was loyal to Schlitz malt liquor, a new brand of beer which had a Minoan-looking bull on its label; whereas Randy's loyalty was to Budweiser, a swankier beer, with its ornate red label like a stock certificate or some guarantee of antiquity and value. He and Wayne once pressed beer bottlecaps into the bark of the oak, as escutcheons, or territorial claims. They supposed that, as the tree grew, its flesh would grip the bottlecaps and they would become permanent buttons; so they found some rocks and pounded the caps into place in the corky bark,

Wayne's primitive bull on the east side, Randy's red Bud disk
on the west side. The tree was at a far end of the lot, where
cars at night seldom parked. If ever they found a car parked
in their space, they exacted the guerilla punishment of letting
the air out of the tires: sneaking like commandos beneath the
level of the fenders, pressing a pebble or a twig into the iron
nipple to suffer that screaming hiss long enough for the tire to
soften, and then running off, never staying to witness—preferring to imagine—the stylized comedy of the pricked towns-
man whose property renders him vulnerable. But usually the
parking space was empty, a soaked oilspot dusted dry at the
center of its parallelogram beneath their bare soles. It wasn't
part of the more desirable real estate in the parking lot. Most
of the activity was further down toward the west end of the lot,
where juniors and seniors parked with both doors open to make
the stereo speakers audible. Red taillights came and went all
evening. If Randy or Wayne knew anybody with a driver's
license, he might take them cruising.

Randy remembered now—and slowed work in the reminis-
cence, standing up to lean on his hoe and draw his forearm
across his brow—that there was a spark plug he had found,
an ordinary spark plug, which he had discovered in the roadside cinders beside the Johnnie's Esso in the days before the
new freeway-exit cloverleaf. He had carried it around in his
pocket for weeks, for some reason, probing and pinching it in
the linty sweat of his pocket until his fingers knew its porcelain
surface as completely as the probing tongue knows a molar. It
was so heavy for its size, there was power compacted there.
His fingers kept discovering and rediscovering the scorched
electrode at its tip. And finally, on a night when Wayne wasn't
there, he buried it shallowly in the instep arch of their oak
tree—under the west side of the trunk, the side with his own

red Bud totem. And then, it seemed, he had forgotten about it totally and immediately. How strange! He hadn't thought at all about it until today, twenty years later.

This was stupid, but he just had to check to see if it was still there. He was already standing here gripping a hoe. Their old parking space was still there across the lot, its asphalt surface lifted ajar with a sarcophagus-lid tilt. The oak still stood there unchanged, not having grown or shrunk at all. Its far-reaching roots, he realized now, were the wooden ropes he had been discovering all morning under the asphalt.

The bottlecaps had of course fallen off. Even back then, he and Wayne had had to keep replacing them. As he began to stab his hoe in and step down on it, he looked furtively around as if he might be caught by somebody from the old days—though the neighborhood had been totally repopulated and the storefronts had gone through many failures as the land kept shedding people. He levered his hoe in the dirt and twisted it, and he found that after he had churned up enough dirt he soon heard a metallic scrape against the blade of his hoe. There it was: the same spark plug. It made sense, that it should remain intact, that the realm of fossils should obey more logical laws, like dreams perfectly preservative. He rubbed crumbs of dirt off with his thumb to discover the same friendly ridges in the porcelain. Even the electrode was unrusted after twenty years in the ground. He palpated it with his thumb as he used to do, and the sensation recalled all his youthful cowardice and courage. As soon as he was able to drive, he had forgotten it. He had been fifteen—the same age as Cindy now. Suddenly the joke of time's passage hit him like a heart attack. Twenty years. The oak tree was supernaturally the same, but he himself was waning. Now it was his daughter who was fifteen. He almost never saw her. Where had she gone? He had been living in a dream. Where had twenty years gone? The tree's hard flesh was still here, but his own immortal flesh, in the form of his daughter, was drifting away as a strange mist.

"Randy?"

He turned to see Arthur Van Sichlyn hobbling toward him over the pavement, his bicycle parked at the shore of the shattered pond.

"Arthur!" Randy said, pocketing the spark plug. His soul rushed back into his body. He was filled with gladness to see Arthur's scowl. "You're back!"

"Actually, I'm returning tomorrow." He gestured around at the demolition. "What is all this?"

He began to describe Kevin's problems with the Fairfax Improvement Committee—watching himself again being inexplicably jolly for a condemned man. Was Cindy in school at this moment? Was today a weekday? Did she ever think of him? He had called her two days ago on the pretext of asking her what she wanted for her birthday, and all she could say was *Nothing, Dad, really, I'm fine*, too engrossed in a television program to pay attention to their conversation.

"I see," said Arthur skeptically. "Last I heard, you were paying for it."

"No, not exactly. We're moving this one and paving a real parking lot in its place."

"What is the future of *this* parking lot?"

"We're moving it to Dallas. In fact, be careful. Don't knock any crumblies off the edges. The asphalt doesn't really stick to the cement. All these pieces will be crated up in sand."

"My son! If it weren't for the credulousness of people like you, he'd have to develop some integrity."

"He got a lot of publicity, see."

"Yes, it was mentioned in *The Guardian*, briefly. But in a rather light tone."

"See, there's a museum in Dallas that saw one of the articles, and they've come in between. Now Fairfax has agreed to let me buy it for them, and then they're turning around and selling it to the Dallas museum. Then they're paving a new parking lot here, and they'll have money left over." Something like an English accent was creeping into Randy's words lately, a slight crimp in the vowels. "Because the main thing they want is to get a real parking lot back here. Everybody's parking on side streets."

"It's fucking humiliating," said Arthur. It always increased Arthur's magnificence in Randy's eyes, that he should be able, at his age and social position, to use obscene language with such aplomb. "I wish he were calling himself Greenslade rather than Van Sichlyn. Which is his matronymic, you might say. What about coffee?"

"What. Now?" Randy looked around at the demolition, feeling anchored to the spot by the spark plug in his pocket.

"Little café round the corner. Kevin should be along in a minute. Or he may even be there already. Look here, it must be fabulously expensive to send all these pieces. Why don't you just leave this parking lot here and pave a new one in Dallas? They'll never know the difference."

"That's not the point," said Randy, but losing interest in this old game of the Van Sichlyns'. He had begun to realize that all of Arthur's imprecations against his son were merely a sneaky form of advertisement. Arthur was walking away muttering that Kevin was probably already in the café. So Randy just dropped his hoe and followed, rubbing under his thumb the porcelain ridges in his pocket.

"He's using you, Randy. He ought to have been a lawyer. At least then there'd be some money. I'm so bloody broke I can hardly pay my fare home again."

"How can you be broke?"

"It's about time his silly art projects generated a bit of cash—"

"Arthur, how can you be broke? You own that house."

"My goodness, Randy, don't be lower class." They came around the corner, where a small café, combined with a book-shop, had set wobbly tables out on the sidewalk. Kevin wasn't there. "Alicia! Hallo!" Arthur called into the café. "Two coffees for me and my friend!

"Let me give you a lesson, Randy," said Arthur as he sat down. "About money and class. One difference of the upper class is that we *can* be broke. In fact, you'll be the one paying for this coffee. Now pay attention, because I'm only saying this to improve you. This money of yours may do you more harm than good."

Kevin appeared at Randy's side holding his rolled-up blue-print of the parking lot. "Is he giving you his upper-class–lower-class speech? This is one of his more famous bullshit monologues. He puts on that Kensington drawl, and every other word is ecktually—"

"Ah, Randy, look who's talking about bullshit. The fudge-packer. The turdburglar."

Kevin sat down. "He doesn't do anything anymore. All he's got left is his condescension. Which he's evolved into this elaborate system like Aquinas."

The café girl appeared with their two cups of coffee. "He's lucky I still call him my son."

Kevin leaned confidentially toward Randy. "Now he's going to tell you I'm not his natural son."

"It's true. His mother went through an awful stage when she would fuck anything that moved. I loved that woman, Randy, but she was difficult. As far as I can calculate it was an Italian, who called himself a count, like every other Italian that ever existed, which would account for the low cunning in his character. These things are in the blood. It may sound racist to you, Randy, and I'm aware that racism is not now fashionable, but the older you get the more you can see . . ."

Randy dipped his head to sip evasively. More and more their comedy seemed tinny and vaudevillean—especially this morning, when everything was coming to him muffled by an illogical dreamy sensation of liberty that went along with his nearing conviction.

"Are you going to go back to the old country with him?" Kevin said. "He's not like this when he's in his natural element. And he's happier out-of-doors. No doubt you'd take little walking tours of the countryside. In the pouring rain. He brings along a stick to strike down small mammals."

"Don't listen to him, Randy."

"It's true. He sees himself as some sort of ecologist . . . "

Randy realized he would go immediately to visit Arthur in England, and he would bring Cindy. He could still recover her. They would have to leave now—maybe today—before Ludex had a chance to find evidence of a "crime." In a red Ferrari, he would rescue her from her school and from her mother. It wasn't too late. He asked Arthur, "When are you going back?"

"Tomorrow morning." Arthur reached across the table to take Randy's wrist in an old man's iron pinch. "Just tell me: Once he gets this parking lot all the way to Dallas, how many art lovers are going to travel there just to look at it?"

"Plenty of people," said Randy, captured.

Kevin said, "Well, actually, Randy, it won't be assembled."

"It won't?"

"No, the gallery bought it, but the real owner is E. F. Hutton. It's complicated," said Kevin, reaching over to lift his father's coffee and take a sip—an incursion that Arthur didn't protest at all, or even seem to notice. "It's a tax write-off apparently for an investor that E. F. Hutton is representing. But the investor wants it to appreciate in value, so for a few years it will be in storage in the museum vault."

Arthur leaned forward rapping the tabletop. "So nobody will even be able to look at the damn thing!" He threw himself back in his chair and started crowing silently.

Kevin spoke in anger to Randy so that the words would rebound off him to the old man: "Look! It's a particular parking lot! It's a parking lot!"

"He's such a charlatan," Arthur moaned. "All these pieces of cement will be sitting in the dark growing more and more valuable . . ."

Kevin clapped his hands once in air. "It's not art! It's a parking lot."

"You can't talk to him when he gets like this."

His thumb probing the numb porcelain landscape of the spark plug in his pocket, a tactile planet revisited, Randy had receded deep into thought behind a glazed expression: he could probably get passports for himself and Cindy within twenty-four hours. There must be a way to quicken the process. If necessary, they could stay in a London hotel for a few days, until Arthur was settled again in the country. And he would have to talk to Dan McBride, to be sure he wasn't legally bound to stay in this country while the investigation was going on. Airplane tickets would be easy to get. And packing would be easy. He most relished the actual elopement, the scene itself, picking up Cindy at Mary's tract house in the red Ferrari neither of them knew about yet. It was a quick rush of ancient anger that made him stand up, saying "I'll be back in a minute. I've got to make a phone call."

There was a phone booth in the gas station on the other side of the street, across the demolished parking lot which he trotted over gingerly, avoiding stepping on the edges. Perhaps that had been an abrupt way to leave the table. But Arthur and Kevin, who still knew nothing of his predicament, must have come to ignore, by now, inexplicably odd behavior in him. They seemed to accept him uncritically, their vision too obstructed by the in-looking squint of their own self-dramatization. He dialed directory information to get the number of the People's Attorney in Berkeley. Finally Judy, the long-haired serious Berkeley girl who occupied the front desk, put him through to Dan.

"Hi, Dan. Two things. First of all—"

"Wait, Randy," said Dan. "Are you calling from home?"

"No, a phone booth."

"Listen, I've been trying to get you. They found this person Bim Auctor."

"They did?"

"Yeah, I just talked to Frank Hodges this morning. Ludex is very efficient. I have some notes."

"Where is he?"

"The full name is Archibald Auctor," said Dan. "I've got it all written down somewhere here." Randy could hear him groping through his drawer, pinching the many pieces of stiff, pimpled paper he had run through his braillewriter.

"Where is he?"

"First of all, he was crazy. Here, I found it."

"*Was?*"

He was dead. Randy's intuition had told him all along that Bim was dead, but now the fact, replacing the idea, was harder than he'd expected. He faced the cleaving wall of the phone booth with a sense of abruptly halted momentum.

"Yeah, he died of blood poisoning, way last April. But he was crazy. That's the crucial legal fact. He was totally crazy. They've decided they'll never figure out what he intended to do with the money, because he was too totally out-there. Apparently even his computer hard disk is encoded in some gibberish of his own invention, like Leonardo DaVinci, which they've given up trying to decode. In fact, boy, was *he* a Renaissance man! Did you have any idea how creepy he was? Apparently Archibald Auctor died of blood poisoning almost a year ago. And get this. He was a plastic surgeon, but he hadn't gone to medical school. The State Board of Medical Quality Assurance was really the first lead they had, after the car; because apparently he was what they call a 'cookbook surgeon'—that is, a guy who just *likes* incisions and blood and so he reads up in libraries and sets up a practice of his own. They said at the Medical Quality Board there are lots of guys like this, and they can go undetected for years. Because some of them are pretty good, and they've got satisfied patients. In fact, this guy was supposedly one of the most respected cosmetic surgeons in Marin County. Under another name. They wouldn't give me his alias . . . "

There was a click and a moment of silent vacuum on the phone. Then an operator's prerecorded voice said, "Your first three minutes are up." The close pane of silence was smudged by his own breath. He was all alone now. While, with a rattle and a ding, the phone digested his quarter, he heard Dan saying, "Are you there?"

"Yeah, I'm here. How did he die?"

"I just told you. He got blood poisoning. They found him lying in bed in his house. But here's another odd detail . . ."

"Where's his house?"

"In Marin somewhere. But listen, here's another odd detail. His body wasn't discovered for a long time because it didn't decay. He must have led a healthy life. His corpse was completely uncorrupted after all these months. Apparently he was a health nut. His cupboards were full of squirrel food, and he went running every day with a surgical mask. That's what his neighbors said. Never without his surgical mask. Did you know how strange he was? Apparently he had formaldehyde jars around the house of his favorite experiments. Hodges says it was like little jars of monsters. So he actually died of an infected fingernail. The coroner says it was just an ordinary staph infection that traveled up and got onto the valves of his heart. Which, you'd think, he could have taken care of, because he had a D.E.A. number to prescribe drugs for his patients. The Medical Quality Assurance guy I talked to said the Drug Enforcement Administration assigns each physician his own number, so a cookbook doctor has to make up his own. . . .

"And, what else . . . They've given up on decoding his hard disk, and they're just calling him crazy, which is a break for you. And the finger infection is called a paranicia; I'm not sure I got the word right; apparently it's the most ordinary infection in the world—like when your cuticle gets red. And what else. He was very rich but died intestate, which means all his money will go to the state after some period. And there's also some information about how he made the actual twenties. But it's sketchy."

"Do they think it's counterfeit?"

"Well, everything was on his computer in this uncrackable

insane code. But they were able to track down some warehouse space in the South Bay that he was renting under an assumed name. And they found clues there, just clues, which make them think they know how he made the money—more or less. But it's nothing they can bring into court."

"It's really counterfeit?" said Randy.

"Okay, I'll tell you what they told me. They think it was lasers. Because the new renters in the warehouse have cleared everything out. There were just a few things in a closet. Everything else was literally hauled off as junk. But they think it was argon lasers. The place was wired for the sort of voltage you'd need. And they found some sort of lens which focuses laser beams to microscopic smallness. The laser would etch the image of the bill on plates, which they think weren't steel plates like at the mint, but some sort of plastic which holds ink exactly like steel."

"Lasers."

"Computer-driven lasers. Right. They think he would take a photograph of a real twenty-dollar bill with some sort of camera that didn't create any lens distortion. Because there were these trestles on the floor for the bellows of a big camera. He'd photograph it, blow it up huge, and scan it. He'd blow up the image to wall-size, like fifteen feet tall and thirty feet across. And then he'd scan it with this system—they called it a 'flying spot' scanner. Supposedly, the reproduction was so perfect he even captured every microscopic flaw in the engravings. Then a computer would reconstruct the bill on a smaller scale using the information from the scan of the huge bill. And then it would etch the plate with a laser beam. Because one thing they did find was a kind of table. They called it a coherent isolation table. It has pneumatic air-filled legs, or oil-filled legs, or something—so it can't possibly jiggle. Like when a truck goes past. They figured the table alone must have cost him twenty thousand dollars."

"Bim had resources," said Randy.

"Yeah, the lenses alone were probably another ten thousand. It's the kind of laser they use for cutting chromosomes and gene splicing. I mean, Randy, this is precise. They measure the depth of the etch in angstroms. They think he must have picked up the technology because of his medical experience. It's mostly surgical technology. They use these for surgery on capillaries—"

"What about the paper?" said Randy.

"The theory with that is, he was bleaching the ink out of one-dollar bills to get the paper, and then printing higher denominations on it."

"Can you do that?"

"I suppose so. Sodium sulfate is a highly unstable bleachy chemical Hodges mentioned. You have to freeze-dry it or something. That's why they think it was sodium sulfate, because they found some special canisters or something for freeze-drying it. They actually brought somebody out here from the Institute of Paper Chemistry in Wisconsin. I think they've had about thirty people on this, but not one of them was told the whole story."

Randy imagined a needle of ruby light burning a portrait into a plastic surface, a wisp of smoke curling away like a wood shaving. Bim must have devoted years to the research.

"Oh, and another thing," said Dan. "This is more in the circumstantial area. The warehouse was fitted out with what they call a 'clean-room' system. It's this elaborate ventilation apparatus that keeps dust out, with air-locks in the doors.

Because it's a delicate process. Also, the laser etching has to take place in some sort of buffer gas. I don't know what Hodges meant by that. I've got 'halide gas' written down here."

"How did he die?" said Randy. He wanted to see the house. See the place where Bim had lived and worked. See where he ate and slept. See where he died.

"Blood poisoning, Randy. I told you."

"How do they know? You can't just die of blood poisoning."

"The coroner was able to deduce it. I suppose he found staphylococcus bacteria on the heart. If your white blood cells don't fight it off, it runs around in your blood. But look, Randy, let's not waste time. This changes our strategy somewhat, because now is when they'll get a search warrant and impound everything."

"And he looked good? He wasn't all rotten?"

"Randy, do you realize what this means?"

"Am I charged with a crime yet? Because I want to take a trip to England."

"Why?"

"I feel like it. Just for a week or two. Am I legally stuck here?"

"Randy, you can't go anywhere now."

"I'll give you the address where I can be reached in England."

"Are you aware of what this means? United States currency can now be perfectly reproduced. This makes Bim Auctor a government unto himself."

"He's dead."

"That's just a technicality. He's not dead in the State Department's mind. Or the *idea* of Bim Auctor isn't dead. This is serious, Randy. They knew this would happen someday, but they're just not ready for it. They'll take you into custody as soon as they can find you. If you go home now, this very minute, you might find Ludex's people there. I mean, it's possible. They might even arrest me, simply because I know about it. Do you know what money *is?*"

"Dan, this is something I just have to do. You're my lawyer."

"No, wait, Randy—"

"I'll send you my address."

He hung up and walked away from the phone: walking out into a world absented of Bim. Staph bacteria like microscopic milky caviar clung to every ordinary surface; but Bim Auctor had pricked his finger and died of it. He was "crazy"; Randy pictured the magnetic nap of the computer hard disk swarming with the language of chaos unintelligible to the Secret Service's computer experts. Bim was "crazy." That was a "crucial legal fact."

The phone started to ring—the operator would want more money—so he started back to the phone booth, then stopped and turned to walk away again.

Then on second thought he stopped and ran back to the phone. A recorded voice was saying, "Please deposit—sixty—five—cents."

He held the phone on a twisted shoulder, his hand burrowing deep in his jeans pocket, down beneath the spark plug, to find three more quarters. It would be necessary to stop at home. But he could go straight from there to Terra Linda to find Cindy. And then to the passport office. Where, with enough money, he could persuade them to issue passports without the usual bureaucratic delay. There were the big cardboard Sebastiani boxes full of bundled twenties in the closet in the guest bedroom. And there was the separate Safeway bag of cash in the linen closet.

He went to the curb and stood there. Now it was just him

alone. And Cindy. During all the years when she was little, he could always restore her to himself by promising Disneyland; that easily disappointed light would come back into her eyes. For years he kept her unfairly tethered to him by the mere mention of the word *Disneyland*, which yanked her back from the hostile teenage sullenness that had begun to set in for no reason. His own father had taken him to Disneyland when he was young, and it had seemed a fitting thing for him to do with his daughter. But each unkept promise had lowered her value incrementally. Well, now he would do better than Disneyland, he would take her to England. He would get her anything she wanted. The most important thing was that Mary should be at home to witness her daughter's abduction to a better life.

He had to hurry. Where was his red Ferrari? He was a government unto himself. Across the street he dug up the earth at the foot of the oak tree. Dropping to his knees, scooping up the loosened dirt, he gouged and stirred with a twig that happened to be lying there; and when the stick broke he resorted to using his fingernails. At last he slipped the spark plug back into place, covered it over, and stood up to press the soil down with the sole of his shoe, looking around to see that he had not been observed. The Ferrari was parked by the laundromat. He jogged back to the café to tell Arthur and Kevin about his plans, jaywalking nimbly, a fugitive now, shrinking to sly smallness against the expanded, newly geographic dimensions of this mirage, thinking, *Bim, protect me now*.

# 21

The window shades were drawn and the bedroom door was locked. Cindy had disemboweled her Kermit the Frog, releasing all the years' accumulation of suicide notes and ransom demands from the zippered compartment in his rump to spread them out before her on her bed in a small heap like tinder— crumpled or folded many different ways, written on many different kinds of paper, from her old pink "Rainbow Unicorn" stationery to the more recent graph paper, in various stale inks of other semesters—but all in that same perfect floral handwriting, "her" mortal handwriting: carefully laid down, vine-like, each i dotted with a round seed, executed in study halls within the guarding curl of a forearm, and in the shelter of impossibility. Somehow she had outgrown this time of inex-

plicable clotted pleasure, but the evidence of it remained to
be destroyed.

Her mother, who had stopped by to pick up some things,
making drawers bang and hangers jingle in the next room,
didn't know she was home. Cindy was hiding until she left,
saving her the awkwardness of the usual greeting and conversation. After she had gone back to her boyfriend Harry's house,
leaving behind only the diminishing whine of the Porsche engine, Cindy could begin burning the notes one by one in her
wastebasket. To avoid triggering a clang of the bedsprings, she
sat coiled and motionless, listening in the artificial twilight;
the effort of secrecy had invoked the audience who lived hov-
eringly in presumption just outside her peripheral vision, who
came to crowd her solitude more and more lately now that she
was a more serious person. Quietly she crept off the bed and
went to the mirror to check on the progress of a pimple on her
chin, which was the minute circumstance that, in the first
place, had opened the luxury of sadness today. It had developed a white punctuation mark, which she held now between
the expert pinch of thumb and finger permitting herself the
unwise pleasure of expressing the white curd within; and in
the dizzying stillness of held breath she applied the exactly
appropriate pressure. The ointment of unhealth emerged in a
fattening drop. Suddenly feeling light-headed in the mirror's
infinite misted vacuum, she sat down on the floor and closed
her eyes to feel herself rise through applause as through confetti. The white crumb she brushed off against the seam of her
jeans. She had been gaining weight, letting her permanent
grow out, neglecting her grease-fragrant shoe box of makeup.
The constant complex responsibility of being foxy, of turning
heads, of moving at the center of a trembling web of vision,
had grown so irksome, she had begun to find relief in plainness,

getting better grades, giving away her expensive clothes to charity and wearing instead the sort of sexless jeans and virginal sweaters Kim Paschke wears, indulging a new fondness for Milk Duds, an entire box every day after school, the grip of caramel on her molars like sin—and all the while nourishing the new certainty that it's nicer not to be touched at all. There was sure peace in being alone, eating in front of the TV, a cholesterol film on her vision letting her relax. Each day after school, she never quite felt relief until the front door had closed behind her in the empty house and she unbuttoned the top button of her jeans and went to the refrigerator, turning on the TV as she passed, letting her zipper part. She filled the house.

When would her mother leave?

She decided impatiently to burn just one letter now. She had been waiting until her mother was gone because the smoke might drift under the door. Even burning a single letter, there was a risk of being caught.

But more and more these days she felt herself obeying the twitch of perversity. She got a matchbook from her drawer and set the empty metal wastebasket in the center of the floor, and knelt before it with a nice sense of ritual. The first note that came to hand was an early ransom demand, which she uncreased by ironing it under her palm against her thigh. She struck a match, whose flame tasted the edge of the paper, took hold trembling, and began to grow. The absurd words "Place one million dollars in the phone booth by Hagen-Das Ice Cream" turned to weightless gray fringe at the advancing edge of the page. The picture of herself—as if viewed from a camera above, kneeling alone in the dark with her burning note—was so sad, her heart firmed; it was almost a feeling of sexual arousal, the deep tragic feeling of satin sliding on satin; the pleasure of sorrow had set candles in her eyes.

The flame started to throb rhythmically, to leap to dangerous heights, swallowing itself upward. She dropped the final, unburnt corner of the page into the bottom of the wastebasket where, with a last convulsion, it curled into ash. A pleasant toast smell filled the room. She pushed herself up to her feet to find that a horizon of smoke had settled at eye level—which she ducked under to grab the bed and find another note for burning. It had begun to seem urgent, this destroying of the notes she had written with moist palms. She fell against the steep bed imagining herself crawling against weariness in the canyon of the whole world's collected regard, unable to quite reach the heap of precious notes, leaving behind a trail of shining scarlet—the price she had paid. Kim Paschke had popped up and jealously stabbed her. And everyone had seen it. Boulders thwarted her progress. As she writhed toward the goal, she felt again the sliding of satin in her bowels. Her public dying was sexy. The spending of her blood was the purchase of a more perfect beauty in her reaching fingertips, which trembled in light-saturated slow motion as they failed to reach the notes . . .

Then she heard the front door open and swing with exactly the rhythm of her father. It couldn't be anyone else. He who never answered his phone anymore, who never showed up at his apartment in San Anselmo, who had dissolved into rumor. All the feelings came back, of like living in a house with one missing wall but pretending nothing was odd. The front door slammed, with her father's recognizable push. And then, frozen in this new breeze, she heard his voice:

"Cindy?"

She sprang to her feet.

"Hello, Randy." Her mother's voice, in the kitchen, was clearly pitched to indicate that his many months' disappearance was an insult, only gradually to be forgiven, in a long chain of insults that had been passing back and forth over the years. "How have you been?"

"I thought I'd take Cindy on a trip," he said. "Is she here?" His footsteps were sounding on the kitchen floor, near the window: he was looking out into the back yard.

"What sort of trip?"

"I just want to take her out of school for a week or two. Go to Europe."

"Oh, Randy," she said.

Cindy knew immediately that her mother wouldn't let her go. Europe was a shining mist that would vanish on approach. A kind of familiar stage fright came back as she began to face the duty of going out there.

"Anything to eat?" said her father's voice.

"Randy, wait a minute. Hold still. What kind of trip? Here. Here's corn chips."

"Europe. England." The crunch of Fritos. "Just for a week or two."

"Would you please just stand still for a minute, Randy?" said her mother. "I can never talk to you."

"Actually, I'm in a bit of a hurry." His footsteps were moving out into the living room.

"This charming-rogue routine worked when you were younger."

"Charming Rogue, what is that? Is that one of the nine basic male types in some book you've been reading on Games Men Play? Is there also the Sexy Stud? And the Serious Sam?"

"Randy, I won't communicate with you when you're like this."

"I see you put in new carpeting."

"Please just be here with me. Can you do that? You just

want to take her out of school on the spur of the moment and go to Europe? How do you intend to pay for it? Where do you intend to stay in Europe? Have you thought this out? Where did you get the money, for instance?"

"Oh, you'd be surprised, Mary. I've been getting pretty lucky. It's the usual combination of luck and skill."

Cindy raised the blinds admitting a chute of sunlight, and she opened the window to let the smoke out. The suicide notes, still heaped on the bed, she stuffed back into Kermit's rump while he smirked blissfully. In the mirror, her face was pale; she patted her cheeks and blew into her cupped hands. Her father would notice that she'd gained weight. She lay back on the bed to put drops in her eyes that were supposed to dissolve the threads of red; and, blinking blindly, she got up and went to her shoe box to find some powder and a little bit of blush.

She could hear her father through the door, his voice rising as he moved farther into the living room: "I suppose she's at the Paschkes'?"

"Randy, I'm going to have to actually assert my custody rights. Randy? Is your soul in the room? I'm telling you right now that she can't go, because I say so and I'm her mother and I have custody. She's in school. Do you know how easy it is for you to destroy everything I've built up? Just by being this charming asshole who comes visiting every once in a while?"

"Did you win this couch on a game show?"

"Randy, pay attention. Cindy isn't going anywhere."

She put on a sweater, and she retousled her hair and returned to her door to gently slide the bolt, and then waited listening for the right moment to enter the living room yawning casually.

But she heard only a prolonged silence. For a long moment

there came no sound from the living room, where the air seemed suddenly to be thinning.

Finally, her mother said, "Randy?"

"Interesting article," said her father's voice—apparently he was flipping through a magazine.

"Randy, I'm her mother." How soft was her new tone! "All these years I've been here authentically. You don't understand this. You think this is all just bullshit from my est training. But love is *being* here, Randy. Love isn't showing up every once in a while to act generous. Love isn't supposed to be fun or nice. It's a fact, it's like eating and sleeping and going to the bathroom. I've *been* here."

With every word her mother was losing power: Randy's invincible coolness made all her desperation bead up around him. Her mother's idea of love was so sticky; all these years of "sharing" in this house, of menstrual periods, and notes describing how to fix dinner, and the pressure to recount what had happened on a date; the sadness of hearing cars turn distant corners on summer nights.

Randy said, "You know all about love, don't you?"

After a moment, her mother said, "I'm sorry." Then: "Things are things."

"Exactly. Things are things. And nothing is nothing."

"I'm sorry," her mother said again.

"You've got all the words. That's what you've got, Mary. When the real thing disappears, words appear."

"Do you have to make things so hard?"

" 'Authentic'!" He almost coughed it. Cindy realized this trip to Europe might be actual.

After a long silence, her mother said firmly, "Randy."

Saying his name made him disappear, was Cindy's thought—

as if, entering the kitchen now, she would find him magically
banished. Her fingers, deep in her jeans pockets, had discovered a pill of thread at the bottom of each pocket, which she'd
been rolling and pinching: she realized that, in her tension,
her shoulders had risen to a weird arch.

It was time for her to enter the room, in this lull. She was
the agent of their rescue. She relaxed her winged shoulders,
opened the door and shuffled out into the living room, closing
the door to keep the levitating mattress of smoke inside, and
rubbing her eyes with her wrists as if she'd just awakened from
a nap—which might also excuse their redness.

"Cindy!" said her mother.

"Hi, Mom. Hey, hi, Dad!" She seemed surprised.

"You're home. We thought you were out someplace."

Randy, sitting on the couch, set aside the magazine in his
hands and opened his arms in embrace. "Whoa!" he said with
a staggering expanse of his arms, to indicate he liked 'em fat;
which he probably thought was a cheery way to greet her. As
always babyish again in his presence, she went through the
necessary ceremony of landing in his lap and letting him set
the harsh brand of a daddy's kiss on her cheek. Was the money
counterfeit or not?

"Want to go to England, honey?" he said.

"Really?" She wriggled around to look at him. "When?"

"No, Randy," said her mother.

"Now. Right this minute."

"Randy, I'm putting my foot down."

Her father whispered in her ear, "We can get you a passport
in three hours. Run and pack a few things. But don't pack
much, because we'll want to buy clothes when we get there."

"Randy!" said her mother. "She's in the middle of a se-
mester. I think there's something wrong with you."

He went on whispering, "We can buy anything you want when we get there."

"I'm calling the police," said her mother, and Cindy knew Randy had won.

"Mom," she said, in the two tones of exasperation.

"Cindy, he can't afford a trip to England. There's something totally inauthentic about this."

"Mom, vacation is soon."

He stood up, dumping her off his lap. "Skip the packing, Cin. Let's leave now. Just grab essential things." He turned to Mary. "I'm the girl's father."

"I'm not joking, Randy."

Cindy's snug heart swelled as she was tugged toward the front door, the tattoo of her father's kiss on her skin. He was a criminal. The expanding glamour of it suddenly became fearsome. As if rising through layers of a dream, the idea of going to Europe began to seem wrong.

"Randy, where in the world did you get that car? Is that your car?"

A low-slung red sports car stood out front. "Dad!" She was scared. She didn't want to go.

"I'll explain it all, Cin," he said. "Let's get out of here. She really is going to call the police."

"Randy, wait a minute," said her mother. "What is going on?"

He hustled her around to the passenger side, and she got into a low flat seat that made her recline uncomfortably. This was one of those hundred-thousand-dollar cars. He said, "You don't happen to have a pen in your back pocket, do you? That's how leather upholstery gets ruined."

"Randy," her mother was saying from the doorstep. Fear had come into her voice, which Cindy had never heard before. "Randy, come on."

He got into the driver's side. "So long, Mary. Have fun with your magazines."

"My magazines!"

He started the engine, and the dashboard radio began to play rock and roll at top volume. Her mother ran inside and the car pulled away with a lurch. The neighborhood tore past. She was pinned back to the seat by the struggling weight of her heart. The loud music of KRQR on the radio united them by isolating them. Now she was as guilty as he. But this would somehow give her new poise. As casually as if she owned the car, she turned down the volume on the radio.

"Mom is such a bitch," she said. It was a kind of test she was throwing out; but of what?

"Is she?" he said, faintly in distraction, wrestling the steering wheel. She took a risk and went straight to the point.

"So tell me, Dad. I'm curious. Is it really counterfeit?" Her heart beat.

He looked across at her, then looked back to the road as he swung out onto Freitas Parkway with a screech of tires.

"Where did you hear anything about counterfeit?"

"It is, isn't it." The sensation was of the passage of power from her mother to herself, to her own narrow shoulders. She stretched her spine against the seat and tried to look relaxed.

He said, "Cindy, it's a long and complicated story, and I promise to tell you the whole thing. But right now we have to get some passports and book a flight. Your mother really will report you as kidnapped. I know her. But I promise I'll explain the whole thing." He looked over at her again. "Okay?"

"Fine. I trust you," she said.

He looked at her.

"Cindy, I want to stop at the Paschkes' for a minute, and I

want you to stay in the car. Is that clear? Under no circumstances can you tell Kim we're going on a trip."

Yes, of course she would tell Kim. It was perfect. The possibility of being glimpsed by somebody from school faded as they got onto the freeway; the flat low car sped through the yellow stoplight by Northgate II and gouged a paring curve out of the entrance ramp.

He said, "Cindy, how do you know about the money?"

"It's right there in the Paschkes'. But don't worry, Dad, I'm proud of you."

He glanced at her. "How did you get the idea it's counterfeit?"

"Everybody knows it's counterfeit, Dad."

"What do you mean 'everybody'? Who's 'everybody'?" The car was slowing.

She was saying the wrong thing.

"Everybody at school. But it's cool, Dad. You're famous. You're a legend."

"At Terra Linda?" The car kept slowing down. "There's a group of kids at T.L. walking around saying I'm a counterfeiter?"

"They can keep a secret." She had said the wrong thing, and now she was ruining her chances.

"Who's 'everybody'?"

"Dad, don't worry. They won't say anything." He had already begun to find her more trouble than she was worth. He could easily drop her off in disgust at the next exit.

But the car sped up again. He began to jam impatiently from lane to lane among the slower drivers.

"I'm a legend," he said to himself with fear.

# 22

At midnight on the night of the month's-end deadline, while Laura slept on her imperturbable pregnancy, Wayne lifted a beer alone in his garage in dark toast to his shortcomings; and the following day, the first day of the month, he took the boxes of coins to a collectors' shop on Fourth Street. The dealer, seeing the logo on the boxes, said right away, "Uh-oh, Marketrend, right? I can only buy a couple of those, my friend. And I won't be able to offer near what you're expecting." But Wayne was weakened enough to be stubborn, and the dealer finally agreed to take the whole pile of coins for a lump sum of seven hundred dollars.

Which wasn't enough for rent. So he had made a deal with his landlord to paint the exterior in exchange for two months' rent, a clever barter agreement which the landlord was willing

to record falsely on his books, though the cleverness was probably all on the part of the landlord, who would gain some
inscrutable tax advantage. It was just another example of being
on the wrong side of the money river. When his RBV tally,
on the last day of the Marketrend Month, was still way below
goal, he spent the final hours at his workbench not even trying
to make any calls, staying at his desk merely to preside offi-
cially over the last moments. Amidst the cigarette smoke, the
mystic certainty kept coming back: that it was his genes, not
Laura's, which contained the joke. And in painful spasms of
clairvoyance he foreknew that, when the amniocentesis nurses
drew the fluid from Laura's belly into a syringe and they examined the DNA under shimmering granular magnification,
they would find in the microscopic bracelets, just as in Kim's,
the same broken facets, decayed links. And then there would
be the decision about whether to go ahead with the pregnancy,
while on lawns all over Marin County realtors' pickets were
being driven into the turf and Wayne was reduced to working
on his own house.

So on Friday night he bought eight gallons of latex at the
True Value by Shakey's. And on Saturday morning he got up
and started smoking cigarettes at his desk in the garage, pon-
dering the eight cans on the floor. But even painting the exterior
felt like an evasion, for the very house itself was imperiled by
Randy's ever-present fissionable crate. Nothing could be done
wholeheartedly until it should leave the garage. Twice when
Laura was at work and he was home alone with it, he had been
drawn to break the pink seal and lift the lid to see the money,
as if only to scare himself, and then he'd replaced the seal
with an identical one—from a separate package he had bought
himself and kept in his tool box, not wanting Laura to notice
that another seal was missing from the original package in her

drawer. Laura left for work each morning now with irony—with a glance toward the kitchen wall that separated them from the crate. It had made everything undecidable, meaningless. She had taken it upon herself to place a classified ad in the *Independent-Journal* offering Wayne's services as a house-painter—a hopeless gesture in these times when even the *legitimate* contractors were laying off crew. But even if he got some work, the reality of ten dollars an hour would be rendered merely conjectural by the unreality of two million artificial dollars in his garage. Kneeling over the paint can, he felt himself a marionette—sighed and stood up. He wanted another cigarette.

Instead of smoking, he found an old windshield-wiper blade from the Volkswagen Laura had once owned, and he used it to stir the paint. The liquid revolved like batter beneath the limp rubber blade, betraying no inconsistencies; so he laid the color-glazed blade aglow in the bottomless bushel basket with the baton and hammer handle and doll's-arm. He tipped some of the paint into a smaller bucket, releasing the healing smell of fresh latex.

Outside, the sorrow of Terra Linda sunshine made him squint. The south wall, dusted now by the pollen of the first oblique sunlight, had needed no scraping or priming. His old wooden A-frame ladder, whose steps' edges had been softened over the years by the polishing force of familiarity, was propped against the wall beside Kim's bedroom window—from which the sound of her television had begun to issue:

"In those days, vast herds of trilobites foraged on the ocean floor."

Having shaken the ladder until it felt staunch, he mounted it, replacing the lost ache of the ladder-rung in his instep; and the remembered sensation of work came flowing back—except that now, painting his own rented house while everything in his life had gone systematically to ruin, work didn't feel productive: his Midas touch would meticulously destroy the old house, erase it. He had perfectly reversed Fortinbras Armstrong's wisdom and become a genius of negation, a magician of self-defeat: he dipped the mink-soft bristles of his brush into the golden paint referred to in the hardware store as Harvest Wheat. Holding the brush in his preferred pencil-grip, he set the initial dab of golden salve on the upper-left-hand corner of the wall, which for years had been an unpleasant parched green.

There was always, for Wayne, an untouchable miracle in this moment when the new color began to spread under his urging brush: there was a metaphysical mystery in the borderline between the two colors, which he kept tapping with his brush to move it: things changed identity beneath his gestures. As he worked the border moved out and down, toward the frame of Kim's bedroom window, and a golden house began to manifest itself where once had been a ghost of ashen green. Soon he was painting in long horizontal strokes in the wet glare, sensing the cover by the amount of drag on the brush. A good painter could work just as well if he were blind; it's how the surface *feels* under the moving brush. Patches of resistance cry out like eczema.

There was a small commotion within the house. Someone had arrived at the front door.

Wayne stopped painting, set his brush on the rim of the bucket, and turned his Harvest Wheat–saturated gaze toward the spectral back door, in fear that Buddy should come walking out. Ever since the midnight of his failure, he had lived in fear that Buddy would come over to tell him that all was not lost, there was still hope, something could still be worked out, he might still make Head Broker . . .

But then he heard Cindy Potts arriving in Kim's bedroom, and he returned to his golden wall with a sneaky reprieve—to recover the ache in his uplifted arms, the familiar seraphic sensation of being suspended silently above ground and gesturing over the transformation of his house. Buddy would never call. Buddy was just as embarrassed by Wayne's failure as Wayne himself was.

Cindy's loud voice said, "Guess what. I'm going to England."

"Why? Jeez!"

"I'm working on my modeling career. The good agencies just aren't here. Actually we're in kind of a hurry. Because, my God!"

"Are you kidding?" said Kim.

He began actively to eavesdrop without shame. A certain amount of this might be the product of Cindy's vivid imagination, but not all of it.

"Because we might even leave sometime today maybe. And I don't even have anything like a portfolio. We're going to get our passports really fast, because usually it takes weeks. Usually it's an awful drag."

"Jeez, Cindy," said Kim, still incredulous. Wayne felt a surge of love for his daughter, who had inherited the Paschke gullibility, the Paschke generosity in being habitually surpassed.

"That's where the good agencies are, there and New York. And I'm going to go to one of those English private schools."

"Cindy!"

"My dad is insane."

Wayne heard Laura's voice calling him. He scrambled as

quietly as possible down from his ladder—reaching the ground before she had time to come out into the back yard. He trotted away from the window toward the kitchen door: "Yes? What?"

"Randy's here," said Laura. "I'd better let him tell you."

She preceded him into the house. Randy was standing just inside in the garage, where Laura gestured.

"Okay," he whispered when Wayne came in.

Laura closed the door. The three of them were standing in the near-darkness. She turned on the hanging lightbulb with its foil pie-tin reflector.

Randy said, "It happened just like I said. The Secret Service truly can't tell the difference. But that doesn't mean I'm safe. In fact, it's gotten weirder. So now it's getting like it's every man for himself."

"Where did Kim and Cindy go?"

"In her room."

Randy went on, "Because this is the first time anybody has had the technology to make perfect money. Like for example, if we don't keep this a total secret, you could have the K.G.B. snooping around here."

"The K.G.B.!"

"The dollar is everything, Wayne. The whole world economy depends on the dollar."

"Randy, wait a minute. Are you . . . For instance, are you wanted by the police?"

"No. At least not yet. I'm going to England for a couple of weeks."

"England," said Laura. "Why are you going to England?"

"Look, I don't have much time. Cindy and I are leaving tonight. Let me just explain this to you. You can't say anything to anybody about the crate. And you can't move it or do anything to it. Just leave it here and don't fool with it. The reason

I'm telling you this is so you can protect yourselves. If I go to jail—"

Wayne said, "Randy, the K.G.B. is the *Russian* police."

"Well, okay, whatever. I'm giving you an example. The counterfeit is genuine. Do you get it?" He looked back and forth between Wayne and Laura, waiting for the idea to sink in. The whole thing affected Wayne like the onset of flu with a creeping sensation in his spine.

"Look," said Randy, "money is a certain kind of paper and a certain kind of ink with a certain kind of design. This money has all that perfectly. So it's legally not a counterfeit. This is the whole problem. The counterfeit isn't a counterfeit. Legally."

"Randy, you can't duplicate the paper. It's impossible."

"No, Wayne. Sometime I'll tell you the whole story."

"When is this crate leaving our garage?"

"Well, here's the thing," said Randy. "Somehow all the kids at T.L. know about this."

"No," said Laura.

"Don't ask me how. Probably even Kim knows about it. I'm a hero. I'm Robin Hood."

"Did you ask Cindy if Kim knows? Obviously it's important to us if Kim knows."

"No. But kids always have rumors, right? Like, remember the rumor that there were spider webs in Double Bubble? Nobody listens to kids. Or 'Paul Is Dead.' Remember 'Paul Is Dead'? Or 'Smoking Bananas Will Get You High'?"

Laura turned to Wayne: "Could they sneak in here? And open the crate?"

Randy started patting the workbench for emphasis, saying, "So but you can't mention this to anybody, even Kim. If the police ever do get to this crate, I'll take the total blame. I'll say I lied to you, and you thought it was full of pots and pans."

Laura whispered, "You know, if we put a padlock on these doors, that will be suspicious behavior. They'll say, 'Why did you just happen to buy these padlocks *then?*' "

Wayne was certain that Kim suspected him of a crime. And he couldn't bring it up with her. Was that possible? That only pretense could keep them all innocent?

Randy said, "Because if we move the crate now, or do anything to it, it will look suspicious. You guys will simply have to ride this out."

Laura's eyes slid away into a future distance and her mouth hardened in an expression which, Wayne knew, meant that she'd decided Randy was right.

Randy said, "You can't imagine how sorry I am, you guys. You're my oldest, best friends. I didn't mean this to get crazy like this. The whole story is so unbelievable. I'll tell you sometime."

He looked back and forth between them, then turned away and sauntered aimlessly around the heaped work table toward the far recesses of the garage, hands in pockets.

Wayne said, "I don't want to have to be keeping this a secret from Kim."

Laura said, "Randy, what is this rumor the kids have?"

Randy, distracted by the warped dartboard and the automobile bumper hanging from the rafters, said, "Uh, hm?"

"What is the rumor?" said Laura. "What exactly are they saying?"

Randy reached out to touch Wayne's mother's old Waring blender, which contained the snakeskin from their Sacramento trip with Kim and the old bottlecaps from his brother's collection. "Oh, the rumor basically is that I'm a counterfeiter, and that you guys have a box of money. That's the extent of it. Although there are additional things, like I have a castle in France . . ." He flipped the switch on the blender—which of course didn't grind up the contents; it hadn't worked in twenty years.

Wayne started to resent his prodding around. "Well, look, Randy," he said, trying to divert his attention. "This crate has got to get out of here soon. Why can't you just take it now? This minute. I mean, how long will this continue to go on?"

Randy had turned his back. "You've got a hell of a lot of stuff, Wayne," he said.

"What is happening with your lawyer? Randy?"

Randy said, "What do you need all this stuff for?" He was rotating slowly.

"You've been in here before."

"Yeah, but . . ." He peered into the grime-frosted terrarium in which the tone arm from a childhood record player lay amidst Styrofoam peanuts. "I guess all this might come in handy someday." He tapped on the glass as if to wake a sleeping animal.

"Randy," said Laura in a sharper tone, "this crate is totally messing up our lives."

"Okay," said Randy, focusing his mind, "I'll be back from England in a couple of weeks, and by then the State Department will know what to do with me. But all we have to do is wait. Everything will work out fine if we just leave this crate here." He trailed off, plucking tentatively at the tablecloth that covered the engine block, disturbing the lie of Wayne's father's old hammer. "You've got a hell of a lot of stuff, Wayne."

Wayne said, "I don't understand how they can let you take a trip. You can't go anywhere now."

"I haven't enjoyed any of this money, Wayne. Think of the pussy! Excuse me, Laura, but Wayne, think of the girls!"

Wayne flicked his eyes toward his wife, who had robbed him of all that, who had kept him a nice guy. A man of greater self-esteem wouldn't need to be such a nice guy all the time. His inability to have an affair with that girl in Rumplestiltskins, his cowardice with money, it was all part of a pattern.

Cindy's voice came from the kitchen: "Hey, where'd everybody go?"

"Uh-oh," said Randy. "She can't see me in here. I have to sneak out the back. Let her wander around a little bit, and then tell her I'm waiting out front." He was edging out the far door.

"Wait, Randy," said Laura. "You've got to personally just get this thing out of here."

He smiled and shrugged.

"Randy, come back here."

"Bon voyage," he said and vanished.

# 23

Cindy whispered, "It's me," when her mother answered the phone.

"Well, Cindy Potts! Where are you calling from?" A stagily *bounced* tone in her mother's voice: her boyfriend was there in the room with her.

"I'm in a phone booth."

"What continent are you on now, world traveler?"

"Mom, I'm right in San Rafael. We haven't left yet. But the reason I'm calling is I just phoned the Missing Children Hotline and I'm not listed . . ."

"Where's your father?"

"He's around somewhere. Mom, would you listen?"

"Okay, what's the Missing Children Hotline."

"You know. It's the toll-free number, where it's, like, 'HAVE YOU SEEN THIS CHILD.' "

"You're not listed? Cindy, did you *expect* to be listed?"

"They do it automatically when you're abducted. That's what they said."

"Oh, Cindy, honey, listen. I thought about it a lot, and I talked it over with Harry, and I decided I was being selfish. I actually had a fairly hairy encounter with myself about it. We decided you should *be* with your father. Enjoy yourself. Go to England. Partly I was just *jealous* because I'd like to go to England myself. But Harry is so marvelous, he's just the most patient thing ever. He's here right now. Actually, we were just about to go out."

"Well, but Mom," Cindy went on, climbing against a steep swell. "All I wanted to say was *don't* list me with the Missing Children Hotline. I have the number here, because they said only the mom can have the child's listing taken off. Do you have a pencil?"

"Honey, I didn't call to report you."

"Yeah, but sometimes the police do it automatically."

"I didn't call the police."

"You didn't? You said you were going to call the police."

"Honey, weren't you listening just now? I think it's fine for you to develop a relationship with your dad. It will be good for both of you. And *England?*"

"Yeah, but don't you think it's a little sudden? Suddenly he's just going to England? I mean, *Mom* . . ."

"Yes, which is partly what I was jealous of. But it would be a lot healthier for me to congratulate him on his prosperity. That's the little bit of growing up I've done on this. I have to acknowledge that you get opportunities I don't get, which is fine; and that you have to start having some kind of relationship with your father, which is also fine, even though I may not get perfect integrity from him. And also, we just have to face that in this society an unmarried man is freer to get to prosperity. He's a single man on his own, Cin, which is how he can buy you scooters and take you to England."

"Mom, you *said*."

"I said what?"

"You said you were going to call the police."

"I know I said, honey. But that was a moment of emotion. As soon as you two left, I started thinking. The minute you guys drove away, I knew."

"Mom!" Cindy, standing in the public phone booth, suddenly felt anger flare out from her flesh, justified by the expensive new dress she was wearing, which she had just bought, and which her mother couldn't see—but which, kept secret from her mother, suddenly became the visible sign of this new feeling that had come over her life: pride and guilt, oddly combined. She had always been guilty of superiority, which perhaps now she might begin just to acknowledge shamelessly. Now that this glamour had come to her, in the form of pre-destined good luck, she felt numbed by it, actually her skin numbed by it, as if she were an actress on television bathed in unnaturally bright light. She had always been lifted by a saving, destructive selfishness.

"What," said her mother, "don't you want to go? Think of the cultural advantages, honey."

"No, Mom, it's just weird. It's pretty sudden." But she knew even as she spoke that her queasiness was unreasonable; her mother lived in an inaccessible world of reason and light—all the more inaccessible to *her* now that she had been finally spoiled by good luck. She gave her hair a bitchy shake and, while her mother went on talking predictably, she looked around with impatience at the Corte Madera Shopping Center, through the cloudy, graffiti-scrubbed glass of the phone booth. The narrow cut of this dress would be an incentive to weight loss.

". . . Cindy, you've only got a week of school before vacation. And in any case, going to England would be much *better* of an education."

"This week just *happens* to be final exams. If you miss finals you don't get credit for the whole course."

"I'll write a note. They'll let you take a makeup, I'm sure. Teachers are reasonable people, even if they *are* grown-ups. They'll understand. They know you're only young once. Which is something *you* seem to forget. I mean, my God, Cin, you're such a little old lady. You make everything into such a big deal. Lighten up. Start to have a little fun. Be young and carefree. Okay? Harry and I have to go now, hon."

"Mom, can you just write down the Hotline number? Just in case?"

"Okay. Then I'm going."

"Do you have a pencil?"

"Yes."

"It's 1-800-843-5678."

"Okay, now have a good trip, honey. And honey? Is that all?"

"Yes, Mom."

"Because I'm serious, you should tell me everything you feel. You know my philosophy on this. This is an area with me. I don't want it ever said that I wasn't open to communication. I mean, isn't it nice to be going to Europe? And getting to know your dad? Aren't you excited? Let's have a little communication here."

"Yes." Her mother was right, of course, but this angry clog she felt in her mind was incommunicable, illogical, a kind of preexistent headache of selfishness she couldn't possibly explain.

"If you have anything to say, please feel free, any time. As long as the lines of communication are open, everything is okay."

"Yes, Mom, I will."

"Okay, then. Harry says hello. Bye, love."

"Bye."

# 24

England turned out to be so boring that when he got a telegram from Dan McBride after only two days telling him to return for a meeting at Stanford, he was glad to cut the trip short. He and Cindy had done nothing but sleep and watch TV for one dim, hostile day in a London motel, both sickened by the unfamiliar ugliness of everything, or by jet lag, or by the cosmic permanency of discovering that even the other side of the world can be boring; and they'd paid one afternoon's visit in the constant rain to the Van Sichlyns' "estate," where Arthur lived in three back rooms in the servants' quarters and helped tourists. Which seemed to be his *job*. It was embarrassing, his clinging to a few antiques. Even the famous Van Sichlyn oak was on somebody else's property now, to be glimpsed only through a chain-link fence—which they didn't even bother to do, it was raining so hard. Even as they bid him good-bye, he was distracted in polishing a tabletop with his elbow. And they'd driven past Buckingham Palace, and they'd glimpsed Big Ben and the Tower of London, and they'd seen a tall red bus and a tall red phone booth; so they just went back to the motel, which had a TV. Except for the TV commercials, which were a lot better than in the U.S., London was like Oakland. When they got back on the plane at Heathrow after less than two days, Randy thought Cindy, too, was glad to end it.

Home's hot air gripped him pleasantly. At the Stanford campus after the airport, he was so invalided from too much travel as to feel himself a leper in the sunshine. The campus was Californian, photogenic, inaudible. Shuffling along with Dan McBride on his elbow, wearing a falling-apart trench coat he'd bought in an airport, he was a cheap transatlantic ghost, and more of an invisible father now, irrelevant to these beautiful girls in their satin running shorts. "Look for a noisy-looking building," Dan said. When finally he had led Dan into a messy student café and sat down in the shade, he felt reconstituted by the camouflage. Dan, his head listing—grinning ceaselessly the faint unconscious grin of the blind, which in Dan usually meant worry—said, "Cream, no sugar," and as Randy brought the two brimming coffees, he discovered a new elderly hunch in his shoulders, a clamp against disintegration. The words "Use Seat Bottom Cushion for Flotation" churned prayerlike in a corner of his mind.

The reason for coming home was to meet this Eddie Mensinger, whose name had been mentioned portentously in last month's discussion at the Secret Service offices, but who was leaving for Taiwan tomorrow and thus could only be consulted today—and who, Randy guessed, must be the tall, arch-browed man with spraying needles of red hair, a baggy plaid suit, and huge shiny shoes, now sneaking up behind Dan with a finger to his lips to warn Randy to silence. He had risen from a corner table, where he had been sitting when they entered. Dan, looking conspicuous this morning in a bright orange nylon shell with the words BLIND SKIER on the back, was unaware of him as he lifted Dan's coffee cup from the table and, clenching his teeth with the effort of stealth, replaced it with a salt shaker. He winked vastly to Randy, a vaudeville scoop of the brow that included him in conspiracy.

"Mensinger!" said Dan irritably.

"Shit," said Eddie Mensinger. "Goddamned nose."

"Eddie Mensinger—Randy Potts," said Dan.

Eddie shook Randy's hand. "The most highly developed nose in Garner Hall," he said. His hand was immense and soft, completely weightless in Randy's grip like a balloon.

"No, I *heard* you," said Dan.

"He's embarrassed about it because it's such a cliché."

"Well, maybe if you'd bathed since 1978," Dan said. "I can even tell you haven't given up masturbating."

"Your immature sense of humor may have had a certain charm at one time, among certain circles . . ."

"Mensinger, how mature is it to torment the handicapped? Where's my coffee?" He was groping over the tabletop. Eddie restored the coffee cup to his palm.

"No fooling," said Eddie, his hand weightless on Randy's shoulder. His eyes were the lunatic lashless violet that red-haired people sometimes have, his huge orange mouth stuck in a permanent smirk. "We were at the University of Illinois together, and I'd come home to Garner Hall, and I'd be walking down the corridor; and Dan would be in his room working on his fucking novel, and he'd shout, 'Hi, Eddie'—just knowing by my footfall. Is this not correct, Dan? Or this is amazing:

We'd go out to the bars—like Ruby Gulch, correct?—and we'd be walking along the street, and he'd point out, 'Here is a lamppost,' 'Here is a wall,' 'Here is a hedgerow.' Entirely acoustic. Because he could only do it if there was traffic on the street. You know what I mean? The reflected sounds would set up an acoustic field. If we stayed out until closing time, we'd come home when there wasn't any traffic on the street, and he couldn't do it anymore. Is this not correct, Fingers? Fingers?"

Dan was grinning hugely, blindly. "How the hell is Stanford, asshole? The Lost Dutchman! We used to call him the Lost Dutchman."

"Crummy-looking campus. Big budget." Eddie sat down, lowering his voice a little. The two men had been shouting at each other, making Randy cringe. "I can do anything. They believe in me. But look, I have this meeting now, which will take forever. Why don't you stick around for the day? Stay at my place tonight. Meet my wife. Both of you."

"I can't," said Randy, thinking of Cindy alone at home in Ross, unsupervised in that big house and capable of any mischief, like maybe calling her mother to brag about the trip. And, too, he wanted to take the phone off the hook and sleep for twenty-four hours. Sleep kept hardening about him if he sat still for a minute.

Eddie said, "Dan? I'll drive you back to Berkeley tomorrow. Kick around old times. The thing is, I'm supposed to be at this meeting right now. I have to justify my existence. But I got your thing." He pulled out of thin air a cardboard envelope marked COURIER. "It's marvelous. I know a guy at Battelle who's been trying the same thing. So I talked to him about it, and he said you've got the souring agent wrong; it must be sodium hypochlorite. But no such flying-spot scan will work, because the closest resolution is three hundred pixels per inch. It's basically primitive; the light beam actually scans by bouncing on a revolving polygon of mirrors. He said there's a new one with a resolution of twenty-five hundred pixels per inch, but even that isn't good enough for perfection. You're talking perfection here."

"Wait, Eddie," said Dan.

Eddie turned squarely to Randy: "I could have told you all this in a letter," he said, and with a huge orange grin like a baseball mitt, he shuddered.

"Eddie, wait," said Dan, "I don't even know what a pixel is. Let me explain this situation to you."

"It's a dot, McBride. There's no such thing as continuous optical scanner storage. All the systems are discrete. Because it digitalizes it. It digitalizes the image. Things are made of dots. Everything is made of dots."

"Would you just relax? My letter doesn't say everything. For one thing, the bill could be photographically enlarged. Like big. Like as big as a barn door. And *then* scan it."

"There are people who have been trying the perfect counterfeit for years, McBride. It's everybody's hobby. For one thing, this bleaching?" He was rubbing with his finger at an invisible rectangular specimen on the table. "You'd have to use peroxygen compounds at some point, and the paper would be damaged. See, that's the big problem: the ink is organic: you have to break carbon bonds to bleach it. But the paper is carbon bonds too, so you'd have to find a souring agent that would attack the ink only. And even then there'd still be traces. My friend at Battelle, his name's Abner, Abner says he gave up on bleaching real bills. The paper isn't paper. It's cotton and flax. You keep melting it. Abner's advice was, give up. He tried it for years. But the sodium hypochlorite was new to him. I could tell it was a good idea, because he resisted it. He was actually angry, which is a good sign when you're dealing with research. The truth always gets them angry. Do you want a beer or something? I'm going to get a beer. I have to justify my existence, but I've got five minutes."

"Eddie, first of all, this has to be confidential. This 'Abner' person is not to hear anything more about it." Dan turned to Randy. "Do you have one of the bills?"

Randy, starting to dislike Mensinger, got out his wallet with the anticipatory satisfaction of playing a trump card which would shut him up.

"Now listen here," Dan said. "We're going to tell you about this because we have to. Because you know the State Department. But Mensinger, this is a great big fat secret."

Randy set a bill on the table.

"Really?" Mensinger laid a finger on the bill, an expression of such exaggerated suspicion on his face that he looked sleepy. His lower lip sagged, and he redraped himself over the chair. His shoulder shuddered again.

Dan said, "That's the whole point of those lab reports. Those reports were on *this* bill."

Eddie turned to regard Randy with a new respect. The crayon-scribbled hair, the amazed arch of the eyebrows, the fruity voice, the hyperactive squirming and twitching of his unmuscled frame in his baggy plaid clothes—Eddie didn't look like a genius but like one of those dull giants distorted by hormonal imbalances. In Randy's sleep-deprived vision he seemed at moments to inflate.

"Lasers," he said, picking up the bill to examine it.

"Lasers on silicon," said Dan. "Or some polymer."

"Well, this was inevitable. Shit." He started scraping at the ink with a fingernail. "The design is archaic, you know. It's

intaglio engraving on steel plates. It's nineteenth-century—
which makes it the most easily counterfeited currency. In fact,
did you know they're coming out with a new design soon? But
this is truly wonderful, you fellows. Can I keep this? This is
going to set Abner Kreisner's underwear on fire."

"No, Eddie, listen. Abner Kreisner must never hear about
this. This isn't a counterfeit anymore. It's literally U.S. currency. Do you see?"

"It was the bleach," said Eddie. He spun the courier envelope to show some pencil jottings on its face: "*Sodium hypochlorite, NaClO. Anhydrous NaClO extrmly explosive, but in
aqu. solution stable—Eau de Javelle—Anhydrous: freeze-dry
in vacuum.*"

"See, that's what pissed him off: the vacuum," Eddie said.
"You should have seen how angry he was: I knew the idea had
merit because he was really furious. He called it the stupidest
thing he'd ever heard."

"Mensinger, listen. Don't tell your friend about this. Is that
clear?"

"Research! There's nothing they resist more than the solution. I'm sure this is what Abner would never think of. Just
*explode* the ink in a vacuum chamber. With this *gaseous* sodium
hypochlorite. How amazing! Something from nothing! Or nothing from something!"

"Eddie, listen. You absolutely may not tell anyone about
this."

"Okay, fine. But Jesus Christ, Dan!" He turned to Randy.
"Did you do this, Randy? Who did this? I want to meet the
guy. Is he government or industry?"

Dan said, "We're not giving you any more facts, Eddie. The
guy who made it is immaterial now."

"Dead?"

"Immaterial."

" 'Immaterial'—you fucking lawyers. You're a fucking lawyer now, McBride."

"Eddie, the Secret Service knows about this. But they can't prosecute, because the bills are so good they don't provide evidence of a crime."

Eddie just looked at Dan.

"Hey, Randy?" said Dan. "Would you get Eddie his beer?"

"Pay for it with this," said Eddie, sliding the bill. "I've got to see the miracle work. You guys are up shit creek. You guys . . . We're not having this conversation. I don't know you guys."

"That's what we want to talk to you about. The State Department is involved with this now."

"The State Department!" Eddie dropped back in his chair and rubbed his scalp with his palm, making the pink quills stand up sharper. "You guys are fucked. I'm putting everything I've got into precious metals as soon as I get home. You guys are fucked."

"Eddie, this is not funny."

Randy had heard all this before—the "international monetary system" was going to "collapse"—so he rose through weariness and left the table to buy Eddie's beer. He was so tired he didn't feel responsible anymore; and Eddie Mensinger, gravity-free like an animated character drawn on film, made him even more tired. He no longer felt blamable for any of this catastrophe, especially now as it grew to such imponderable proportions. He felt himself merely another victim of it. The girl at the counter—her cute coed lips as hard as sugar-dusted bubble gum—seemed to catch his eye flirtatiously. He said, "Draft, please," and she turned away with a faint smile as if they'd shared a secret. But she wasn't Mary. She was just a girl, made of resilient new cartilage, and Randy had become too tired, too complicated. When she returned with the mug, he averted his eyes as if all this money was an illness rendering him temporarily impotent. Damp English weather still clung in the weave of his clothes. He wasn't all here. He had never meant to cause all this trouble. He just wanted to go home to bed, and hand the fate of the international monetary system over to smart-asses like Eddie Mensinger. When he came back to the table, carrying this carbonated student beer in its faceted plexiglass mug cheated of weight, the atmosphere at the table had changed. Finally Eddie had started to listen, head bowed, kneading one ear with his fingers and pulling on it.

"No solid evidence," Dan was saying. "Just circumstantial and conjectural. So he himself isn't findable. It's what we call a mope defense."

Dan waited for a response from Eddie, who looked like he was trying to tear his ear off his head. Finally Eddie said, "Depends on what Captain Nemo does with it."

"Captain Nemo is immaterial. He won't do anything. Nonexistent."

"Well then it depends on what he *would* have done with it."

"Okay, suppose Captain Nemo is crazy. Suppose he doesn't want to get personally rich off this."

"He's a philanthropist."

"He wants to buy a lot of foreign currency," said Dan. "Suppose."

"Speculation?"

Dan didn't answer.

"Buying particular currencies? Or a mixed basket?"

"Mixed basket. Everything. Suppose."

"And he can produce as much as he likes?"

"Could. He's out of the picture now. But yes, he could

produce these rapidly, and never duplicate serial numbers. This laser moves faster than the human eye. He kept calling the first twenty million a pilot project."

Eddie said up straight and reached around to his back, through his armpit, to grasp his shoulderblade. Then, with a shiver, he sat back and scowled armless at the beer Randy had brought. "Ralph Conlin," he said at last.

"With the State Department."

"Handsome guy, right? Presidential haircut?"

"Don't ask *me*," said Dan.

"He may seem like just another government twerp but he's okay."

"Would he have sole responsibility in this?"

"Probably. Undoubtedly. I wish I could ask my uncle about this. I have an uncle who's an offshore banker. He knows all about currency."

"I don't think this is speculation. From everything we know about Captain Nemo, he wasn't profit-oriented. He was insane."

" 'Was'?"

" 'Is.' Whatever. He's immaterial."

"You know, Hitler tried this."

"What, *count*erfeiting?" said Randy, surprised by a frog in his throat that made him squeak—surprised to find himself a bit offended, loyally, that Bim should be compared to Hitler.

"He produced millions and millions of British pound notes, which he was actually going to bomb London with. But the operation fell through in some way. In times of war—or during World War II you could say the U.S. government counterfeited its own currency. Or you could say that any Keynesian administration is counterfeiting its own currency. Like the Kennedy and Johnson administrations. I mean, in the late fifties somebody in Miami was making Cuban currency—what is it, pesos?—which the Eisenhower administration just sort of winked at."

Dan asked, "Do you suppose the State Department is afraid of this?"

"People say that's what Stalin did to Hungary. It's hyperinflation. Worse than the German hyperinflation. You just keep printing money. So that, in Hungary, you had gold-chain shops on every streetcorner. Although gold itself is only valuable for its worthlessness."

"Eddie, do you suppose the State Department is afraid of this?"

Eddie looked out the window, petting his necktie. "Well," he said, "the Federal Reserve would intervene. They would buy dollars to support the price. But that's really a joke." He began to shake his head slowly.

"Why? What's a joke?"

"The Fed's currency reserves are in the low billions. But the dollar! *Hundreds* of billions of dollars cross the counter every day. Because, see, the dollar is now the key currency. And it's a key currency in a degenerate stage. There's already a tremendous overhang out there. In Eurodollars. And in domestic deposits by foreigners. More than half of U.S. deposits is owned by foreigners. So the banks would all fail in a day. In an hour. Instantaneously. Gresham's Law: Bad money drives out good. It's like one of those snow shelves, one of those cornices where you only need a teensy explosive charge to start an avalanche."

"And so would other currencies become valuable?"

"Plus, it would happen faster than Captain Nemo would have thought possible. Because the money in the Third World Mattress would come into circulation."

"Which is . . . ?"

"The Third World Mattress. Something like sixty or seventy percent of all the U.S. cash is stuck outside the country. In exile. It's collected in countries with high inflation rates—in Israel, Argentina, Brazil. It's literally in people's mattresses. And it's in government vaults in asshole countries. Like probably Lebanon and Iraq have vaults of dollars. And South American drug dealers have warehouses full of hundred-dollar bills. But everybody would be stung by dollars, and all the Third World Mattress money would come out. The avalanche would bury the Fed. The Fed would be undercollateralized, in effect. I'm sure this is why Conlin has been assigned to this." He turned to Randy. "They're afraid of you."

Dan pursued, "So then, Eddie. So then, other currencies would become valuable."

"No, they'd all go down the tube. It would be the Middle Ages."

"And precious metals would become valuable—"

"Russia would become the dominant world power. The Soviet Union has four fifths of the world's gold deposits. *More* than four fifths. The Russians could put an end to all this cold-war negotiation with us and simply buy us."

Dan said to Randy, "All this is just conjectural."

"Yes," said Eddie, pushing himself away from the table to tip back on two chair legs. "Yes." One huge shoe swung up onto his knee. A silence fell over the table. He stared deflated at his beer, which he had ignored. Finally he said, "I'm going to deny ever having had this conversation."

"Oh, it'll never come to that," said Dan. "This is all just talk. Randy, don't take Eddie too seriously. They keep him in a tank."

Another silence swelled among them, the three of them

looking off in different directions. Randy suddenly began to feel oddly deserted, or betrayed. The other two men were drifting away from him at the table. The country would be purchased by the Russians with their caves full of barbaric yellow metal. The jukebox separated them further by turning itself on to play a new song—one of the songs Cindy liked, with the new Teflon-surfaced sound of beeps and thuds that rock and roll had become in this decade. Her music on the stereo, her Lancôme pencil on the couch cushion, the Cambridge Plan diet powder caked on the blender, her scampering on the stairs, the clues that she'd been snooping in his drawers—it was as if he'd let a mink into the house. He would have to sue for parental custody: he'd realized it in a moment, on the plane, when, in exasperation over not being allowed to order a double Scotch on the rocks, she'd tossed her hair and whined, "God, Dad!" The realization had rendered him suddenly mortal.

Eddie let the forelegs of his tilted chair fall with a bang back to the floor. "How many people know about this?" he said.

Dan said, "We three, the Secret Service officer whose name is Ludex, a Treasury lawyer named Hodges, that Conlin—"

Randy said, "And all the kids at Terra Linda High School."

Dan said, "You're joking."

"No, my crazy daughter. You know how kids get wind of things. They snoop around—"

"You're joking, Randy." Dan was grinning with fear.

"But hey, who listens to kids?" pleaded Randy. He looked at Eddie. "Who listens to kids?"

Eddie shrugged, staring down at the table and pulling on his ear again.

"Come on, you guys. This week it's smoking bananas will get you high. Next week it's Paul McCartney died. The week after that it's God knows what. Nobody cares about what kids say."

Eddie said to Dan, "You should call the Secret Service right now, and ask if they've assigned any prosecution."

"Right now?" said Dan.

"McBride, there are certain markets, like stocks and commodities and the money market, which we call 'perfect.' Meaning there's no lag. News like this has an instantaneous effect." His arm floated toward the window indicating, Randy supposed, everything that was at stake. "It's not the specific Captain Nemo. It's the fact that this is now obviously possible." His hand remained suspended behind him.

"I'd rather not call Ludex. He's very good. As much as possible, I prefer to let things glide."

"Well, fuck," said Eddie, springing to his feet so quickly his lapels flopped. "I have to go justify my existence. Can I just say I'll meet you back here at twelve thirty? I'd like to call some people. I know a guy at the San Francisco Fed. We could frame our questions vaguely . . ."

Randy said, "I have to get home."

Eddie turned on Randy. "Well, I suggest you call Ludex or the T-man, and just ask who would be prosecuting you."

"No," said Dan, still seated, "I insist—"

"Dan," he said, touching the bill on the table. "This is now possible."

"We'll talk, Eddie. Go justify your existence."

"Will you just stay here?"

"Fine. I brought work."

"Not me," said Randy, making a wiping motion before himself in air. He was tired; he wanted to get home and make sure Cindy was okay. And obviously nothing could be done immediately.

Eddie stood back to regard Randy. "Can I have this bill?" he said.

"Sure. But I'm driving back to Marin now . . ."

"Just relax, Mr. Potts. This is fiction."

I'm relaxed, he wanted to say. Don't worry about me, I'm the mope in the mope defense, all I want to do is go to bed.

Eddie held the twenty-dollar bill up to the light, sighing.

"Eddie?" said Dan. "You'd be willing to testify?"

"Closed hearings only." He began rubbing a corner of the bill against his courier envelope, leaving a faint smudge of scrubbed-off ink. "This is a masterpiece. Did they check the face-plate numbers with the Bureau of Engraving and Printing?"

"Eddie, the lab report is in there."

"I just can't believe it. Who is this guy?"

"Go justify your existence," said Dan. He lifted his briefcase. "I'll stay right here, I've got work I can do."

"Okay," said Eddie. "If I'm not back by twelve thirty it means I don't exist anymore. And Randy, just forget about all this. Bullshit."

He strode toward the door, his plaid suit flapping; then he stopped and came back. "No! You'd need at least two bleaches," he said. "One to break the ink bond, and another to break the ink-paper bond. And then just simple water would restore the fabric. Just Brownian motion. Abner told me the dollar-counterfeiters in Milan have been rinsing with water— though certainly not this well." He shrugged and raised his eyebrows, and then he ran away, his big shoes squashing air.

"So," said Dan inconclusively.

They sat for a minute. Randy stared at nothing, the ambient noise waxing harsher and thinner in his ears while sleep grew rapidly like an ash around him. Eddie Mensinger had been an illusion, an invention of Dan McBride, a hired clown. Use seat bottom cushion for flotation.

Saying how tired he was, he pushed himself up from the table to excuse himself and get out on the road, glad to be irrelevant now, already entering the stupor he deserved. Dan promised he would call if further talks with Eddie yielded anything important, and Randy waved him away as he turned toward the door. Outside, the hot air was muffled. His car would be parked in the sunny lot beyond the row of buildings— probably ticketed by the campus police because he'd parked in a reserved space. And the drive home on 101 would be swift, and Cindy would be at home, and he could take a long nap. The heavy stone buildings of the campus revolved past him in silence. He was moving in a dream, protected by the deafness in the central vacuum of the storm. His car was still there—not ticketed—and the putty upholstery was hot when he got in. Don't worry, this is fiction. Everything is made of dots. He turned on the radio and followed the signs back to the freeway—101 NORTH, SAN FRANCISCO—feeling better as the hot upholstery transmitted California warmth to his England-chilled spine. It was a relief to be back home on the freeway playing the radio loud—with an appetite, he realized, for a sweet trashy pizza, and with the rhythm to a Chuck Berry song pulsing in his thumb, whose knuckle tapped on the steering wheel as he gradually became more alert, driving, and lost his jet-lag stupor. He accelerated toward the Golden Gate Bridge as Chuck Berry's guitar, in solo, began to twank louder.

He was free. The whole idea of Bim was now cartoonish. Bim was "insane," his disk indecipherable. Nobody would believe it. No jury would believe it. He pictured Bim folding his tiny legs like a child in the seat of that unbelievable car. He pictured Bim's careful affectionate bottled-fetus hands bleaching the epidermal rectangle with tender insidious chemicals so that even the microscopic red and blue capillaries would remain intact. He pictured the dollar in a bell-jar vacuum, the explosion of its ink into a black mist. And he himself didn't believe it. Bim, he thought as he regarded the blue sky above, had always felt like a contrivance, fundamentally unrealistic. The money was real. It was money.

As soon as he got back home, he would telephone Ludex himself, to ask about his prosecution. If he had to give up the money, he would—almost gladly. He had always known that the essential, saving thing about him was that he was forgivable.

When he pulled into the driveway, Cindy's bikini-clad corpse was lying on the front lawn on a beach towel, with her radio and her suntan oil and her book and her cucumber. He pulled past her on the gravel, receiving not the faintest wrist-twitch of greeting; at times she was, admirably, capable of total cold-blooded inactivity.

The Ferrari was running badly again, despite its recent tune-up, and as he pulled up, the idling engine took on a disturbing shudder. He parked by the back door and went inside with the flat box of the pizza he'd stopped for, and eaten most of already. In the kitchen, he untucked its cardboard tabs and unpeeled one more triangle from the cardboard disk; but he didn't really want it. It was the *idea* of a pizza he'd wanted— that moment of ritual conviviality when everybody lifts a wedge, and strands of melted cheese unite everybody in spokes. He should have shared it, should have brought it to the Paschkes, while he was still a millionaire, in the clear.

Get it over with.

He threw the floppy triangle back into the box.

The phone book was on the kitchen shelf, where he found the number of the San Francisco Secret Service office. But he decided to run upstairs to the hall telephone to make the call, because although Cindy knew a lot about his present legal problems, he didn't want her to overhear anything more.

The telephone was on a table beneath a window in the hallway. He stood over it for a minute to catch his breath, having taken the stairs two-at-a-time with the phone book in his arms, and he took off the shoes and socks that had been on his feet since London, and wriggled his bare toes in the waxy new carpeting. Below on the lawn, he could see Cindy lying with slices of cucumber on her eyes like coins. What did she want? She didn't seem to want anything. Even a trip to England seemed to annoy her. He'd asked her on the returning plane what she would want if anything were possible, and after many evasions, she'd ended the whole discussion by saying sarcastically, "Braces, Dad," and returning to her reading. It was a new kind of heartache. She'd eaten almost nothing on the trip, crazily dieting.

He rested his forehead against the window frame and took courage, dialing the Secret Service number, rehearsing the crucial question, *Which government agency has been assigned my investigation* . . .

But he got only a busy signal. He hung up.

Suddenly he realized what was wrong with the scene on the lawn below. Kevin Van Sichlyn's grass-clippings installation wasn't there. Cindy was lying right where it should have been. The pile of clippings was nowhere to be seen. Either she or the gardeners had thrown it away. And a photographer from some magazine was supposed to come out next week to photograph it. Hadn't he told her not to fool around with it?

No, actually, maybe he hadn't. But at least, he remembered,

he had instructed the gardeners that it was art, and was not to be tampered with—instructions which the gardeners had accepted with surprising casualness as if they were accustomed to eccentricities in their clients.

The only thing to do was to gather together some more grass clippings and heap them where the old pile had been. They would be greener and higher-heaped than the old pile, but soon they would sink and wither, and nobody, not even Kevin, would know the difference.

As he stood in the silence waiting, his eyes closed, his consciousness shrank to lenslike compression, and a cloud of imaginary noise rose to envelop him. The air barked startlingly. He was more tired than he thought.

He picked up the phone to call the Secret Service again. There was nothing to worry about. He would simply give up the money if he had to.

The line was still busy. He breathed a deep breath and went downstairs and poured himself a cup of coffee, already brewed by Cindy, and he went outside by the back door, hobbling bare-heeled on the gravel so that his elbows jabbed out in air and he sloshed his coffee. "Cindy?" he said, when he'd made it to the soft lawn.

She didn't answer.

"Cindy, this is important."

He sat down cross-legged beside her towel. One of her new books—*The Mind: A Time-Life Introduction*—lay beside her. Reading on the plane home—as she had read savagely throughout the trip—she had looked up once to say, "Dad? Do I have extreme mood swings or regression to infantile behavior?"

He felt stranded alone with her here. This shining lawn was eternity. Squinting above his coffee cup, he watched the grass glitter in the breeze.

"What," she moaned finally.

"Did I mention this pile of grass clippings that was here?"

"Don't have a cow, Dad. All I did was move it a little. This is the only place in the yard with decent sun." She rolled, letting the cucumber slices fall away. Randy hid his eyes from the awkward beauty of her tying her bikini strings. He wanted her to meet lots of boys, boys who were crazy about her and would do anything for her. Boys who would reform themselves to try to be worthy of her.

"I only moved it," she said. "The landscapers threw it away."

It was easy to see now where the turf had been crushed in an oval.

"Honey, did you know how valuable that was?" He chose, for the moment, not to approach the whole issue of her lying out here in her bikini while the landscaping crew was working.

"We can always get some more grass. I'll do it right now if you want. Sheesh!"

"Did you know there's a photographer coming out next week to take pictures of it?"

"Dad, *I'll* get some more. There's a lawn mower in there."

Randy dipped his nose into the rim of his cup and, speaking into his coffee so that humidity condensed on his face, he said, "Okay, I'll help you."

"Nobody will know the difference. I bet even your stupid artist friend."

He had to call Ludex. The telephone was still sitting poised on the hall table inside. The daze of jet-lag was coming over him again. He was falling asleep.

"Just a minute, hon," his own voice rose to wake him. "I have to make a phone call."

He stood up and went back inside. All the furniture and carpeting and paintings incriminated him pleasantly as he passed, and he got to the upstairs telephone and dialed the Secret Service number again. This time it rang.

"United States Secret Service," said the voice of the receptionist.

"I'd like to speak to Mr. Ludex," Randy said.

"Please hold."

The phone clicked into silence again.

He looked up to see Cindy standing in her kimono on the landing of the stairs, listening with curiosity.

He said, "Cindy, you're not interested in this."

"Yes I am."

"Just go away, will you?"

"Okay, okay," she moaned, descending the stairs slowly.

The phone was picked up: "Ludex."

"This is Randy Potts, Mr. Ludex."

There was a pause. "Mr. Potts, I'm not sure we should be talking without your lawyer."

"I was just with my lawyer—"

"This telephone conversation is being recorded," said Ludex, "and anything you say may be brought into a court of law."

"Mr. Ludex, this is easy. All I want to know is who my prosecution has been assigned to."

"There is no prosecution at present. You are not accused of a crime."

"Come on. We both know—"

"Randy . . ." He paused. "I'm going up to Terra Linda today, Randy, to wrap up the problem of the tenth crate—which is the last mystery. Although it seems like every child in Terra Linda knows about it . . ."

Grief foreknown came rushing into him. The Paschkes would never forgive him. Laura—for whom he had always borne a love almost husbandly, from his sleazy bachelor's distance—Laura would never forgive him.

"They didn't do anything, I swear. I didn't even tell them what was in the crate."

"Are you referring to the Paschkes?"

"They had no idea. I told them it was full of magazines."

"So you are referring to the Paschkes," said Ludex. "You've just put the last piece in place for us."

As if the phone were red hot, he went on holding it for a moment and then hung up. He had to get to Wayne's house to remove the crate once and for all. Now they had enough evidence to get a search warrant. Ludex might be on his way there right now.

As he ran down the stairs, he discovered Cindy standing below the landing.

"Are you going there?" she said. "I'm coming with."

"Cindy, mind your own business."

She flew up the stairs to her room. "Hang on, I just need to put on some clothes."

# 25

Cindy ran into her room and found a pair of jeans and started hopping toward her bathroom on one foot, while the other foot stabbed and stabbed inside her jeans against a flop in the leg which had twisted like a knot. There was a shirt on the bathroom floor. There was also a pair of shorts, which she put on instead of the irksome jeans. She wouldn't bother with shoes.

"Stay here, Cindy," her father's voice rose from the staircase below. "I'm leaving now."

"No, wait, Dad. Wait. I thought of something."

She flew down the staircase buttoning her shirt. Her father was already going out the back door, and she caught up with him on the lawn. "Dad, listen, I figured out the solution. You should turn yourself in. You know?"

"Honey, you can't come. Look, you're all covered in suntan oil. You know what it does to the upholstery."

"I'll sit on my butt."

"You can't come with me, Cindy."

But he wasn't stopping her as she opened the car door and slipped in. "I promise," she said, "my legs will never touch the leather. Same with my arms. You'll see."

"Cindy, you have to stay here." He got in on the driver's side. "That's my final word."

"Okay, listen. If this money is supposedly so perfect, here's what I think." She sat on the leather seat hugging her knees in a forearm lock beneath her chin, while her father went through his mysterious ritual adjustments to the dashboard. "If this money is so perfect, why don't you just turn yourself in? You and Kim's parents and everybody. We all turn ourselves in. Then they won't be able to get us and—*I* think— we'll be able to keep all the money. Because they said it *can* be real money, and if it *can* be it *is*. And they can't take money away from you. It says in the Constitution. Look at Wayne. Who is going to think *Wayne* is a criminal?"

"Your leg is touching," he said as he turned the key.

"No it isn't. Come on, we have to get there."

"I'm serious. That oil leaves permanent stains."

"Dad, would you please get going? We don't have much time."

"If I see one inch of skin come in contact—"

"It won't."

He turned the key again. The car made a grinding noise, and then there was nothing. He tried again, and this time there was only the sound of the starter. "Shit. It was running uneven on the way home."

Only now did she remember the few harmless Milk Duds

that, on the day they left for London, she had dropped into the gas tank casually, thoughtlessly, looking away—as if by not considering the consequences she could be unblamable.

But she refused to consider it specifically any further, turning away from the problem with an enhancement of her physical beauty by having caused expensive trouble—a calmer smoothness of the brow. That was just the kind of person she would turn out to be, fortunately. Next, she would call the Missing Children Hotline: the immediate crisis would get worse if her father was on a list of kidnappers somewhere and there was a warrant out for him. He kept twisting the key in the ignition until the starter began to slow from a high drilling sound to a feeble grind. "Let's take a fucking taxi," he said.

"Are you going to call the Paschkes?"

He leaped out of the car. "First I'll call a taxi."

Of the few things she had sneaked back to retrieve from her mother's house, the most important was her Kermit the Frog, who now lay upstairs under her bed. While her father dialed the kitchen phone, she slipped unnoticed up the back staircase and crawled under the bed to pull him out from the embrace of a discarded sweater, his soft green cloth, as always, an old bandage to the touch. The zipper on his underside released the tinder within, among which she found the number of the Missing Children Hotline, 800-843-5678, jotted on a faint grocery receipt. Her father's voice could be heard downstairs, speaking in sharp tones to the taxi people, trying to persuade them to send a car quickly. If he had put in her own separate phone line she would have been able to call right away without waiting. He hung up and started dialing again, calling the Paschkes this time.

She stuffed the ransom demands and suicide notes back into the soft frog—all of which she could have burned by now. But she hadn't. And it entered her mind that maybe she never would, finally. To do so would be like burning scrimped cash; cash which, however, she could never spend, like souvenir money from a foreign country. Maybe she would just hang on to the cloth bladder of notes forever as a kind of memento, a kind of dimly recalled fragment of a dream that seems important to preserve in spite of its daylight loss of meaning. It looked ordinary among her other stuffed animals. It could abide with her indefinitely without anyone's ever thinking to snoop into it. Her father's voice rose through the floor from the kitchen, and though he spoke indistinguishably in murmurs, just the tone of his voice—anxious, embarrassed, earnest—told her that he wasn't going to be put in jail. He was just too obviously simple-hearted to do anything against the law, you could hear it in the sound of his voice resonating in the floorboards of the house and communicating with her bones, her spine.

At the sound of his hanging up the phone, his swift footfalls crossed the house to the front door. She ran out to the hall window to see him walk outside on the front lawn looking for the arrival of a taxi, stepping heedlessly on the sacred spot where his stupid pile of grass clippings had been, beside her cucumber, radio, and body-imprinted beach towel still spread out on the lawn like the police-staked spot where a crashed corpse had lain, seen from high above. He, too, was barefoot, vulnerable-looking for a father.

800-843-5678.

She picked up the phone on the hall table—watching him as he limped barefoot to the curb with his hands thrust shyly, foolishly into his pockets and looked down the street for a taxi that probably wouldn't arrive for twenty minutes—but as she held the receiver, something in just the old plug sound of the dial tone deterred her from calling, and she set her forehead and her palms against the window pane.

She could imagine it: the voice of one of the little old ladies at the Missing Children Hotline would answer, warmed by the usual charitableness of an unpaid volunteer; and Cindy would inquire about the case of Cynthia Potts, identifying herself as the girl's mother and asking that Cynthia Potts be removed from the list of the missing; and the little old lady would ask routinely if this was a runaway or an abduction; there would be some clicking of computer keys on the other end; and finally she would say no such girl was listed. Her mother hadn't called. Her mother had already developed a constructive attitude toward Cindy's leaving. And she herself—who, by her own radiance, had driven her parents apart in the first place—was alone now in the gap she had created, watching her father from high above, again the only angel charged with the responsibility of rescue but, as always, stifled, frozen behind the window, silenced on the nether side of that mural of light which separates angels from mortals.

# 26

At that very moment, Wayne was sitting alone at the bar at Rumplestiltskins wearing his smartly tailored sport coat from the European Shoppe, which pinched him erect. As he watched his reflection in the back-bar mirror, one hand on his beer, he slipped the other hand inside his coat to feel the inch-thick bundle of twenty-dollar bills in the inner pocket. In the mirror he looked like the kind of guy that comes into these places, his face deceptively impassive as he touched himself in the secret excitement of anonymity. The bundle of money had been in his pocket today while he bargained with the owner of the house in Tiburon who had answered Laura's housepainting ad in the *Independent-Journal*; its compacted weight at his breast had helped him to impersonate an actual painting contractor and confidently underbid the competition. They'd stood in the back yard where the lawn was treacherously dug up in swells, and he'd told the owner with self-assurance, "The wood is so mushy up there, we'll have to do some carpentry first," inventing a *we* on the spur of the moment as if he possessed an entire crew—and immediately picturing Kim's sketchy friend Eric DeBono being brought in to play the part—while he evaded sincerity by keeping his eyes fixed on the rotten eave above as though it were a just-out-of-reach rescue to be grabbed for. The owner turned to him and said, "All right, Mr. Paschke, do you subcontract that?" and he found himself swimming further out into fiction: "No, we always do it ourselves."

The amulet of money lent him a tough entrepreneurial new squint, a welted hardness around the eyes, which was visible now in the back-bar mirror. At happy hour they served free hors d'oeuvres—broccoli and cauliflower dip, coin-sized quiches, cheese on toothpicks—so that you could eat like a gourmet for free. He had audibly ordered a four-dollar imported beer when he came in. But it was a slow afternoon at Rumplestiltskins. At this hour, he was almost the only customer; too much sunlight entered the bar. He had always pictured this moment as dark, shadowy. How else but among shadows and darkness could he approach the seductive, flawed blonde, whose specific name now was erased in the yellow of her sweater and the blur of a toss of her hair. His face in the mirror was an oval as featureless as a fingerprint—somehow, in its solitude, *mocked* by his smartly tailored jacket, squeezed pink. This was the only day of the week when Laura had the late shift at Denny's. She wouldn't be home until seven thirty, and would never know he'd been alone at Rumplestiltskins with two thousand dollars wearing his European Shoppe jacket. She hardly even knew of the existence of Rumplestiltskins. Her dented Pinto—with its unique ruptured-manifold-gasket purr

and its disintegrating seat that cupped safely the mandolin of
her body, its seatbelt placing a diagonal stripe between her
breasts—had other routes around town, and seldom came this
far out Fourth Street. Would it be possible for her to determine
that one of the bundles was missing from the crate? He knew
she sometimes opened the crate herself. He knew she had risen
restlessly from bed to go into the garage and unscrew the lid
and take out one of the bundles, merely to count it and replace
it: he had followed her and spied on her through the crack at
the door's hinges, and had gone skidding on stocking feet back
to bed ahead of her when, with a sigh, she put back the money
and began to screw the lid back down. She always replaced
the pink seal on the lid, from the supply in her own package
in her sewing drawer.

He ordered another beer, setting four dollars on the bar.
"Dortmunder, please." He was down to seven dollars of his
own cash. A group of girls came in the door, and he watched
them in the mirror. Probably office workers. It was just the
hour when secretaries would be released. Three of them. An
older one with lacquered hair—either married or divorced,
judging by the set of her mouth—and two younger ones, probably never married. One of the younger ones moved brazenly
toward a table, perhaps having been here before, while the
two others, already fearing pollution by Rumplestiltskins' reputation, hung back bashfully at the shore of the empty dance
floor. Wayne chose the younger of the bashful ones as his.
Lint-haired, quiet, she had the proper imperfection, the skepticism of one willing to be hurt. For that must be how the more
confident males in bars choose their women: there must be
something tragic—which goes unmentioned, which is indeed
unmentionable—in a woman you pick up. And then you keep
things superficial. He recalled the image of the gerbil-faced

blonde—Tina, that was her name—tipsy and sad, she had averted her eyes as she tugged her sweater down over her hips giving him permission to let his glance slip lower while her face was turned away unhappily smiling. A fundamental sadness seemed to be essential to the whole process of picking up women in bars. He drank deep from his new bottle of beer, brutally. His shoulders broadened again in the mirror. He was drinking fast and had begun to tower above his former life— capable of all this new boldness *because* of his impoverishment, because there was no longer a safety net. He felt swung upward as if, in the void beneath him, his now-fantastic indebtedness were a helping counterweight.

It was courage. His reflection in the mirror, despite the temporary astigmatism of the beer, was the image of a man rendered cruel and unprincipled by two thousand dollars. He would need a victim of equal sophistication, *numbed* by sophistication. Somebody like Tina, whose eyes were hidden by the sexy bruise of tragedy; not like this innocent secretary with the linty hair. He was a real contractor now. He had spent the afternoon discussing thousands of dollars with the owner of a big house in Tiburon. The owner was one of these shrewd types who have been taking over Marin; he had bought the house just to fix it up and sell it at a profit, and had ornamented it with plastic cornices and scrollwork from Builder's Emporium, which inscribed the plain façade with wealth: "You spend forty-nine ninety-five on plastic," he had confided, "and you can add another twenty thousand dollars to the market value." That was how the world worked. In revealing such a secret, he had contaminated Wayne with the assumption—because of the smart jacket, or because of the magical spell of the hidden cash—that Wayne was as sharp an entrepreneur as himself.

And there was also, today, the shrewd gain of forty flagstones, now outside in the bed of his truck. The mason on the house had said they were leftovers, free for the taking, so he had—after the owner left—hung his European Shoppe coat on the rearview mirror and loaded them onto the truck, thinking of using them in the back yard at home, creating a series of stepping stones through the sometimes marshy area of the yard beyond the patio.

More people entered. Rumplestiltskins was beginning to fill up. He ordered another Dortmunder, and he swiveled around to regard the room. The bundle of money in his pocket had an evil weight. The last time he had seen Tina here, she had moaned, "Wayne, you've come back for me!" and garlanded herself swooning along the bar. It was amazing that a girl so young and pretty, with such intelligent sexiness like a coed, could find him attractive. Maybe it was true what they say about older men being more interesting—in spite of his paunch; the few orange-peel pores in his nose; his baby-hair on top.

A pair of narrow hands covered his eyes from behind. A voice—Tina's voice! summoned!—said, "You've come back for me!" Turning to greet her, he knew he was in trouble, exactly the trouble he'd asked for.

"Tina!" he said with surprising composure. She was wearing jeans and that same tight yellow sweater, her hair drawn back from her face. The slightly receding chin was made voluptuous by lipstick outlining her mouth.

He said, "Have you been here the whole time?"

"I live right across." Somehow she had already generated the feeling that she was clinging to him, enlarging him—though in fact she had slid away against the bar with her head tilted affectionately, her hips slanting. Her breasts, obviously un-brassiered since her one bare shoulder showed no strap, were supernaturally buoyant in air before him. He detected wine on her breath—which, in his new incarnation as a lowlife, he would have to think of as an early advantage. He would have a few more beers himself, and soon it might be possible to want her with a desire so towering, so righteous, that he could fall upon her with no thought of the consequences.

"You know I live right across at Hillview, because I told you that before, didn't I? I saw you come in with your truck full of rocks like a caveman. And I said, There goes my caveman."

"Oh, those," he said. "Those are just some materials for a friend."

"So buy me a drink, caveman. . . . Rick? Dubonnet and Sprite?"

"Friend of mine who's a mason. I promised him I'd do him a favor and pick up some flagstones for him." He couldn't see, for the blaze on his cheeks.

She said, "You know, I dreamed about you the other night."

"You did?" He could only keep looking away. Down at his drink. Over at the empty bandstand. "What did you dream?"

"Do you think it's polite for a man to ask a lady what she dreamed about him? It might be embarrassing." She squirmed up onto the stool and touched his arm. "No, I'm only joking."

"Be four," said the bartender, setting down her red drink and walking off.

Wayne got out his wallet but discovered only three dollars. Hadn't he had more? He started this afternoon with seventeen.

". . . It had something to do with that guy on 'Mod Squad.' Remember 'Mod Squad'? I was on 'Mod Squad' and I was making that horrible Noodles-in-a-Cup stuff. For some reason everybody wanted Noodles-in-a-Cup, and *my* Noodles-in-a-Cup was the best in the world . . ."

Patting his hip and breast, dipping into his pockets, he found nothing—only his measuring tape, the twist-tie from an extension cord, last winter's Kleenexes, one of the matchbooks from when he was a heavy smoker, a receipt from somewhere. He couldn't pay for the drink. It seemed, for an irrational moment, like the end of the affair.

"Do you have a dollar, Tina?" he said. Fortunately, he told himself, he was drunk enough to ask this without too much embarrassment. It was the kind of thing lowlifes get away with. "I've messed up my money today somehow. I thought I had seven dollars."

"I'm broke," she said. Then she set two fingers on his wrist and said, "Let's just ditch this place and go across to my apartment. We can drink for free there. I got a whole big bottle of this crap. You can tell me how your numismatic investment scam is going."

"Well, sure, okay. Except we still have to pay for this." The moment of striking the bargain had passed, and immediately his stomach was stabbed with the thrill. The bartender was at the other end of the bar; he would have to get his attention when he came back. In the mirror, his face looked poached. He drank the last of his beer. "Okay."

Tina said, "I don't mean 'scam' exactly. Last time I felt like I wasn't being very supportive. I thought about it after you left the bar, and I decided, What the hell, maybe I'm wrong, maybe numismatic coins will be the wave of the future."

"No, no, you're perfectly supportive." He would be an adulterer. She had revolved toward him on her stool showing him the shield of tight denim at her crotch where the seams met; he noticed a faint food stain on the hip of her sweater; it had been there the last time he saw her here.

"Maybe it's just my limitation, I decided. I personally

couldn't sell coins, because I'm so crummy at anything to do with sales. But I ought to give credit to somebody who can. I didn't mean to imply that there's something unethical about this CoinTrend, or whatever it is. After all, caveat emptor. It's a free country."

"Don't worry, you're supportive." His eyes fell to the stain.

She said, "My feeling is, anything that needs a salesman isn't worth having. If people have to be *persuaded* they need something, well then . . . But heck, this CoinTrend may be different."

The bartender came near, and Wayne said, "Excuse me. I only have three dollars. I thought I had more. I've never been in this situation in my life, honestly . . ."

"Don't be a tightass, Rick," said Tina.

"Got any credit cards?"

"No, not exactly. But can I leave something? Like I could leave my driver's license or my watch, or something valuable? Because really, this is not the usual thing for me."

The bartender swept the untouched drink off the bar to set it on a shelf beneath. "I can serve this to somebody else."

"Well, do you think that's okay?"

"Anything for Tina." He turned away to wait on another customer, before Wayne had a chance to thank him. The place was starting to get crowded.

"Okay, let's go to mine," said Tina, grasping her purse.

For the first time today, he wanted a cigarette: that old hunger for the rough suffocating yawn, the expanding gray balloon in the chest. His cravings had been less frequent lately. He'd been getting almost to the point of quitting altogether.

He slipped off the stool onto the springy feet of slight intoxication. Tina, walking beside him, was pecking through her purse, and he glimpsed at her neckline the hard slope of her breast. She was indeed wearing no brassiere. The star of alternating creases at the center of her jeans gathered over a raised pubis. But his eyes kept seeking the stain on her sweater, like a small patch of gray felt in the yellow nap. And even the yellow sweater itself—he hadn't consciously realized it until now—was the saddest thing in the world, her favorite sweater.

"Anyway, it's a ridiculous dream," she was saying as she walked. "Here I am hauling around gallons of those kinky little noodles, moving them around with a pitchfork like."

"Oh, you smoke," he said when she pulled out a pack of cigarettes. "Can I have one?"

"Of course," she said—in a new tone that, for the first time, implied sex—and she handed him the package. He felt sensitized all over by jeopardy: plenty of things could go wrong now. His confident walk was unnaturally levitated. When they got outside, the grasp of the warm afternoon air steadied him: it was an ordinary day. The parking lot was covered in golden late-afternoon light. It seemed possible not to go through with this, to part from Tina in summery innocence.

She handed him a lighter and readjusted the strap of her purse on her shoulder. He lit the cigarette and pulled smoke into his lungs, with gratitude for the old scrape in the throat, the rapid rubbery numbness in the brain.

"Yeah," he said. They were passing his truck full of flagstones. "I'm getting involved with houses. Fixing 'em up and selling 'em."

"Does this mean you're less devoted to coins?" Her wrist slipped through his arm. Ahead across the parking lot were the Hillview Apartments, tortilla stucco with motel-style aluminum windows. He was still too sober. He would have to drink a lot more at her apartment.

"Oh, the investment market is slowing down, so I got out."
How long would this take? Laura would be home at seven
thirty. The disturbing thing was that the sun was still high. It
couldn't be sexy if they were to gaze on each other's nakedness
in daylight.

"I detect a bit of understatement," she said. "Is the market
for these coins 'slowing down' kind of fast?"

"Yeah, you might say that."

"I see. But hey, renovating houses sounds interesting. And
it sounds like a lot more fun."

They arrived at a door. She lived in a ground-floor unit
immediately on the parking lot. And indeed it was depressing.
The door was heavy and armored like a motel-room door,
turquoise, with rust pimples crowding the base. And inside
was a smell like scented tissues. The carpet was as orange as
Tang, so astonishingly orange that he set foot on it warily.

"Here's my humble palace," she said. He tried to recover
the memory of her breasts, their gravity-defiant bulk unbras-
siered. But her favorite yellow sweater had lit his soul with a
sad light.

"Do you want a drink? I've got a French Colombard that's
good in my opinion. By my presently reduced standards." The
jug was sitting out on the table in the sun, beaded with the
sweat of recent refrigeration.

"Sure. Yeah. Nice place." The orange rectangle beneath
his feet had raised him into fear—so orange that it isolated
the few pieces of furniture. The orange, too, would kill passion.
Would she peel up her sweater to release her buoyant breasts
so that their undersides would be bathed in reflected tangerine
light? The same light that now tinted her underchin, her under-
forearms?

She was pouring two glasses. Now that she had turned her

back, he could see the contour of her body in the jeans. Her hips were athletic and childishly mobile, constantly taking up unexpected slants.

"It's nice to have you visit," she said.

"Yes," he said. His voice had turned slightly furry.

"Here," she said, crossing the orange surface and handing him a glass.

"Really convenient," he said, and he cleared his throat. "Living here, I mean. I mean, you've got parking. You've got Rumplestiltskins. You've got the happy-hour hors d'oeuvres. You've got the freeway. You've got the 7-Eleven, which basically has everything. I mean, you don't have to even *leave! Ever!*"

She didn't respond. He'd sounded hysterical. A silence froze time, while she looked down into her wineglass, then set it aside.

She said with her eyes on the floor, "You know, Wayne, we don't have to, uh."

"Oh?" he said. He couldn't feel his feet planted firmly.

"Let's just visit," she said. "Okay? I really do want to hear about the coin business, Wayne. You actually made it sound interesting. We could go back to the bar if you like, and I'll just run a tab. If you'd be more comfortable there."

"No?" He was trying to pretend feebly that he wasn't sure what she was referring to.

She turned and went to stand beside a big chair of wide-wale blue corduroy, and she set one knee on its arm. Everything in the place was arranged carefully: a box of designer Kleenex; the latest *Us* magazine and *TV Guide;* pussy willows in a jug; a mushroom-shaped deodorizer. Slanting direct sunlight hit the carpet and bounced irradiating everything with that fakey vitamin color. It was hot and stuffy. "Can we just talk for a while?" she said. "Just ramble? Like, whatever comes up?"

His mind was empty. What time was it? Would somebody steal his flagstones from the bed of his truck? Finally he said, "You never told me what you do. Besides being a student," he added, because he recalled she'd told him about taking classes at a junior college in Novato.

"I work at a drive-in pharmacy. It sounds dull, but I like it. I like the people."

"That must be interesting," he said, his eyes hooded. He was still standing in the middle of the room with his wineglass. The only place to sit down was in a chair at the dinette table, which, when he lifted it, turned out to be so light in his adrenaline-inspired grip that it felt like a toy, a little girl's tea-set chair. He sat down on its edge.

"Actually, it's more like being a drive-in psychiatrist. All our customers are old people and invalids who don't have anybody else to talk to."

"You know I'm married," he blurted out.

She said, "I know, Wayne. I figured. But that's okay. I like you, Wayne. I'm not a floozy. I like you. It's okay whatever happens."

Wayne, sitting slouched within the pinch of his European Shoppe coat, couldn't raise his eyes from the rubber carpet-protector on her chair leg. He managed to tear them away and glance once at her, then up to the framed Porsche-and-champagne poster above her head.

She said, "God, I sometimes wish there were no such thing as sex."

"I'm sorry."

"No, you misunderstand. There's nothing to apologize for. You're a lucky fellow, Wayne Paschke."

"Oh yeah?" he said.

"No, you were born lucky. Even if the coin business isn't so hot."

"I guess this was a stupid idea, huh?" he said.

"No, Wayne, nothing is stupid."

"I'm sorry. I really like you. I didn't mean."

"Don't be sorry. Hey, Wayne, look at me." She was smiling. "Lighten up, Wayne."

"I guess I should go," he said. "I'm sorry."

"Wayne, you don't understand. You haven't taken anything away from me."

"Still." He was already thinking guiltily of getting away, back out into the fragrant air of rush hour, where his wife had been pregnant for so long now that, even if they did get an amniocentesis, it was too late to do anything about it if the report showed deformities.

"Wayne, don't be sorry. You mustn't apologize. You may not understand why, but it's very important to me that you don't apologize."

"Okay, I'm sorry. Really."

On the drive home as if in a tunnel, he never changed lanes and stayed inside the speed limit, not wanting to get caught out at this last moment before the money was reunited with the crate. Occasionally he felt for it in his pocket, but discreetly, without removing his elbow from the armrest, in case a police car might be near. He imagined himself stopped, searched, caught with two thousand dollars in counterfeit bills, jailed. As he came off the freeway and into his own neighborhood, he relaxed, permitting himself the prayerful rinsing shiver of having just averted danger, of a near miss. The forty flagstones banged and crunched together as he pulled over his driveway curb. He longed to get to work moving them, setting them in earth as oaths.

Laura's Pinto was in the driveway. She had come home from work early.

And a yellow cab was parked idling across the street. The driver was sitting behind the wheel reading a newspaper.

Wayne turned off his engine. Laura came out in her Denny's uniform, her hands poised interrupted at kitchen-counter height, her belly now clearly pressing out against her apron. It must be too late for an amniocentesis.

"Randy is here," she said.

"Randy?"

"And Cindy. They want to take the crate away. We have to hurry, because he says the Secret Service might come any minute."

His adultery had not been actual but, which was just as effective, mental. The panel of counterfeit money over his heart might be making a slight bulge, so he took off the jacket and left it on the seat of his truck.

"Where is he?"

"He's in there. He says Cindy has known about the crate for a long time. And Kim has known about it too."

"Where's Kim?"

"She's here. They're all in there."

Even Eric DeBono's ten-speed bike was lying on the lawn.

"My God, Laura!" he said, feeling as if he were faking his astonishment. As he looked into her eyes his gaze flickered crucially; he turned away from her to walk inside. He would begin to deserve her again after a few days had passed. After he had set the stones.

Inside, Randy was standing by the kitchen table. He looked

different, all rumpled and irritable. Money changes people.

"Okay, Wayne, my lawyer is going to call back," he said. "I called him right away, but I couldn't reach him. So I left a message." He was backing into the garage in Wayne's path; for some reason he was barefoot. "Here's what's happening. I've given them enough evidence to get a search warrant for this place. Accidentally, Wayne. Accidentally. So now they know you exist, and they know there's a crate here. But we can get it out of here fast, and they might not have time. I don't know how long it takes to get a search warrant. For all I know, they may be on their way over here right now. My lawyer will know what to do. I tried calling him all over. But I left a message at his office, and they say he'll call in soon."

Wayne was looking around the garage seeing that nothing had been disturbed, still shrugging his way back into fidelity as if his marriage alone could save him from Randy's crime. "I never got why we couldn't move the crate in the first place."

"Because I thought it would work, Wayne. I thought it would work. Nobody knew about this crate. Not even you. Do you think my motives weren't perfectly honorable the whole time?"

The three kids were standing around the crate. Wayne said, "I wish you guys would get away from there." They ignored him. Cindy was saying something about how the seal was just a price sticker that could be bought in any stationery shop. She too was wearing no shoes.

"Hey. You kids get away from that crate," he said, and they broke up their huddle a little bit. "Let's all get out of here. I just have to take a minute to understand this." He spread his arms usherlike to let the three kids precede him; and as he walked out to the kitchen, his voice resonated oddly as if this were TV dialogue: "You say you want to move the crate. Right?

But what good will it do? If they already know it's here. They'll be able to prove it, won't they? They'll have detectives find little molecules of wood from it on the garage floor. Or they'll have witnesses. Won't they? I mean, aren't they always smarter than you think? They go in with their microscopes."

Randy said, "Come on, just help me, Wayne. Isn't it worth a try? It's too heavy for me to get out there by myself, and that fucking driver refuses."

"Is that your cab? What happened to your Maserati or whatever?"

"It wouldn't start. But listen Wayne, we have to hurry. Isn't it at least worth a try? Eric, I bet you could help. You're a big strong boy."

Laura, who was standing at the window, said, "There's those kids again. I saw them a couple of times before."

Five or six high-school kids were approaching the house shyly in the usual leather and rags, scraped hair and discolorations.

"That one in the leather jacket," said Laura. "I saw her a few days ago when I went to work. They were just hanging around, but it seemed suspicious."

Cindy spoke up. "That's Heather Jamison. She's a major hosebag."

"Just you stay here." Wayne went out on the lawn. "Do you kids want something?"

"Is this where the money is?" The speaker was a shaven-headed boy in a hospital gown with a swastika Bic-penned onto his scalp.

"We're here to see the money," said the girl in the leather jacket, the bold one among the cowering group. Her makeup was so thick she looked dead. In fact, all the kids looked like

victims of a war, or of atomic radiation. It was the fashion at
T.L. these days, which Kim seemed to be immune to, fortunately.

"There's no money here," said Wayne. The whole scene felt
like Halloween. "Who told you there was money here?"

"Come on, old man," said the girl. Beneath a knotted ban-
danna, her hair was dyed cellophane blue. "We just want to
look through the fucking mail slot."

"There's nothing to look at here," said Wayne. Suddenly
like a giant held down by a thousand threads, he realized how
hopeless his situation was. There was nothing to do but surrender wholly to the mercy of the legal system. Obviously,
Terra Linda High School kids had been paying regular visits
here, to peer with curiosity through the mail slot at the famous
crate of money. In fact, he should call the police right away
and turn himself in. That way they're easier on you. Aren't
they? Except of course, that might put Randy in worse danger—they should first try to telephone his lawyer again . . .

"Now you kids just run along and play."

"Bite my crank, old man," said the girl.

"What?" said Wayne, amazed. One of the kids tittered.

"Suck my big weenie," she said.

"Shh!" In his mind, this girl had turned into a zombie of
shame sent by Tina to his very home. "Now you just keep your
voice down, and get the hell out of here. There's nothing to
see here."

"Eat my wonk," she cried, and the whole group ran off. He
turned back to the house with the pretense that nothing had
upset him. The encounter at Rumplestiltskins had left a re-
sidual film on his skin which unfitted him to be arbiter here.

He found Laura inside in the kitchen with Randy, scolding

him. "We're the last piece in the puzzle? Randy? Well then, obviously! Randy! Do you realize!" She tore off her apron and whipped it down on the table, turning her back and going to the refrigerator, while Randy hung his head in remorse. Wayne, as he stood in the doorway unseen, felt an unmistakable twinge of jealousy: *How had Randy and his wife become intimate enough to quarrel?*

No, that was crazy. There couldn't be anything between Laura and Randy. The solvent of this money had broken down all the usual logical bonds among things. He was emotionally overwrought and beginning to hallucinate. He had to relax. "Why don't we just . . ." He grasped a chair. "Laura, would you make some coffee?"

"I already am. Randy?"

"Black. But I think we should get our ass in gear."

"Can I have some? With cream and sugar?" said Cindy—who was sitting with Kim and Eric by the window.

"No coffee for young people," said Laura.

"Look, Randy," he said, taking his place at the kitchen table in his swivel chair, husbandlike. "Has this rumor spread all over Marin?"

"Yeah, but all I'm saying is, maybe we have a chance if we move the crate now. Maybe there's some legal technicality we don't know about. Like if it's not literally on the premises. I should try calling my lawyer again. Maybe we could page him or something. He's down at Stanford University somewhere. Because, see, what you guys don't know is that the government thinks this is a very big deal."

"What would happen if Laura and I went to the police with the crate and told them the whole story. Would that hurt your case?"

"Wait. Wayne?" said Laura. "You haven't heard the whole thing. Eric and Kim have been sneaking in there taking pictures of the seal. They put the seal on."

"*They* put the seal on!"

They were sitting together by the window. The boy's hand was on his daughter's waist. Suddenly the irrelevant knowledge came to him that the two children had had sex. His daughter. In a way, it was fitting, that the father should be ignorant. Probably Laura had been aware all along.

The boy said, "And Mr. Paschke, the photographs are dated by Fotomat."

His mind was faint with distance. "What?" Wayne had never quite liked Eric, he was a smart aleck. What did Kim see in him?

"You see, every time you develop pictures at Fotomat, they put the date on. So there's evidence once a week that the seal is still on."

Glances passed among the three adults.

Randy shrugged.

Laura finally said, "I bet it won't stand up in court."

Eric said, "Also, Mr. Paschke, I mailed the pictures to myself—so there's a postmark on the envelopes. It was an extra precaution. The envelopes are all still sealed."

Cindy said wearily, "Just call that Secret Service agent. Ludex. Obviously this Ludex already knows everything, so you can't hurt anything by just calling up and asking."

Laura said, "Just ask if Wayne and I are supposed to be accomplices. I mean, if he already knows there's a crate here . . ."

Randy picked at his knee seam. "I'd rather wait till my lawyer calls back."

Wayne began to feel angry. "Randy, if he was going to come and arrest us, wouldn't he be here by now?"

"Can you just trust me, Wayne?" Randy said.

"Look, I'll call him myself. I'm a citizen. If they think I've done anything wrong, I have a right to know." He wasn't guilty of anything, he wasn't rich, he had a wife and child. And now a job too.

"No, if anybody is going to call . . ."

Wayne reached for the phone. "I'm so tired of this fucking crate."

"Okay!" Randy got to the phone first. "I'll call. I'll call."

Laura said, "Randy, just ask if they think we're accomplices."

"Jesus fucking Christ," he muttered, dialing. "He probably won't even be there—he's probably on his way here now."

Laura said, pouring water, "Just call, Randy."

He asked information for the Secret Service number. Wayne stood up and wandered over to look out the front window, feeling, as in a movie, that he would be scanning for cops outside darting from bush to bush with crackling walkie-talkies. Kim and Eric were whispering together. Lovers. How could his daughter be sexy? She seemed all baby fat and gristle. How could they know about love, its patience, its responsibilities? His wife Laura stood over three cups of hot water measuring teaspoonfuls of black Maxwell House crystals which glittered with the frost of having had their flavor freeze-dried in. This could be his last cup of coffee at home. Any minute, the police would arrive. What does the government do with a "perfect" counterfeit? It just wasn't possible. They always get you by the paper. He decided to go into the bedroom to listen in on the extension, wanting to hear it firsthand.

What should be done with the bundle of twenties in the truck? There might not be any way to reunite it with the crate. If the police seized the crate, he would have to reveal that bundle of cash. Wouldn't they search his house? And his truck? He picked up the phone beside the bed to hear the Secret Service receptionist say, "I'll connect you. Just a moment please."

"Okay, thanks," said Randy's voice.

After one ring, an agent answered the phone: "Ludex."

"Mr. Ludex, this is Randy Potts."

"Just a minute," said Ludex, and he put Randy on hold. Silence.

"Wayne, are you listening?" said Randy.

"Yes."

"Well, don't say anything. Don't even breathe. Okay?"

"Okay! Jesus!"

"Could you keep your mouth away from the phone?"

"I won't say anything, Randy!"

"Do you realize we're probably being recorded right now?"

"Okay! Well then why did you even begin talking to me?"

"All right! Then just be quiet!"

Ludex came back. "What can I do for you, Mr. Potts?"

"I just have a question about my case. I need to know if you consider Wayne Paschke an accomplice, because that's the one thing I'll fight for in court . . ."

"I'm sorry, Mr. Potts. We don't have a case on file for you."

"This is important—"

"I don't think we've met," said Ludex. "I'm in a conference at the moment. If you have a crime to report, then I'll return you to the receptionist and it can be assigned to an agent."

"I'm talking about my case," Randy said.

"We have no case for you. Maybe you were thinking of another office. I'm sure we've never met."

"Never met! What about those meetings?"

"Mr. Potts, there were never any meetings. I'm going to return your call to the receptionist, and if you want to report a crime—"

"You came to my house. I came to your office."

"Mr. Potts, are you listening? There is no record of the investigation you're describing—"

"There isn't?"

"There is no record in this office or in any other government office. Do you understand?"

"What about . . . ?"

"I'm not going to receive your calls anymore. Do you understand?"

Randy said, "No," after a pause.

"I want you to listen closely. You have a voucher for certain property impounded, a certain amount of U.S. currency which was brought here for examination. You bring that voucher to the proper office, and you'll have your property returned to you in full, and the Evidence and Accounting file will be routinely shredded. Do you understand? The receptionist will tell you to bring the voucher to Evidence and Accounting downstairs."

"If you don't have any record of an investigation, where did all this impounded money come from?"

"Mr. Potts, you're not listening. After this, I'll no longer accept your calls—"

"I talked to you just an hour ago. Remember? You said everybody in Terra Linda knows."

Ludex paused. "I've never heard of you until this minute."

"Okay, but here. Can I have your assurance that no police or anybody is going to come out here?"

"There is no reason. There is no case."

Ludex hung up. A receptionist immediately opened the line again and said, "May I help you?"

"I want to talk to Mr. Ludex."

"He's in a conference right now. May I help you?"

"He's not in a conference, I was just talking to him."

"Maybe if you can explain your problem to me . . ."

"I want to talk to Hodges. Somebody Hodges. Ed Hodges?"

"I'm sorry, there's no Mr. Hodges at this office. May I help you?"

"No. Yes, how do I recover seized property?"

"Do you have a blue voucher?"

"Yes."

"The Evidence and Accounting office is open every weekday from nine to four thirty. It's in Room 213 of the Golden Gate building. You may present your voucher there for redemption."

"Let me just talk to Ludex."

"I'm sorry, Mr. Ludex is in conference for the rest of the afternoon. If you have a crime to report—"

"Thanks," said Randy, and he hung up.

Wayne listened for the second click. Then he set the phone back in the cradle and went out into the kitchen.

Randy was sitting there running his finger around the rim of his coffee cup.

"What?" said Laura.

"He says he's never heard of me."

"It might be a way of stalling for time while they figure out how to sneak up on us," Wayne said. He found himself irresponsibly excited. The three kids were still sitting against the wall by the window like an audience. Kim, beside Eric, chewed on a tress of her hair.

"Kim?" he said. "How long have you known about this? Why did you put that seal on the crate?"

"We thought it would prove everybody was innocent."

"I want a complete story from you both. Tonight."

"Can Eric and me go to Jack-in-the-Box?"

"Tonight? Are you joking?"

"I mean, if the police don't come."

"No you may not."

"Yes, Wayne, let them go," said Laura. "I think it's a good idea. But tomorrow we'll talk, Kim. Tomorrow is Saturday. The three of us." She fixed Kim in her gaze, and Kim shrugged assent.

"It's 'Eric and *I*,' " said Laura.

Kim rolled her eyes.

The phone rang, and Wayne set a claiming hand on it, then picked it up.

"Hello?"

"I'm looking for a Mr. Randy Potts. I'm returning his call."

He handed over the receiver.

Randy said, "Dan, am I glad you called! I've just been talking to Ludex, and now I'm here at the Paschkes' house. We've got real trouble. Now the thing is, there's one more crate I didn't tell you about . . . Randy . . . Randy Potts!" He looked up into Wayne's eyes. "Dan!" he said. "I was just talking to you this morning . . ."

He was looking around the room as if he'd lost something valuable. Wayne caught Laura's eye.

"I'm your client, Dan," Randy said. "We've been working on this for weeks. I was talking to you just this morning at

Stanford. Yes? Yes?" He dropped into a chair. "I can't keep it, it's counterfeit. It's counterfeit. Don't you remember? It was laser-etched . . .

"Well, you certainly didn't think it was ridiculous this morning. Dan, I don't believe this. I can't keep it. It's counterfeit. I'm your client. Randy Potts. Randy Potts . . ."

He stood up, angry. "Okay, I'm going to find out what's going on. You've been talking to Ludex, haven't you. What did Ludex say to you? I'm not going to just disappear." He hung up.

Wayne said, "What?"

Randy said, "He tells me he's never heard of me."

Nobody said anything. A car went past outside. In the distance its diminishing engine sound was like a wave receding from a dry new shore. Wayne sighed.

Laura said, "It might be best if we moved the crate. As Randy says, there might be some legal technicality we don't know about—like we're less guilty if we're not caught in physical possession of the crate."

"You know what he said?" Randy was warming his palms over his coffee. "He said, 'Of course I remember, Randy, but now I forget.' It's pretty obvious to me that he talked with Ludex. Now I feel like I have to hire a lawyer to protect me from my lawyer."

"Do you have that blue voucher thing?" said Wayne.

"Yeah. You know what he said? He said, quote, Don't be a fool, unquote."

"Fine, but nevertheless," said Laura.

Cindy said, "Randy, don't be a dildo."

So the time came when they moved the crate of two million dollars out of Wayne's garage. It floated between them as they carried it out to the yellow cab, with the three kids as the only spectators. And Randy was apologizing for the fact that he would probably never be able to tell them the true source of the money because it was real money now, and he had to keep it that way. And now he would hire an investment specialist to help him use it wisely—probably investing in art, which he'd heard was a wise method of tax avoidance. He would probably lose a big chunk of it in taxes even if it were declared as some sort of "windfall," but a shrewd lawyer could help him keep most of it. Wayne never mentioned the separate bundle of two thousand dollars—which he had decided would fit, undiscoverably, into the cylinder of the old engine block beneath the tablecloth at the far end of the garage.

So after Randy and Cindy had driven away in the yellow cab with the crate between them on the seat, and after the two young lovers had walked off toward the mall to have dinner at Jack-in-the-Box, Laura and Wayne stood arm-in-arm on the lawn in the red glow of sunset. "Neither of them were wearing any shoes," said Wayne. Laura tightened her embrace and said, "Meat loaf," and broke away to go inside to the kitchen, where he heard her turn on the TV. She always liked to have it on softly when she was cooking, not to watch but just to get the cozy background sound of TV havoc. It restored peace. And Wayne, still replaying the events in his mind with an effort of suspended disbelief, pushed up his shirtsleeves and took down the rear gate of his pickup, to move the flagstones around back. He covered his shirt front with white rock flour carrying them in small armloads and stacking them in heavy rocking piles in the Tudor aluminum shed in the corner of the back yard. They took up so much room inside the shed, he had to temporarily disarrange things. But next weekend he would set the stones in earth and restore all the tools to cover their usual shadows; and the stones, after a season or two, would sink solidly into the soil of the back yard.

"I got the job," he said, finally coming into the house a bit damp at the hairline—and carrying his cash-contaminated jacket casually. He picked up the day's mail from the kitchen table.

"In Tiburon? You did? My God, Wayne!" She came up and, while he sorted through the mail, hugged him from behind. "I completely forgot."

"Also, I got some free flagstones. I thought I'd put in a walkway by the patio."

The mail—*Free Beverage with the Purchase of a Western Bacon Cheeseburger, Marin Medical Center, Whole Fryers Coupon*—slipped through his fingers.

Her ear lay against his spine, and she squeezed his middle. "I can't believe it," she sighed, releasing him, and she returned to her bowl on the counter.

He started opening the mail, while carrying the coat—a few ounces too heavy—into the garage on a hooked little finger, to drop it casually over his workbench chair. Later he would slide the cash into the cylinder bore.

The bill he had opened was from Marin Medical Center, a summation of unpaid-for services stretching far back into Kim's history with plastic surgeons, printed by computer in sprayed needle-point dots. It was becoming more obvious every day that they wouldn't get an amniocentesis; the subject was rendered all the more conspicuous by its never being mentioned. So if the fetus was being poisoned by a chromosome, it seemed that he and Laura had apparently agreed to be irresponsible together, to let the last conceivable chance for an abortion pass them by without even discussing it. As if by not mentioning it, they could magically exclude it from possibility.

"Is that Marin Medical?" said Laura.

"Amazing," he murmured, referring to their indebtedness.

"Well, Kim's done. And San Francisco General will only be a thousand if there aren't complications."

He raised his eyes to regard her through the doorway. She pushed back a tress of hair with her wrist as she bent over the vegetable drawer, and he was reminded of the times when they used to sneak away from fifth period to be alone together in Steve Cantrell's borrowed Dodge van with a green shag-carpeted interior, and shining strands of her hair would be snagged and combed through the nap of the resilient carpet.

He said, "She's doing it with the DeBono boy, isn't she."

"Well, Wayne, I wish you wouldn't put it that way." She was puncturing, with her thumbnail, the cellophane film on a bar of ground beef.

"Hm," he said.

"Wayne, she's really happy. She's worried you'd be mad if you knew. But she's being smart about it. She's a smart girl."

Wayne said, in a voice weak and distant, "No, I'm not mad." And in fact the confirmation made him feel merely vague, increasing the vagueness that seemed to be the main lesson of his life these days as his bald spot grew and the yellow margarine collected around his heart and he got a housepainting contract of his own. It turns out that getting older feels like dissolving at the edges, getting ever vaguer by the inclusion of everything. It made sense that his daughter should be having sex already, and it made sense that her vague big father should be unaware of it.

"I guess she talks to you about it?" he said. He was sitting in his swivel chair.

"Yes, which is understandable. It can be scary."

"Especially for Kim." His voice was coming to him from a great distance.

"You know what? She tells me Eric *likes* her prostheses."

"He does? What does he do?"

"Well, honey, I don't need to be specific." Laura returned to her bowl and patted the ground beef. "Listen, Kim must never know I told you."

"Sure, of course. But what does he do?"

"Wayne, I don't want to discuss it specifically."

"He's kinky!"

"I think he really loves Kim, which is the important thing. And I think he's a gentleman."

"Yeah, but still. I was thinking of hiring him this summer. It's too weird. What do they do anyway?"

"Would you just stop asking? Why don't you have a beer. Would you like a beer?"

"No." He folded the Marin Medical Center bill. She was right, there was no use in his knowing about his daughter's sex life. "How about one of your Diet Cokes? I've got to go on a diet."

"You're neurotic about that." She set a Diet Coke in front of him unopened. "A hundred and eighty-five is fine."

He rattled the doctor's bill in his fingers. "It's really a miracle." He saw, as he had seen painfully many times before, the picture of his daughter lying prostrate beneath the needle, her eyes closed and her lip lifted. But now Kim's lip was flawless, satin, a constant invitation to a boy's kiss.

Wayne got up and leaned against the counter beside Laura, watching her shake breadcrumbs into a measuring cup. He had always liked the feeling of his own regal irrelevancy, standing beside her in the kitchen while she worked with a paring knife or a mixing bowl. But now he felt nervous, undeserving. He watched her for a while—the familiar sight of the ground beef in the mixing bowl, and the breadcrumbs measured atop the beef, and the egg yolk slipping down over both of them.

With a sudden resolve that stopped up his ears, he simply came right out and said, after all these weeks, "It's too late for the amniocentesis, isn't it?"

She looked at him. How seldom their eyes met anymore. But how beautiful her irises were.

He went on, "I mean, it's not too late for the test, but it's too late to do anything about it *if*."

She sighed and deserted him at the counter, to cross the floor and open a cupboard and take out an envelope of soup powder. Then she said, "Wayne, who*ever* he is."

They had agreed on the pronoun *he* months ago, hoping for a boy; Kim especially, wanting a brother, kept insisting on it as a family rule, correcting them when they used *it*. Laura came back to the counter and tore open the foil packet, dumping the contents into the bowl.

"Look at Kim," she said.

Yes, look at Kim, he thought, immediately strangled with repentance.

"I just decided," Laura said. "Who*ever* he is."

He broke away and—putting his hands in his pockets to look nonchalant—he walked with a stinging face out into the back yard.

He leaned against the aluminum shed, whose thin, sprung wall boomed at the touch of his shoulder. Its plywood floor elevated above the ground on cinderblocks, its Tudor cross-planks stamped into the aluminum, he had bought it years ago at the Sears Garden Center for $89.95, and had screwed it together himself in an afternoon. The coolness of the aluminum against his wrist—and then against his forehead as he turned to lean against it—healed him. The neighborhood, at this hour when the light was fading, had grown still.

Laura came outside.

"Is that okay?" she said. She was still holding a spoon.

"Yes. Wonderful." He put his arms around her, and she wiped her tears on his shoulder. They hugged over the obstacle of her pregnancy.

"Don't squish him," she said. "You'll make his eyes bug out."

It struck Wayne as funny. When he made a little laugh, she sniffed, realizing it was funnier than she'd thought.

She said, "He'll come out all flattened like a flounder."

"We'll have to move him around with a spatula."

Laura lay her forehead against his neck and sighed. "We're weird."

"Is Kim coming home after dinner?" he said.

"Yes, but later." Laura shifted her chin on his shoulder.

"Will she end up as weird as us?"

"Obviously she already is."

She kissed his neck and went back inside with her wooden spoon.

Wayne pushed his hands deep in his empty pockets to raise his shoulders, stretching his spine, and he walked aimlessly around the side of the house into the front yard. With the loss of the money he had regained the neighborhood. At this deep hour of dusk, everything radiated its color from within—the sticky-looking red paint on a fire plug, the bright sulphur tickets running down the center of the asphalt road. Which connected to other roads. Which connected to yet other roads.

Laura's twin biers of meat loaf would be baking at 350 degrees on the usual cookie sheet, and she would give him the four scabby end pieces, which he preferred. Later, while she was doing something distracting, he would creep into the garage and draw back the tablecloth and slip the rolled bundle of twenties into the cylinder bore of the engine block. Then Kim's unmated Adidas sock—which had lain for three years over the rim of the bushel basket—could be set on top of the cloth as a sealing weight.

After dinner, he offered to do the dishes, and Laura went into the bedroom. The meat-loaf cookie sheet, glazed with black enamel, was daunting. He gave it a squirt of soap and filled it with a sliding pane of gray water, setting it aside to soak overnight. The plates and glasses and utensils were in the sink, which he filled with sudsy water. As he glided his Tuffy pad around on the plates, the drug of slumber climbed on him— so that after he had scrubbed everything, he couldn't resist dropping his elbows onto the sill of the sink for a minute, his gaze widening on the water.

His failure at Marketrend had, somehow, opened a space in the world for the unborn child to come into. In theory at least, Armstrong's system of the cosmos made sense. Everything works out. Everything gets what it desires. Even the little colony of clinging suds floating in the dishwater, even *it* was getting what it desired. So how could there exist, in the cosmos, such imperfections as the oilstain in his driveway? Sometimes it seemed his life was governed by a single glad feeling, that feeling of deciding not to do an algebra assignment, of flunking, gratefully. In his sleepiness, the hum of the refrigerator grew to surround him.

He pushed himself up to the altitude of a grown man, and one by one he rinsed the two plates, the handful of utensils, the two glasses, until they squeaked under his rubbing fingers.

In the silence after turning off the faucet, he dried his hands on his hips and went to the bedroom. Laura was pulling her nightgown over her bare shoulders, and he stopped outside the door unobserved. Sometimes there were these moments of common clarity, when he could see how luminous was the alien flesh legally in his possession. The legal institution of marriage could never rub the strangeness from their cohabiting.

Knowing he was there, she said, "Is the front light on?"

"Yeah. You know, it does seem almost possible the Secret Service will let him alone now."

He almost felt he needed a response of some kind to confirm that the bizarre events of the afternoon had actually occurred.

He watched her fingers ascend, pinching each button into its slit on her nightgown. He said, "What do you think he'll buy with all his money?"

"Champagne . . ." She picked up her hairbrush and began brushing out her hair. "Caviar."

He hung his pants over the back of a chair.

She said, "When should I set the alarm for?"

"Six thirty. The mason gets there by seven."

His wristwatch, his pocket change, his shirt, all fell away.

He said, "I didn't believe any of that. What did you think about all that? About the economy collapsing because of Randy's money?"

She ducked forward to brush her hair away from the nape of her neck. "Well, Wayne," she said. "I'm setting the alarm for six thirty."

It was a harsh reply, which she amended, "Oh, Randy Potts"—dismissing the whole idea of him, but affectionately.

When he lay down in the dark beside her—having only left the room for a minute to brush his teeth—she was already asleep. He also would be quickly covered over by sleep. He soothed himself with visions of the inside of his shadowy toolshed, which next weekend would be restored to its usual arrangement: the clippers atop the burlap tarp, the empty gas can in the corner, the seed envelopes on the lawn mower.

And the heavy flagstones. Lying where swatches of turf had been cut away, they would be sinking imperceptibly into the earth, which, boiling with worms and beetles, would congeal around the stones over the years to lock them in as solid as fossils. He felt himself sinking into sleep as solidly as one of those stones—until a thought struck him that woke him up.

He had been drifting back to the astounding grafted porpoises of Tina's breasts, almost sickening in their beauty, which to touch was forbidden. And he was thinking of the serene fact that he could never have had an affair with her, because his physical body was legally, literally, in the possession of Laura. But then he thought: one part of him was owned by somebody else. His brother had claimed his kidney. And suddenly it dawned on him that he actually wanted to give his kidney away. It was what he had *always* wanted. It was a kind of good fortune. The thought surprised him so much that it woke him up.

It wasn't really "his" kidney, after all. Looked at one way, it was merely in his custody for a few years. He was lucky to be able to give it away. In fact, the whole idea—of having temporary protectorship of something that would belong to his distant, lost brother—made him so happy that he couldn't fall asleep again, and he just lay there beside Laura feeling owned by different people.

# FOR THE BEST IN PAPERBACKS, LOOK FOR THE

In every corner of the world, on every subject under the sun, Penguin represents quality and variety—the very best in publishing today.

For complete information about books available from Penguin—including Pelicans, Puffins, Peregrines, and Penguin Classics—and how to order them, write to us at the appropriate address below. Please note that for copyright reasons the selection of books varies from country to country.

**In the United Kingdom:** For a complete list of books available from Penguin in the U.K., please write to *Dept E.P., Penguin Books Ltd, Harmondsworth, Middlesex, UB7 0DA*.

**In the United States:** For a complete list of books available from Penguin in the U.S., please write to *Dept BA, Penguin*, Box 120, Bergenfield, New Jersey 07621-0120.

**In Canada:** For a complete list of books available from Penguin in Canada, please write to *Penguin Books Ltd, 2801 John Street, Markham, Ontario L3R 1B4*.

**In Australia:** For a complete list of books available from Penguin in Australia, please write to the *Marketing Department, Penguin Books Ltd, P.O. Box 257, Ringwood, Victoria 3134*.

**In New Zealand:** For a complete list of books available from Penguin in New Zealand, please write to the *Marketing Department, Penguin Books (NZ) Ltd, Private Bag, Takapuna, Auckland 9*.

**In India:** For a complete list of books available from Penguin, please write to *Penguin Overseas Ltd, 706 Eros Apartments, 56 Nehru Place, New Delhi, 110019*.

**In Holland:** For a complete list of books available from Penguin in Holland, please write to *Penguin Books Nederland B.V., Postbus 195, NL-1380AD Weesp, Netherlands*.

**In Germany:** For a complete list of books available from Penguin, please write to *Penguin Books Ltd, Friedrichstrasse 10-12, D-6000 Frankfurt Main 1, Federal Republic of Germany*.

**In Spain:** For a complete list of books available from Penguin in Spain, please write to *Longman, Penguin España, Calle San Nicolas 15, E-28013 Madrid, Spain*.

**In Japan:** For a complete list of books available from Penguin in Japan, please write to *Longman Penguin Japan Co Ltd, Yamaguchi Building, 2-12-9 Kanda Jimbocho, Chiyoda-Ku, Tokyo 101, Japan*.